"It's not easy falling in love with a wizard who keeps putting romance on hold to save the world. But it's fun reading about it."
—*The Dallas Morning News*

"Swendson's unique take on the paranormal genre is a standout. . . . *Damsel* is full of romantic and magical twists and turns."
—Parkersburg *News and Sentinel*

"Trying to start a romance with the world hanging in the balance is not optimal, but it sure is funny. . . . This is mayhem at its most enchanting!"
—*Romantic Times*

"Shanna Swendson has returned with a third delightful book. . . . Readers will eagerly await Katie Chandler's next adventures. Fans of both chick-lit and Harry Potter should not miss out on this series."
—freshfiction.com

Once Upon Stilettos

"[A] modern-day fairy tale."
—KNIGHT RIDDER/*Tribune* News Service

"The winning follow-up to *Enchanted, Inc.* . . . [This] smart, snappy novel will delight fans that loved the first installment and win over new readers, too."
—*Booklist*

"Once again Swendson offers a fresh spin on a genre in this exceptional Manhattan fairy tale, 4½ stars."
—*Romantic Times*

Enchanted, Inc.

Don't Hex
with
Texas

Don't Hex
with
Texas

A Novel

Shanna Swendson

Ballantine Books
New York

A Ballantine Books Trade Paperback Original

Copyright © 2008 by Shanna Swendson

Published in the United States by Ballantine Books, an imprint of The Random House Publishing Group, a division of Random House, Inc., New York.

BALLANTINE and colophon are registered trademarks of Random House, Inc.

Library of Congress Cataloging-in-Publication Data

Swendson, Shanna.
Don't hex with Texas / Shanna Swendson.
p. cm.
ISBN 978-0-345-49293-7 (pbk.)
1. Chandler, Katie (Fictitious character)—Fiction.   2. Family-owned business enterprises—Fiction.   3. Magic—Fiction.
4. Wizards—Fiction.   5. Texas—Fiction.   I. Title

PS3619.W445D66 2008
813'.6—dc22
2007043426

Printed in the United States of America

www.ballantinebooks.com

4 6 8 9 7 5 3

Book design by Katie Shaw

Don't Hex
with
Texas

One

It had been months since I'd needed rescuing from anything—no dragons, hideous monsters from hell, evil wizards, not even a really bad blind date. That was one small benefit I'd gained in moving away from New York City. No matter what else I might say about my hometown of Cobb, Texas (population 2,500), I definitely had fewer threats to my life here than I'd faced recently in Manhattan.

On the other hand, these days I seem to be doing a lot more of the rescuing, myself.

"Katie!" a voice screeched from the other side of the office door. I took a deep breath and counted to ten as I waited for the inevitable. As I expected, a badly bleached head appeared in my office doorway. It was my sister-in-law, Sherri, otherwise known as The Evil Bitch Queen of the Universe. (And the fact that it was my other sister-in-law, Beth, the one who loves all mankind, who dubbed her that says a lot about Sherri.)

Luckily, I'd dealt with worse than Sherri during my time in New York. When you've fended off not only harpies but also my ex-boss

Mimi, Sherri is in the minor leagues of evil. "What is it, Sherri?" I asked with exaggerated patience.

"You'd better go rescue a customer from your brother. I noticed his eyes were starting to glaze."

I wasn't sure what special skill I had that enabled me to take care of this when she couldn't. Considering the way she was dressed—a blouse dipping dangerously low and a pair of jeans that would probably cut her in two if she tried to do something crazy like sit down or bend over—she was well equipped to create a good diversion so the customer could escape. But that might almost be work, so Sherri had to delegate it to me.

With a deep sigh, I got out of my desk chair and headed out into the store. "I'll take care of it." I didn't have to ask which brother it was, even though I had three of them. Frank, the eldest, didn't usually string together words in groups larger than five, which meant he couldn't trap a customer for long, and Dean, Sherri's husband, was as allergic to work as his wife was, so him tending to customers was highly unlikely.

That left Teddy, the youngest of the boys. Teddy took the feed and seed business very, very seriously. He was always conducting experiments to determine the absolute best fertilizer for each soil type or crop or to figure out which seed got the best results in various conditions. The problem was that he loved to share his knowledge in excruciating detail with anyone who had the bad luck to ask even the slightest question.

Sure enough, he had an elderly man cornered, and the poor man was most definitely in need of rescue from a classic Teddy dissertation on plant nutrition. "Teddy!" I called out as I approached them. I smiled as I took my brother's arm. "Sorry to interrupt, but have you got the network connection up and running again?"

Teddy blinked at me. "Oh, I guess I got sidetracked." He turned back as though to excuse himself from his victim, but the customer had already grabbed some plant food and was headed to the checkout and a put-upon-looking Sherri. I had a feeling she'd soon have to take a half-hour break to recover from the strain of serving a customer.

That was the kind of rescue work I'd been doing lately. Instead of spotting magical threats so my wizard friends could deal with them, I was rescuing customers from my overeager brother, rescuing the cash drawer from my evil sister-in-law, rescuing my brothers from my mother, rescuing my mother from her mother, and generally keeping things relatively sane at home and at our family farm-and-ranch supply store. A few months back here in Texas had made me realize why I'd been so good at juggling all the magical wackiness in my old job: it was downright calm compared to what I had to deal with back home.

"I should have this connection back up and running in no time," Teddy announced as he slid under my desk.

"Great. I have to do orders this afternoon, so I'll need Internet access." That was true, but what I was really desperate for was the lifeline to the world I'd left behind. I got antsy when I had to go too long without news from my friends in New York, especially news about a certain person in New York.

He was the main reason I'd come back home. Not because he'd broken my heart or jilted me or any of the other things that usually send women running for the comfort of home and hearth. No, Owen Palmer had proved his devotion to me to an extent that most men never have the chance to. He'd had to choose between stopping the bad guys and saving me, and he'd chosen me.

While I'm totally in favor of not being burned by magical flames, him choosing me was not a great move for our cause. Not only did it mean that the bad guys got away, but it also meant that they knew for sure what his greatest weakness was. Me. Being the hero's greatest weakness might sound wonderful in a romance novel, but in real life it's not nearly as much fun. For one thing, it tends to make you a target. For another, it means that you can't help but feel responsible for everything the bad guy does, since it's because of you that the bad guy is still on the loose.

So, I'd done what any noble heroine with her eyes on the big picture would do. I'd removed myself from the equation, leaving him free to fight the renegade dark wizard and his cronies without having to worry about me. As a result, I'd broken his heart by walking away. At least, I thought I might have. Not that I'd heard from him. I didn't really see him as the type to beg me to come back, and even if he was, I had a feeling he was under very strict orders from his boss not to go after me, but that didn't stop me from jumping whenever the phone rang or daydreaming about him walking into the store.

The phone rang, and as always my heart started racing, even though I knew there were thousands of other reasons for the store's phone to ring . . . and ring. Sherri had apparently taken that break I'd predicted, so I picked up the call from my desk. "Chandler Agricultural Supply," I said briskly. "How may I help you?"

"Katie, is that you?"

"Marcia!" Marcia was one of my New York roommates, and hearing her voice nearly brought tears to my eyes. Is it possible to be homesick when you're in the place where you grew up, surrounded by family? "What's going on?"

"I tried e-mailing you a couple of times this morning, but it keeps bouncing."

"Yeah, there's something wrong with our server or network, or something."

"It'll be fixed soon," came Teddy's muffled remark from under my desk.

"It should be fixed soon," I relayed to Marcia. "Is there something going on?"

"I had dinner with Rod last night, and I've got a little news." Rod Gwaltney was Owen's lifelong best friend, and he'd started dating Marcia at the start of the year. Considering that his previous relationships could be measured in hours, that meant that this was looking very serious, indeed.

"Oh, do tell. The kind of news that involves jewelry?"

"What? No! God, no. We're still not even calling each other boyfriend or girlfriend. Talking about rings would really send him running."

"Wow, you do have him figured out."

"Owen's been coaching me some."

My heart started pounding again, and I got a funny feeling in my stomach. "So you've seen him? How is he?"

"My, but someone sounds eager. I'll tell you if you stop asking questions."

"Sorry! Go on. I won't say another word."

"So, as I was saying, I had dinner with Rod last night, and I have a status report for you." I was dying to ask questions, but I bit my tongue because I knew I'd get the answers quicker if I kept my mouth shut. "There's been no news on the bad guy front, to the point that it almost looks like they've gone underground. Owen thinks something big's about to happen, and the bad guys are changing gears."

"Yeah, that's usually how it goes. Do they have any idea what might be coming?"

"Not yet, but Rod's getting worried about Owen. He's working really hard. He's not getting enough sleep, and while we're all trying to make sure he eats, I think he's losing weight, and you know he wasn't a huge guy to begin with."

That answered any question I might have had about his dedication to the cause. "Has he said anything about, well, you know, me?" I cringed inwardly at how pathetic I sounded, but I had to ask.

"Not really. Sorry. But you know, he doesn't say much about anything." I wasn't sure what I was looking for there. I knew I couldn't go back unless the bad guys were well and truly vanquished, no matter how much he begged, and I knew he wouldn't beg. That didn't mean I didn't miss him.

"Thanks for the update," I said with a sigh. "Keep up the good work and keep me posted about him . . . and about you and Rod." Marcia had only recently learned about the magical world, but she'd proven herself a gung ho sideline participant in the efforts to stop bad magic from spreading, even if her role thus far seemed to be relaying messages and making sure overworked wizards got a good meal every so often.

"Don't worry, I think you'll know if Rod makes a move toward commitment. Heaven and earth might be rent asunder. Not that I'm looking for a deep commitment at the moment. We're having fun. We have plenty of time to worry about getting serious. Besides, I'm not even sure I want to hook up with a wizard on a more permanent basis. That may just be a lot of hassle."

"Yeah, you could be right about that." I knew from personal experience that dating a wizard had its complications, especially if he was leading the fight against dark magic. "But keep me in the loop. I miss you guys."

As I hung up, I remembered that my brother was still under my desk, tinkering with modems, servers, and whatever else he had rigged together to create a computer network for the store. I didn't think I'd said anything that gave away my magical connections from my side of the conversation, and besides, Teddy was probably the best brother to talk around. If he was focused on solving a problem, World War III could have broken out in the office without him paying much attention.

Even if Marcia was right about wizards being trouble, she could walk away from all things magical if she wanted to. I wasn't sure I could. She wasn't magical, one way or another, while I was in the special class of people who are immune to magic. The fact that magic has no effect on me under most circumstances made me a valuable player in the magical world. I'd been recruited by a company called Magic, Spells, and Illusions, Inc., to help them detect magical trickery in their business dealings, which ended up putting me in the middle of the ongoing fight against a rogue wizard and his mysterious supporters. I wouldn't claim to have actually saved the world, but I had helped prevent some pretty bad stuff from happening.

But if I was so valuable, what was I doing running the office in a small-town farm-and-ranch supply store? This town was so utterly non-magical that I hadn't learned about my magical immunity until I'd moved to New York City. There had to be a way I could help the cause beyond simply staying out of Owen's way. I couldn't imagine sitting on the sidelines with a magical war on the horizon.

A bell sounding from the front counter interrupted my brooding. Sherri should have been back from her break, but this was Sherri I was dealing with. I pasted a smile on my face and went out to ring up the customer. Then another customer needed help making a decision about the right soil additives for her rosebushes. It wasn't my area of expertise, but I'd absorbed enough over the years that I probably had fertilizer in my veins.

I returned to the front counter to find Dean toying with the cash register. "I think it's broken," he said.

"Why, what's wrong with it?"

"The drawer won't open." He tugged at the cash drawer to demonstrate.

"That's because it doesn't open unless you've made a transaction."

A flicker of irritation crossed his green eyes. "Oh. That would explain it."

"Was there something you needed?"

"Nah. I guess I should get the money out of petty cash, anyway." In other words, Mom's purse, since I wasn't letting him near the store's petty cash, and he knew it. Still, that didn't stop him from trying. He gave me his most charming smile. "You could spot me a twenty, couldn't you?"

"Sorry, Deano, but I'm immune to your charms." When you've spent enough time around a wizard like Rod, who used every trick in the book to charm people, normal smooth-talking loses any impact it might have had.

He shrugged. "Hey, it was worth a shot. You seen Sherri?"

"She's been taking a break for half an hour. If you see her, maybe you could tell her she needs to get back to work."

I barely made it into the office before the phone rang again. This time I answered it on the first ring. "Hey, girl, can you get away for lunch?" the voice at the other end of the line asked. It was Nita Patel, my best friend from high school.

"You're working days again?" She worked in the motel her family ran, and she was even more trapped by the family business than I was. At least I'd made an escape, no matter how temporary, to New York.

"Yeah, something happened last night that really spooked my brother, so they freaked out and put me on days. Now I'm stuck here at the front desk all day. It's not like anyone's going to check in anytime soon. But it would really brighten my day if you could pick up some lunch on your way over and join me."

A glance at the front counter assured me that Sherri had finally returned. "That sounds like a great idea. What are you in the mood for?"

"My dad's gone for the day. What do you think?"

"Okay, Dairy Queen it is. Double cheeseburger, no onions?"

"You read my mind." Needless to say, Nita wasn't a very good Hindu. Since moving to Texas, she'd developed a taste for hamburgers that she had to indulge behind her more traditional father's back.

"I'll be right over." After I hung up, I nudged Teddy's jeans-clad leg where it stuck out from under my desk. "I'm going out to lunch. Back in about an hour."

"Okay," he said, and I doubted it had even registered on his brain.

I got my purse and headed out. The pickup truck handed down to me from Dean when he got his new one sat in the gravel parking lot in front of the store. My New York friends would probably be equally fascinated and horrified to know I was driving something like this. It had definitely been a change from commuting to work on the subway. The feed store was on the edge of town, but in a town our size, it took less than a minute to get to the Dairy Queen on the edge of downtown.

The lunch rush, such as it was in Cobb, had only just started at the Dairy Queen, so I didn't have to wait too long to get burgers for Nita and myself. Once I had the food, I headed over to the motel on the outskirts of the other side of town.

Once upon a time, the town had been on one of the main routes between Austin and Dallas, but the interstate had been built about fifty miles to the east, which meant nobody came to this town who didn't absolutely have to. It wasn't the most profitable place to run a motel, but the Patels had been doing a good job of it ever since they'd moved to town. I'd been in fourth grade, and the teacher had assigned me as a buddy to Nita to help her get used to life in a new country. We'd quickly become best friends, and now Nita was probably more Americanized than I was.

"Omigod, I just had the best idea," she said as soon as I walked into the lobby. She opened the little gate that let me go behind the front desk as she kept talking. "I'm thinking we could put some potpourri in each of the guest rooms, have bagels and juice in the lobby, call it a bed-and-breakfast, and raise our rates by about twenty bucks a night."

"Sounds like a plan," I said. "But who in their right mind would come to Cobb on purpose?"

She took a big bite of her burger, pausing to savor it. "That's the genius of my idea. We hook up with the antiques stores in town, put together a brochure and a website, and advertise antiquing weekends. We could also throw in a spa package. Do you think Kiki at the Kut 'n' Kurl knows how to do facials?"

"More important—would anyone want a facial from a place called the Kut 'n' Kurl?"

"Good point. I'll give it some more thought." I smiled, imagining it would probably get about as much thought as any of her previous wild schemes, which included theme-decorated rooms and taking the motel's look back to its 1930s glory, complete with the metal lawn chairs she'd found on eBay. I recognized her impulse as the urge to do something bigger and better with her life than sit around in a small town and work for the family business. She wanted to stretch and grow, but she didn't have an outlet for it. I knew the feeling. Not for the first time, I wondered if I'd made the right call leaving New York.

As I suspected, Nita was ready with a new plan before she finished her burger. "What do you say we take off and get out of here? We could get a place together in Dallas or Austin! I'm sure you and I could get jobs." I looked at her expectantly. "Okay, so my dad might declare me no longer a member of the family, but I'm almost twenty-seven years old, so it's not like he could bring me back forcefully, and I'm sure he'd get over it eventually, especially if I managed to find myself a nice Indian boy to marry, since it's not like this town is crawling with them. I just know if I have to stay here one more second, I'm going to explode from boredom."

"If you do, at least the explosion would give the rest of us something to talk about for a while."

She threw a salt packet at me. "You know what I mean. What I don't get is why you came back here. You'd escaped. You were free! New York can't have been so bad that you had to come back."

Nita had been my friend forever, and I hated lying to her, but the existence of magic was a secret I wasn't allowed to share. "Things got complicated," was all I said.

"Then what do you think about going to Dallas, hmm?"

In the back of my mind, I hoped to move back to New York eventually. There wasn't any particular reason why I had to live out my exile in Cobb, but it wouldn't be fair to Nita to agree to move to Dallas with her, only to run back to New York at the first opportunity.

Fortunately, before I could come up with a way to say so without hurting her feelings, she was on to something else. Unfortunately, that something was me. "Now, really, what was it? Broken heart, love affair gone wrong? I know! You had a hot affair with your boss and had to leave your job when he dumped you for someone else, like Bridget Jones." We'd had this conversation about once a week since I'd been back, and her theories were getting increasingly wilder. Her version of my life was starting to sound more exciting than the reality, even with all the magical warfare.

I looked away, trying to think of something I could say to distract her, and noticed the side window with plastic sheeting taped to it. "Is that what happened last night that spooked your brother?" I asked.

"Yeah, it was the weirdest thing. I was on duty, and I went into the back right before midnight to check something, then when I got back out here, the window was gone."

"Was anything stolen?"

"Not that I could tell. The computer, TV, and cash were all here. I called Ramesh over, and he sent me home. He didn't want me working alone at night if stuff like that was going on, so he switched shifts with me."

"I guess you had a bit of cleanup work to do."

"That's the weird thing—there wasn't any glass. No rocks or bricks inside, either. It was like someone just took the glass out of the window. Isn't that spooky?"

"Yeah." She had no idea how spooky it was. I'd actually seen something like that happen once before. Owen had zapped the glass out of a window when the restaurant we were in caught on fire and the doorway got jammed with people trying to escape. Somehow, though, I doubted that was what happened here. Not only were there no magical people in this part of the world, but nothing was missing, so why would someone even bother? "You know, it was probably some senior class prank, part of a scavenger hunt," I said to reassure her.

"You're right, but don't tell Ramesh. I hate working nights, so this new arrangement is fine with me. Well, I hate working here, period, but until my dad enters the twenty-first century and lets me move away, or until some nice Indian boy drops by to take me away from all this— or until you agree to run away with me—I'm stuck."

I was afraid she'd go back to nagging me about why I'd left New York, but she didn't. We chatted about how much we hated our current jobs until it was time to force myself to head back to the store.

Sherri hadn't waited for me to get back from lunch before taking her own lunch break, but Beth, Teddy's wife, had come to my rescue, ringing up customers with a baby on her hip. She flashed me a smile as I squeezed past her to get to the office, then once I'd put my purse away, I took the baby off her hands. Babysitting sounded a lot more pleasant to me at the moment than dealing with the store.

"Thanks," I said when the minor rush subsided. "I guess Sherri was hungry."

She rolled her eyes. "That girl needs a keeper."

"That girl needs a jailer."

"Ted said to let you know that the Internet access should be working now. Frank will be here in a moment for the afternoon shift, Dean's MIA, as usual, your dad's making a delivery, and Ted's off checking his test crops."

"So everything's about as under control as you can get around here."

"Exactly. So go sit down and catch up on paperwork. I've got the register if you'll watch Lucy."

Lucy was teething, so she tended to eat paperwork, along with anything else that came anywhere near her mouth, but it still sounded like a good trade-off to me. It was hard to concentrate on the bookkeeping, though, when all I could think about was Nita's missing window. When Owen did that spell, the window had returned a while later. I wondered if that would happen this time. And then I reminded myself that it couldn't be magic. We didn't have magic around here. I was immune to magic and I'd never seen anything magical being hidden from other people. I'd discovered during my parents' visit to New York last Thanksgiving that I'd inherited my magical immunity from my mother, and in her whole life in Cobb she'd never noticed anything that made her think of magic. That was one of the reasons I'd come here when I needed to get away. It was the last place where my magical problems were likely to follow me.

"Katie!" Beth called from the front. Her voice was a lot more pleasant than Sherri's screech. "Someone's here to see you." I got the impression from the teasing singsong of her voice that whoever was there was male and good-looking. My heart rate went bonkers, and I could practically feel the adrenaline rushing into my system. I kept an extra-tight grip on Lucy as I stood, for fear my suddenly rubbery limbs wouldn't be able to hold her.

When I got out into the store, that surge of emotion deflated instantly. The man waiting to see me wasn't dark-haired, blue-eyed, and just a little shorter than average. He was tall and blond, though he did have blue eyes. "Well, if it isn't Miss Katie Chandler, come back home from the big city," he drawled.

"Yes, I've been back since January," I said, shifting Lucy's weight and trying to get her fingers untangled from my hair. If I wasn't mistaken, this guy was Steve Grant, the quarterback, football hero, and otherwise big man on campus from my high school days. "How's it going? Is there something I can help you with?"

Steve took in the baby I held. "I guess that's why you're back, huh?"

It was an interesting assumption to make, considering that Lucy was her mother made over, bright red curls and all, and looked absolutely nothing like me. "Um, no. This would be my niece."

He looked immensely relieved. "Well, whatever the reason, it's good to have you back. Say, we ought to get together some time, you know, catch up on old times."

As far as I could recall, we didn't have any "old times." We'd had a class or two together, but otherwise, our interactions had been limited to me playing in the band while he played football. The dating pool must have really dried up if he was resorting to asking me out. "I guess this means I'm the only single woman left in town," I said with a laugh.

"Whoa, what? No! That's not what I meant. I mean, well, I saw you in the DQ earlier today, and I think the city's been good for you. You're so . . . sophisticated."

I wasn't sure the word "sophisticated" applied to someone wearing faded jeans and a seed company T-shirt with her hair coming out of a halfhearted attempt at a ponytail. "That's awfully sweet of you to say, Steve, but I'm not really interested in dating right now, thanks." I hoped he didn't press me for details because it was hard to explain that I was still hung up on the guy I'd left behind in New York and he couldn't possibly compete. It's not like I was planning to join a convent if circumstances didn't let me get back with Owen, but I just wasn't ready to move on yet. "Is there anything else I can help you with? We've got a sale on lawn tractors."

"Nah, not today. But if you change your mind, give me a shout. I'm sure you know how to find me." He gave me a wink before strolling out of the store. I had to admit that his backside in Wranglers wasn't anything to sneeze at, but he wasn't Owen, and I doubted anything else would do for a very long time.

I hadn't even made it back to the office before my mother came running up the front steps and burst into the store.

"You are not going to believe what I just saw!" she shouted.

Two

I flashed back to Thanksgiving in New York, when I'd spent much of the holiday trying either to hide magical things from my mother or rationalize the things she did see. Then I remembered where I was. More likely, Mom had seen one of the local preachers making out in the backseat of a Chevy with the church secretary. Now, that would be news worth reporting, and she could most definitely be counted on to report it. I'd never seen a fairy or elf here, so I could safely rule that possibility out.

"What is it, Lois?" Beth asked cheerfully. I tried to take her cue and calm down. She acted like this was an everyday occurrence, and with my mother, it probably was.

"I was at the drugstore, and Lester Jones actually gave someone his prescription for free!"

I immediately relaxed. Lester Jones, the town pharmacist, was a notorious skinflint. If you were at his house for dinner and asked him for an aspirin, he'd charge you a nickel for it. Beth raised an eyebrow. "Hmm, that is interesting. Maybe he's had a change of heart and is trying to make up for all those years of overcharging. They did have a revival last week over at the Second Baptist Church."

"I didn't know Lester was a Baptist," Mom said with a disapproving tone. "I didn't think he was anything."

"All the more reason he might have been 'saved' if he went to the revival," Beth reasoned.

"Who was the lucky customer?" I asked. "Maybe it was someone who has some dirt on Lester, or someone Lester owes money to."

"It was that weird kid—the one who got a scholarship to A&M and then flunked out. You know him, Beth, the one who used to be friends with Teddy."

"Oh, you mean Gene Ward?" Beth asked with a frown. "That would explain a lot. His dad does own half the town. I wonder why he needed medicine."

"Well, the boy did have his hand bandaged. It was probably antibiotics or something for the pain." That solved Nita's mystery as well as Mom's. From what I knew about Eugene Ward, he'd probably tried to take out the window so he could rob the motel, and then Nita had startled him so he'd run away before getting anything. He thought he was smarter than everyone else and could get away with anything, but he was also a big scaredy-cat. If he had been caught, his daddy would have bought off the Patels and bailed him out. He'd probably already paid off half the merchants in town after Gene's assorted foolish stunts.

My oldest brother, Frank, showed up then, and his presence settled things down. "Hey, Mom," he said, giving her a hug and a quick kiss. "What brings you down here?"

"I was out running errands and thought I'd drop by to see if y'all wanted to come over tonight for supper after you get done with work. Are Dean and Sherri around?"

"Sherri left a little while ago," I reported. "Dean was here before lunch, but I have no idea where he went."

"I guess I'll have to track them down and make sure they're coming.

It wouldn't be a family dinner without them. I'll see everyone around seven-thirty."

Beth turned to me once Mom was gone and said, "Now, I believe you're off duty, if you want to hand Miss Priss back to me."

I gladly handed over the baby, who clung to my T-shirt with damp fingers until she realized she was going back to her mother. "I'll check my e-mail and handle a few orders before I go, now that the network's fixed."

I had one message in my personal in-box, a chatty message from Trix, the MSI executive receptionist, catching me up on all the office gossip I was missing. Most of it was complaining about my replacement, Kim, and what Trix would do to her if Kim weren't immune to magic. There was no mention of Owen. I updated orders with our major suppliers, then logged off and headed home.

The house was empty when I got there, which meant Mom was probably at the grocery store. I probably should have offered to help her, but I'd be helping make dinner, so I needed to take what time I could get to myself. I'd also hauled home some of the office paperwork so I could actually get it done without the typical interruptions I faced at the store.

One way my current life beat my New York life hands down was in living space. You could have fit my entire New York apartment into my family's living room—and three of us had shared that apartment. Funny, though, that I felt less crowded sharing that small apartment with two friends than I felt living at home with my parents.

I'd barely settled onto my bed with a stack of receipts when I heard a voice from downstairs. "Yoo-hoo! Anyone home? I thought I saw Katie's truck outside." It was my grandmother.

Perhaps this house felt more crowded because it was kind of like living in the middle of Grand Central Station—spacious, but you couldn't get a moment to yourself.

I put my work aside and headed downstairs to find my grandmother in the kitchen. "Hey, Granny," I said. "Did you need something?"

"Just dropping by. I was out running errands. Is your mother around?" Without waiting for an answer, she darted into the living room. She carried a cane, but I couldn't remember her ever leaning on it. She mostly just waved it at people.

"I think she's at the grocery store," I said as I ran after her. "She should be home any minute."

She whirled and headed back to the kitchen. "You wouldn't happen to have any coffee ready, would you?"

"I don't think so, but I can make you some if you like." Before I finished speaking she was already putting a filter in the coffeemaker and dumping in some coffee. "Or you could make yourself at home," I finished under my breath.

"Katie!" my mother's voice called from outside. I detected a hint of panic, probably because she'd seen my grandmother's block-long old Oldsmobile parked in the driveway.

"There's Mom now," I said cheerfully. "I'll help her unload the groceries while you make the coffee." Without waiting for a response, I ran out the kitchen door and down the steps from the back porch to the driveway.

My mother looked like she'd swooned against the side of her car. "Please don't tell me my mother is here," she said.

"Well, then I'd have to lie. She's making coffee."

"I did not need this today, not with everyone coming over for dinner tonight."

I reached into the trunk and grabbed a few grocery bags. "Weren't you going to invite her?"

"Of course I was. But I wasn't planning to have an audience while I cooked. She'll criticize everything."

"Why don't I call Molly and tell her to bring the kids over when they get out of school? They can distract Granny."

"Oh, you're brilliant. How did I have such a brilliant little girl? It's too bad you haven't had children yet so you could pass on those brains to the next generation." It was a sign of how long I'd been back home that I let the remark about children roll right off my back. When you're hassled about marriage and children on a daily basis, you tend to get used to it.

"By the way, Beth said Steve Grant came by the store to see you," she said. And there she went again.

"Yeah, he saw me in Dairy Queen and wanted to know what I was doing back in town."

"He's still single, you know. I can't believe some smart young lady hasn't snatched him up yet."

"Yes, I know." Then we were inside the house. I dumped my groceries on the kitchen table and hightailed it back to Mom's car for another load while Granny started in on Mom. It was one of those cases where discretion really was the better part of valor.

When I got back inside with the next load, Mom was saying, "And would you believe Lester gave it to him for free? Beth thought it had something to do with Gene's daddy owning half the town."

As I went back outside, I hoped the subject had changed by the time I got back with the next load of groceries, since I'd finished emptying the car and I wouldn't have any more excuses for sneaking away. "That's the last of it," I said, dropping the bags on the table.

"Katie, I was just telling Mama about what I saw outside the grocery store. I swear, there were people dancing in the parking lot, right there on the courthouse square. It reminded me of that deli you took me to in New York, the one where the waiters all did the dance routine."

I got a sick feeling in my stomach. That hadn't been the kind of restaurant staffed by hopeful Broadway actors. The impromptu dance routine had come about because of Phelan Idris, the rogue wizard Owen was fighting, casting a spell on everyone in the deli to make them dance for his own amusement. "Are you sure it wasn't the drill team doing

some danceathon fund-raiser?" I asked. Magic was supposed to be absolutely impossible here, wasn't it? This town certainly wasn't the kind
of place where people started dancing in the streets for no reason.

"No, it was most definitely *not* the drill team. Everyone who came
out of the store got into it. It was absolutely ridiculous."

"Ah, spring fever," Granny said, pouring herself a cup of coffee.
"Back in the day, in the old country, we'd welcome spring by dancing to
the spirits of the earth and air." Her Texas drawl mutated into something
out of a Lucky Charms commercial.

"Mother, you've never been in the old country," Mom pointed out.
"You were born in Texas, and you've never left the state. How on earth
would you know what they did back in Ireland?"

"Just because some of you have forgotten the old ways doesn't mean
all of us have," Granny muttered.

"The only old ways you know are how to get on my last nerve,"
Mom said under her breath.

"I'll go give Molly a call," I said, figuring that my great-grandchildren
distraction plan would be a really good idea about now. I didn't relish
the idea of breaking up yet another fight between my mother and grandmother. Mom was younger, bigger, and stronger, but Granny was armed
and usually meaner.

Before long, the house was swarming with my niece and nephews,
Frank's kids. They clamored over Granny in the living room, showing
her everything they'd done in school. Mom, Molly, and I took advantage
of the relative quiet to get dinner ready. Mom was still going on about
the weirdness in the grocery store parking lot.

"Can you believe such a thing?" she asked Molly.

"Did you see anyone else around?" I asked. "Maybe they were film-
ing something, like a commercial for the store."

"That could be it."

"Funny," Molly said, "I was just there on my way over here, and nobody said anything. You'd think that would be the talk of the town."

"And that's not all," Mom said. "I could have sworn one of the antique lampposts on the courthouse square disappeared right in front of my eyes, and then came back."

Molly laughed. "You probably just blinked. Things do tend to go away for a second when you close your eyes."

"I know what I saw," Mom snapped, causing Molly to flinch and then cast a worried look in my direction. I shrugged in response, not sure what to do. While I knew that it was entirely possible that Mom was going nuts, I also knew that there was such a thing as magic and that the things Mom described could actually happen.

I might have been out of the center of the action, but it looked like I was back to investigating. If I saw something weird around town, then I'd know something magical was going on. If I didn't, we'd either have to get Mom to a doctor or find her a hobby. Neither possibility appealed to me.

Once dinner was over and all the guests were gone, I announced that I was going out and hoped that the fact that I was an adult who had lived for more than a year in Manhattan would mean nobody felt the need to ask where I was going or why. At any rate, I was out the door before anyone had a chance to ask. I drove into town, parked at the courthouse square, and got out of the truck to walk around.

As far as I could tell, everything was where it should be. All the antique lampposts and replacement antique-looking lampposts were in place, as were all the statues and monuments to various wars and local heroes. The gargoyles on the courthouse roof stayed still. Not one of them winked at me. Looking at these lifeless carvings made me miss Sam, my gargoyle friend from New York. Even one of his less-capable colleagues would have been a welcome sight.

I closed my eyes for a moment and tried to open my other senses, straining to feel the tingle that told me magic was in use. That wasn't any special power I had. Anyone could feel the charge in the air that meant someone was using magic nearby, but since most people don't know magic is real, they write off that feeling as a shiver up the spine. Nothing here gave me shivers other than the thought that Mom might really be losing it this time.

The grocery store across from the courthouse had closed for the night, so the parking spaces in front were empty. Owen would have been able to detect traces of residual magic, but I couldn't sense anything. I decided it was time for the next-best weirdness detector in a small town: the Dairy Queen.

On a warm night like this one, odds were that a fair number of people would have gone out for a banana split or a malt, and if anything even slightly out of the ordinary had happened, they'd certainly be talking about it. Sure enough, the parking lot was nearly full, and there were people crowded around all the outdoor tables. I went inside and ordered a brownie Blizzard, then looked around for a place I could sit and overhear as many conversations as possible.

"Hey, Katie, over here!" a deep voice called out. I turned to see Steve Grant sitting with a couple of his buddies. For a second, I had a high school flashback. There'd been many a time I saw the same group of guys sitting at the same table in the Dairy Queen. Of course, back then they weren't calling me over to join them. I'd have probably died on the spot if they had. In high school, guys like that didn't talk to girls like me, unless they wanted help with their English homework.

The group looked a little different these days. We hadn't been out of high school for ten years, but already the hairlines were starting to recede and the waistlines were starting to expand. I didn't want to give Steve any false hopes, but their table was centrally located, and if anyone in town would have the scoop on anything going on, it would be these guys.

I wandered over to the table, pausing to take a bite of my Blizzard every few steps, so I'd look properly casual. "Hey," I said. "Fancy meeting you here."

"What are you up to?" he asked.

"Escaping from my parents. And eating ice cream."

Steve patted the space next to him in the booth. "Care to join us? I saved you a seat."

"That was sweet of you." I perched on the end of the booth, as far from him as I could get, which wasn't very far, as he made no effort to scoot over and give me room. I had a feeling that was more deliberate than inconsiderate of him. I took a bite of ice cream to stifle the giggle that threatened to come out. The last time I had men like him all over me like that, I'd been wearing enchanted shoes. Somehow, I doubted my raggedy old tennis shoes had any kind of attraction spell on them. "So, guys, what's the news in town tonight?" I asked.

"Nothin'," the guy across the table from me grunted. I couldn't remember his real name. In school, he'd been called Tank, and it looked like as an adult he was making every effort to live up to his nickname. His nearly monosyllabic response reminded me why I hadn't been that impressed with the football studs in school.

"Wow, exciting," I quipped, unable to hold back the sarcasm.

"Not really," the third guy said. I wasn't sure I'd figured out who he'd been in school—probably one of the interchangeable second-string jocks who'd flocked around Steve. Clearly, he didn't quite grasp the concept of sarcasm.

"So I guess nothing much has changed while I've been away," I said.

"Very, very little," Steve said, stretching his arm along the back of the booth. "But you sure changed."

I was fairly certain he was flirting with me, but I wasn't sure how to respond. Part of me wanted to hear how he thought I'd changed, and part of me knew for sure that I'd changed in ways he'd never be able to see. "That does tend to happen as you grow up," I said. Before he could come back with another attempt at flirtation, I added, "I suppose they still roll up the sidewalks pretty early around here. No dancing in the streets, or anything like that."

They all looked blank, so I could only assume that either the parking-lot dance Mom had talked about hadn't really happened, or if it had, it had been a good enough spell that nobody remembered it enough to be able to talk about it. That was the way those things tended to work. Since I'd found no other absolute evidence of magic thus far, I was leaning toward the former.

"I guess the big, bad city chewed you up and spit you out, huh?" Steve said, giving me a pitying look.

I nearly choked on a chunk of brownie. "What?"

"I mean, well, you came home awful quick. What was it, a year you spent up there?" He reached over and patted me on the thigh. "But don't worry, nobody thinks badly of you. Some people just aren't meant to go off like that. You're a hometown girl. You belong back here with us."

"I—no—not—what?" I was too stunned to form a coherent sentence, which was probably for the best. If I'd said something, it would have been to give him a tongue-lashing for the ages. By the time I formulated an appropriate response, I'd calmed down to the point I no longer wanted to scratch his eyes out. "Actually," I said coldly, "the company I work for is doing some restructuring, which meant my position was put on hold temporarily. My dad needed a little help at the store, so instead of temping in New York until the company needs me again, I thought I'd come back here and help out." I'd told the cover story often enough that I almost believed it, though it was getting harder and harder to convince myself or anyone else about the "temporary" part.

"Whoa, hey, didn't mean to get you all riled up. I'm just glad to have you back. We should get together sometime."

"Sorry, I really don't think I can fit it into my schedule."

"What, you have a boyfriend or something?" The guys all laughed.

"As a matter of fact, I do." Well, technically I didn't, as I'd broken things off with him for the greater good, but I was still hung up on him, which sort of counted.

"And I guess he's still in New York, huh? Well, what he doesn't know won't hurt him."

I gave him a smile with my teeth bared. "But it could hurt you."

"Big, tough guy, huh?"

I gave Steve an enigmatic smile and finished my Blizzard quickly enough to give myself an ice cream headache, said a hasty good-bye to the guys, and headed home.

Things settled back to normal after a few days. The following Tuesday morning, Sherri was late, as usual, so I worked the front of the store for the first hour, before I even had a chance to check e-mail and get my office work started. When she finally showed up, I took the opportunity to sit down at the computer. I handled the work stuff first, checking the status of my supply orders and notifying customers who'd have deliveries.

A sudden commotion from the front of the store jolted me away from my work. I hurried out to see Mom leaning heavily on the front counter, shouting for help. Sherri, of course, was nowhere to be seen.

"Mom, what is it?" I asked, rushing to her side. She was deathly pale, and her face was beaded with sweat. She opened her mouth as if to speak, but then her eyes rolled back in her head and she went limp. I barely caught her as she fainted dead away.

Three

I lowered Mom to the floor as gently as I could, shouting, "Teddy? Sherri? Anyone? I need some help here!" Trying to remember everything I'd learned in the first-aid class I'd taken during Girl Scouts, I checked her pulse and her breathing. Both seemed to be fine, if a little rapid. I leaned over her and tried gently touching her face. "Mom? Mom, can you hear me?"

Sherri chose that moment to wander back in. She took one look at Mom lying there on the floor and screamed her head off. I thought for a moment she might faint, herself, and waited for her to hit the ground, but, unfortunately, she didn't oblige me. Teddy then came running in. "What happened?" he asked, sinking immediately to his knees next to Mom.

"I'm not sure. She looked like she'd seen a ghost, then she keeled over on me."

"You think it has anything to do with all that stuff she was saying yesterday?"

"I have no idea."

"She's never been entirely normal, but this is odd, even for her."

I started to agree, but then I noticed Mom's eyelids twitching. Little wonder—Teddy must have been unloading fertilizer, and the chemical smell on him was strong enough to work as smelling salts. Her eyes fluttered open, and she whispered, "What happened?"

"You fainted. I don't know why. You didn't get to that part before you passed out." She struggled to sit up, and I pushed her back down. "Maybe you'd better take it easy for a while. Give the blood a chance to get back to your brain." I turned to ask Sherri to go get some water, but she was nowhere to be seen. If I knew her, she was probably out having her own fainting spell on the front sidewalk where more people might notice her.

Fortunately, all the family comings and goings at the store meant someone else—someone more useful—was bound to come along at any moment, and sure enough, Molly soon showed up, dragging a whimpering four-year-old. When she saw Mom lying on the floor, she went pale and steadied herself against the counter. I hoped she didn't faint on me, too. "What happened?" she asked.

"Mom just had a little fainting spell. She seems to be fine now, but could you go get her some water?"

"Of course." She released her son's hand and said, "Mommy needs to go get Gramma some water. Be a good boy and stay here with Uncle Teddy and Aunt Katie." As soon as she was out of sight, he quit whimpering and went to work emptying all the nearby shelves he could reach. I had too many other things to worry about to bother stopping him.

Teddy, however, had less patience. "Davy!" he scolded. The kid looked at him, weighed whether or not to test him, raised a hand toward the next item on the shelf, took another look at Teddy, then backed away and put his thumb in his mouth.

Molly then returned with a glass of water, and I helped Mom sit up to drink it. "I'm fine, I'm fine," she insisted after she drained the glass.

"People who are 'fine' don't pass out," I said. "Now, what happened?"

"I was on my way to the beauty shop, and I passed the courthouse square. There was a man on the square wearing robes. He looked like he was doing some kind of a dance, waving his arms around. And then the statues started moving, I swear. Not much, but more than statues are supposed to move. But nobody else seemed to see it, and there were a lot of people on their way to work in the courthouse, so there were people there. All they did was give the guy money as they went by him."

"It must have been an illusion, like that David Copperfield guy," Teddy said. "You know, the one who does things like make the Statue of Liberty disappear on TV. He was probably panhandling with his magic."

"Were you even listening to me?" Mom snapped. "I said no one even looked twice at the statues. If they didn't notice the statues moving, then why would they give him money? It was so odd, I had to tell someone as soon as possible."

With his mother back in the room, Davy resumed gleefully destroying the display at the front of the store. "Oh honey, don't do that," Molly moaned, but that didn't slow him down.

It was a sign of just how out of it Mom was that it took her a full minute to turn and tell her grandson, "David Chandler, you stop that this instant or you won't be allowed in Grampa's store anymore." That did the trick with Davy, and it seemed to have snapped Mom out of her daze. The color returned to her cheeks, and her eyes sparked with life.

"So, as I was saying, it was the weirdest thing. I felt like I was in the middle of a dream, where all these odd things were happening, and I was the only one who noticed—or maybe I was the weird one and everything else was normal." I knew that feeling very well, myself. It was the way I often felt at work—at my real job as one of the few magical immunes working for a magical company. But that's not the way it was supposed to be here. This place was supposed to be entirely normal.

"Maybe you were dreaming," Molly suggested. "Sleepwalking, or something like that. I've heard of people who make meals or go driving in their sleep."

"I was not asleep," Mom insisted. "I saw it."

Sherri came running in then. "I brought you some coffee," she said. She must have gone to the Starbucks in Waco to get it, considering the time it took and the fact that there was a full coffeepot behind the front counter.

"Oh, bless your heart," Mom said, taking it from her. "You're such a doll to look after me that way."

Sherri preened, then as she straightened, she swayed and placed a hand against her forehead. "I think the room is spinning. Maybe there's something in the air. We're all being poisoned."

It took everything I had not to laugh at her, and I knew I didn't dare meet my brother's eyes. We'd lose it entirely, and then Mom would be furious with us. "Help me up, Katie," Mom said. When Teddy moved to help on her other side, she said, "Teddy, hon, you smell like a chemical plant. You're probably what's making Sherri dizzy." Back on her feet again, she shook us off and said, "You should have seen it!"

And then she proceeded to act out the whole thing. She was in the process of imitating the mysterious robed man as he cast his spell on the square when a customer came in. And not just any customer. It was the minister at my parents' church. He took one look at Mom dancing and waving her arms and frowned, but before he could say anything, Sherri was on him. He was pretty young, in only his second job out of seminary, and not bad-looking. I somehow doubted, though, that Sherri had any idea he was a minister. It wasn't as though she darkened the doors of any church very often.

If he'd had a response to Mom's quickly ended antics, it was soon overshadowed by his response to finding a bleached blonde in painted-on clothes wrapped around him. Sherri sold gardening supplies like she was selling expensive cars, which is to say that she used sex appeal, though really, to be honest, she was mostly selling herself. I waited for Mom to react to Sherri's behavior, but it seemed that was a lost cause. If I hadn't been certain that Mom was immune to magic, I'd have sworn that Sherri really was a witch who'd cast a spell on Mom. It was like watching Rod pick up women back in his pre-Marcia days.

In spite of Sherri's "help," the minister got his vegetable seeds and left. We picked up where we left off, except Mom had quit trying to act out the courthouse square scene. "You don't think it was a stroke, or anything like that, do you?" Teddy asked me under his breath.

"I don't think so. She's not acting like someone who's had a stroke. I think she just got overexcited."

"Maybe you should take her to see the doctor, just in case. I really don't think she should be driving until we're sure what happened."

"Do you think maybe she's got diabetes?" Molly asked. "Doesn't that sometimes make people pass out?"

"I thought that was only after they were on insulin, though," Teddy said. "That's what makes their blood sugar drop."

"It could be epilepsy," Molly suggested.

Mom put her hands on her hips and glared at us. "I'll thank you three to stop talking about me like I'm not here. I just got a little light-headed from excitement, is all. You don't need to go diagnosing me."

"Yeah, I can't believe you're being so rude to Mom," Sherri cooed. "You should treat her with more respect."

I might have had trouble resisting the urge to claw her eyes out if Davy hadn't chosen that moment to push over the shelf he'd emptied with a loud squeal of delight.

"Oh, Davy," Molly moaned. In a preemptive strike to prevent more disasters, Teddy picked a protesting Davy up and moved him away from the scene of the crime as Molly headed over to straighten everything up.

"I still think you should—" Teddy began, but was interrupted when Mom shrieked.

I said a silent prayer for sanity and patience before turning around to see what was happening now. What ever had made me think that life would be quieter and simpler back home? The newcomer turned out to be Gene Ward, the subject of Mom's pharmacy gossip.

"Hey, Teddy," he said, hooking his thumbs in his belt loops. One of the loops immediately tore off.

"Hey, Gene," Teddy responded as he continued trying to settle Davy down. "Can we help you with something?"

Gene had been in Teddy's graduating class, which meant he must have been around thirty. Aside from clearer skin, a couple of fine lines around his eyes, and a hairline that had just started to recede, he looked like he'd been stuck in suspended animation since high school. In fact, he seemed to be wearing some of the same clothes he'd had then. He'd been something of a nerd—smart, but with next to no social skills. He might have been the first male under the age of sixty that Sherri didn't throw herself at as soon as he came through the door.

"My dad sent me in for some stuff," he said with a shrug as he handed a list to Teddy. Even there, he was stuck in a time warp, acting like a resentful teenager running errands for his parents.

Mom was still staring at him like she expected him to sprout horns, and he glanced warily at her a time or two while Teddy handed Davy back to his mother and went to put together Gene's order.

I decided that pulling Mom away from the situation was probably the smartest course of action. We didn't want to face the fallout that would happen with Gene's dad if she said or did something crazy. "Mom, I need your help with something in the office," I said.

She tore her gaze away from Gene. "Okay." She sounded a little shaky, and far too meek.

Once we were out of earshot from the front of the store, I asked, "What was going on with you out there? Was Gene the guy you saw in the square?"

"I don't know. I couldn't see his face. I'm pretty sure he wasn't wearing those shoes."

"Then why did you scream when you saw him? And why were you giving him that funny look?"

"My nerves are a little on edge right now. He just startled me. And as for a funny look, have you ever seen a boy who deserves a funny look more? He's Teddy's age, and he's still living with his parents, still doing nothing with his life, and going nowhere." I declined to point out that I was only a few years younger, and I was still living with and working for my parents.

"Well, you really gave us a shock. I think maybe you ought to go to the doctor, and I don't want you driving until we figure it out." I knew that the things she described were entirely possible, and they sounded an awful lot like the kinds of things my enemies liked to do. Come to think of it, my friends had done similar things when they tested my immunity in the first place. They'd made weirder and weirder things happen until I'd had no choice but to react so they could be sure I was seeing things that were magically hidden from normal people.

The problem was that things like that didn't happen here. In New York, you expected weird stuff, magical and otherwise, but I'd been assured by no less than Merlin himself that my hometown was practically a magic-free zone.

Even if this was all caused by magic, I wasn't allowed to let anyone else in on the secret, so there wasn't much I could do about it. If I started agreeing with Mom, everyone else would think I was as crazy as she was. But someone needed to get to the bottom of this, and it was probably best to rule out the simplest explanations. That was the way Owen tended to approach problem solving.

"Come on, Mom, I'll take you to the doctor so we can be sure you're okay."

"You need to take me to the beauty shop first. I'm only a little late for my appointment."

It was one of those situations where arguing would only cost me time and effort, so I decided to just go with it. Mom handed me her car keys, and we took her car to the town square, where the beauty shop was. Although the smell of permanent solution and hairspray usually made me sneeze, I hung around in the salon while Mom got her hair done so I could eavesdrop on the gossip. If anything at all had been happening on the square that morning, these women would be chattering about it. I noticed that Mom kept her mouth shut. She must have been tired of people treating her like she was crazy.

Unfortunately, the topic of conversation in the salon had nothing to do with weird goings-on on the courthouse square. Instead, I was the star of the show. "Lois, you're so lucky your little girl came back home," one woman said as the stylist wrapped her hair in tinfoil.

"I guess she didn't find herself a husband when she was off in New York," another one shouted from underneath a hair dryer hood.

"We thought at Thanksgiving that she was getting close," Mom said, "but that didn't work out. It was a real shame, too. He was a lawyer, and he had a Mercedes."

"It wasn't my idea to break up with him," I muttered, then realized I'd admitted to being dumped, which wasn't much better. I'd been the one to break things off with Owen, but as I'd never told anyone in my family about Owen in the first place, I had to keep my mouth shut about that.

"Well, you know, some girls are just unlucky at love," the stylist said, giving me a pitying look. I wasn't entirely sure if she was pitying my sad state of romantic affairs or my hair, which needed a good cut. That was something I wasn't likely to find here, so a ponytail was fine for the time being. It was certainly better than a big-hair bouffant or tight sausage curls, the two specialties of the house.

Mom finally emerged with her very own bouffant, and I drove her to the doctor's office a few blocks from the square. She was likely to get in with the doctor and then suddenly claim to be fine, so I insisted on accompanying her into the exam room. Dr. Charles had been my doctor when I was growing up, and I still couldn't look at him without thinking of booster shots.

"What seems to be the problem, Mrs. Chandler?" he asked, looking at us over the top of his reading glasses.

"Oh, I'm just fine," Mom said.

I knew it. "She had a fainting spell a little while ago," I said. "She passed out in the store and was out for several minutes. We thought it would be a good idea to have her checked out."

"Hmm, yes, I would think so." He went about checking her blood pressure and pulse, listening to her heart and lungs, and all those other little doctor tests. "Your blood pressure's a bit low," he said, "but otherwise you seem to be okay. Do you have any idea what might have brought on the spell? Did you have some kind of emotional shock?"

She looked at me, frowned, then looked back at the doctor. "I thought I saw something that gave me a bit of a start. Frank would say I let my imagination run away with me."

"Well, fainting after a shock happens more often in movies than in real life, but it does happen. I'd suggest taking it easy for a while. Put your feet up and make all those boys wait on you. Let me know right away if it happens again."

"I told you it wasn't anything serious," Mom said.

"Hey, better safe than sorry," I replied. "Thank you, Doctor."

"You were right to bring her in. It's best not to take sudden unconsciousness lightly."

Although the doctor had told Mom to make the boys wait on her, I knew exactly who'd be stuck with that thankless job. I could do paperwork at home or at the store, so we stopped by the store on the way home to let everyone know what the doctor had said and to pick up some things for me to work on. At home, I got Mom settled into her bed with some hot tea and a few magazines, but she stopped me before I could leave her room.

"You don't really think I'm going crazy, do you, Katie?"

I gave her what I hoped was a reassuring smile. "Not any crazier than usual."

"I swear, I *did* see all those things. It was almost like when we were in New York and it was so weird and wonderful. I just never expected to see anything like it here."

"Maybe that trip made you better at seeing unusual things, so you notice them more now."

She shook her head. "But then why didn't I see these things until now?" With a nervous laugh, she added, "I wouldn't be surprised if I am letting my imagination run wild. I mean, look at Mama. She's not always entirely there, and I'm not sure she ever has been, what with all her talk about the old country and the wee folk, and all that. If I am crazy, I certainly come by it honestly. As they say, the nut doesn't fall too far from the tree."

It occurred to me right then that my grandmother might be magically immune. Owen had said that the trait was genetic. It would certainly explain a lot about some of the wild tales she told. She really might have seen wee folk and fairies. "I guess I'm doomed, then," I told my mother.

"No, you're my levelheaded one," she said. "Who says the craziness is limited to women? It'll be one of your brothers in your generation. You're far too sane to take after your mother and grandmother."

If only you knew, I thought as I left her room.

Sherri showed up in mid-afternoon, probably to avoid other work while also taking advantage of a kissing-up opportunity. I left her with Mom so I could head back into town. If Mom's mysterious cloaked man had been going after money from the morning commuters at the courthouse, he'd surely be there for the afternoon rush, and I wanted to see it with my own eyes. Before I left the house, I went up to my bedroom and unlocked my jewelry box. I ignored the tinny song it played and the ballerina that twirled when I opened the lid while I retrieved the item I needed.

Owen had given me the locket for Christmas, but it wasn't the sentimental value I needed at the moment. Rather than being a significant piece of relationship jewelry, it was a magical tool. It amplified the sensation of magic in use so that I had more to go on than an ambiguous tingling sensation. I clasped it around my neck and tucked it under my T-shirt before taking Mom's car downtown.

I found a parking space at one corner of the courthouse that allowed me to watch two sides simultaneously. The only people I saw were ordinary county workers in suits or business-casual clothes. No statues moved, no one wore robes, and no one behaved at all oddly—other than me, of course. Sitting alone in a vehicle in front of the courthouse for no apparent reason wasn't exactly a normal way to spend the afternoon.

I was beginning to wish I'd stopped by the Dairy Queen for a malt on my way over when I saw something that made me do a double take. If I wasn't mistaken, one of the Art Deco relief sculptures of a buffalo on the newest wing of the courthouse had moved its head. I blinked, trying to bring it into focus, but it went back to being just another sculpture. Staring at anything for too long after being out in the heat could make anyone think they were seeing things, I decided. My necklace hadn't so much as trembled, so it probably wasn't magic. Of course it wasn't magic, I reminded myself. This was Cobb, not New York. We didn't have magic here.

I got out of Mom's car to walk around, hoping the fresh air would clear my head. It was hard to tell what on the courthouse really belonged there and what might be new or unusual, considering what a mishmash of architectural styles it was. Different parts had been built in different eras, with the older parts remodeled in odd ways over the years, so that there were Gothic gargoyles perched on Art Deco arches. I remembered all the lectures from junior high art class when we'd taken field trips to sketch the courthouse. Too bad I didn't still have those drawings, I thought. They'd have helped me be more sure of what I was seeing.

At the far side of the courthouse, near the gazebo that was part of the Civil War memorial, I saw a figure that didn't seem to belong. He wore a rough, hooded robe that made him look more like a Jedi Knight than like a wizard. Then again, I hadn't ever seen any wizards wearing robes, except at a costume party. Even Merlin wore business suits these days. I hid behind a crepe myrtle bush to watch him.

He danced around, waving his arms, and I thought I heard something that might have been chanting, though I was too far away to hear it clearly. He was certainly putting out more effort than I ever saw from the wizards I knew. They usually just waved a hand and muttered a few words to get what they wanted. My necklace hummed slightly against my chest, but it was perhaps the weakest response I'd ever noticed from it. After a while, the arms on the statue in front of the robed figure shivered, and the statue seemed to wake up. The robed figure then jumped up and down for joy. While he was jumping, the statue went back to its usual position and froze. I could hear his groan of frustration quite clearly when he noticed that.

The clock in the courthouse tower chimed five, and soon all the county workers came spilling down the front steps of the courthouse. The robed figure turned to face the sidewalk and waved his arms vigorously. My necklace shivered ever so slightly. Nobody seemed to notice that there was anything unusual happening. Every so often, one of the workers would go glassy-eyed for a second, and then he'd put some money on the ground in front of the robed figure before heading down the sidewalk. A few steps later, the worker would stumble, look disoriented for a second, and then go on his way.

I bit my tongue to keep myself from gasping out loud. I'd seen something like that once before, when Owen had tested one of Phelan Idris's control spells.

I wouldn't have believed if I hadn't seen it for myself, but it looked like the least magical place on earth now had a town wizard.

Four

My first impulse was to run at the wizard and tackle him to pull off his robes and uncover his identity, but I held back. His spells might not have been able to hurt me, but physical sticks and stones could break my bones. Not to mention the fact that assault and battery were considered crimes, and I was in the town square where both the county sheriff's department and the city police department were housed. I didn't think "but he was doing magic" would count as a valid excuse for an attack.

And then I realized that spying on the guy the way I was might not be the best idea, either. The wizard was definitely veiling himself and his activities from nonmagical people, judging from the lack of reaction to him. I had no such protection. Anyone who walked past would see me lurking around the courthouse grounds for no apparent reason. I guessed I could have approached him to talk to him and find out what his intentions were, but in case he wasn't one of the good guys, I didn't want to expose myself as a magical immune. That was my secret weapon, my ace up the sleeve. I'd need to know more before I could take any action.

A woman leaving the courthouse gave me a funny look, and I made a show of bending to examine a flowering bush. Then I smiled at her and said, "That new plant food we sold the county sure made the azaleas do well this year." When she'd walked past, I turned back to see what the wizard was doing, but he was gone. I didn't see a sign of him anywhere around the square. I somehow doubted he'd magically teleported away, given how weak his magic seemed to be, but he could have taken off his robes while my back was turned and blended into the flow of courthouse workers leaving for the day.

I made a circuit of the square, pausing to look at various plants I passed along the way so I'd have a good cover story for my strange behavior. Teddy did that kind of thing on a regular basis, so no one should have found it particularly odd for me to do it. Sometimes there are benefits to coming from a family known for its share of oddities. Finally convinced that I'd let my quarry get away, I headed to Mom's car so I could drive to the feed store.

It proved to be empty of customers at closing time, but full of family. Even Dean was hanging around, leaning against the front counter. He had almost enough sweat beading on his forehead for me to imagine he might have done real work that afternoon. Mom and Sherri were the only ones not there. "Wow, did someone decide to throw a family reunion without letting me know?" I asked.

"We were talking about your mother," Dad said solemnly.

"Mom's fine. She just got a little overexcited."

"It's not the first time," Molly said softly.

"She's acting like she did in New York, when she kept talking about seeing things," Dad added.

Of course she'd seen things in New York. She was magically immune and in a place full of magical people. "Well, New York can be weird," I quipped. "You don't really think she's crazy, do you?"

I looked around at the others, who all appeared deeply concerned. Even Beth was frowning, and she was usually the most optimistic one in the bunch. "We're worried that she might be putting her health at risk," Teddy said, putting an arm around his wife. "That fainting spell today wasn't a good sign."

"So, what are you proposing we do?" I asked. "Put her away somewhere?"

Dad shook his head. "No, not that, not yet. But it might be good for her to get some professional help. They could find out what's wrong with her and do something to make her better."

The funny thing was, the treatment they'd give her probably really would make her better. That's because antipsychotic medications tended to have a dampening effect on magical immunity. If they put Mom on drugs, she'd stop seeing things, one way or another. It would certainly make life easier for the family, but would it be good for Mom? With a possible magical war brewing, I liked the idea that magic couldn't be used against my mother. Most of the danger I'd gotten into had been during times when my immunity had been altered. Plus, there were side effects to long-term use of drugs like that, and I didn't like the idea of her taking them when she wasn't really sick.

"That still sounds a little extreme considering that she's just had a few bouts of flightiness," I insisted. "Heck, Granny's been talking about the wee folk for years, and we haven't drugged or committed her."

Beth crossed the room to take my hands in hers. "Katie, I know it's hard to think this way about your mother, but we really do have to consider what's best for her."

Under other circumstances, I'd have been the first to admit that Mom could be a bit on the crazy side, but that was just her personality. Now I knew for a fact that Mom was most definitely not crazy, that everything she'd seen had been real. Unfortunately, it was impossible for me to explain that Mom wasn't crazy without sounding even crazier than she did. It's one thing to announce that you've seen something odd. It's another entirely to say that you know exactly what the odd thing was and that it really was magic.

"We're not talking about shipping her off to the state hospital tomorrow," Dad said. "We just want to keep an eye on her for the next few weeks and make sure she's okay."

"She's probably a little overtired and stressed-out," Beth said reassuringly, giving my hands a squeeze. "A week or so of rest, and she'll be right back to normal."

She most definitely would be, if I could do anything about it. "Okay," I agreed. "Two weeks, and then we'll discuss this again. And now, I probably ought to catch up on some work while Sherri's watching Mom." The circle split up as everyone headed off to their respective jobs to close the store down for the night. Fortunately, no one followed me to the office. I didn't need an audience for what I was about to do.

There was only one way I could ensure that Mom stopped seeing things that would make her sound crazy, and that was to deal with the magic. Magic wasn't normal around here, and I was pretty sure my former boss would want to hear about the situation. Making life easier for Mom would be a bonus.

With one last look over my shoulder, I picked up the phone and dialed my old office. It was after business hours in New York, but my boss had a way of knowing when something was going on, and since he lived in the office building, there was a chance he'd still be around.

Sure enough, a deep voice answered the phone after one ring. "Hello, Katie. It's good to hear from you." When I'd first met Merlin, he'd had an indecipherable accent, but at the time he'd only recently been awakened from a long magical hibernation and had just learned modern English. Yes, I mean *that* Merlin, the one from Camelot. He's my boss—well, former boss. His accent had faded considerably in the time I'd been gone. He barely sounded foreign anymore. "Now, what seems to be the trouble?"

I checked over my shoulder one more time before launching into the whole story about the wizard on the courthouse square. "And now the family thinks Mom is crazy. I can't let her be medicated or locked

away when I know that what she's seeing is real. Are there even supposed to be wizards in this area?"

"There are none I've heard of. I shall have to check with the regula-
tory body to see if one has registered. I do, however, find it very suspicious that one has appeared in your hometown at this time."

"Do you think Idris and his gang figured out where I am and followed me to stir things up? That was exactly what I was trying to prevent by leaving New York, you know."

"We don't yet have enough information to know, but we should at
least investigate. Given our ongoing problems with rogue magic, I
would prefer to be safe rather than sorry."

"Thank you. I had a feeling this was something you'd want to hear
about. So far, this guy doesn't seem to be doing anything all that dangerous other than stirring up Mom and maybe bilking the courthouse workers out of a dollar or two. I guess I'm mostly worried because his spells
look awfully familiar, like the type of spells Idris has been trying to sell. At
the very least, it might tell us if he's going after a national market."

Idris had once worked for MSI but was fired for spending too much
time developing ethically questionable spells. He'd then gone into business for himself marketing those same spells out of back-alley shops,
and we'd managed to put a stop to that by making sure he couldn't sell
anything he'd developed as an MSI employee. He'd made a comeback
with some serious financial backing, this time selling a wider variety of
spells, but still focusing on the kind of magic MSI avoided, like using
magic to influence others for personal gain.

"I will send someone to investigate as soon as possible," Merlin said.

"Great!" And then because I couldn't resist, I added, "And how are
things going otherwise? Any new developments?"

"Mr. Idris is being his usual elusive self. We have had no new encounters since you left, which has made it difficult to make much headway."

"Maybe all I need to do is stay out of town and you won't have any
trouble at all," I grumbled.

"I hardly think that is the case. He and the people he apparently an-swers to have likely been working on something new that will surprise and confound us, as always."

"Oh. Well, keep up the good work."

After I got off the phone with Merlin, I got online to check airline schedules, just out of curiosity. If whoever Merlin sent took half an hour or so to wrap things up at the office, he could be home within an hour. He might need half an hour to pack, and then it could take at least an hour to get to LaGuardia at this time of day. That is, if he used normal transportation. Magical folk had other means of travel at their disposal, things like teleporting or using flying carpets, but I decided to estimate on the safe side. I looked for flights within a couple of hours of that time and saw that there were several options throughout the evening. They arrived at the Dallas–Fort Worth airport very late at night, and then it was about a two-hour drive to get here.

I forced myself to stop creating a mental itinerary before I drove my-self crazy. I had no idea how big an emergency they considered this to be. Nobody was going to rush straight to the airport and hop a plane just because I'd called with a report of odd things going on in a small, out-of-the-way town. Besides, I doubted it would be the person I most wanted them to send. Why would they send one of their top guys to check on a little bit of amateur wizardry in a backwater like this? Owen would be in New York, heading up the overall efforts, not running off to Texas to put out minor fires. They probably had specialists for dealing with new wizards in unexpected places. And did I really want to see him, anyway?

Well, yeah, I did want to see him. I got a flutter in my chest just thinking about it. The question was, would seeing him be a good idea? I was able to feel noble and stoic for my brave decision to walk away from a man I was falling in love with in order to further the greater good. If I saw him again, it might not be so easy to be noble. There was also al-ways the chance that he didn't want to see me. I had no idea what he thought about what I'd done, whether he understood or was angry. So I guess that made Owen both the person I most and least wanted to see.

I held my breath all morning at the store the next day, and I nearly jumped out of my skin every time I heard the front door open. It was entirely possible that whomever Merlin had sent could be here by now. But each time, it was only a customer. I spent more time in the front of the store than I usually liked to; I was far too edgy to stay in my office.

By lunchtime, I'd come to the conclusion that a watched pot never boiled, so the surest way to make the person from MSI show up would be to take off for a while. I picked up lunch at the Dairy Queen, then went over to the motel to eat with Nita. She was sitting behind the front desk, her nose buried in a pink book with a martini glass on the cover. She jerked to attention when the bell on the front door jingled as I entered. "What brings you here?" she asked.

"I needed a break from my crazy family," I said, in all honesty. "Sometimes I worry that I'll get caught up in the madness and become just as bad as they are."

She groaned. "Tell me about it. You should have seen the ceremony my mom did this morning. Incense, chanting, all that."

I thought the room smelled different—not the usual scent of surface cleaner and pine air freshener. "Why? What happened?"

"My dad watched the security tapes from the other night, when the window vanished. There wasn't anyone on there for half an hour before and after the time I'm pretty sure I heard something. The tape's too grainy to tell exactly when the window went away. Of course, Mom had a big freak-out. I actually think the time on the security camera is off. It didn't get set for Daylight Savings Time a few years ago, and it hasn't been right since, but she'd prefer to believe there were evil spirits."

"Your mom and my mom must be drinking the same Kool-Aid," I

said as I joined her on her side of the counter. "My mom's become convinced that there's something very odd going on in town." Never mind that she was right. It was her enthusiasm for finding oddities—and the possibility that it would get her into trouble—that worried me. And now I wondered if the missing window might have something to do with our town wizard.

"It's because this town is so incredibly dull that you have to imagine things to find any excitement at all. If my dad had to conform to every cultural stereotype and run a motel, why couldn't it at least have been one in a real city? We could have been near Six Flags. Or maybe the Alamo." Nita waved her book at me. "It's no fair! Why can't I have this kind of life—having cosmos at a bar after work with my friends and going on lots of hot dates with successful men? And to think, you were there and you left it behind!"

"It's not quite the way it seems in books."

"So you didn't go out with your friends and you didn't go on dates?"

"Well, yeah, I guess I did. But it wasn't as fun as it sounds in books. I got set up on a lot of blind dates that never went well. Some of them were real disasters."

"You know what they say, you have to kiss a lot of frogs before you meet your prince."

I shuddered. "That's not as effective as you'd think," I muttered under my breath.

"What's that?"

"I mean, quantity doesn't necessarily mean you'll ever find quality." Plus, men who'd been turned into frogs tended to have some lingering issues once you broke the spell and turned them back into men.

"It still sounds better to me than spending my life sitting behind this desk. Is one date too much to ask for?"

"You've never been on a date?"

"Oh, come on Katie, you were there in high school."

"Yeah, but surely since then?"

"Okay, maybe one or two in college when my parents didn't know. But nothing since then. Who would I date around here?"

"Steve Grant is apparently still single."

She laughed out loud. "Oh, good one! He's exactly my type!" Once she got herself under control she said, "Well, if you aren't willing to run away to the city with me, maybe we can take a trip for a couple of days and do some girl stuff like go shopping and have drinks and flirt and all that. What do you say?"

"I say it sounds like fun. I just have a few family things I want to straighten out first."

"I heard about your mom's fainting spell. Is she okay?"

News really did travel fast in this town. "Yeah, the doctor said she's probably fine. We're keeping an eye on her for a while, just in case."

"Okay, then I'll start angling for a couple of days off, and then we can hit the city! What do you think, Dallas or Austin? Dallas has the shopping—not that I can afford much, but it would be fun to look— and Austin has the nightlife. I know, I'll look it up in the tourist guides and see what looks good."

And she was off. This was a plan she might actually carry out, I thought as I noticed the way her eyes shone. I knew how stifled I felt around here and could only imagine what life must be like for her. "Let me know what you decide, and I'll try to swing some time off myself."

I heard a car drive up in front of the office and whirled to look. It was a relatively new, bland sedan that was probably a rental. My heart started racing. Maybe he'd stopped to secure accommodations and then freshen up before meeting me at the store to get the scoop, and this was the only motel in town. The only other lodgings were in a bed-and-breakfast in an old mansion near the square. Unfortunately for both Nita and me, the man who got out of the car was neither young and Indian nor Owen. He was just another middle-aged traveling salesman type who must have pissed off someone in his company to get assigned this cruddy territory.

I shook my head at my own silliness. Why was I still getting excited to see a rental car when I was fairly certain it wasn't going to be Owen? Deep down inside, I supposed I still hoped that he'd insist on being the one to come investigate because he wanted to see me as much as I wanted to see him. Nita didn't have a monopoly on romantic fantasies, it appeared.

While she checked the salesman in, I arranged our lunches on the desk behind the counter, then picked up one of the many magazines she kept in a nearby basket and flipped through it. It was one of those regional tourist magazines they put in hotel rooms, with a few articles about local attractions, a calendar of events, and a lot of ads. The articles were the same in almost every issue, so I went straight to the ads, hoping to find something interesting to do in there. What I saw was more than interesting. It was downright weird.

On the page full of ads for area private schools, there was one that said, "Can you read this?" Since I could, I kept reading.

If you're one of the few, select people who can read this ad, you may have special abilities! With the right training to develop your natural talents, fame and fortune are practically inevitable!

It reminded me of those ads that said if you could draw a turtle cartoon, you could get training to illustrate children's books. Except this ad didn't ask for anything other than the ability to read it. I leaned closer to the page so my necklace practically touched it, and then I felt the faint vibration from a very weak spell. The ability they were looking for was magic, I was sure. The ad must have been veiled so that only people with magic powers—or the complete lack thereof—could read it. I had a feeling I knew where our local wizard must have come from. Someone around here was training people to use magic.

Nita sent the customer off on his way to his room, then we settled down for lunch. I left the magazine open on the desk, the ad clearly visible. "What do you think of that?" I asked, pointing in the general direction of the ad in question.

She leaned over and squinted at the page. "'Miss Rochester's Academy for Young Ladies,'" she read. "'Training girls in social deportment for a refined way of life.' You have got to be kidding. I am so glad my mom never saw anything like this when I was in high school. If she thought she could have shipped me off to a private school to teach me to be demure, she would have."

If Nita couldn't see it, the ad must have been veiled, and this also meant that Nita was neither magical nor magically immune. "It sounds kind of Victorian, doesn't it?" I said. I finished my lunch, then made excuses about getting back to the store. "Mind if I take this?" I asked, picking up the magazine.

"Why? You think you need to learn social graces?"

"No, there's an article I thought Teddy would be interested in."

"Sure, take it," she said with a wave. "I get a stack of them every month. The idea is to give them away."

Once I got into investigation mode, it was hard to stop myself, so on my way back to the store, I detoured by the courthouse square to see if anything was going on. It appeared to be the kind of day that put the "sleepy" into "sleepy little town." Not much of anything was stirring, especially not a robed wizard. The statues remained reassuringly still.

Then I took another look at the roof. There were gargoyles on part of the courthouse, but I didn't recall ever seeing any on this side. I tensed as a gargoyle unfurled its wings and soared down to ground level. That was certainly something I'd never seen the courthouse gargoyles do. It was, however, something I'd seen gargoyles do often enough in New York, particularly this one.

"Sam!" I cried out and ran to hug him. I had to bend a little because gargoyles aren't generally that big, and he folded his wings around me in a hug. I realized then that I'd never touched him before. He had an odd texture, simultaneously rocky and leathery. "I'm glad they sent you," I said when we broke apart.

"Hey, wouldn't have missed it for the world, doll. Besides, who'd you expect them to send other than their top gumshoe?"

"I'm glad they sent the best."

"What appears to be the deal?"

I explained quickly about the things Mom had seen and what I'd observed. When I finished, Sam nodded. "Okay, looks like I'll be staking out the square here for a while, get an idea what the perp's up to, and then I can figure out what to do about it."

"Sounds like a plan. I've also found something I want to check out." I told him about the magazine ad.

He made a whistling sound, like the wind blowing across the top of a Coke bottle. "That's not good. You think that's what our local wizard is up to?"

"Could be. There's a Web address, so I'll go look it up, and I'll keep you posted on what I find. Want me to stop by on any particular schedule?"

"Nah, don't worry about it. I'm officially on the case, so you can stand down. I'll find you if I need you. This place ain't a tenth the size of Manhattan, and I can find you there." Actually, the incorporated landmass of the town wasn't too much smaller than Manhattan Island, but I knew what he meant.

"Okay, then. Let me know if you need anything. Oh, and remember that you might have to be careful. People are more likely to notice little oddities and ask about them here than they are in New York. News spreads fast. Plus, my mom's immune, and I think my grandmother might be, too. I have other relatives around, so there's no telling how far that trait spreads." It would be ironic if this town turned out to be the nonmagical capital of the world from being the home of more immunes than any other place. That would actually explain a lot about how boring the place was.

"Got it. Now shoo so I can get on with my stakeout."

Once I got back to the store, it took me awhile before I had time to look up the magic school. We were busy with customers, and then even when the afternoon rush died down, I kept having family members pop into my office. They finally got busy again with their own work, and I pulled the folded-up magazine out of my bag, then typed the Web address into my browser.

It took the site forever to load, which made me wonder how much bandwidth magic required. The initial page looked a lot like the ad, but instead of the contact info in the ad, there was a button to click on if you could see the ad and wanted to know more. I clicked on it, then waited for the next page to load.

When it came up, the Spellworks logo was at the top of the page. My stomach did a backflip before tying itself into a square knot. That company was our enemy, and that meant Phelan Idris was behind whatever was going on in town.

Five

I had to hold my breath while I read so I could concentrate, and moving my computer's mouse was difficult with my hands shaking. The Web page said that if you could read this site, you had magical powers—which wasn't entirely accurate, as I very well knew, but I didn't expect them to explain the concept of magical immunity in their initial "magic is real" paragraph. There had to be something else in the site to weed out people like me. It went on to describe all the benefits of having magical powers, including the usual stuff like wealth, influence over others, and making the world work the way you wanted it to. Of course, there was no mention of learning the proper context for using your power, but then a code of ethics wasn't something I'd expect to see in a sales pitch, so I didn't count the ethical lapse against Idris this time.

For an introductory fee of five hundred dollars and then a monthly fee of two hundred dollars, you could learn to use your powers. The site promised that within two months, you could start using magic to more than make up for the amount you spent on the lessons. Lessons would be taught online using streaming video, with message boards for interacting with the instructor and with other students. The rest was the usual "act now" stuff, including info on paying by credit card for automatic monthly payments.

I clicked around on the page, trying to find more information, but everything appeared to be password protected. Oddly, I didn't see anything to click on in order to sign up for the classes. That must have been their trap to weed out immunes. The "sign up now" button was probably an illusion that I couldn't see.

This was big. If Idris was out to teach people how to do magic his way, the world could be in a lot of trouble. On a whim, I tried Googling every phrase I could think of that might lead me to magic lessons, but I didn't ever get the Spellworks site in the search results. At least it didn't look like random people playing around on the Internet could stumble on the site. The question was, how widely were they advertising this? Was it just around here, and what was the purpose in teaching a bunch of amateurs to do petty parlor tricks?

When I'd wrapped up my work for the day, I headed straight to the courthouse to find Sam. I took a magazine stuffed with printouts from the Spellworks website and sat on a bench, trying to look like I was just casually sitting there, reading the magazine. Sam flew down from the roof to join me. "The perp must've heard of my reputation and took off," he said with a grin on his grotesque face. "Not a single sight of 'im. And boy, is this town of yours slow, or what?"

"Tell me about it. Believe it or not, this is pretty exciting as things go around here. But I have something you need to see." I pulled the pages out of my magazine to show to him. "It's not quite what was on the website—maybe magic doesn't come through on the printer—but I think you can get the idea. They're recruiting new wizards. Can they do that? Are there really people out there who don't know they have magical powers?"

He shrugged. "Hey, that's not my area of expertise. I just do security, you know? But there's gotta be someone out there who doesn't know he's really a wizard. We can't catch 'em all. This definitely looks bigger than a single rogue wizard to me. It might be easier to put a stop to this here than in New York."

"Why's that? All our people and resources are in New York."

"But there's no power here. The magical lines are weak in these parts, which is why you don't have a big magical community. Magical folk tend to settle around lines of power. We get a few of our big guns down here who are highly trained and who've got their own reserves of power, and fighting off the bad guys will be a snap. In New York, there's enough power flying around to put everyone on a more even footing. We just need to figure out who our local wizard is, grab him, and then we can use him to draw Idris out."

"Cool."

"Hey, ain't it funny that you headed down here to get away from all that, and then it comes to you anyway?"

"Yeah, it's a real scream." From what Sam had said, it didn't sound like the specifics of my decision to leave had been widely broadcast. I may not have escaped from magic, but I had still separated myself from Owen so he wouldn't be tempted to make the wrong choice in a show-down, so I figured I'd still accomplished something by leaving. "You'll tell headquarters what's going on?"

"Don't worry, I got it under control."

Before I could respond to him, someone called my name from across the courthouse grounds. I turned to see Nita waving at me. Then she ran full throttle toward me, so fast that Sam had to scramble to get off the bench before she plopped down on top of him. "What are you doing here?" she asked me.

I tried to keep my eyes from following Sam as he flew back to the courthouse roof. "Oh, you know, just hanging out."

She raised an eyebrow. "At the courthouse?"

"The grounds are nice. It's like a park. And my family isn't here."

"That would be the important part."

"So, what are you doing here?"

"Mom sent me to the grocery store. It's my day to get off 'early.'" She formed air quotes with her fingers. "That means I get to go home at a normal hour after working a normal day, and Dad works the desk until Ramesh gets to start a little later on the overnight shift. This is practically a weekend for me." She whirled a finger in the air in a halfhearted show of celebration. "Whoopie. Hey, I have an idea. We should do something tonight."

I looked around at the sleepy town square, then spread my hands to indicate all that nothingness. "Like what?"

"We could eat out and go to a movie. It's a Tom Cruise movie this week."

"Eww." I made a face. "I can't stand him." Besides, the last thing I wanted to do right now was look at a dark-haired, blue-eyed man who wasn't Owen.

"Your lack of aesthetic sense is not my problem. He's pretty as long as he keeps his mouth shut. And it's not like we have a lot of options. There's one movie screen in town, and that's what's showing. Otherwise, we could watch Bollywood musicals with my mom or crime dramas with your dad, or I guess we could find an empty motel room and watch HBO."

We'd actually had some cool slumber parties doing that when we were kids, but the idea wasn't as thrilling now as it had been back then. "Okay, you win. Dinner and a movie it is." Plus, being out and about would help me spot any additional magical weirdness that might ensue. It was almost like I was getting to be part of the investigation.

Nita bounced off the bench. "Cool! Now we just have to get some groceries and take them home to Mom, and then I'm free."

"I could wait here for you." I wanted to talk to Sam some more, and the wizard seemed to be most active at this time of day.

She shook her head vigorously while she grabbed my arm and tugged me off the bench. "No, I need you with me so I can escape. If you're with me already, Mom won't be able to come up with an excuse for me to stay in."

We picked up the groceries, then rode in Nita's ancient Escort to the little house behind the motel where the Patels lived. Mrs. Patel greeted me with her usual combination of warmth and suspicion. I always got the feeling that she liked me but didn't quite trust me not to get her daughter in trouble—never mind that it was almost always the other way around. Moving a mile a minute, Nita dashed through the kitchen, putting away the groceries she'd bought and chattering nonstop about our plans so that her mother couldn't get a word in edgewise to object. When we were back outside in the car, I was out of breath just from watching her performance.

The café on the town square was practically full when we got there—not that there were too many tables to begin with. Dean and Sherri were there, seated front and center. I gave them a wave as we headed to our own table but didn't stop to talk. "I still can't believe he married her," Nita said when we sat down. "He was so hot, he could have had anyone."

"Nita, he's my brother."

"So? He's still hot, and I'm not related to him. Okay, so he's a bit of a jerk, and I could have thrown myself at him naked and he wouldn't have noticed, but that doesn't mean I don't like looking at him." She craned ever so slightly in her seat to get a better view.

"Between this and your Tom Cruise thing, I really think you need to get out more."

"Thank you! I've been saying that for ages."

She reluctantly ordered the vegetable plate, saying that her dad was bound to get a report if she ordered pot roast and was seen eating it in public. I ordered the pot roast, with plans to sneak her a piece or two. We chatted about her latest scheme for updating the motel while we waited for our meals, and our food was served before she could get sidetracked into talking about my love life. We were enjoying lemon pie for dessert when a commotion arose from one of the front tables. I cringed when I realized Dean and Sherri were at it again.

"I swear to God, Dean Chandler, you have got a hole in your pocket!" Sherri shouted. Every head in the room turned to watch the fight.

"You get a paycheck, too. Why do I have to be the one to buy your dinner?"

"Because I buy the groceries and pay the bills—since you can't be bothered. And because you forgot my birthday. Again. You owe me a dinner."

"Sherri, this is not the time. I don't have any cash on me, so just pay the damn check."

She threw a few bills on the table, then stalked out of the restaurant. He sat back down after she'd left and asked the waitress for another cup of coffee. As soon as the show was over, all the spectators turned to look at me, as if to see my reaction. I shrugged and rolled my eyes. "Hey, who knew we were going to get dinner and a show," I quipped to Nita. "No need to see a movie now."

"You're not getting out of the movie that easily."

The theater was a relic from the past—no stadium seating, digital projection, or surround sound. It was the same theater where my parents had watched a double feature of Westerns for a dime on Saturday afternoons when they were kids, and it hadn't changed much since then. About the only difference was the ticket prices, which were still a real bargain compared to movie theaters in New York. Here, I could afford to buy snacks after buying a movie ticket. Nita and I bought popcorn and candy, then looked for two adjacent seats in the theater that weren't broken or with springs coming through the worn velvet. There were about ten other people in the auditorium by the time the movie started. (Of course, the tallest one sat right in front of me.)

I zoned out and ate my snacks, barely paying any attention to the movie, which seemed to mostly involve a lot of running around and stuff blowing up. The sound system was as vintage as the theater, but they made up for it by cranking up the volume to the point that my whole body vibrated. Nita was engrossed in the film, I was sure. But then I turned to look at her and was surprised to see her sound asleep. She must have been working long hours lately, I thought. But then the head of the tall guy in front of me drooped forward. A loud snore came from the row behind me. It wasn't the best movie ever, but it wasn't an insomnia cure, either.

That was when I noticed a figure sneaking through the theater. An explosion on the screen revealed the cloaked and hooded wizard, and he was aiming for the tall guy sitting in front of me. I slumped down in my seat, fished a Junior Mint out of my candy box, and flicked it at the base of the tall guy's neck. He sat up with a start, rubbing his neck, and the wizard hit the floor. The wizard must have been trying a sleeping spell to make it easy to pickpocket the audience. I elbowed Nita hard in the ribs.

"Welcome to the Cobb Inn!" she blurted as she popped back to life. Then she blinked and looked around. "Did I fall asleep?" she whispered to me.

"You picked the movie," I said with a shrug. She went back to gazing dreamily at Tom on the screen, and I noticed the wizard moving around the theater again. I leaned over to her and whispered, "I'm heading to the bathroom." She barely nodded in acknowledgment, her eyes stuck on the screen.

I duckwalked to the end of the row, trying to keep my head below the level of the seats while avoiding getting any part of my body other than my feet on the theater floor, which was coated in decades' worth of spilled soda. When I got to a place where I was safely hidden but still had a straight shot at the other audience members, I started throwing Junior Mints at the sleeping people to wake them up. Soon the theater was full of people sitting up and rubbing their heads. I hadn't noticed the buildup of magic—probably because any vibrating from my necklace would have been lost in the boom of the sound system—but I felt its absence when the spell apparently ended. Just at that moment, I turned to see the cloaked figure slip out through the emergency exit in the front of the auditorium. I was tempted to follow him, but I knew I wasn't equipped for taking down a wizard. Sam was outside in the square, watching for cloaked figures, so I left it to him and went back to my seat.

Once the sleeping spell was gone, I was the one who had to be elbowed back to life at the end of the movie. As the lights came up, someone in the back of the theater shouted, "My wallet!" Then at the front of the theater, someone yelled, "Is this it?" Owner and wallet were soon reunited, although the wallet had been stripped of cash.

"It was probably some kid," Nita said as we left the theater, still munching our leftover popcorn. "The crime rate has really gone up in the last year or so. Some of the kids have even tried to form a gang. Not that they know what to do with a gang, but it's a lot of pranks like that. I remember when you could leave your purse on the seat beside you during a movie and it would be totally safe."

"Yeah, kids these days."

The two of us were still giggling about sounding like old-timers when Nita shrieked. "What is it?" I asked.

She didn't bother answering. Instead, she grabbed the wooden advertising sign from in front of the antiques shop next to the theater and beat it on the ground a few times, all the while shouting, "Take that, and that, and that!" Then she grabbed my arm, shrieked again, and took off running across the square. I had to struggle to keep up with her.

"What is it?" I asked again when she'd slowed down enough to talk.

She pointed shakily toward the sidewalk near the movie theater. "Snake! There! Sidewalk! Dead now!"

"You killed a snake on the sidewalk by the movie theater?" I translated.

She nodded furiously, and I couldn't help but look for something high to stand on top of. "What kind of snake was it?"

"Dead. If you really want to know, you can go look for yourself, but I don't think much of the head is left."

"I'll take your word for it." I had a feeling there wouldn't be anything to find, though. I hadn't seen a snake at all. I suspected it had been little more than an illusion, but was Nita the target, or was I? I looked up to see Sam sitting on a tree branch nearby, and I felt a lot safer. His job was protecting people against magical threats, and I had a feeling he'd know what to do with a snake, too. "Are you okay?" I asked Nita.

"I need ice cream," she announced. "Killing snakes makes me hungry." We got into her car and went to the Dairy Queen for sundaes, then headed back to the courthouse square so I could get my truck and go home. Unfortunately, my truck wasn't there.

"Boy, you were right about the crime," I said, staring at the empty parking space. I didn't care enough about the old truck to be too sad about it being stolen from me, but it was going to be inconvenient.

"Look, there's something on the curb," Nita pointed out. A piece of paper sitting on the curb fluttered from under a rock placed on top of it.

I retrieved the paper, then moved under a streetlamp to read out loud: "Sis, borrowed the truck since Sherri left me stranded. I still had a key. I'll get it back to you later. Get a ride home with Nita. Dean." I looked over at Nita. "Can I get a ride home?"

"No problem. That just keeps me out later, which is okay with me. Too bad there aren't any bars in town so we could make it a real girls' night out."

"We both have early mornings tomorrow," I reminded her, "and seeing as we both snoozed a little during the movie, I don't think we're up for a late night. Besides, your mom would kill you if you went out drinking, and then she'd be convinced I led you to your ruin."

"I have *got* to get away from here. I'm too young to act like a senior citizen. Well, come on, let's go."

When we were back in her car, I said, "Drive by Dean's house first. It will make life easier if I can pick the truck up now." But the truck wasn't there, just Sherri and Dean's cars. It looked like Dean had started and then forgotten some kind of ambitious building project on the front of the house, which might explain why Sherri was peeved at him. "Oh well, never mind. I guess you'll have to take me home. I wonder where Dean is."

The truck was parked in the driveway at my parents' house, which wasn't a huge surprise. Dean ran straight home every time he and Sherri had a fight. Nita glanced over at me and said, "We've got empty rooms at the motel if you need a place to hide."

I unbuckled my seat belt. "Thanks for the offer, but this shouldn't be too bad. I'll just go to my room and ignore it all. And thanks for the night out—it was fun."

"No, it wasn't really what I'd call fun, but it was about as close as you can get around here, and thanks for coming along. See you soon!"

I got inside to find Dean sitting at the kitchen table, being consoled by Mom with various pastries. "Someday she'll learn to appreciate all the things you have to offer her," Mom was saying as I crept through the kitchen. The only time Mom ever said anything against Sherri was when Dean and Sherri were fighting, which meant I got to hear Mom criticize Sherri at least once a month.

"'Night, everyone!" I said casually once I was safely in the living room.

"Did you have a good time at the movies?" Mom asked.

"Just fabulous. And how did you know?"

"I saw you heading over there after you left the café," Dean admitted. In other words, he'd blabbed about my night out, even though I was an adult and allowed to go out with a friend. On the other hand, that meant Mom had known where I was and hadn't panicked, so I decided not to complain this time. I was a lot more disturbed by the magical activity I'd seen, some of which was actual criminal behavior instead of just the semi-benign manipulation the wizard had been doing earlier.

As soon as I was sure everyone in the house was sound asleep—including Dean in the bedroom he used to share with Teddy—I did something I hadn't done since I was in high school. I opened my window and crawled out onto the porch roof, then went from there to an adjacent tree that allowed me to climb fairly easily down to the ground. The boys had made far more use of that escape route than I had, but I'd been dragged along once or twice. It was the only safe way to get out of the house without alerting my parents because there was a really squeaky spot on the stairs that woke everyone up if you hit it, and we'd never figured out a way to avoid it.

Dean had left the truck parked far enough away that I could start it without waking everyone, so I drove back downtown to the square, where I found Sam. "I never saw you as a night owl," he said when he landed next to the truck.

"I needed to talk to you, and I figured this might be one time when I wouldn't be interrupted. It's nearly impossible for me to get away for any length of time around here." I told him what had happened in the theater and then with Nita's snake outside the theater. He flew quickly over to that stretch of sidewalk, poked around a bit, then flew back to me.

"Nothing," he reported. "If there was any blood or if anything had died over there, then someone must have done a really good cleaning job. The sign's kind of banged up, though. Say, do you think the bad guy is targeting you?"

"If he's targeting me, it can't be because he knows me from my work at MSI. He'd have known I was immune to magic and wouldn't have seen an illusion of a snake. It was probably random, targeting two women who would probably react to a snake by screaming and running. He just didn't count on Nita being so violently anti-snake."

"I still don't like it. It hits a little too close to home. Why here, and why do all these things seem to be happening around your family?" I opened my mouth to answer him, but he held up a wing to silence me. "Answerin' those questions is my job. You're out of this. Keep your eyes open, of course, but this ain't your fight anymore. Now you go home and get your beauty sleep, and I'll take care of everything."

Getting back up on the porch roof was a little more difficult than getting down, but I made it safely back to my bedroom with only a scratch or two. I was out of practice for that kind of sneaking around. It was hard getting to sleep, but I kept telling myself that Sam had things under control. All I had to do was keep Mom from seeing anything she shouldn't until Sam had wrapped things up and caught the bad guys.

Over the next day or so, I resisted the urge to run by the square every time I needed to go through town, and made more offers to run to the grocery store for my mom than I used to when I was in high school and had a crush on one of the bag boys. That was the only way to keep her completely away from the area of maximum magical activity.

Friday morning, I had the pleasure of dealing with some of the less glamorous aspects of the business (which was pretty nonglamorous to begin with). Dean wasn't to be found and Dad was making deliveries, so I got to help Teddy and Frank unload a shipment. By the time we were done, I was drenched in sweat. I found a T-shirt advertising cattle feed left from a vendor's visit in my office and changed into that so I wouldn't be too hideously smelly for the rest of the day. I was afraid to look in the mirror at what my hair and face looked like, so I hid in my office, catching up on paperwork.

Just after lunch Beth showed up. I took Lucy off her hands while she worked the register. I was getting ready to head home when Beth called me from the front of the store. "Katie, someone's here to see you."

I had the usual reaction to being told that someone wanted to see me—racing pulse, pounding heart, a bit of a shiver down my spine—but it went away more quickly than usual. With Sam in town and on the case, the odds of anyone else showing up were pretty slim. It was most likely a salesman or, God forbid, Steve Grant.

Boosting Lucy up on my hip, I made my way out to the front of the store, a fake-pleasant smile plastered on my face as I prepared to deal with a salesman. And then I froze in shock and horror.

Owen Palmer was standing live and in the flesh in the middle of Chandler Agricultural Supply.

"Oh. You," was all I could think of to say.

Six

We stared at each other for a long moment. I'd thought I'd become pretty good at reading Owen, but I hadn't the slightest idea what was going through his mind. Normally I could gauge by the color and intensity of his blushes, but given sun exposure and the Texas climate, I couldn't tell how much of the redness on his face was an emotional blush and how much was possibly sunburn or heat.

Beth, being the sensitive soul that she is, beat a strategic retreat to the other side of the store, where she busied herself straightening shelves that were already in good order. It was nice of her to do so, but it didn't seem to do Owen and me much good since neither of us managed to say anything.

Finally, he cracked the slightest hint of a smile, and a spark of humor lit his eyes as he gestured toward Lucy. "I know you haven't been gone that long."

It took me a second to realize I was still holding the baby. Meanwhile, I let my breath out in a big whoosh of relief. It certainly didn't sound like he hated me. "She's my niece," I explained. "She belongs to Beth, the one who made such a nice show of giving us some privacy. Beth's married to my youngest brother."

In all the scenarios I'd daydreamed about the reunion I couldn't help but hope for one day, I hadn't ever imagined it this way, with me explaining my family tree to him. I also hadn't looked quite like this. Why did he have to show up when I was at my worst, wearing grubby jeans, a T-shirt three sizes too large, my hair straggling out of a ponytail, and no makeup? It wasn't fair at all.

The store's phone rang, but it only rang once, which meant Beth must have picked it up and couldn't be eavesdropping on us very intently. I decided to take advantage of that. "I wasn't expecting you," I said. "I mean, with Sam here already."

"With Idris involved, this isn't a one-man job anymore. I want to get to the bottom of this." He kept his voice low, which was probably a good idea, since Beth's ears were practically out on stalks as she tried to listen in, even if she was on the phone. I thought I detected a note of bitterness in his voice, but that could have been my guilty conscience playing tricks on me. He wasn't scowling or looking angry.

"Well, um, it's good to see you," I said.

He opened his mouth, but then saw Beth heading back our way, closed it, then after a pause said, "It's kind of hot here, isn't it? I mean, for April."

"It's just April in Texas," I said with a casual shrug. Actually, we were in the middle of a bad heat wave and it was unseasonably hot, but this was a game we Texans couldn't help but play with Yankees who complained about the heat, even if we were suffering almost as badly.

"Katie, I need your help with something," Beth said as she reached us. The apologetic look on her face appeared to be genuine.

"Excuse me for a second," I said to Owen and turned to follow Beth, but she stopped and frowned.

"You'll need your hands free." She took the baby from me and handed her to Owen. "Here, would you mind holding her for a second? Thanks."

I should have intervened on Owen's behalf, but Beth dragged me away too quickly. I didn't think he had much experience with babies or small children. He was an only child, and all of his friends that I knew of were childless. Sticking him with a baby was cruel and unusual punishment, but Beth was such a natural with kids that she didn't realize not everyone else was.

"What did you need?" I asked Beth before she had a chance to ask me about the incredibly handsome guy who'd come to see me.

"A customer's going to be coming by to pick something up, and it's on that top shelf."

I knew right away what Beth needed. Her one flaw, as far as I could tell, was that she was deathly afraid of heights. She didn't even like climbing up on a stepladder. "Okay, I'll get it. Tell me what you need."

"I'll hold the ladder steady," she hurried to offer. "I need that cedar bird feeder up there."

"You mean the one left over from the fall? The one we didn't manage to sell? What does someone need a bird feeder for at this time of year?"

"I don't ask. I just sell. And I guess there might be people who feed birds year-round so they can look at them."

I was halfway up the ladder when she asked, "So, who's the guy?"

I wasn't sure what to tell her. Explaining Owen's presence was a no-win proposition. If I said he was here on business, they'd want to know what business could possibly bring him here, and then they'd ask about the business. If I said he was my boyfriend, he'd have the whole family ganging up on him, and it would be incredibly awkward for both of us, considering that I was the one who'd broken up with him and it didn't appear that he'd come to beg me to go back with him. The truth was, of course, out of the question.

"He's someone I know from New York. I haven't yet had a chance to ask him what he's doing here, since someone had to drag me away to climb a ladder for her."

When I got back down with the bird feeder, she had the good grace to be blushing prettily. As a fair-skinned redhead, she could almost out-blush Owen in the rare instances when she was embarrassed about something. "Sorry about that. And no, it was not a ploy. I really do need this. Mr. Ward is coming by to pick this up, and you know what he's like. If it's not waiting on the front counter when he gets here, the whole town will hear about how lousy our service is. I wouldn't put it past him to run stoplights and speed to try to get here before we can have it ready for him, so I didn't dare wait."

"It's okay. Don't worry about it. I just hope Owen survives your daughter."

Much to my surprise, Lucy was snuggled up against Owen's shoulder, looking utterly blissful. I could hardly blame her. Even at nine months old, she had good taste in men. Owen didn't look quite as comfortable as she did, but he wasn't as panic-stricken as I'd feared.

"Sorry about that," Beth said to Owen as I put the bird feeder on the counter. "Minor business emergency. And now I'll relieve you of my daughter." She reached for Lucy, who whimpered and clung desperately to Owen's shirt. "Oh, come on, you're not abandoning me already, are you?" she asked the baby. "Come back to Mama. You can play with . . . um?" She gave me a pointed look.

"Beth, this is Owen Palmer, a friend from New York. Owen, this is my sister-in-law, Beth. And your new biggest fan is Lucy."

"Nice to meet you, Owen," Beth beamed. "Lucy, you can play with Mr. Owen later, okay? Right now, I'm sure he and Auntie Katie would like to talk."

It took all three of us to detach the whimpering baby from Owen's shirt, and Beth whisked her away before the whimpering could escalate into a full-scale tantrum. "My, but you do have a way with the ladies," I teased. The quick flush that spread across his cheeks was a great relief to me. It meant he couldn't have changed that much since I'd been gone.

But he had changed in other respects. I saw what Marcia meant about him looking thin and tired. That made him look older and more serious than I remembered him being. "So, I guess you flew here?" I said. "I mean, not like flying, just . . ."

"American Airlines," he finished my sentence, another one of those sparks of humor lighting his dark blue eyes and almost making me swoon. It looked like the effect he could have on me hadn't changed at all.

"Good, good," I said, nodding. "And you had a good flight? I guess you flew into DFW and drove down?"

"No, for that leg of the trip I got out my flying carpet."

"Really?"

Then he really smiled, for the first time since he walked in the store. "No, not really. That takes a lot of energy, and the magic lines here are weak enough that I thought I'd better save my strength. I got a rental and drove. It was an interesting trip. I guess I got to see a good part of the state."

"Yeah, that's a nice drive, a good cross-section of Texas." I wanted to scream with frustration, even as I kept the small talk going. I'd missed him desperately for the past four months, and here we were talking about his travel arrangements instead of talking about us or even talking about the situation that had brought him here.

And then it was too late to get into the good stuff because my family started swarming. If I hadn't been absolutely certain that Beth would never do such a thing, I'd have halfway suspected her of calling them all to tell them about my visitor. As it was, I had a feeling it was pure, dumb luck. First, Sherri showed up, at least half an hour late from her lunch break. She tottered in across the store's uneven wooden floor in high-heeled sandals. Her skin-tight pedal-pusher jeans gave the impression that they once might have been regular jeans but had shrunk severely in the wash. She took one look at Owen and sucked in her stomach while inflating her chest.

"Well, hello there," she cooed. I could hardly blame her for noticing him, since he was quite the hottie. He wasn't what I'd really consider a hunk, since to me that implied big and brawny. Owen wasn't all that big, and he had a slender frame, but he had a good amount of muscle packed onto that frame. At least, I was pretty sure he did. I hadn't seen him without his shirt on, except for one time when I was bandaging an injured shoulder. But when he hugged me or even put an arm around me to steady me on the subway, I could feel that he had some solid muscles under his clothes. To go with that body, he had a face straight off a sculpture, all square-jawed and strong-cheekboned.

What I could blame Sherri for was flirting openly with him while being married to my brother. Fortunately, Owen wasn't impressed at all with Sherri's type, yet another reason I was so crazy about him. He took a subtle step away from her and gave her the kind of look he usually reserved for unsavory things left on the sidewalk. "Sherri, this is my friend Owen from New York," I said stiffly. "Owen, this is my other sister-in-law, Sherri. She's married to my middle brother, Dean, and she works here, too."

Before she could properly throw herself at him, Teddy ran through from the back of the store, waving a piece of paper. "I think I've figured out the formula!" he shouted. "Twice the growth, and no weeds! Is Dad around? He'll want to see this!" Then he was gone.

"That was Teddy," I explained to Owen. "My youngest brother. Whatever you do, never ask him about fertilizer, how to grow greener grass, how to get more yield from your crop, or which seeds to plant. Trust me on this."

Owen looked the least bit shell-shocked as he nodded. Molly then showed up, dragging a screaming Davy. "Is Frank around? I need him to watch Davy for a while."

"Last I heard, he was making deliveries." I very pointedly did not offer to watch my nephew, even though it might have been interesting to see what Owen could do with him. He'd tamed dragons, so a bratty preschooler couldn't have been too much more difficult.

Just then, she noticed Owen. "Oh, I'm sorry, was I interrupting something? I shouldn't barge in on you like that when you're with a customer."

I dutifully made introductions. Sherri sidled up to Owen and said, "So, how long are you in town for?" But before he could answer, George Ward came into the store and Sherri was all over him like white on rice. Mr. Ward may have been older and married, but he was rich, which moved him up the scales in Sherri's world. Little did she know, but Owen probably could have bought and sold George Ward a few times over. I didn't intend for her to find out, or else Owen might end up clubbed and dragged off to her lair.

"I'll go see if Beth can watch Davy," Molly said. "She and Teddy are good with him. It was nice meeting you, Owen."

Owen looked dazed. "Do you have a chart?" he asked softly.

"I'll draw you one."

Our momentary respite ended when Mom showed up and things really got interesting. I wasn't sure what she was doing at the store when she was supposed to be resting, but she had a radar for detecting interesting or embarrassing events in her children's lives. She headed straight toward us, as though she already knew Owen would be there.

Then she managed a double-take reaction that was almost too good to have been unplanned. "Oh!" she said when she saw him. "My! Katie, who's your friend?"

If I hadn't already introduced him to the rest of the family I might have tried to pass him off as a customer before hustling him away from the store. Instead, I gritted my teeth and repeated my rote introduction. Owen didn't have Rod's natural (and sometimes unnatural) charm, but he was the kind of guy mothers can't help but like, all clean-cut and polite. "It's nice to meet you, Mrs. Chandler," he said.

She actually blushed, which may have been a first, as I would have thought she was incapable of being embarrassed. At least, she always acted like she didn't understand the concept of embarrassment around us. "Oh!" she said, fluttering a hand, "Please, call me Lois. So, you came all the way from New York to see our Katie. You must be a *very special* friend, indeed." Her tone left no doubt as to what she meant by "very special."

It was Owen's turn to blush, and I could feel my own cheeks flaming. I wasn't sure what to say. While I froze and panicked, Owen took a step closer to me and said, "Well, Katie is rather special." I was afraid I'd drop to the floor and die, right then and there.

"Ohhhhh!" Mom said, her eyebrows shooting up to her hairline. "Now, where are you staying while you're in town? Of course, you'll have to stay with us. We have a couple of extra bedrooms since the boys have all moved out. Katie's the only one of the bunch who still isn't married—*yet*." She fluttered her eyelashes and gave Owen a meaningful look on the word "yet," leaving no doubt that she expected him to step up to the plate and propose at any moment.

"That's very kind of you to offer," Owen began, shooting hesitant glances between her and me.

"I insist! You don't want to stay at that crummy old motel."

"Mom!" I hissed. "My friend runs that motel." It wasn't exactly four-star accommodations, but it was clean, neat, and safe, except when the office windows disappeared, and even then, nothing had been stolen. Even better, my parents didn't live there. And I didn't live there. I wouldn't have to be constantly aware of him under the same roof, seeing him first thing in the morning, and generally being reminded of all the reasons I hated that we couldn't be together. I also didn't think it was a great idea for him to have that much proximity to me. That is, if he didn't hate me now. For all I knew, he'd have no trouble resisting my nearness.

"I'm sure it's nice enough, but we have plenty of room, and it's so much homier."

"The motel does have free high-speed Internet access," I pointed out. Nita called it her lifeline. "And cable. HBO, even."

"Katie, I'm sure Owen didn't come all this way to play on the Internet and watch TV," Mom said, taking Owen by the arm. "Of course you'll stay with us. I'll be insulted if you don't."

She looked like she was about to drag him physically out of the store. Dad came to his rescue by showing up just then with Frank Jr. "I hear Teddy got that formula figured out," Dad said.

"Frank!" Mom said, dragging Owen over to him. "This is *Owen*. He's Katie's *friend*. Here from *New York*." She emphasized every few words, as though trying to impart some kind of extra significance.

"That's nice," Dad said. "Good to meet you, Owen." Then he turned back to Mom. "And what are you doing out and about? Aren't you supposed to be resting?"

"I'm not sick, Frank. The doctor said so. I had errands to run."

Before this got too crazy, I stepped forward. "If Owen's going to stay with us, I ought to get him over there so he doesn't have to hang around here all day." Mom was too busy being pleased about winning the argument to notice him escaping from her. "You can follow me to the house," I told him. "It's just on the edge of town."

Mom jumped right back into action. "Oh, why don't you ride with him, Katie? I'm sure someone can get your truck home for you. You wouldn't want *him* getting *lost*, now, *would you*?" There she went, emphasizing words again. This time, I was fairly sure she was telling me not to let this one out of my sight, ever.

Owen didn't need any encouraging to get out of the store. As we settled into his rental car, he said, "I see you moved to New York for the peace and quiet."

I laughed, and the strange tension between us eased. "I've missed you," I said. I might have hugged him, but he was driving and I had the strangest fear that he'd dissolve into a magical mist if I broke the spell by touching him.

"Which way do I go?"

I directed him back through town toward our house, trying not to feel stung by the way he'd ignored what I'd said. "You're probably going to regret staying with us. You'd have been much safer, and you'd have had more privacy to work if you'd gotten a room at the motel."

"It didn't sound like I had much of a choice."

"No, you probably didn't. She might have kidnapped you from the motel. Then again, it might not have been such a good idea to give her any sense that we might be involved."

"How else were you going to explain me being here? It doesn't look like there's much to do here on business, and it's not a tourist center. The only reasonable explanation for my presence is if I'm your boyfriend."

It was the first time he'd ever used the b-word with me, but it wasn't the best context for it. This was definitely not the way I'd imagined our reunion. Of course, I'd tended to picture us running toward each other across a flower-dotted mountain meadow or him walking into the store, sweeping me off my feet and carrying me away, so my ideas of the reunion were highly unlikely. Still, even my sanest, most rational versions of the reunion fantasy had been nothing like this. I'd been rather partial to the one where I secretly went back to New York, then showed up at a meeting at work as though nothing had happened, much to his shock and delight.

I'd had a lot of time for daydreaming over the past few months, and I'd spent it well.

"Okay," I said, nodding as though we were agreeing on a business deal. "You're my boyfriend here to visit me from New York. How do we explain the fact that I've never said anything about you?"

"You haven't?"

"You met my mother. Would you tell her anything?"

"Probably not."

"And you thought your folks were scary." His foster parents had been a little intimidating, but they weren't likely to give anyone a nervous breakdown, unlike my family.

"I guess I must have broken your heart, which sent you running back home to your family, and you kept it a secret because you didn't want pity for your heartbreak."

"But that still makes you sound like a bad guy, if you broke my heart so badly that I had to run home. That wouldn't go over well with my brothers, and *that* would certainly get in the way of you getting any work done. How about something closer to the truth, that we'd just started getting to know each other when I had to leave because of work, and then you realized how much you missed me and came to see me?"

"That works, too. Okay, let's go with that one." Great, I could finally call him my boyfriend, and it wasn't even for real. Fate could be really cruel sometimes.

I pointed him toward the road to our house, and it was silent in the car for a long moment. "It was the exact opposite, you know. I mean, about you breaking my heart," I said softly.

"I know." I had a feeling there were layers of meaning in those two words. It kind of sounded like he meant that I wasn't the one whose heart had been broken.

"I didn't mean to hurt you. I was trying to help you." He didn't respond to that, and I chewed on my lower lip the rest of the way to our house. When I spoke again, it was to direct him to turn in at the driveway and then park in back.

As he got out of the car, he looked admiringly at the house. "Wow. And you were impressed by my house," he said. Our house was a rambling Victorian farmhouse with wraparound porches.

"It's just a farmhouse," I said.

"Is that a historic marker?"

"Anything in Texas that survives more than a few years is considered historic and gets a marker. I wouldn't be surprised to find out that my grandmother has one tattooed somewhere on her body."

He took a small suitcase and something that looked like an oversized briefcase out of the trunk, and I led him through the pack of curious dogs into the house through the kitchen door. "I'd bring you in properly through the front door, but I'm honestly not sure it opens anymore. We never use it. I think I'll put you in Dean and Teddy's old room." We went up the stairs, and I guided him to the largest bedroom, which had two twin beds and lots of science fair trophies in it. "It's not our usual guest room, but it has the advantage of being easy to escape from."

He looked out the window. "Onto the porch roof, then onto the tree branch and down the tree?"

"You got it."

"Is there a problem with the stairs that makes this necessary?"

"They squeak like crazy, worse even than that spot in the hallway at your folks' place, and it's several steps in a row, so you can't just skip the squeaky ones. Mom and Dad's room is right by the stairs, so no one can get up or down those stairs without being caught."

"With four kids—and three of them boys—I bet your parents kept them that way on purpose."

"Exactly. I'm still not sure Mom and Dad know about the escape route, and boy, did Dean make use of it. The one downside of putting you in this room is that Dean's the one most likely to need it. He still moves back home every so often, but he can take Frank's old room if Sherri kicks him out while you're here."

"Complicated relationship?"

"Don't ask. Now, there are a couple of bathrooms off the hall here, and there's one downstairs under the stairs. Mom will tell you to make yourself at home and get anything you want to eat or drink from the kitchen, but she'll spend the entire time trying to force food on you, so that probably won't be an issue. And now before the whole mob gets here, we should probably talk. The store closes at six today, so that holds off most of the family, but Mom could be back sooner. She's probably making the rounds to let everyone know about her future son-in-law, so we have a little time. However, my grandmother could show up at any moment."

He blanched a bit at my recitation of family likely to invade us, and I could tell that he was reconsidering the offer to stay with us. He sat on one of the room's twin beds, braced his hands on his knees, and asked, "You haven't had any more encounters with our suspect, have you?"

I thought I detected a hint of worry in his eyes. "No, nothing since the other night, and I still don't think that was targeting me, specifically, for who I am. You don't attack a magical immune with an illusion." I fought back a shudder. "For all I know, the guy was flirting with me. What's Sam found out? I haven't talked to him since Wednesday night."

He went into professional mode, the way he was in meetings at work when he seemed to disconnect his emotions from the situation. "Sam observed the suspect over the course of two days. He hasn't been able to identify the suspect yet, so we may have to confront him or her directly."

"So, magical duel on Main Street?"

"Not if I can avoid it. I'd rather have a friendly chat about the responsible use of magic and the need to be registered centrally, then see if I can use him to get to Idris. If he or she isn't receptive to that, then I might have to take other measures. Having power means you have to abide by the code, whether or not you know about it."

"I guess this means some detective work for us, huh?" I felt my spirits lifting at the thought of it, and I realized how bored I'd been away from the magical world.

"It means some detective work for me. You're not a part of this anymore." I winced inwardly, but before I could say anything in self-defense, we were interrupted.

"Hello! Who's there?" my grandmother's voice called from downstairs. "I don't recognize that car, so if you're robbing us, you should know that I'm armed."

"And that would be my grandmother," I said with a sigh. "I knew we wouldn't have long." I got up and called downstairs. "It's just me, Granny. I've got a friend visiting."

"That Indian girl from the motel?"

"No, Granny, a friend is visiting from out of town." I gestured to Owen, and he got up and followed me downstairs. "Granny, I'd like you to meet Owen. He's here visiting me from New York. Owen, this is my grandmother, Mrs. Callahan."

Owen tried to shake her hand in greeting, but she braced both her hands on the top of her cane and gave him a good, long stare. "With coloring like that, you must be Irish," she said. "It's good to see someone from the old country."

I bit my tongue before I echoed my mother's usual reminder that she'd never been to the old country, but I figured her Texas accent—she hadn't yet gone to Lucky Charms land—was clue enough for someone as smart as Owen. "I'm not entirely sure what my heritage is," he said. "I suppose there could be some Irish." Owen actually didn't have the slightest idea who he was. He'd been orphaned young and didn't know anything about his parents. I didn't know the whole story, but I pictured him as a baby left in a basket on the front steps of a church. That's the way it always happened in books.

"Ah, you're Irish, I'm sure of it. I think you may even have a touch of the magic running through your veins." And there she went into the land of marshmallow stars and clover. "I'd guess you often see the wee folk, as well." She tapped the corner of her eye with a gnarled finger. "I can tell, I can. They say I have the Sight."

"Mother, you're not telling those stories to Owen, are you?" My mother's voice came from the kitchen. She then appeared in the living room. "Mama, would you mind making us some coffee? I'm sure Owen could use a pick-me-up after making such a long trip." Granny gave Owen a long, searching look before she wandered back into the kitchen. Mom then dropped her voice to a whisper and said, "Don't let her fool you. She's never been outside Texas. We are of Irish descent, but everything she knows about the old country, she learned from watching movies. And if she has the Sight, well, then it's got cataracts on it as bad as the ones she had on her eyes."

"She's very seldom right," I agreed, but she had been right about Owen having magic in him. Had she actually seen that, or was it more of her usual blatherings?

"Now, if you'll excuse me," Mom said, "I need to start getting things ready for dinner. I've invited the whole family over to get to know you better."

It looked like getting time to investigate—let alone time to work out whatever was going on with us—was going to be a real challenge.

Seven

Fortunately, Owen didn't react in the way I wanted to, which was to run screaming from the house. He also didn't react in the way I halfway expected him to, which was keeling over in a dead faint. Instead he said softly but with a firm undertone to his voice, "That's very nice of you, Mrs. Chandler, but I was looking forward to catching up with Katie tonight." With that he put his arm around me, proving finally that he was here for real and wasn't just a cloud of magical mist. Oh yeah, he was definitely real and very solid, and I wanted even less to spend the evening with the entire family. I'd forgotten just how good it felt to have his arm around me.

Mom faltered. "Oh. I suppose I could see that. Yes. I'm sure you're tired from traveling, anyway. You already met the whole family. I should let you rest before you have to keep them all straight. You two go on and have fun catching up."

"Thank you for being so understanding. Now, I think I'll go finish unpacking, and then I'd like Katie to show me around the town." With his arm still around me, he steered me back toward the stairs.

"Wow, that was some trick," I said once we were safely up in Dean and Teddy's old room. "I'd have suspected you of using magic if I didn't know she was immune. Though I suppose you are the dragon whisperer, and Mom isn't too far from that."

"You met Gloria. I learned a lot from her. That's the way she always gets her way, by being polite and firm at the same time and by asking for something that they'd look like a heel for saying no to." Gloria was his foster mother, and quite a formidable woman. Putting her in the same room with my mother could possibly be dangerous—or else result in a cage match to which we could sell tickets.

"Well, you really pushed my mother's buttons," I said, sitting on one of the twin beds. "The only thing she wants more than to show you off to everyone is to give us enough time alone to make sure something eventually happens. And by 'something' I mean an event involving a church, flowers, and a white dress. Fair warning."

He hung his clothes in the closet, shoving aside the coats and other winter wear stored there. "Don't worry about that. I've got plenty of experience there, too. You saw what Christmas was like."

When we'd been in his hometown for Christmas, the mothers of all the local marriageable young women had literally fought over him. Yeah, there was magic involved, but I got the feeling the inclination hadn't been buried too deep beneath the surface. "It's never a dull moment, is it?" I said.

"I daydream about dull moments." He knelt beside the large case and asked, "Is there a safe place to hide this where we don't have to worry about anyone trying to get into it? Normally, I'd shove it under a bed and make it invisible, but with your mother being magically immune, that won't work."

"I think my grandmother may be, too. Or crazy. Or maybe both. Why, what is it?"

"Supplies, some reference material. Basically, everything magical I have with me. It's locked, but if I were a host, I might be suspicious about a locked case like this."

"You can hide it in my room. She might get nosy and poke around in here to see what she can learn about you, but she thinks she already knows everything about me."

"Good idea. Thanks."

I stuck my head in the hallway to make sure the coast was clear, then gestured to him and led him down the hall to my room. Only as he crossed the threshold did I rethink my offer. This meant he would see my childhood room. It was pink. Very pink, as in explosion at the Pepto Bismol factory. Everything was all ruffles and lace, like a room fit for a fairy-tale princess. I'd tried to temper the effect as I got older by covering the pink floral wallpaper with posters, but since the posters were of castles or were from romantic movies, it didn't help much. I'd barely been aware of my surroundings since I'd been back, but walking into this room with Owen, I couldn't help but be slapped in the face with how awful it was.

"I'll have you know, I picked out the decor when I was five," I said in a preemptive strike.

"I didn't say anything."

"You were thinking it."

"But I know better than to say anything. Where should I put this?" He hefted the case. "I wouldn't want it to clash with your decor."

"Very funny." I lifted the pink ruffled and flounced bedskirt. "Here, slide it under the bed, up by the head. Even if someone gets crazy enough to vacuum under the bed, it should be hidden somewhat there because of the nightstand."

He knelt and placed the case as I directed, then stood up and looked around the room. "I never really saw you as the pink type."

"That phase only lasted a couple of years. Two years later, it was purple, but Mom wouldn't let me redecorate. In high school, I wanted to go all modern with red, black, and white. Now I think I'd do it in pale blue and white."

He raised an eyebrow, but refrained from further comment. "Are you ready to go?"

"Can you give me five minutes to change clothes? I'm kind of a mess from work." Once I had the door shut with him safely on the other side, I frantically pulled off my clothes, then put on a nicer pair of jeans and a clean shirt. I tugged the ponytail holder out of my hair and ran a brush through it. I limited makeup to a little lip gloss because I didn't want to look like I was trying too hard.

Feeling much better about myself, I found him in Teddy and Dean's room. I gave him a quick tour of the house, avoiding the kitchen where Mom and Granny lurked. In the backyard, the dogs ran to greet us, going straight to Owen. I was a bit insulted at the snub by my own dogs. The dogs escorted us to the edge of the yard where we could see the fields, which were laid out in stripes in various shades of green. "We don't really farm as a business anymore," I explained, "but those are Teddy's test crops. He plants different kinds of seeds and tests them with all kinds of fertilizers to see what works best."

"That would be the formula he was talking about?"

"Yes, and like I warned you, don't ask him about it. It's like someone asking you a question about how magic works. Now, over there is the barn, which mostly serves as a storage shed. We have a few head of cattle—again, for comparing different kinds of feed—and some horses that are more pets than anything. And there you are. So I guess we need to go talk to Sam?"

He produced the keys to the rental car and said, "Yeah, we're set for a meeting in fifteen minutes."

"Then I am part of the investigation, huh?"

"Only because it would be suspicious if I went off by myself so soon after getting here. That would raise too many questions with your family."

That wasn't exactly an enthusiastic invitation, but it didn't stop me

from getting into the car with him. I couldn't blame him for being a bit
hurt and upset about the way things had happened, but I was sure he'd
understood. And hey, it hadn't been a picnic for me, either.

As we drove away, I noticed the kitchen curtains moving and knew
we were being watched. Mom and Granny probably thought we were off
for a big, romantic night, but except for the one moment when he'd put
his arm around me, he'd been acting anything but romantic. He seemed
almost as distant as if he were still in New York rather than right there
beside me.

"I guess we're heading to the square," I said when the silence in the
car grew oppressive.

"No, that's too public for a meeting. It takes too much power to
conceal something that complex. We're meeting somewhere else." It
was my hometown, but he seemed to know his way around already,
turning onto side streets without hesitation. We pulled up in back of the
town's Catholic church, where a lone gargoyle sat on the roof ridge. He
swooped down to join us.

"Ah, that's more like it," Sam said. "I need a little recharge from
perching on a church every so often. I was afraid if I sat on that courthouse much longer, I'd turn into a lawyer. So, what's the plan, boss?"

"You haven't been able to identify our culprit?"

"Hey, Katie-bug here's the local." He turned to me. "You know the
townfolk. Did old Prances in Robes ring a bell with you?"

"There wasn't anything particularly distinctive about him—or her. I
guess it would help if he'd walked with a limp or had a certain gait that
looked familiar, or maybe wore personalized cowboy boots under his
robes so they showed when he took a step. I don't think I even saw his
feet."

"What's your assessment of our local wizard?" Owen asked Sam.

"Pretty basic magic. Really rough, not a lot of power or control. I'm
most worried about him using magic as a pickpocketing tool."

"Yeah, that does put things closer to the dark side, which isn't a good introduction to magic," Owen mused. "I'm curious to see these lessons and how well they work. We don't often see people learning as adults."

"How do people learn they're magical?" I asked.

"It's an inherited trait, so parents are generally magical and then they know to look for the signs in their children."

"But what if someone slips through the cracks and doesn't find out that they're magical? Couldn't that happen?"

"I suppose there might be someone with latent magical talent out there who never knew. Families can drift apart and lose traditions, and if they're not in a place with strong power lines or other magical people for them to learn from, they might not ever realize what they're capable of. I imagine that's what we're dealing with here, someone who figured out he could do strange things that were useful and is enjoying the power."

"Which is what we gotta put a stop to," Sam growled. "It ruins things for all of us if some wacko goes out and shows off."

Owen took my hand then, and shivers went all up and down my spine—not the magical tingle I had from Sam's veiled presence. I heard a car drive by on the adjacent street, more slowly than normal. "That's the third car in the last few minutes," Owen said. "They can't see Sam, but what they do see looks like us having a deep conversation."

I was all for giving them a show, but holding my hand seemed to be as far as Owen was willing to go at the moment. "By this time, my mom will have already heard that I'm with a guy in back of the Catholic church."

Owen turned back to face Sam, and I saw that the gargoyle's stone face was etched with amusement. "We'll check around and see if someone shows signs of being our culprit. You keep an eye out for magical activity and let me know if anything else happens."

Sam saluted him with one wing. "Got it, boss."

As we got back into the car, Owen said, "If you're showing me off around town and introducing me to people, that gives us an excuse to talk to any suspects. Do you have any suspects?"

"Not many. There's this weird guy who used to be Teddy's friend. Mom swears he made the pharmacist give him his prescription for free. I'm still not sure if that's another one of the magical things she spotted or if that one's all in her head. Frankly, I can't see him working hard enough to learn how to do a real spell. If he flunked out of A&M, he's not going to be able to learn magic. Then there's Sherri, I guess, but she's not the magical kind of witch."

"This isn't witchcraft we're dealing with, anyway. It's entirely different."

"The first place we have to go is the motel so you can meet Nita."

"Is she a suspect?"

"No, but she's my best friend around here, and wouldn't it look funny for me to show off my handsome New York boyfriend to everyone in town without first introducing you to my best friend? Besides, something weird happened at the motel a few nights ago. A window disappeared entirely, like that time you made the restaurant windows vanish. There wasn't any broken glass lying around, and nothing was stolen."

"The motel is the pink place on the north side of town, right?"

"That's it."

"You must really like it, then."

I groaned. I'd clearly never live down the pink room. At least Owen was showing signs of a sense of humor instead of being more stone-like than Sam.

Nita was sitting behind the front desk, reading a pastel-covered book with a stiletto-clad foot on the cover. She glanced up when the front door bell jingled, took one look at Owen, and her jaw dropped. It seemed to take her a full minute to realize I was with Owen, and then she looked even more shocked. Owen, as usual, blushed furiously, which had the effect of making him even more adorable.

"Hi, Nita," I said, wondering if I needed to do CPR or at least check for a pulse. "You've got to meet Owen, my friend from New York who's here for a visit. Owen, Nita and I have been friends since fourth grade."

Owen hit her with one of his heart-melting smiles and said, "Nice to meet you."

"Huh? Uh, New York, yeah," she stammered. Then she pulled herself together. "And you left New York? With him there? And you never told me about him?"

Owen's blush deepened. "It's a long story," I explained. "I didn't really want to talk much about it."

Her eyes got even wider, then she narrowed them meaningfully at me. In other words, we would be talking later. Now recovered fully and back to her usual perky self, she asked Owen, "So, how long are you in town?"

"A few days."

"Do you need a place to stay? We have vacancies. Lots of vacancies."

"Mom already got him," I said. "He's in Dean and Teddy's old room."

"I'll have to talk to her about competing with me, but I don't blame you. We don't have breakfast here. I'm still trying to convince my dad that we should turn it into a bed-and-breakfast."

I looked over and saw that the window was back in place, the plastic gone. "Hey, you got the window fixed."

"Yeah, Ramesh must have done it last night when he got bored enough—goodness knows the night shift gets boring. It was like that when I took over this morning."

Owen wandered over to the window in question and placed a hand on the glass, as if out of idle curiosity. While he was occupied, Nita flipped up the desk gate to run into the lobby, grab me, and pull me off to the far corner. "Oh my God, Katie, he's, like, gorgeous! Why didn't you say anything? I knew it was a broken heart! And now he's come to get you! You'll have to tell me everything when you get a chance."

"Later," I promised her. Then I raised my voice to a normal speaking level. "I guess we'd better move on. I'm showing Owen around the town today."

"And hiding out from your mom, I bet," Nita added. "How big a family dinner did she try to plan for tonight?"

"The works, but we scored a one-night reprieve."

She smiled up at Owen and extended a hand to shake his. "It was very, very nice to meet you. Have fun!" As we left the lobby, I glanced over my shoulder to see her miming, "Call me!"

"Well?" I asked Owen once we were in the car.

"Magic," he confirmed. "It was sloppy, oozing all over the place, but I think I recognized the remnants of the spell."

"So if our guy isn't actively, knowingly using bad magic, he's at least trying to use magic to commit crimes. Why else would he have removed the motel window? He was probably trying to rob the place, but Nita almost caught him."

"This could get ugly," he muttered.

"Next stop should probably be the pharmacy," I said. "There are a couple of possible suspects there, and that's the place where Mom thought Gene was getting prescriptions for free. But I think that if anyone in that transaction was using magic or would use magic to shake people down for money, it was Lester, the pharmacist. He's a mean old skinflint. Think Scrooge before the ghosts, only with less hair and with a stockpile of drugs."

"Who's your other suspect?"

"This one's a stretch, but there's a hippie chick who runs the card and gift part of the store. She's someone I could totally see trying to explore magic. I could certainly imagine her wearing robes and dancing around the courthouse square. I'm just not sure I can imagine her doing anything mean or greedy. Though I guess she might have been collecting the money for charity. How does this work, anyway? Can you tell someone's magical just from talking to them?"

"Unfortunately, it's not quite that simple unless I've been around them actively using magic. Right now, I'm getting a sense for things. Then I might know how to go about testing."

I directed him to park on the square, and then we walked over to the pharmacy. A blast of incense hit us as we entered, and not far behind it was Rainbow, which I was pretty sure was not her real name.

"Greetings and blessings!" she trilled. "Is there anything I can help you find? I got a new shipment of healing aromatherapy candles that you might enjoy. There are some that balance your energy into harmony, and others that encourage the full bloom of love."

Owen turned bright red again, but I wasn't sure if that was because of the suggestion of encouraging the full bloom of love or because he was coughing and gasping for breath from the heavy, scented smoke in the air.

"No, thanks," I said. "We just dropped in to get him some allergy medicine." Then I dragged a still-coughing Owen back to the more sterile-smelling pharmacy part of the store.

Lester was around the pharmacy counter before we reached the first set of shelves, not so much because he wanted to offer great customer service, but because he was afraid we might be shoplifters. Never mind that he'd known me almost since birth—the word "trust" wasn't in Lester's vocabulary.

"What do you need?" he demanded. If one of the chains moved to town or if someone else decided to open a pharmacy, as long as they had the basic customer-service skills of the Soup Nazi, Lester would be in huge trouble.

I grabbed a box of Benadryl off a nearby shelf. "Just getting some antihistamines for him. It's his first time in Texas." Owen coughed obligingly, and Lester glared at him.

"What are you doing here?" he asked.

"Visiting Katie from New York," Owen wheezed.

That was the wrong thing to say. Lester didn't trust the townfolk he'd known his whole life, so he certainly didn't trust a Yankee. He snatched the box from my hand and went back to the register to ring it up. Owen paid for the purchase before I could get my purse open, and the sight of money thawed Lester ever so slightly. "You in town long?" Lester asked.

"Just for a visit," Owen said vaguely.

"If you need something stronger than that, I have some prescription antihistamines. You normally would need to see a doctor to get them, but I'm sure we could work a deal."

Owen took a deep breath before we crossed through the gift part of the store and didn't let it out until we were safely on the sidewalk. "Please don't buy any of her aromatherapy," he said as he gasped for air. "I'm not sure I could take it."

"Her aromatherapy doesn't exactly encourage the full bloom of romance in you, huh?"

"Well, there is some magic in it, but it's not done right, so the effect on a magical person isn't quite what's intended."

"You mean, that stuff is for real?"

"There's a bit of a benign influence spell on the candle she was burning. You wouldn't notice the effects, of course. On a normal person, it might promote a feeling of well-being. To a magical person it's like . . . Well, it's like being a person with perfect pitch and listening to a singer who's just slightly off-key. Other people might find it perfectly pleasing, but someone with perfect pitch would be climbing the walls."

"I guess she's one of our suspects if she's selling magical products."

"Probably not. If she can tolerate it, she isn't magical. It could be something the supplier has done, and she has no idea that magic's involved. All she might know is that the candles make her feel good. Just in case, you'll need to go in there without me and buy one so the company can investigate. I can't go in there again."

"Hey, there's a test for our magical person. We herd the whole town through the pharmacy and see who goes into convulsions."

"That actually could work. Maybe you should buy a couple of candles and we could set a trap."

"It's also a good sign that Lester isn't our rogue wizard. He seems to be selling prescription meds under the counter, but he couldn't be magical and survive spending all day around those candles."

"Unless maybe the constant exposure to those candles is what makes him so irritable. What's next on your agenda?"

"The grocery store. Mom swears people were dancing out in front, but nobody else seems to recall it happening. Idris did do that while Mom was in New York, so I thought it sounded like one of his spells. If it happened."

We walked around the square to the grocery store. He stepped off the sidewalk into one of the empty parking spaces in front, then shook his head and rejoined me on the sidewalk. "If there was any residual magic there, it's faded by now. But if it did happen, perhaps someone who works in the store could be our culprit. They'd have access to the square, which seems to be the focus of magical activity. That in and of itself is proof this person doesn't know what he's doing. The square is the weakest magical point in the area. They'd be much better off in that park along the creek."

Frankly, I couldn't imagine anyone at the grocery store resembling a mischievous rogue wizard. They were all nice, small-town folks who knew their customers by name and greeted everyone like a long-lost relative. I had to introduce Owen at least half a dozen times, and I knew they'd all know his name the next time he came into the store. We bought a couple of nonperishable items to explain our visit, then left.

"That was a bust," I said with a sigh. "I guess all that's left is the Dairy Queen. We can get dinner while we're there. We'll have to be careful what we talk about, because a conversation there is as good as dictating it to the town newspaper, but we can overhear a lot. It's also one of about three restaurants in town, so it's our best shot for a dinner out."

"Just point me in the right direction."

I'm not sure I would ever have imagined Owen Palmer fitting in at the Cobb Dairy Queen. He was so shiny and handsome, like a movie star, and even if you didn't know he was a powerful wizard, you couldn't help but sense that there was something special about him. But amazingly enough, he blended in almost as well as I did. The women all noticed him, of course, but no one seemed to regard him as an outsider. I supposed he was a small-town boy himself, even if he was from another part of the country.

Steve and his gang showed up not long after we'd ordered and found a table, and I couldn't help but enjoy the look he gave when he saw Owen with me. Having a man with matinee-idol looks sitting across from me was quite a personal coup. I hoped Steve would accept his defeat and move on, but he came over to our table after he placed his order.

"So, Katie, who's your friend?" he asked, hooking his thumbs through his belt loops and adopting a challenging stance.

"This is Owen, who's visiting me from New York, and Owen, this is Steve. We went to high school together."

They called our number from the front counter, and Owen got up to go get our food. "I guess I'll leave you two alone on your hot date," Steve said. If he'd been an air quotes kind of person, he'd have put air quotes around the words "hot date." Then he moseyed off. I could have sworn he was giving his behind a deliberate sway for my benefit as he walked away.

"Ex-boyfriend?" Owen asked as he returned to the table with two steak finger baskets.

"Hah! Back in school, I'm not sure he knew I existed, other than as the younger sister of my brothers. I'm merely one of the few single women in this age range left in town, and the few others aren't impressed with his type, either, so he's getting a little desperate."

As we ate, we assessed the other patrons for their magical potential under our breath, not entirely seriously. "Silver-haired lady at three o'clock—your three o'clock," I muttered. "I know she's got a heck of an herb garden. She's probably brewing potions."

"How about the junior vampire scouts on your right? If they could do magic, you know they would."

I turned my head ever so slightly to see the group of teens dressed all in black with white makeup and black lipstick—boys and girls alike. "Nah," I whispered. "If they're dancing in robes at the courthouse, they're doing it at midnight, not broad daylight, and they'd be doing it in a group. Nonconformity is no fun unless everyone else is doing it."

He grinned, and I felt for the first time since he'd shown up that he really was my Owen, the guy who'd become one of my closest, most trusted friends even while I had a huge crush on him. I'd always been at ease with him, in spite of the shivers he sent up my spine with every touch. That's what had been different about him when he walked into our store today, I realized. He'd been closed off from me.

"You know, I really did leave because I thought it was best for both of us," I said. "I didn't want to put you in that kind of situation again."

"I know. I got a lecture or three about it."

"So you understand?"

He paused for a long moment, his eyes searching mine as if trying to find the exact words to say. Finally he said, "I can see why you felt you had to do it."

That hadn't quite answered my question. He was still sidestepping the issue, and I still couldn't tell what he really felt about me. But maybe I wanted too much, too soon. He was barely off the airplane. "Thank you for coming," I said, trying to pour all my sincerity and all my feelings into my words.

He turned an almost purple shade of red and shrugged. "Any time you need me, I'll be there, you know that. No matter what."

His intensity was enough to take my breath away. "I do," I managed to whisper. Then, as much as I wanted to stay in that moment, I couldn't help but be distracted. "Don't look now, but one of our prime suspects just walked in."

Eight

"I'd like to talk to him," Owen murmured. "See if you can get him over here."

I waited until Gene finished at the counter, then called out as he passed, "Hey, Gene! What's up?"

He looked around as if trying to figure out who was calling to him before he focused on me. Then he looked suspicious. "Why?" he asked, a defiant, challenging tone in his voice. I made a mental note to ask Teddy if their friendship had actually broken up or if they'd just drifted apart over time. He hadn't seemed too hostile with us the other day in the store, but the glare he gave me now made me wonder if he had issues with the Chandlers, with Teddy, or maybe even with me.

"Just saying hi," I said with a shrug. "Oh, this is my friend Owen from New York. Owen, Gene and I were in high school together."

Owen stood and stuck out a hand as if to shake it, but Gene ignored him. "I was way ahead of you in school," he mumbled.

"Yeah, he and my brother Teddy were big-shot seniors when I was a lowly freshman. But we were all in marching band together."

"Yeah. Well, see you," he said with a grunt and wandered off.

"He seems nice," Owen said, his lips quirking like he was trying to keep from smiling.

"Very charming guy. I think Teddy hung out with him mostly because he was the only other kid in the school who could understand what he was talking about. So, are you ready to head out, or do you want ice cream?"

"Can we get ice cream to go and then take a walk? I'd like to check out that creek with the walking path alongside it."

"Sure. I recommend the brownie Blizzard."

We were watching the girl behind the counter make our ice cream treats when Dean came in. Every female head in the place turned to watch him. I usually didn't notice it, since he was my brother, but he was almost as good-looking as Owen. "Why, if it isn't my baby sister," he said, grabbing me in a one-armed hug and kissing the top of my head. "Looks like you escaped for the evening. And this must be that boyfriend I've heard so much about. Hi, I'm Dean, the middle brother."

I wormed my way out of his grasp and introduced them.

Dean held out his hand for Owen to shake. "Welcome. We're glad you're here. We may torture you some to make sure you're good enough for our little Katie, but it's just a formality. It's rare enough for her to get a guy that we don't want to risk scaring him off—unless he needs to be scared off."

"Dean!" I protested, elbowing him in the ribs.

"Just kidding, Kitty-Kat. You know I love you. Say, are you two here for dinner?" I suspected Dean was really angling for an invitation to join us for dinner that would result in someone else paying for his meal.

"Sorry, brother of mine, but we just ate. And now we're on our way out, since it looks like our Blizzards are ready. But don't worry, Mom is planning to kill the fatted calf and throw a huge shindig tomorrow to celebrate the fact that I have a live one on the hook, so you can grill Owen then."

Owen handed me one of the cups of ice cream that had just been put on the counter for us. "It was nice meeting you, Dean," he said. "I'm sure we'll talk later." Once we'd strolled out of the parking lot and were heading down the sidewalk to the park, he said, "I get the feeling he's not as nice as he seems. You really tensed up around him."

"Wow, you are good. Actually, he's not bad. He just tries to slide by on charm rather than bothering to develop any other skills. He makes Rod look like a rank amateur. We got along fine growing up, but I think his wife has been a bad influence on him. He might have made something of himself if she hadn't been so much like him."

"His wife was Sherri, right? The blonde in the tight clothes?"

"Hey, you may not need that chart, after all."

"I'd still like it before the big family dinner—names and relationships annotated."

"Okay, I'll get to work on it. Now, what was it you wanted to see down by the creek?"

"The sense of magic is stronger here."

"Really? So we're not entirely empty of magic?"

"No place is entirely empty of magic. There's just more magic in some places than in others. In this area, the magic is concentrated in a few spots, including areas around running water. The power comes from the earth rather than from the atmosphere, so it's highly localized and more difficult to draw upon." At the creek bank he bent over the water, holding a hand out with his eyes halfway closed. He dipped his hand into the water and let it flow around him for a while, then stood up, shaking the water from his hand. Then he went over to a nearby tree and put a hand against it.

I ate my ice cream as I watched him. "Is there something I could help you find?" I asked him after a while when he seemed to have forgotten I was there. It looked like he'd gone back to being distant. Or maybe he was focusing on work, I reminded myself. After all, he hadn't come just to see me.

"Did you ever see anything unusual around here?"

"I've told you, I saw nothing to do with magic until I came to New York. Was there something in particular I should have seen?"

He continued looking around, nudging clumps of grass with his foot and poking into bushes. "Any unfamiliar creatures? Or were there any local stories about seeing something odd down here at night?"

"Creatures? You mean like fairies and stuff?"

"Not quite like you've seen before. These would be wilder. There may be a few isolated species in the area."

"I don't know. I've never seen any, and I used to play down here all the time."

"Did you ever come down here after dark or during twilight?"

"No. It was a big make-out spot back in my school days, which left me out, and now I hear it's where kids go to drink and use drugs."

"Then you wouldn't have seen anything."

"I guess it would explain all of my grandmother's talk about the wee folk. It also says something about how she must have spent her youth if she was here to see them. Go, Granny!"

He looked around some more, and I wondered if I should have been helping, but he hadn't responded to my offer of help, so I left him to it since I had no clue what he hoped to see. "They may not be here anymore," he said at last. "The drinkers and drug users might have driven them away. They'd have been drawn by the auras of the lovers, but the drinkers have a more negative energy."

"What good would it do to find these creatures?"

"They could be allies. They also might have seen something that could help us. It was just a thought, since we don't have much to go on."

"I guess we could always get a few of those candles, set them up around the house, and then get Mom to throw a big open house and invite the whole town."

"Hold on to that idea. We may need it later."

"Do you have any ideas about any of our suspects?"

"Not really. And there's always a chance that it's someone you don't know."

"There aren't too many people around here that I don't know. This isn't the kind of town people move to on purpose."

"I think it's a nice town. It's like something out of an old movie."

"Yeah, lost in time, that's us. We're the Texas version of Brigadoon. And now we even have the magic to go with it. So, what do we do next?"

"We wait for our wizard to make another move and see if that tells us anything."

We walked back to the Dairy Queen where his car was parked. Dean's flashy new truck was still outside, and I felt a tiny bit guilty about being relieved when he didn't come out while we were there. The relief grew stronger when I noticed Sherri's little convertible parked nearby. If she'd joined him for dinner, I really didn't want to run into the two of them.

That desire grew even stronger when I looked through the windows into the restaurant and saw Sherri and Dean yelling at each other, having yet another one of their very public fights. "Uh-oh," I said. "You may have to move into the other guest room tonight, unless Dean doesn't mind using Frank's old room."

"Why?"

"He and his wife are at it again. They do this all the time. They have a big fight, then she kicks him out. A few days later they make up and start all over again. I guess it works for them, but it sounds like hell to me."

We got home and chatted a little with Mom and Dad, then Owen called it a night. I stayed downstairs to get the interrogation over with. Mom barely waited until he was at the top of the stairs before she started in on me. "Why didn't you say anything about him?" she demanded.

"Well, the last guy I dated didn't stick around too long, so I didn't want to say anything this time before I knew for sure where we stood.

His visit here was a complete surprise." Pretty much all of that was the truth, more or less.

"But to come all this way, just to see you! He must really like you. Or is there something else going on?" She elbowed Dad. "What do you think, Frank?"

Dad moved his attention briefly from the television. "He seems like a nice enough kid. But maybe you should wait awhile before booking the church. Don't want to get ahead of yourself." Then he went back to watching people sift through crime scene evidence.

"How do you two know each other?"

"From work. And before you ask, we hadn't been going out that long. We started dating a week or so before Christmas, and then I moved back here right after the new year, so things hadn't gone very far. We haven't even begun discussing marriage plans, so get that out of your head. I spent Christmas with his parents, who were very nice. Is there anything else you wanted to know about him? The floor's open for questions."

Mom opened and closed her mouth, and I escaped before she could think of something else to ask.

I woke in the middle of the night to hear a tapping sound on my window. It persisted, so I crawled out of bed and pulled back the pink ruffled curtains to find Owen crouching on the porch roof. I opened the window and mumbled, "What is it?"

"Sam says our suspect is up to something."

"And you couldn't have knocked on my door from inside the house to tell me this?"

If it hadn't been so dark out, I'm pretty sure I would have seen him turn bright red. The moonlight glinted off his glasses, making it hard to read his eyes. "I didn't want your parents to catch me sneaking into your room."

"But they'll be okay with you crawling around on the roof, I'm sure."

"You did tell me how to sneak out of that room."

"Give me a second to put some clothes on, and I'll be right out," I said, a little less crabby now that I was fully awake. I pulled on jeans, a T-shirt, and sneakers and redid my ponytail so it didn't have so many scraggly bits hanging off it before I climbed out the window onto the roof. Owen kept to the outside of the porch roof as we made our way over to the tree. He dropped down first, then waited as if to catch me in case I slipped on my way down. As old a pro at this as I was, I didn't need his help.

His car was parked far enough away from the house that the sound of the engine starting wouldn't wake anyone up, and his rental car's engine was much quieter than my truck's. It took only a couple of minutes before we were downtown. He parked a block away from the square, and then we went on foot the rest of the way.

There wasn't anyone dancing in robes under the moonlight on the square, but we could tell right away that someone had been there. The "whoop, whoop" of the security alarm at the jewelry store was the first clue. The front windows on most of the businesses on the square were missing. It looked like a lot of the goods inside were gone, too.

Sam joined us from his vantage point on top of the courthouse. "I only noticed him at the last place he knocked over," Sam said. "He was pretty stealthy about the whole thing—may even have been veiling—so I didn't spot him sooner. Sorry about that. And then when I tried to catch up with him, he vanished. Seems like he's learned how to veil himself even from magical folk, but he can't multitask and do serious veiling while working magic."

"He's not here now," I said. "I don't see anything."

"He can't have gone too far," Owen said. He held his hands up and said something in a foreign language. I felt a surge of power, but saw nothing change.

"Hey!" Sam protested. "You're blowing my cover. I thought the boss told you not to pull that stunt again." I assumed that meant Owen had just removed every magical veiling in the area, including Sam's. The last time Owen had done that, it created a real stir in midtown Manhattan and got him into a bit of trouble.

Owen waved a hand at Sam, restoring the veiling illusion. "This is the town square at midnight, not Times Square, so it's not like there's anyone to spot you. Now go see if you can find anything."

Sirens sounded in the distance, probably responding to the jewelry store's burglar alarm. "We'd better get away from here," I said. "If someone sees us here, we'll be the suspects."

"They won't see us."

"Oh, right. Magic, invisibility, and all that." Since I could see us, I didn't feel great about standing in front of a burgled store with missing windows when I heard police sirens approaching. Owen didn't seem at all bothered. He just stood there, scanning the sky for Sam.

The gargoyle returned a moment later. "I didn't see anything. He must have gone to ground. Aerial surveillance isn't foolproof, you know. You only have to crawl under something and *poof,* you've vanished."

A police car rounded the corner into the square. "Then I guess we'll have to hunt on the ground," Owen said as he knelt and placed his hands flat on the ground. I felt another surge of magic coming up through the soles of my feet. The approaching police car slowed to the point it was almost motionless. Owen rose and said, "Split up and search the next couple of blocks."

Sam tilted his head to one side. "Are you sure—" he started, but Owen cut him off.

"We'll discuss it later. Go!"

I certainly wasn't going to argue when he sounded like that. Even though I knew he could do nothing to me magically, he still sounded powerful and intimidating. I chose the side of the square where the grocery store was and ran to investigate the parking lot in back. Nothing was moving, and not just because it was the middle of the night in a small town that tended to be still and quiet at high noon. Not even the things that usually moved were moving. A plastic grocery bag being tossed by the wind hung suspended motionless in midair. An alley cat stopped in mid-pounce, inches away from a paralyzed mouse. This was totally freaky, walking through a frozen landscape. Unfortunately, I didn't find anything human-sized and frozen, so I returned to the square.

Owen returned next. I could see his frustration in the set of his shoulders and the way he clenched his fists. "You didn't find anything, did you?" he asked.

I shook my head. "Sorry. And what is all this, anyway?" I gestured around the motionless square.

He ducked his head in what looked a lot like embarrassment. That was a relief. At least he had the good grace to seem a little abashed by having done something so incredible. "It was a theory," he said with a shrug. "It has to do with energy feedback and inertia manipulated magically."

I was rescued from the Mr. Wizard—literally—explanation by Sam's return. "Didn't see a thing," he reported. "That spell spread, what, three blocks? Our guy probably made it farther than that. So maybe you ought to set time right again before things get really odd."

Owen knelt and put his hands on the ground again, and everything changed. When the evening breeze hit my face and I heard all the little night sounds that had been silent, I realized just how still things had been under the spell. The police siren came back as the car lurched forward and then stopped across a row of empty nose-in parking spots in front of the jewelry store. Owen gestured toward where we'd left his car, and we ran in that direction, Sam flying low behind us.

As soon as we were back at the car, Sam lit into Owen. "What in the blue blazes was that stunt supposed to be?" Owen opened his mouth to respond, but Sam cut him off with the wave of a wing. "I don't wanna know the theory. I just wanna know what you thought you were doing even going there. That's not stuff you play with, even if you're about the only one who could pull off something like that."

Good. So I wasn't the only one who was a little freaked out. And now I was even more freaked out because I'd never seen Sam that upset. As well as Sam knew the ins and outs of the magical world, if Sam was worried about what Owen had done, I knew I had reason to worry.

"It was a calculated risk," Owen argued once Sam let him get a word in edgewise. "This is a nonmagical area, and there weren't a lot of civilians around. The sooner we catch this guy, the lower our risk for exposure is. I know what I'm doing, and I thought it was worth a chance. Time is of the essence here, Sam."

Sam folded his arms across his chest and his wings against his back. "Hmmph. Just don't get cocky, kid. One rogue wizard is enough."

"I don't think I'm in any danger of being drunk with power. I'm actually kind of exhausted."

"We do have to stop this guy," I put in, hoping to steer this conversation back to the reason we were here in the first place. "Our local wizard is even worse than Idris in a way, since I don't think we ever caught Idris using magic to actually commit a crime. Idris's spells may be on the darker side ethically, and he may encourage others to do bad things, but we've never seen him use magic to steal, have we?"

"He doesn't have to if he can get other people to do the dirty work for him," Owen said. "He's probably charging a commission."

"So, we'll stay on the case," Sam said. "I'll keep an eye on the place, see when the glass comes back, and make sure nobody else tries to take advantage of the situation. You two get out of here before anyone sees you."

"And before my parents realize we're not there," I added.

The next morning, I got up early enough to try doing something with my hair other than the usual ponytail. It had grown past my shoulders, and it didn't seem to want to do anything other than lie lifelessly against my head. I even went all-out and put on a bit of makeup. Owen might have caught me off guard the day before, but I wanted to show him that I hadn't let myself slide completely. I knew it was a bad idea to even think of getting back together with him. We had to keep our relationship strictly business, but I'd want to look nice for a business relationship, as well. At least, that's what I told myself as I put on some lip gloss.

I got downstairs to find Owen already sitting at the kitchen table, sharing a newspaper with my dad while silently drinking coffee. Mom was cooking an elaborate breakfast. She jabbered on while the men more or less ignored her. Every so often, Dad would pass a newspaper section on to Owen. From what I could tell, nothing in what Mom was chattering about had anything to do with any suspicions about where we'd been the night before.

"Katie!" Dad greeted me as I entered the kitchen. Owen looked up at me and flashed me a smile. He was fully dressed, complete with contact lenses.

"Good morning, everyone." I headed straight to the coffeepot to pour myself a cup before I took a seat at the table next to Owen.

"Why don't you take the day off to spend with your friend?" Dad suggested. "You've been working harder than you ought to, considering I haven't been paying you a real salary other than room and board and spending money. Besides, it's Saturday, and we're only open half a day, anyway. Someone comes in all the way from New York, you should spend time with him." I took that to mean that Dad thoroughly approved of Owen.

"Well, okay, twist my arm," I said. "Though I'm not sure what we'll come up with to do. We saw all the local sights yesterday. Both of them."

"I'm sure you'll think of something," Mom said.

"I know what we could do today," I said. "Maybe we could get a tour of the courthouse. It's got some really interesting architecture, and there's that little museum of Cobb County justice."

"That sounds like fun," Owen said, catching my eyes and giving me the slightest of nods to show he knew that I really didn't have that warped a definition of fun. "I think the courthouse square is definitely worth checking out. And then I'd like to explore some of the surrounding countryside. I don't think I've ever seen this much open space."

"I'll pack you a picnic lunch!" Mom chirped. "Oh, Frank, doesn't that sound romantic?" Dad just rustled his newspaper as he turned the page and folded it over again.

It did sound romantic, but I forced myself not to get my hopes up. So far, romance didn't seem to have entered Owen's mind. "Speaking of romance," I said, "did Dean come over last night?"

"Why would he do that?" Mom asked.

"I saw him and Sherri in the Dairy Queen having one of their knock-down, drag-outs. Usually he comes crawling home after one of those because she kicks him out. I wonder where he slept last night if he didn't come here."

"Stop saying such things about your brother. His marriage may be a bit rocky, but it's nothing for you to gossip about. Now, give me a few minutes, and I'll have a picnic all packed for you two. Just don't stay out too late. Tonight's the big family dinner, and you'll want to get back in time to get cleaned up and changed. I'm sure Owen would like to see you in something other than jeans. Surely you don't dress like that in New York."

"In New York I don't have a job that involves moving around bags of fertilizer and cattle feed," I muttered. I glanced over at Owen, and he looked like he was about to burst a blood vessel from trying to hold back his amusement. I rolled my eyes at him, and he went into a coughing fit that sounded suspiciously like laughter.

When we were safely out of the house with a picnic basket that could have fed an entire scout troop, I said, "It was so much easier at your folks' house."

"For you, maybe."

"Oh, don't start that. Yeah, you got a lecture or two, and they're not exactly cuddly, but they weren't that bad. At least we didn't have to try to hide or cover up anything."

"That's because they already know everything, and I do mean everything. There's no point in hiding anything from them."

"Well, compared to my family, they're sane."

"I'll give you that one." This time, it was my turn to fight a smile. He was thawing ever so slightly, getting back to his old self in his more relaxed moments.

We went straight to the courthouse square, with the pretense of taking that tour we'd mentioned. The local police department must have used up every piece of crime scene tape they had to seal off most of the storefronts on the square. All the windows were back in place, and a crowd had gathered around the perimeter of the taped-off area.

I led Owen through the crowd to where one of the local deputies was trying to keep the crowd back. I'd gone to high school with him and had seen him around town since I'd been back. "Hey, Jason!" I called out. "What happened here?"

He grinned as he pushed back his hat and wiped the sweat off his forehead. "Damnedest thing—oh, sorry, didn't mean to curse in front of you. Anyway, most of these stores were robbed overnight, very select things taken, no sign of forced entry."

"Really? What kind of stuff was stolen?"

"Oh, the kind of stuff you'd take if you had five free minutes in a store—and a criminal mind, of course. Some jewelry from the jewelry store. Not the really good stuff, because that was locked up, but a few of the pieces they had on display. Some of their china. A few of the more expensive knickknacks from the pharmacy's gift shop, that kind of thing. They didn't seem to be after drugs, and they didn't even take the over-the-counter stuff that can be made into crystal meth, which is what we see in most drugstore robberies these days."

"Wow, that's amazing," I said. "Thanks for the scoop."

He tipped his hat to me. "Any time, Katie."

"So, there we are," I said as Owen and I wove our way back out of the crowd. "It's almost like this whole correspondence course is on how to use magic to get rich quick."

He scanned the crowd. "I bet our culprit is here right now. They say a criminal always returns to the scene of the crime. Someone who's pleased with himself for doing something so clever wouldn't be able to resist watching the aftermath."

"There's one problem with that: Everyone in the whole town is here. I already see at least two of my brothers and every single one of our suspects."

In fact, Gene was walking right toward us, though his attention was elsewhere, so I doubted he was really aiming at us. The clock in the courthouse tower chimed, and he frowned and glanced at his watch. "The clock is five minutes slow," he announced to no one in particular. "Someone should do something about that." He changed course and headed off, apparently to do just that.

Teddy came up to us in Gene's wake. "This is something else, isn't it?" he said. "Who'd have thought this town would have its own criminal genius?" Then he frowned and looked at Owen. "Do I know you?"

"Teddy, this is my friend Owen, who's here from New York. He was in the store yesterday when you were running around talking about your formula."

The light dawned in Teddy's eyes. "Oh yeah, I thought you looked familiar." He shook Owen's hand. "Welcome. So, you're friends with my little sister, huh? I'm glad to hear she has friends up in New York."

"Teddy," I groaned.

Dean then joined us. "Hey, it's practically a family reunion," he said, draping his arms around Teddy and me. "My favorite sister and my second-favorite brother."

"Second-favorite?" Teddy knew the routine well enough to act affronted. Then he turned to Owen and asked, "Do you believe this guy?"

"Whoa, no forming outside alliances," Dean said with a laugh. "I thought you and I were supposed to gang up on the new guy to make sure he's good enough for our baby sister."

"I think Katie's smart enough to choose for herself."

I stepped out from under Dean's arm and blew a kiss at Teddy. "And that's why you're my smartest brother," I said. "Now, we have things to do. You can torture Owen tonight at dinner."

Once we were in the car and pulling away from the square, Owen said, "I'm glad my intentions toward you are totally honorable. It looks like you're well defended."

"They're all talk. You have nothing to worry about, so you don't have to keep your intentions too honorable." I couldn't help but smile when I saw the flush that spread across his cheeks.

We drove out to a roadside picnic area on a creek bank, complete with sheltered table. I hated to admit that my mother was right, but it really was the perfect spot for a romantic picnic. Mom had even packed the picnic basket accordingly, with dainty finger sandwiches, strawberries, and other foods that were perfect for feeding to each other. She'd also included a tablecloth and plastic dishes. I set the table, wondering if maybe, just maybe, he had some other agenda in bringing me out here. We could have talked work almost anywhere, but this was the perfect place to talk about us.

"It's nice out here," he said as he sat at the table. "I guess that creek over there is the same one that runs through town."

"Yeah, that's the one." I passed him the plate of sandwiches. "Do you think the magical creatures are there?"

He took a few sandwiches and passed the plate back to me. "Maybe. They've probably moved out of town, but we wouldn't see them at this time of day. They tend to be nocturnal."

"I guess we'll have to come back at night, then." I could certainly go for that.

"If we need them, we will."

I tried not to sigh in frustration that the conversation was stuck on work, but I couldn't think of a way to bring up anything else. Life was so much easier in junior high when you could hand a guy a note that said, "Do you like me? Check yes or no." Not that I'd ever had the nerve to do that kind of thing, even when I was in junior high. I picked up a strawberry and put it to my lips, trying to eat it as seductively as I could. The juice dripping down my chin to stain my shirt probably didn't help the image I was trying to project.

Still, he did react. His eyes went wide and the tip of his tongue touched his lower lip, at the same spot where the juice dripped from my lip. Then he blinked several times, looked away from me, cleared his throat, and said, "So, how do we catch our culprit?"

With a sigh, I got out a notebook and started to take notes. I'd been a secretary—or administrative assistant—long enough that it had become habit, and it didn't look like he was yet ready to move out of the business arena with me, no matter how much I tried to tempt him. "Do we keep trying to uncover him, or try to catch him in the act and then unmask him?"

"In the absence of any definitive clues, we might have better luck trying to catch him and unmask him. Unless he's some freak prodigy, I don't think we have to worry much about me not being able to beat him magically. Even if we're equals, power-wise, which I think is highly unlikely from what I've sensed, I have years of experience and a lot more spells at my disposal than he could ever get from a correspondence course." He frowned and stared off into space for a moment, then said, "We could always set a trap—give him something he can't resist. But what do we use for bait?"

Nine

"I'm guessing it'll take more than a hunk of cheese to trap this rat," I said. "What we need to do is figure out what he wants, what's really driving him, and then make that available somehow."

"Or not make it too available," Owen replied, his eyes a little unfocused as he brainstormed. "Make it a challenge. He does seem to want money, but what it looks like he's really enjoying is getting the chance to one-up everyone, to feel special and know he's the only one around who can do this."

"Shows how much he knows, with you in town," I quipped. "Maybe we can use that, though. How likely do you think it is that our culprit even knows there are magical immunes like me?"

I saw the spark light in his eyes and knew he had an idea. "Not very likely. That's seldom in Magic 101. He may know there are other magic users, but he probably doesn't think there are any in this town. I'd bet the knowledge would disturb him. He wants to be the best."

He grabbed my notebook and pen and went straight to work, outlining a plan in his textbook-perfect handwriting. "See, we find something he can't resist that he's sure to try to get into, then magically ward it. That should intrigue him enough to stop and study it. I doubt they've yet covered wards, so he won't know what's going on. Then we can grab him. He'll probably try using magic to defend himself, but it won't work on you, and I can deflect it. He'll think he's outclassed and outnumbered." He looked up at me and grinned. "See, this is why I need you around. You make me think better." Then he blushed furiously and looked back down at the notebook. "Well, most of the time. When you're not in immediate danger."

At least he'd acknowledged that he needed me, even if he'd felt the need to throw in the part about me in danger. That's what had tripped us up the last time, and I didn't like the reminder. "Then maybe we should just lock me up in a bank vault, and you can come visit me when you need to brainstorm."

He completely missed my sarcasm in his excitement. "That's it exactly! You know he'll want to hit the bank. Emptying the safe would be the ultimate magical robber challenge. I should ward the bank. I'll do it tonight, while he's still probably recovering from last night's activities and before he hits again. If I'm tired from what little I did, I'm sure he's exhausted from making all those windows disappear."

"Looks like another night without much sleep for us." And it looked like we'd be spending more time alone together after dark. That was a big bonus.

Since we had our work out of the way, I would have thought we had the rest of the day after we finished lunch free for sightseeing or even just spending time together and really catching up, but Owen wanted to go back to town and check out the bank and surrounding area. I hoped that meant he wanted to get his work taken care of so he could focus on me, but I was afraid he just wanted to get back to New York.

We got home in plenty of time to help Mom prepare the huge feast. She'd already fried chicken, had chicken and dumplings stewing, and there was a roast in the oven. She set us to work snapping beans while she made a pie. Granny came over an hour early with a tuna salad. "Because it's healthy to have salad with your meal," she said, and Mom shot us a pleading look.

"Granny, Owen was fascinated with some of the local history. You've lived here a long time. I'm sure you have stories," I said, moving her out of the kitchen and into the living room, where she regaled him with tales I was sure were mostly fictional, but still interesting, or would have been if I hadn't heard them dozens of times. They were new to Owen, though, and he seemed to be paying attention, even taking mental notes whenever she lapsed into Lucky Charms land and started talking about things like the wee folk. He seemed determined not to let himself go off duty.

Then the rest of the clan started arriving, and the usual Chandler family chaos ensued. Beth and Teddy got there first. Beth greeted Owen with a kiss on the cheek, which momentarily flustered him. "How are you enjoying your visit?" she asked him.

"I really like Texas," he said. "I'm enjoying the open spaces."

"Very diplomatic," she said with a laugh. "I guess the family can be a little overwhelming. I find them overwhelming, and I went to school with Teddy and Katie, so they weren't strangers to me."

That got him even more flustered. "That's—that's not what I meant . . ."

She turned to me. "Katie, he really is the cutest thing. I think I approve." The only thing that saved Owen from dying of embarrassment on the spot was Lucy stretching her arms out toward him and whimpering. She practically wiggled her way out of her mother's arms, and Owen caught her just in time. "Well, will you look at that," Beth said, putting her hands on her hips as Lucy contentedly sighed and snuggled against his shoulder. "Katie, sweetie, you may have competition here for your man. Owen, you don't have to hold her. I'll take her back."

"No, this is okay, for a while, I guess." He looked a little lost, like he wasn't quite sure what to do.

Teddy clapped him on the back. "I may give my sister credit for thinking for herself, but my daughter doesn't yet have much life experience, so I'll be watching you, buddy."

Beth slipped a burp cloth between Lucy and Owen's shirt. "She's teething, so she drools," she explained. "Let me know when you get tired of holding her, or hand her off to Katie." Then she darted off to help in the kitchen.

"You do know that's going to set my mother off," I said to him. "I'll never hear the end of how much she wants more grandchildren, and how you seem to be very good with babies."

"This may be the first baby I've ever touched."

"That would be a dangerous thing to say around my mother. She'll say you're a natural. I bet it has something to do with the way you are with animals."

"Yes, because babies and dragons are so much alike," he said, the sarcasm obvious in his voice.

"You really haven't spent much time around babies, have you? They're basically the same as dragons, only smaller, without the wings, and with a different skin color."

"She smells better."

"Not all the time."

It was only when I looked up as Frank, Molly, and their three kids showed up that I noticed my grandmother looking at us oddly. We'd been talking softly, and I was sure she was practically deaf, but the look on her face told me she'd heard the whole conversation.

Once everyone had arrived and we sat down to eat, the meal progressed without major disasters. Everyone was polite to Owen, and they didn't ask too many embarrassing personal questions about him or about the nature of our relationship. As the meal went on, I quit stressing about what to say about him and about us.

But I shouldn't have let myself relax. Mom was offering seconds when Granny asked, "So, how much time do you spend with dragons up in New York? I didn't know they were still around. You'd think it would make the news if they were running free up there."

Owen looked completely blank, and I stifled a gasp as he looked to me and two pink spots formed on his cheeks. "Mother!" Mom snapped, and I then noticed that everyone was looking at Granny instead of at us. We were lucky she was known for saying crazy things like that, or we would have been busted.

"He was talking about dragons," Granny insisted.

"Mama, you know your hearing isn't so great, so it's easy for you to mishear things. Now, if you'd let me take you to get a hearing aid, you wouldn't have these problems."

"I don't need a hearing aid. My hearing is perfectly fine. He's got magic in him, so it's natural for him to talk about dragons." She turned to face Owen. "My da used to tell me stories about dragons, but he said they were only in the old country."

He looked at her for a long moment, then said, "Actually, Katie and I were talking about dragons, so you did hear correctly. But we were being figurative. There were some people at work we called the dragons. It was kind of a joke. I'm sorry if we alarmed you." He then gave her a smile guaranteed to melt a woman's heart, no matter how old or young she was. It was a good thing he was oblivious to that particular power or he could have been truly dangerous if he was ever tempted to use it for evil. "You know, though, New York might be the one place where dragons could live without anyone noticing. I wouldn't be surprised to learn there were whole nests of them living in the sewers and subway tunnels. There's no telling what's down there."

"Forget about the subway tunnels," I threw in, "there's one who lived downstairs from us. She was a nightmare." Everyone at the table laughed, but Granny just stared at Owen. Her eyes still measured him shrewdly, but I could tell he'd won an ally by deflecting the conversation away from her hearing problems or mental health. She'd still be watching him, but she wouldn't try to expose him to Mom and Dad. I was rather impressed with him, myself.

After dinner, he got stuck with my dad and brothers in the living room while the women cleaned up. I knew it was a sexist division of labor, but ever since Dean had broken one of Mom's good china plates, she wouldn't let the men wash dishes. I always suspected that Dean had done that on purpose. Owen offered to help, but he was shooed away as company. I thought I should have been allowed to stay with him, since he was my guest, but I got drafted by the kitchen crew. I figured if he got into trouble with my dad and brothers, he could always blow something up as a diversion. With Granny on his side, he was probably safe anyway.

Mom and Molly put away the food, Beth washed the dishes, and Sherri and I dried them. Actually, I dried them and Sherri leaned against the counter. She shoved her hair back with one hand, then scratched her neck, and then surprised me by reaching up to open a cabinet so I could put a dish away. Molly, passing by, paused and said, "Wow! Look at that!" Only then did I notice the bracelet on Sherri's wrist.

"Oh, this little thing?" she said with a laugh as she gave her wrist a shake. It wasn't dripping with diamonds, but it was still a nice piece of jewelry, maybe even real gold, with some gemstones set into the charms. I did the payroll for the store, so I knew exactly how much money Dean and Sherri made, and I doubted it was enough for them to afford jewelry like that on top of their expensive car and house payments.

"Present from Dean, or did you treat yourself?" Molly asked.

Sherri gave a canary-stuffed-cat smile. "I'm not telling."

"I'm guessing the former, judging by the, um, healthy glow you two had when you got here," I said.

Sherri snapped me on the shoulder with a dish towel. "Oh, you! Don't be naughty. How do you know that getting this for myself didn't make me feel all sexy?"

I tried to study her face without looking like I was staring so I could tell whether or not she was telling the truth. Unfortunately, she could convince herself that anything she wanted to believe was the truth, and therefore when she said it, she didn't think it was a lie. I was fairly certain she could beat any polygraph test.

The timing of her getting new jewelry clearly out of her price range the day after someone had robbed the jewelry store was awfully suspicious. Maybe Sherri really was a witch, in more ways than one, and *she* was our suspect. Of course, it was equally likely that the culprit was now selling jewelry and other stolen items out of the trunk of his car, and that was how she was able to afford it.

"You must have bought that at Murphy's," Beth said, drying her hands and leaning over to get a good look. "I think I saw something like that there the other day when I went in to get my watch battery replaced."

Sherri laughed for no apparent reason and tossed her head back. I thought she looked uncomfortable, but I couldn't tell if it was the discomfort from having stolen it and her sister-in-law recognizing the source or from having it recognized as stolen property she'd purchased illegally. Wearing stolen jewelry in a small town wasn't the brightest idea. It was too likely that everyone would know exactly where it came from.

After a while, she stammered, "Well, I mean, uh, it's really not that unique. They probably mass produce these in China and ship them over by the boatload."

"What are you girls looking at?" Mom asked, joining us.

Molly grabbed Sherri's wrist and held it out for Mom. "We were just admiring Sherri's new jewelry," she said.

"Oh, that is nice. I think that's the one I saw in Murphy's. I even thought about what a nice birthday gift it would make for you. But I guess I'll have to think of something else, now that you already have it. Dean and I must share the same taste."

Sherri held out her other arm and shook it. "I have two wrists!"

Beth turned back to the sink and plunged her hands into the hot water, then began scrubbing furiously. Molly drifted away, and I fought to keep my mouth shut. I had to struggle to keep up with Beth's increased washing pace, but I didn't mind because I couldn't wait to get to Owen and tell him what I'd discovered.

When I finally escaped from the kitchen, I was surprised to see Owen looking perfectly at ease. He and Teddy were chatting, and while they shared a similar mind-set, I couldn't imagine what they had in common to talk about. There was some chemistry involved in magical potions, but there weren't too many other crossovers between Teddy's agricultural work and Owen's magic. I got close enough to overhear and found that they were talking about books. They both liked the same spy thrillers and mysteries and were exchanging reading suggestions.

I loved my family, but I wanted more than anything for them to go away—and soon. Granny left first, since she didn't like to drive at night. Then Molly and Frank left to get their kids to bed, and Teddy and Beth weren't far behind them, sneaking out with a still-sleeping Lucy before she could wake up and demand to be held by her new hero.

You could have knocked me over with a feather when, as she and Dean were saying their good-byes, Sherri said, "You two should come over for Sunday lunch tomorrow. We barely got to chat at all with so many people here tonight." She was supposedly talking to me, but she didn't take her eyes off Owen when she talked.

Based on prior experience, I knew she probably wanted a chance to get her hooks into Owen, but I couldn't be bothered to stir up any jealousy. Even if she really was a witch of the magical persuasion, I doubted she could overpower Owen. And if she was the other kind of witch, she was so far from his type I doubted he even noticed she was a woman. Owen's obliviousness had gotten us in trouble in the past, when someone managed to throw herself at him without him noticing her enough to even reject her and she turned against the entire company in order to get revenge.

"We'd love to," I said, ignoring the dismay on Owen's face. It would be the perfect opportunity to see if there was any other magically stolen loot in their possession. I tried to give him a significant look to show him I knew what I was doing.

"Then how about we see you at twelve-thirty? Don't bother bringing anything. I've got it all taken care of."

When the house was finally empty of everyone but us, Mom, and Dad, I suggested to Owen that we go sit out on the porch swing and enjoy the lovely evening. As soon as I was certain we weren't being spied upon—at least not closely enough to be overheard—I shared my conclusions. "I have a new suspect for us," I said.

"One of your family?"

"Only indirectly. Sherri was wearing a new bracelet tonight, one Beth remembered having seen in the jewelry store on the square. Sherri seemed uncomfortable and was really vague about how she got it. I know she and Dean can't usually afford stuff like that."

"You think she's our rogue wizard?"

"Either that, or she knows who it is because she's buying hot goods from him at a discount."

"So *that's* why you accepted the invitation."

"Exactly. Normally, I'd avoid it like the plague, but we might be able to see what else they have in their house, and you might be able to tell if there's any magic going on. I don't suppose there'd be any way to expose her as the thief without revealing the magical angle, huh?"

"It might be difficult."

"Rats. I know it sounds awful of me, but I'd have loved to convince Mom that she didn't hang the moon. Frank and Teddy have such great wives, and I'm glad to think of them as sisters, but I don't know what Dean was thinking. He wasn't thinking with his brains, that's for sure."

"She's not even that attractive. She just looks cheap."

I desperately wanted to hug him for that. I'd forgotten where I'd left off on the list of things I loved about him, but that needed to go on the list. Too bad a hug would be totally inappropriate for the strictly business relationship he seemed to be trying to maintain.

"I guess we rig the bank tonight after everyone else is asleep. How will we make it so that the customers and employees can still get in and out but our wizard can't?"

"I can set it to only block people with a certain magical level. Someone who can actually work magic has to be beyond a particular threshold. If we hear reports of people being unable to get in the bank, we'll know there's more magic in this town than we realized. But if I'm right, he'll try to hit the bank tomorrow night, so we'll have everything taken care of before customers become an issue."

"I take it we're crawling out the windows again tonight."

"I'll have to get some things from my case first. I really hope your parents are heavy sleepers."

We went back inside and made a big show of heading off to bed. Once I was safely in my room for the night, I changed into black jeans and a black hooded sweatshirt, made a dummy out of pillows so that my bed looked occupied, and pulled Owen's case out from under my bed. Then I read by flashlight until shortly after midnight, when Owen tapped on my window.

He was also dressed in black. I moved to hand him the case, but he shook his head and crawled in through the window. "I don't need the whole thing." He knelt by the case, opened it, then dug around in it, putting various items into a black backpack that came from inside the case. I tried to get a look inside the case, but it was too dark to see much, and the magical light he used to illuminate his work was angled the wrong way to give me a good look.

After he had everything he needed, he relocked the case and shoved it back under the bed. Then we made our way out the window and down off the porch roof. We parked behind the Dairy Queen and walked the rest of the way to the bank, which was a block off the town square. It was a solid Art Deco building that must have gone up just in time for the banks to fail at the start of the Depression. The building had proved far sturdier than the institution, as it was still in use by a branch of a national conglomerate. Sam waited for us in front of the bank.

"Do you think you can manage a veil long enough for me to get this done?" Owen asked him. "I don't want us accidentally fingered as suspects."

"Got it covered, kiddo. I'm not sure it'll be strong enough to block out our local wizard, but the cops on patrol won't spot any suspicious activity. Just make it snappy. There's not a lot of power to draw on around here. I spent a few hours on a church today, which helped, but it's not as good as being able to tap into a real power source."

"Is a church a good source of power then?" I couldn't resist asking. "If it is, this town may be more powerful than you think. We have a church on almost every corner."

"That's gargoyle-specific, doll, only 'cause we was created to guard churches in the first place. Most of your churches here don't have much power, since they weren't built with gargoyles in mind. A big oversight, if you ask me."

Owen was already at work, pulling things out of his bag and placing them around the bank's front entrance. "Is there a back door?" he asked as he worked.

"No, one way in and one way out. This place was built during a time when bank robberies happened all the time. You didn't want to give them much of an escape route. Is there anything you need me to do?"

"Thanks, but not yet. I'll need you when it comes time to set these. Help Sam keep lookout."

I couldn't help but hold my breath and hope that Sam's veil was good when I saw headlights approaching. It looked like the police were patrolling the square extra carefully after the previous night's events. The lights turned as the car circled the square, and I let my breath out. A few minutes later, they reappeared, heading down the side street the bank was on. I flattened myself against the building as the car passed, and the officer drove so slowly that I saw his head moving back and forth as he scanned the streets for suspicious activity. Surely a gargoyle standing on the sidewalk and two people dressed in black near the bank's entrance would have been enough to make him pull over if he saw anything, but he kept on going.

"You didn't trust me, did you?" Sam asked, sounding offended, as I let out the breath I'd been holding.

"No offense, but since your magic doesn't work on me, I find it very easy to forget that it's there," I said, surprised at how badly I was shaking. It reminded me of the one time I'd joined in a teenage prank when we toilet-papered the home of our chemistry teacher. I'd been too scared of being caught to get any fun at all out of it, so I decided to avoid that kind of activity from then on.

"I'm trying to work here," Owen snapped. He did tend to get testy when he was concentrating on something. That was about the only time he lost his usual calm. Sam and I looked at each other, and Sam shrugged.

Behind us, Owen began chanting softly in something that sounded like it might be Greek. He scattered a shimmering powder across the bank's threshold as he spoke. I shivered at the tingle of strong magic in use nearby, and I was glad I hadn't worn the magic-amplifying necklace. He took a step backward, paused for a moment, then said, "Okay, now to set it and fine-tune it. I'll need your help for this."

"My help? But I have no magic at all."

"Which means you have a lot of pent-up energy that I can tap into. Setting wards like this requires a massive burst of power, and with the power lines here so weak, I need another source if I don't want to deplete myself entirely. You should barely notice the effect." He held out his hand to me, and I stepped forward and took it. His hand was firm and warm, and I was sure mine was cold and clammy.

He adjusted his grip so that our palms were tight together and our fingers were laced, as much skin as possible in contact between us. "Now you need to relax. You don't have to do anything but stand there and keep breathing. Okay?"

I nodded, then found my voice to croak, "Okay."

"Okay, then. Sam, stay on lookout, and make sure that veil is working. There might be a few fireworks." *Yeah, there sure might,* I thought as my skin tingled from the close contact with him. And he hadn't even started the magic.

I felt like I should close my eyes, but Owen hadn't mentioned it, and I wanted to see what happened. He murmured something under his breath that was somewhere between a chant and a song. There was more melody than in your average chant, while it was still too flat to be much of a song for anyone who wasn't into rap. I didn't understand the words at all, and I didn't think I recognized the language. Then the strongest burst of magic I'd ever felt hit me. It flowed through me, and it reminded me of the very brief time earlier this year when, due to a fluke involving a parasitic fairy, I'd been able to do magic, myself. My hand grew so warm where it touched Owen's that I was sure it would glow red if I looked at it.

I did look at it, and there was a golden aura surrounding our joined hands. But then an even brighter light caught my eye. I turned to see a sheet of white light rise from the powder on the ground to fill the entire bank doorway. The sheet held for maybe a minute, then suddenly all the magic was gone. The doorway went back to normal, with even the powder dissipated, and when I looked at our hands, the aura was missing. I didn't feel the warmth anymore.

Owen took several long, deep breaths, then released my hand. "You okay?" he asked.

"Yeah, I think so." Actually, I felt a little shaky and light-headed, but I didn't think it was because of whatever he'd done magically. It probably had more to do with watching him in action while holding his hand that way. I couldn't help but wonder what it would be like to make love with him, if we ever managed to get back together and get our relationship to that point before some disaster hit us, and then I was glad it was so dark out because my face felt as warm as our hands had. "Did it work?" I asked.

"Sam?"

The gargoyle waddled forward and approached the doorway, only to be thrown backward. "Yep, it works, all right."

"Now what?" I asked.

"Sam starts staking out the bank and lets us know what he sees. And we get to bed before someone notices us missing."

We crept back across town to the car, then began driving home. We'd only gone a few blocks when Owen said, "Uh-oh." I turned around and saw flashing blue-and-red lights behind us.

"Uh-oh," I repeated.

Ten

My heart always pounded whenever I saw a police car on the side of a road and I thought I was doing a mile or two over the speed limit. I'd keep an eye on the rearview mirror for the next several miles until I could convince myself that the officer wasn't going to come after me. Tonight, seeing the police car flashing its lights behind us when we were out in the middle of the night doing extremely suspicious things while a rare crime wave was going on, I thought I'd have a stroke. Or maybe throw up. Tears stung my eyes in the instinctive female response to being pulled over. I never deliberately tried to cry my way out of a ticket, but I couldn't seem to help myself.

Owen, on the other hand, looked totally calm. He pulled right over and rolled down the window. Then he reached across the seat and grabbed my hand. "Good evening, officer," he said, a strange undertone to his voice. "What seems to be the problem here?" I recognized the tingle of magic, and my palm grew warm where Owen held it.

The officer got a glassy look to his eyes. "No problem. Have you seen anything suspicious?"

"Not at all."

"Thank you, and have a nice day." The officer turned and walked back to his car, and Owen drove off, not releasing my hand until the police car was completely out of sight.

As soon as the threat appeared to be over, I went giddy with relief. "These aren't the droids you're looking for," I quoted, ruining my Obi-Wan Kenobi impression by interrupting it with giggles.

"What?"

"Oh, come on, you know, Jedi mind tricks. The Force has a powerful effect on the weak-minded."

"Well, it does. And you'd better be glad I know that trick, or we'd have become the prime suspects. Do they have dashboard cameras in these police cars?"

"Not in this town, so you don't have to zap the tape magically. I thought using magic to manipulate others was wrong."

"It's a gray area. It depends a lot on motive. In this case, I can get away with it because it was crucial to the success of the mission. If I'd made him fix a ticket I'd earned, then I'd be in trouble."

"I guess it would have been bad if we became suspects while we were trying to solve the problem," I admitted. Then I added, "That was really cool how you did that."

"It's not something I have a lot of practice with, and as tired as I am, I wasn't sure it would work."

"What would you have done if it didn't?"

"I guess I'd have zapped him to knock him out and then tinkered with his memory so he didn't recall stopping me." The matter-of-fact way he said that was a little chilling.

He sat in the car for a while after we got back home. He looked utterly exhausted, like he had to recharge before he could even walk again. "Is setting wards really that draining?" I asked.

"Yeah, because you have to give them enough power to run for a while. It's the same amount of power as doing a spell constantly for days. In New York, there are stronger power sources naturally that I'm able to tap into, so warding my home only required a long nap and a day without using magic for recovery. The office has enhanced power sources, so warding my office was next to nothing. Here, though." He shook his head. "Doing much of anything takes a lot out of me. That's why I needed to draw on you. What time will we need to get up in the morning?"

"Church starts at eleven, and normally you'd be expected to go, but if you're not feeling well, Mom and Dad would understand. They'll go to Sunday school earlier than that, but we don't have to get up when they do. Sundays are fend-for-yourself days for breakfast."

"I think your mother would be deeply disappointed if she didn't get to show me off to her friends, and that might affect our ability to get anything done without making her suspicious. I'll be okay, assuming I can manage to get back into the house. A few hours of sleep will get me mostly back to normal."

This time, he didn't use magic to ease the way up the tree. He boosted me up, and then I reached a hand down to help pull him up. He was slender, but he was a lot heavier than he looked. I climbed through my bedroom window first, then held my breath and listened for other sounds of life in the house. When I was sure the coast was clear, I gestured him inside and dragged his case out from under the bed.

He put away the backpack and got out a small vial before relocking the case and hiding it again. Then he asked, "Do you think anyone would notice if I went back to my room through the hallway? I'm not sure I'm up to much more climbing around on the roof."

"If anyone hears anything, they'll assume you're going to or from the bathroom. It's not quite like the stairs."

He eased my door open, looked up and down the hall, then slipped silently away. I waited, holding my breath, until he'd disappeared into his room, then counted to a hundred before I shut my door as silently as possible and changed into my pajamas. It looked like we'd gotten away without being noticed yet again, though that police officer had been a close call. I pulled the pillow dummy out from under my covers so I could get into bed, then tried not to think about what it had felt like when Owen's hand had burned against mine.

He didn't look much worse for wear when he came down to breakfast the next morning. You'd have to know him as well as I did to notice the exhaustion behind his eyes. Mom had left a stack of waffles for us to pop into the toaster, and I couldn't detect a trace of suspicion in the note she'd written, much to my relief.

Owen was dressed the way he usually was for work, in a suit and tie. I should have been immune to seeing him that way by now, but I hadn't seen him like that for a while, and it almost took my breath away, even as it gave me a pang for what I'd been missing. "Coffee?" I asked, trying to hide what felt like a visible reaction.

"Please." He hung his suit jacket over the back of a kitchen chair and wearily took a seat.

I placed the coffee in front of him, along with glasses of orange juice and milk. "Are you sure you're okay?" I asked.

"As long as no one challenges me to a magical duel today, I'll be fine. Our wizard is probably still recovering from the other night's crime spree. The lack of local power sources should impact him—or her—even more than it does me."

Some waffles popped out of the toaster, and I put one on a plate and set it in front of him. "Syrup's on the table. Is there anything else you need?"

"I'm fine. Do you eat like this all the time?"

I put my own waffles on a plate and took the seat next to him. "No, Mom's just showing off for company. Most mornings, we grab a bowl of cereal and maybe some toast." I felt intensely conscious of how snug my skirt had become. A few months of eating Mom's cooking without all the walking I did in New York, and I was in danger of needing to buy an entirely new wardrobe. My only saving grace was the fact that my job here involved more physical activity than my job at MSI had—well, except for when I was being chased by dragons or weird magical creatures. My days in the office at MSI were generally pretty sedentary while I seldom got to sit down for five minutes straight at the store.

Owen ate silently for a while, and then the caffeine hit his system, so he became a little more animated. "I guess we go from church to your brother's house to make sure your sister-in-law isn't our culprit. Then is there anything else on the agenda?"

"You'll be pleased to note that an after-lunch nap is usually on the Sunday afternoon schedule."

"Good. Then we'll be ready for another busy night."

"Another one?" I may have hated the ruffles and canopy, but otherwise, I was quite fond of my bed, particularly in the middle of the night. I wasn't up for all this midnight creeping around.

"Our wizard should have recovered by now from Friday night's capers, and Sunday night would be the ideal time to hit the bank for maximum impact. Imagine the shock and horror when they open the bank Monday morning to find the vault empty. That would give him a real thrill."

"Can you really use magic to rob a bank or break into a safe?"

"I wouldn't try it at a Chase branch in Manhattan, but I could probably get in and out of the bank here with a good amount of money without anyone noticing if I tried. I don't know of any specific spells for safecracking, but there are some good spells for locks that might be modified. With what we've seen so far from our wizard, I wouldn't be surprised if specific bank-robbing spells were included in Idris's course."

"There are times when I'm really glad you're on our side," I said, finishing my waffle.

Mom was waiting for us in front of the church, and I was glad Owen had insisted on coming, no matter how he felt, for she was dressed to the nines, all set to show off. We barely made it inside before she started introducing Owen to everyone as her daughter's *special* friend who'd come all the way from New York to visit her. Owen was a good sport, even though it must have been his idea of hell to be surrounded by hordes of middle-aged and elderly women all fussing over him. I'd seen the kind of treatment he got when he went home for a visit, so I supposed he was used to it by now. At least here, no one was trying to throw daughters at him, since he was here to see me. Then again, my presence hadn't exactly stopped the onslaught in his hometown at Christmas, though there was magic involved in all that mayhem.

I could almost feel the tension leave him when we got back in the car after church. "You held up nicely," I said. "Many a strong man has faltered in the face of the women of the Cobb United Methodist Church."

"Well, I have faced my share of dragons." I knew from the quip that he was back to himself and might even be up to dealing with Dean and Sherri. I gave him directions to their house on the other side of town.

Sherri greeted us at the door in a skirt that could have doubled as a tube top and a tube top that could have doubled as a headband. I somehow doubted she'd been to church that morning dressed like that. She wore her new bracelet, along with a matching necklace and earrings. She grabbed Owen as soon as he stepped through the door and kissed him on both cheeks, European style, missing both times so that her kisses landed on the corners of his mouth. "Welcome to my home!" she said as she ushered us in.

It looked an awful lot like my home—my parents' home, that is. The same family pictures hung on the wall in very similar frames, and if I wasn't mistaken, the furniture was my parents' former living room set.

She'd set the dining table with china that looked suspiciously like the wedding china my mom never used. I made a note to myself to check the china cabinet and count pieces when I got home.

Dean wandered in from the backyard, smelling of charcoal smoke, so I assumed he was grilling something for lunch. When he greeted Owen, he was a little cooler and more reserved than he'd been the night before. He'd probably figured out that his wife had spotted a potential upgrade. Surely he was used to that by now, though, considering she'd broken an engagement with another man to marry him.

His coldness flustered Sherri. She fluttered around, picking up a book of matches and going to light a candle sitting on a side table. I thought it looked a lot like one of the ones Rainbow was selling in the drugstore—the ones Owen couldn't tolerate being around. I'd just opened my mouth to say he had allergies when Dean said, "Don't light that thing."

"Why not?" Sherri asked, still holding the lit match. "It's aromatherapy that will promote a calming environment."

"It makes the place smell like a cheap whorehouse, and it's so strong it gives me a headache."

"Like you'd know how one smelled," she muttered, but she blew the match out. As soon as Dean returned to the back patio to tend his steaks, she said in a voice pitched higher with tension, "Can I get you something to drink? How about a beer? Or we have sodas or iced tea or some lemonade, I think."

"Iced tea is fine for me," I said, wondering if she'd made it herself. On second thought, that might not have been the best choice.

"Iced tea for me, too, thank you," Owen said. He gave the distinct impression that he wished he could get away with wiping his mouth from where she'd kissed him.

Much to my relief, Sherri pulled a bottle of branded store-bought tea from her refrigerator, which meant it was probably safe to drink. As she handed glasses to each of us, she batted her eyelashes at Owen and said,

"You can take your coat and tie off, if you like. We're not formal here. But you do look awful handsome all dressed up like that." She turned to me while he blushed bright red. "Katie, what on earth were you thinking leaving him behind in New York? Or do they grow men like this on trees up there?"

I bit my tongue to force back the impulse to say that actually, the men up there were root vegetables. I knew she'd probably take that the wrong way and say something that would really embarrass Owen. Out of consideration for his exhaustion, I decided to deflect the subject. "That looks a lot like Mom's china," I said, wandering over to the dinner table as if to admire it.

"Yeah, it's the same pattern," she said. "I loved it so much when she had that wedding tea for me that I decided to get some for myself. Wasn't I lucky that Murphy's still had it in stock, all these years later?"

"It's a classic pattern," I said, in the most neutral response I could manage. I couldn't help but wonder how recently she'd acquired the china from the burgled jewelry store—or if maybe there were a few place settings missing from Mom's china cabinet. Then because I couldn't help myself, I asked, "Oh, is that a new necklace? I don't think I've seen it before."

She stuck her chest out to display it better, and I heard Owen choke on his tea. "Do you like it? It goes with my new bracelet. And see, matching earrings, too."

Now I was even more suspicious. Either Dean was selling drugs, she was selling her body, or something very, very fishy was going on.

Dean came back inside with a plate piled with steaks. "Steaks are ready," he said. "How about the rest of dinner?"

Sherri fluttered her hands. "Ooh! I just have to get it on the table." She ran to the kitchen and brought out take-out containers of slaw and baked beans. She dumped the beans into a bowl and put it in the microwave, then stuck a serving spoon in the slaw and put it on the table. I felt a little embarrassed that my family was being so very redneck in front of Owen, but then I glanced at him and saw that he didn't seem to be particularly upset. Of course not. He embarrassed easily, but he wasn't really a snob. Come to think of it, this was kind of the way he lived, eating out of take-out containers, though he did so in a multimillion-dollar Manhattan town house.

Oops, that meant I was the snob. I had to ask myself if I suspected Sherri because she really might be our greedy rogue wizard, or if it was because I was looking for an excuse to see her as my enemy. It was a tough call.

She got the beans out of the microwave and said, "Now, everybody take a seat. Sit wherever you want. We usually sit on the sofa and eat in front of the TV, so it's not like we have usual seats at the table."

Owen took a seat, and I sat across from him. Dean hovered with his platter of steaks. "Do you want yours more rare or well-done?" he asked Owen.

"Do you have anything somewhere in between?"

Dean laughed. "Right answer. I think that's the way all of them are." He sounded friendly enough now, so perhaps his earlier coolness had been about something else. More than likely, he and Sherri had had a spat soon before we got there. He served steaks to the rest of us, then took his seat. Sherri passed the side dishes around, then Dean said, "Dig in!"

Owen had managed to avoid the worst of the family interrogation so far. My parents must have been so happy to learn that I had a man, any man, that they weren't going to look the gift horse in the mouth. My brother, on the other hand, had no such qualms. Dean barely waited until we'd started eating before he went on the offensive.

"So, Owen," he said, "you're from New York, right?"

Owen didn't even flinch. He'd gone into his business mode. "Yes. I live in the city now, but I grew up in a small town not far outside the city."

I held my breath, hoping Dean wouldn't ask where Owen was born. That was a touchy subject, since he didn't actually know for sure, and I didn't want to have to get into that. Fortunately, Dean didn't go there. Instead, he asked, "Where did you go to school?"

Owen gave him an even gaze and said, "Yale, for my undergraduate through my doctorate." He didn't blush, but I felt my own face growing warm with pride on his behalf. Yep, my guy—or ex-guy, or whatever he was—was hot stuff.

Even Sherri seemed to be impressed. "Whoa, so you're like a doctor?"

"I'm not a medical doctor. It's a PhD, and it mostly means I spent a lot of time in school writing a lot of papers."

Dean didn't see the need to back down. If anything, he was more intent on finding and exposing whatever was wrong with Owen. I wasn't sure if he was really being the protective big brother on my behalf, or if he was looking for weaknesses so he could assure himself that he was still the hottest guy in town. "And what is it you do?" I was actually rather surprised that nobody had yet asked the question. The fact that Owen had worked with me had seemed like answer enough so far.

Owen very deliberately finished chewing the bite he'd just taken, then took a drink of tea before answering. "I work in research and development for a company supplying specialized technology resources." I tried to remember that description for future use. Saying "the Microsoft of magic" only worked when I was talking to people who were in on the secret.

Owen held Dean's gaze, like he was waiting for a reaction. Dean was no dummy, but he'd never applied himself, so I knew he was well out of his league, and it looked like he knew it, too. I felt it was time to jump in. "So, big brother dearest," I said, trying to sound fond instead of defensive, "does he pass muster? Or should I have held out for a medical doctor who went to Harvard?"

"That wouldn't necessarily have been an upgrade," Owen said with a raised eyebrow in my direction. "Not Harvard."

"I think he's swell, Katie," Sherri said. "Dean, you should lighten up. Does anyone want seconds?"

Before Dean could say anything else, I piped up again. "I was just admiring Sherri's china. Did y'all get this recently?"

For perhaps the first time in my life, I saw Dean utterly speechless. His mouth hung open, and no sound came out of it. Sherri didn't seem to notice. "It's brand-new," she said proudly. "Y'all are the first ever to eat off it."

"Well, someone's trying to score Brownie points," I continued. "I noticed all that pretty new jewelry Sherri's wearing. I guess one of your businesses hit the jackpot for you, huh?" Dean couldn't resist a get-rich-quick scheme. He was the guy all those Internet spam "make money fast" ads were targeted to. And then, almost holding my breath in anticipation, I went in for the kill that was sure to get me a reaction. "It's lucky you got all that stuff before someone knocked over the jewelry store. It would have been a shame if you'd gotten together the money to buy all these nice things, and someone had swiped them out from under you."

Their reactions weren't at all what I'd anticipated. Sherri couldn't keep a secret to save her life, so I'd expected her to lean forward and whisper to us about buying everything cheap from a guy who'd offered a great deal. Or, if she was our wizard, she'd have started preening, gloating, and acting mysterious. Instead, she nodded sincerely and said, "Yeah, I know."

Dean's reaction was even more surprising. He went totally still, only his eyes moving as he looked between Owen and me, then he said in an ice-cold voice, "And I think it's interesting how the biggest crime wave ever to hit this town just happened to strike the day after your boyfriend showed up."

I wasn't sure how to react in order to convey the maximum degree of innocence. Of course, Owen wasn't the thief, but the mysterious crime wave was related to his visit. I tried for affronted girlfriend and embarrassed sister, which wasn't much of a stretch.

Meanwhile, Owen went even colder than Dean had been, with the eerie kind of stillness that he got when he was absolutely furious. The last time I'd seen him that angry, he'd almost accidentally sent Grand Central Station plummeting three stories underground after generating a shock wave that could have undermined the foundation. "Are you implying anything in particular?" he asked, his voice even and conversational.

"Dean, don't be rude!" Sherri said. "Like he'd need to come here to rob the town. If he was a robber, he could have robbed all kinds of places in New York. Now, you apologize right this instant."

Dean and Owen remained in a staredown, blue eyes locked with green. Under normal circumstances, Owen might have been at a disadvantage because he wore contact lenses and would have to blink, but Owen was anything but normal. I had a feeling that if I'd worn Owen's magic-detecting necklace, it would have been buzzing up a storm, just from the waves of anger that were coming off him. Dean's high school portrait that hung on the dining room wall fell to the floor with a crash. There was a strong chance it was pure coincidence and caused by a slipshod job of picture hanging, but I wouldn't have bet on it.

"Dean, I said stop it and apologize," Sherri said again, her voice shrill. That broke the standoff, and for the first time since I met her, I actually liked Sherri. "You know he's not the robber, and besides, your mom was talking about weird stuff happening days before he got here."

Dean kept his eyes fixed on Owen. "Weird stuff isn't the same as robbery."

"Yeah, but still, weird things were happening around town, so it's not like everything suddenly changed when he got here—except maybe for Katie. I'm sure a lot changed for her." She looked embarrassed as she said, "I doubt y'all will want to stay for dessert after my husband was so rude. It was just a store-bought cake that I got on special, anyway, and you can bet Lois'll have something even better when you get back home." Sherri stood up. "I'm sorry about all this."

This was one of those times when it was best not to get into an argument, so I got my purse while Owen got his suit coat, and then Sherri walked us to the door. As soon as we were both in the car, I said, "I'm sorry about that. He was a total jerk. I don't know what his deal was."

Owen didn't say anything while he started the car, put it in gear, and then backed out of the driveway. He didn't talk until we were halfway home. Then he sighed and seemed to relax a little. "I know he's your brother," he began, "and I realize I know absolutely nothing about what it's like to be part of a family—"

"That most definitely is not it," I cut in.

"But I think we have to consider him a suspect. It was a classic move—you were getting too close with your questions about all the new things he seems to have acquired lately, so he tried to deflect suspicion onto me. I'm sure if he talks to enough people in town about this, it will be easy for him to make the outsider look like the culprit."

"Well, considering that he's got a house full of stuff stolen from the stores in question, and you have nothing on you—and I suspect you've arranged it so nothing could be easily planted—that won't go far. This town may be small and old-fashioned, but we haven't tarred and feathered a stranger before riding him out of town on a rail since I can remember. And how can he be our suspect? He's not magical. Remember, my family tends to be immune to magic."

"I'm not saying he's our wizard, but I think he may know who the wizard is and may be in league with him. He might not know that magic is involved. He may just be serving as the fence."

I shook my head. "No, I don't see it. He can be a jerk, and I could totally see him as a con artist, but I can't imagine him going that far."

"So you still think Sherri is our key suspect?"

I sighed. "No, not really, unless her niceness today was all an act and they were doing a good cop/bad cop routine to get us off the trail. But why would they even think we might be on their trail? There's no reason for them to know that either of us might be investigating magical activity."

"Not unless they've been warned. Idris may have figured out I left New York and must be here."

"You're being paranoid. Dean just felt threatened by you. He's always been the town golden boy, the best-looking guy who could have any girl he wanted. And now he's having second thoughts about the girl he's stuck with, people in town have grown immune to the charm and looks so they expect him to actually do something, and then you come along and show him up. You're better looking than he is—and don't go blushing on me because that only makes you cuter. Yeah, believe it or not, you're hot stuff. Then you go talking about having a doctorate from Yale and a high-powered-sounding job in New York. Sherri was practically drooling all over the table at what a catch you were, and then I went and questioned the goodies he'd gotten her to make her sweet for a little while and ruined that much."

I sighed. "He had to tear you down to make himself look better." When he didn't respond, I added, "You don't know him like I do, and like you said, you don't have any experience with brothers."

He glanced over at me, looking a little sheepish. "I have Rod."

"Yeah, and Dean and Rod are practically two peas in a pod, except Rod isn't allergic to work and never tied himself to any of the bimbos he used to date."

"Because I wouldn't let him."

"Rod feels threatened enough to hide behind an illusion. What do you think he might do if he felt really threatened, if he thought he might lose his standing with someone whose opinion mattered to him?"

"I'm not sure he'd go so far as to be that rude to a guest in his home, but I see your point. I'm sorry."

"He does sound suspicious, I'll admit, but I can't imagine him going that far. If he's involved at all, he's just buying stuff cheap from the guy who did steal it, or from someone that guy sold it to. If worse comes to worst, we could try interrogating him about his sources, but I doubt he'd be too cooperative. I guess we'll find out who it is soon enough, though. Another late night?"

"I'm afraid so."

"This should be our last one. Our wizard won't be able to resist hitting the bank. He'll run into the wards, and then bang, we've got our guy. What could possibly go wrong?"

Eleven

Of course, saying that nothing can go wrong is almost as good as putting a curse on yourself to guarantee that *everything* will go wrong.

It started when we got back home. Mom was waiting for us in the kitchen. "Kathleen Elizabeth, how dare you be so rude to your own brother when you were a guest in his house!"

As I counted to ten before saying anything I might regret to my mother, I realized that Dean must have called ahead in a preemptive tattletale strike. "I? I was rude to *him*?" I sputtered.

Owen was far calmer, which meant he was still very, very angry. "He was the one who was rude, I'm afraid," he said softly. "He accused me of being the thief who robbed all the stores in the town square the night I arrived here."

That brought Mom up cold. Being rude to family was one thing, but you were never supposed to be rude to guests, particularly not the potentially-marriage-material-good-catch boyfriend of your still-single sister. She frowned at Owen, then turned back to me. "Of course Owen wasn't the robber. He was here all night. But Dean said you'd accused *him* of being the robber."

Okay, maybe I had, sort of, but in a very indirect way. "Mom, I didn't accuse him of anything. I simply remarked on all the nice new things he and Sherri got recently. They've got a whole set of china like yours, and Sherri had a necklace and earrings that match her new bracelet, the one she was wearing last night. And then I said they were lucky they got them before the stores were robbed and all the good stuff was taken." I took a breath and continued. "Why, if I didn't know better, I'd think that was his guilty conscience talking. If he didn't have anything to feel guilty about, he wouldn't have assumed I was accusing him, and then he wouldn't have tried to shift the blame to Owen."

It took her a while to process that information. In most families, the middle child is more or less forgotten, but Dean had always been Mom's favorite, the one who could do no wrong. I wondered if it had something to do with how handsome he was. "Well, you're making accusations against him now," she said at last.

"No, I'm simply evaluating his behavior, and I did say that I knew he couldn't really be the thief. I'd just prefer that he not invite me over and then attack my friend. If he had doubts about Owen, he could have talked to me privately."

She sighed heavily. "I'm terribly sorry about that, Owen. Now, would you two like some dessert? I made a chocolate cake."

I never passed up chocolate, and Owen was well aware of that, so we sat at the kitchen table with Mom and Dad and had chocolate cake with coffee. The atmosphere was still a little tense, but after a couple of slices of cake, Owen seemed to have settled down and I was no longer afraid of household objects blowing up. Now he just looked tired.

As Mom took the dishes away, she said, "I don't know if Katie told you, but Sunday afternoons are usually pretty quiet around here. It's a day of rest, and we all try to read and relax or nap. You're free to do what you like, of course, but we prefer to keep things quiet for the afternoon."

"I could use a nap," Owen said. "I know it's not a big time difference, but I think I'm a little jet-lagged, and I had to work a lot of extra hours to be able to take off to come down here."

She smiled and patted him on the arm, as if trying to make up for the way Dean had treated him. "Then you have a good nap, and we'll see you at dinner tonight. Sunday night is casual, so there's no set timetable."

At the top of the stairs, Owen pulled me into his room. "Let's get ready for tonight first," he said, shutting the door.

"You know what my parents are going to think about us being in here with the door closed." I certainly knew what I was thinking about.

"You won't be in here too long, and your hair won't be at all messed up when you leave, so relax. She's more likely to think we're talking about how awful your brother is." He pulled off his tie and sat on one of the beds. I sat next to him. "We need to come up with disguises for tonight."

"Disguises?"

"You're the one who lives here. You have family here. Do you really want to let anyone in town know that you or someone associated with you is involved with magic?"

"No, not really. What kind of disguise were you thinking of?"

"This is probably someone without much experience with magic and an image of magic formed from seeing too many movies. He's been wearing a hooded robe to do his own work. We should probably go with that—dress in hooded robes of our own and act as though we're superior wizards to put a good scare in him."

"Act?" I asked, raising an eyebrow.

He ignored me. "Any spell he tries to do to fight us off won't affect you, and I'll be able to deflect it from me. If we show him how inferior he is and exactly what he's playing with, we may be able to scare him into stopping and then cooperating with us. I guess our problem is how we'll come up with wizard-looking robes between now and tonight."

"Not a problem." I got off the bed and went to the chest of drawers that had been Teddy's. "Teddy probably still has some of his *Star Wars* and Dungeons and Dragons costumes in here. He's the nerd of the family, and the reason I can quote from anything with the word 'star' in the title." I dug around in the bottom drawer and came out with a black hooded cloak with stars and moons on it. "I could have sworn his old Jedi outfit was still in here, but the wizard should work just as well, as long as you don't mind glowing in the dark." I tossed it to him.

"Of course, real wizards wear Armani," he said with a grin and a raised eyebrow as he wrapped the cloak around himself, "but it'll do. It looks very, um, magical. Now, what about you?"

"I should have a cloak that matches that one. Teddy made me go with him to a costume party and we dressed as a team."

He took off his robe and I hung it in the closet so the wrinkles could fall out of it. "And now, I believe it's naptime," I said, "since we aren't going to get any sleep again tonight. Do you need a book? My dad has a pretty extensive collection of spy and mystery novels."

"I'll probably be asleep before you're back in your room," he said with a yawn. "Bang on my door if I'm not stirring when everyone else is up and around."

I knew I'd do no such thing. He looked like he'd been operating on a sleep deficit coming into this, and then he'd had sleepless nights on top of heavy magic use. I wanted him fully charged before we had to go out and trap our wizard.

The old wizard cloak was still in the bottom drawer of my bureau where I'd shoved it about ten years ago. I shook it out, tried it on, then hung it at the back of my closet. Who knew that some of Teddy's nerdy oddities would turn out to be so useful?

I was surprised by how easily I fell asleep, even though I was still agitated from the disastrous lunch. My windows were on the eastern side of the house, so my room was in shadow when I woke up. Owen's door was still closed, so I tiptoed down the stairs, which made their usual squeak of protest. I could understand my parents keeping it when they had teenagers in the house, but with all of us grown, it would have been nice if they'd finally had that fixed. Never mind that I was sneaking out far more often these days than I had when I'd been a teenager.

Owen came downstairs not five minutes later, wearing his wire-rimmed glasses, faded jeans, and a T-shirt that almost perfectly matched his eye color. I could have sworn my mother drooled just the least bit. Goodness knows I was practically swooning. "Did you have a good nap?" I asked him.

"Very good, and you know, I could go right back to sleep now. I must have been tired."

"Country air is good for you," Mom said. "It gives you more restful sleep." Then she proceeded to load the kitchen table with food for a "light" Sunday supper.

When we excused ourselves to go to bed ridiculously early, both of us tried to make it very obvious that we were going to separate rooms, lest we give the impression of being impatient honeymooners. Though, come to think of it, we'd barely given any indication that we were anything more than just friends. While my old-fashioned parents would probably be relieved to know that we weren't sleeping together outside of wedlock, shouldn't they have been concerned that we barely touched each other and didn't act at all romantic? Our relationship confused me, and I was inside it. Anyone else should have been truly baffled if they were paying attention.

I dressed in black and coiled my hair at the nape of my neck before crawling into bed to get what sleep I could before we had to head off and play wizard. It seemed like I'd barely closed my eyes before Owen crawled through my window, his robe balled up under his arm. We got out his case, and he again got his pack full of supplies, to which he added both wizard robes. Then we were off, climbing off the porch roof, down the tree, and onto the ground.

This time, Owen parked behind the library on the other side of the bank, a place that was more sheltered than the Dairy Queen and on a different major road. Sam stood guard in front of the bank. "No sign of 'im yet, boss," he reported.

"How are you for energy?" Owen asked.

"They've been having church services of some kind or another in this town from shortly after dawn until nearly sunset, and I've been basking on rooftops all day, so I'm fully charged." He looked up at me and added, "Gargoyles get extra power when the church is having a service. All that worship really jolts up the juice. I could get to like it here, plenty of sunshine, lots of churches. Hey, boss, too bad you don't got something you can plug into to recharge, other than tapping into the little lady here." And then he gulped audibly and said, "I didn't mean it that way. Sorry."

"We'll be hiding over there at the next building," Owen said evenly, ignoring Sam's last comment. "Signal us when you see something."

Sam perched on the roof over the bank's doorway, and Owen and I took refuge in the doorway of the chamber of commerce building next door to the bank. There, we couldn't help but be close to each other because it was hard to crowd into a doorway recess with another person without touching. I wasn't sure whether I wanted our rogue wizard to hurry and get there or to take his sweet time. The proximity was practically intoxicating, I was so acutely aware of Owen's nearness. I was on the verge of suggesting that I wait in another doorway so I wouldn't be tempted to do anything that might disrupt the fragile balance we had going between us when Sam called out, "I think he's coming."

The wizard I'd seen before rounded the corner from the square. He wore the same homemade-looking robes he'd been wearing the day I saw him, and I couldn't spot anything that might identify him to me. The hood draped so low that his face was hidden in shadows, the sleeves covered his hands, and the robe dragged on the ground, completely covering his shoes. He carried a satchel that didn't have any distinguishing characteristics—no recognizable marks, no logos, and definitely no monogrammed initials, which would have been really helpful.

The wizard hid in the doorway of the building directly across the street from the bank, took some things out of his satchel and spread them around, then took a small booklet out and flipped through it. Referring to the book every so often, he arranged the items in front of him. He lit a couple of candles, using matches instead of the wave of a hand the way Owen might have, and then I felt the tingle of magic building.

He repacked his bag, looked both ways up and down the street, darted across the street, and stood in front of the bank doorway. Raising his arms over his head, he chanted some words in hesitant Latin, and now I was sure it was a he because that was definitely a male voice. Then he stepped forward, and just as he was about to hit the wards, I felt another surge of magic from very close by. The wards flared up in bright light, and the wizard bounced off them, falling on his back on the sidewalk. I knew that wards were usually invisible, so Owen must have added the light show for effect. It would have been nice if we could have seen the junior wizard's face to enjoy his reaction, but the hood hid him completely.

We'd just started to step off the doorstep to confront him when Sam gave another signal, this one silent. Headlights appeared, and a police car came slowly down the street. Owen immediately made the wards quit glowing, but it looked like the unusual light had attracted some attention, for the police car came to a stop in front of the bank. Our wizard crawled through the shadows to the side of the building, then took off running between buildings. I would have chased after him, but Owen gripped my arm.

"I can't keep us hidden if we move very far," he whispered.

We both held our breath as the police officer got out, swinging his flashlight back and forth. I couldn't stop myself from wincing when the beam swept across us, but the cop didn't seem to notice us. He leaned back into the car and got on the radio. "I thought I saw someone in front of the bank who ran off when I got here. I'm gonna check it out," he said. The radio squawked, he paused to listen, then said, "Nah, I don't think I need backup. Probably just some kid, but you never know, could be our mystery burglar." He put the radio away, put his hand on his gun, and went in between the buildings, following the wizard's path, but came back a moment later, empty-handed. He checked around the bank doorway, unaffected by the wards, then returned to his car.

He got back on the radio. "Didn't see anything. It could have been just a dog, or else my eyes playing tricks on me. I'll make one more circuit around town, then that'll be the end of my shift. See you back at the barn."

As soon as the car was gone, I turned to Owen. "We had him. Why didn't we go after him? People walk around with veils and illusions all the time, so I don't get why you couldn't keep us hidden if we chased him."

"Complete invisibility against someone who's really looking takes a lot of power. Most so-called invisibility isn't complete. It's more of a spell to make people not notice something they weren't paying attention to in the first place. It's much harder to really be invisible to someone who's intently looking for you. I know I couldn't have kept the two of us invisible and silent while chasing our suspect. If we'd gone after him, we'd have been the ones who were caught."

"And that would have ruined everything," I admitted. "You couldn't have done that time-freezing thing again, I guess?"

Instead of answering me, he knelt and put his hands on the ground. Then I felt the magic through the soles of my feet. "Not a good thing to do with someone around who's linked to the world outside the spell," he then said. "What if dispatch tried reaching the police officer here while he was frozen? Now, let's see how far our guy got."

I had to pull up the hem of my robe to run after him down the alley where the wizard had disappeared. It would have been nice to get rid of the robes before we had to go running and searching, but I guessed if we found the guy, we wouldn't want to be recognized. The air was as still as it had been the other night, but the only frozen living beings we saw in the alley were cats and rats. I had no idea we had that many rats in this town. It gave me the creeps.

We searched the entire downtown area, weaving between buildings and looking under anything that might have offered shelter from Sam. The gargoyle returned just as we made it back to the bank. "Sorry, boss, I lost him," he said. "He went low, which is where I'm not as good. Scrambled between buildings and then got up under something. That's where I lost him. I checked the area over, but if he got inside somewhere and went building to building and then ditched the robes, well, I'm good, but I'm not that good. You'd have needed a rat to track this guy, and I'm not yet on friendly terms with any of the locals."

Owen looked at me. "Are there any good hiding places here, places where someone might know to hide out?"

"The upstairs rooms in most of these buildings on the square are vacant. You can get into some of them using the fire escapes. Kids sometimes hang out there. But there's also a pretty good chance he got out of range before you had a chance to freeze him."

Sam hopped up onto the trunk of the car so he could look Owen in the eye. "You did it again? I thought things seemed quiet. How long has it been?"

I compared my watch to the courthouse clock tower, factoring in the five minutes from the other night. "Fifteen minutes."

"Drop it now," Sam said. "People'll notice, and it can't be good for you or for the space-time continuum."

"We can catch him!" Owen insisted. "What if he's hiding in one of those buildings?"

"He was headin' away from the square when I lost him. He was probably out of range. And if he's gone to ground, he'll stay for a while. I can go look in the buildings, but you've got to stop playing with the big stuff like that."

With a sigh, Owen knelt again, and soon it was a lot easier to breathe. Sam took off to peek through windows, and we got into the car. I directed Owen down back roads that led away from town before going the long way back around to my parents' house.

"He'll be back tomorrow night, if Sam doesn't catch him tonight," he said after a while, sounding almost like he was trying to boost his own spirits.

"How can you be so sure?"

"Up to this point, he's thought he was invincible because he could do magic. The wards really threw him. Now he has to suspect there's another wizard around who's stronger than he is. He'll spend the day reading his spell book, maybe checking in with his correspondence course teacher. If we're lucky, he might even try casing the bank in daylight to see what the problem is."

"He won't be able to get in, even in daylight, will he?"

"No. Which might even mean we could figure out our culprit that way and not have to stay up all night tomorrow. Is there anything you need to do tomorrow?"

"I should probably put in some time at work so I don't get too far behind. You could come with me and see the joys of the family business. That would keep you away from Mom. I can take off pretty early, though."

"I think I'll help Sam stake out the bank. I'd really like to get this wrapped up."

Sherri showed up on time for work the next morning, which was one of the signs of the impending apocalypse, and she came bearing a gift, which was definitely an omen of the end times. She brought a cake in a foil pan back to the office. "Is Owen here?" she asked. That explained the earliness and the cake, I thought.

"No, he had some things to do today. Why?"

"I wanted to apologize again for what a jerk Dean was to him yesterday. I made him this cake, since you didn't get to have dessert at my house." Her eyes were puffy and red-rimmed, and I actually felt sorry for her.

"You have nothing to apologize for," I said, taking the cake from her and putting it on my desk. "Dean was the one who was a jerk."

"I don't know what to do about Dean," she blurted with a sob. "I think he's got himself mixed up in something bad."

I took her arm and helped her over to the sofa in the back of the office. "What is it?" I asked, sitting next to her and holding her hand.

"I think he's involved with something illegal to make money. You know how he is, this is always going to be the thing that makes him rich, and it just puts us deeper in the hole, but at least all of those have been honest. Sort of. Now, though, he's buying me way too much stuff, and I know I shouldn't complain, but we don't have that kind of money. He's out at all hours, coming and going without telling me, and I think he's meeting with shady people. I don't know what I'll do if he goes to jail." Then she broke down in sobs.

Dean drove me crazy at times, but if she was worried enough to question gifts, I couldn't help but worry about him, even if he had brought his troubles on himself. I just didn't have time to deal with it at the moment, not until we took care of this wizard. Why couldn't my family wait to have a major crisis? Then again, if he was dealing with the wizard, Sherri might be a useful source of information. "Keep an eye on him, and let me know if you notice anything else suspicious, okay?" I said, giving her shoulders a squeeze. "It might help if we knew who he was dealing with and where he got all that stuff. But we will take care of it, I promise."

She collapsed, sobbing, on my shoulder, and I patted her back until she pulled herself together. "Thanks, Katie," she said with a sniffle and an attempt at a smile. "Well, I'd better go fix my face, then get to the register."

I got through the rest of the morning without any additional scenes. By noon, I was able to wrap things up in the office. I took the morning's receipts in a deposit bag and headed to the bank. It really was an errand I'd have to do anyway, but it was the perfect excuse to check in on Owen and Sam.

The bank was busy at noon on a Monday, so I had to park a block away and walk. Owen was across the street from the bank, leaning against a wall with a cup of coffee in his hand. I wasn't sure whether I should speak to him, or if he was invisible to everyone but me. He spoke first. "An errand at the bank?" he asked.

"Yeah, would you believe, I have to make a deposit?"

"Need some company?"

"Sure, if you're that desperate for something to do."

"I want to get a look at the inside of the bank, just in case."

"I take it you haven't seen any customers being forcefully repelled."

"Not a one."

As we approached the bank, I saw Dean heading toward the front steps. I wanted to talk to him some more about what I'd noticed and about Sherri's concerns, but he was the last person I wanted to see right now. Next to me, Owen stiffened. He obviously wasn't too thrilled to see Dean, either. Both of us slowed our pace, holding back so that Dean turned to go into the bank before he noticed us. I sighed in relief that at least one awkward encounter had been avoided when he reached the bank entrance without seeing us. Then he bounced off something invisible and landed on his back on the sidewalk.

Twelve

It was impossible. I never in a million years would have believed it if I hadn't seen him bounce off the wards with my own eyes. My brother was the local wizard. The lying, thieving, con-artist local wizard. I rushed over, Owen right behind me. "Dean? It was you?" I couldn't help but blurt as my brother stared up at me in shock.

"What was me?" he tried as a look of panic crossed his face. He rolled to his side, as if to prepare to get up and run. Owen bent, grabbed his arm, and helped him to his feet, then didn't let go. His knuckles turned white, he was grasping so hard. Dean made as though to pull away, and I thought I felt the tingle of building magic. Dean frantically mumbled words, his eyes growing wider and wider as Owen stayed put and was entirely unaffected by whatever he'd tried to do.

After about a minute of this, Owen's grip on Dean's arm tightened and he said very softly, "Don't even try it. You are so outclassed here that you can't even comprehend the class I'm in." Then, quite suddenly, Owen released Dean and stepped backward. Dean's muscles tensed, ready to run the moment he was let go, but he was frozen in place, unable to take a step. Owen stood there watching him, his arms folded across his chest, not even breaking a sweat.

Then Dean yelled at the top of his lungs, "Hey, this is your burglar! He's the guy who did it!" People kept walking up and down the sidewalk, not giving him more than a passing glance.

"You're not the only one who can hide what you're up to," Owen said mildly. Then he added, "Katie, I'll stay out here and keep your brother company while you wrap up your errand. We have a lot to talk about."

"What are you doing with my sister, you freak? Katie, you come back here, don't do what he says!" Dean shouted. He then began mumbling words and wiggling his fingers at me. I felt the magic but, of course, it did nothing to me.

"Give it a rest, Dean," I said with a sigh. "I need to go make these deposits." I didn't want to leave them alone, but I was holding the morning's receipts for the store, including the checks that had come in over the weekend, so skipping this errand wasn't an option. I headed to the bank, shivering as I crossed through the wards at the threshold, and gave one last glance over my shoulder before I entered. I wasn't sure if the lines were longer than usual or if they only felt that way because I was so eager to get back outside and see what was going on.

My brother was the local criminal wizard? There had to be some kind of mix-up or coincidental misunderstanding. Maybe he'd tripped or slipped on the steps instead of bouncing off the wards. But no, he'd been using magic—or trying to—on Owen and me. There couldn't be any doubt, unless there was another local wizard who'd done all the illegal stuff, but then that wouldn't explain all of Dean's new acquisitions.

It seemed to take forever to make my deposit, and while normally I'd have been glad that the teller double-checked the amounts, this time I couldn't help but drum my fingers on the counter in impatience. I practically grabbed the deposit receipt out of her hand and shoved it into my bag while I jogged across the lobby to the exit.

Owen and Dean were still right where I'd left them, in the middle of a staredown. "All done!" I announced. "Now, where do we go from here?"

"Is there a place we can talk without being overheard or interrupted?" Owen asked.

"In this town? Let's see, Mom will be at home. Sherri will be off work soon, so Dean's house is out. I know, we can talk in the barn."

"Good idea, Katie," Owen said, still sounding calm and collected, but I noticed a small muscle in his jaw twitching.

"Katie, you're siding with this guy?" Dean asked, the faintest hint of a desperate whine in his voice. "Do you know what he is?"

"I know exactly what he is. I'm just not sure you know yet what you're really dealing with, and I guess I don't know what you are anymore."

Owen waved a hand ever so slightly, making an "after you" gesture, and Dean's legs began moving, walking him toward Owen's rental car. Every so often, Dean gave a little jerk, like he was trying to break free, but Owen only intensified his control. He made Dean sit in the passenger seat.

Owen then took a small cell phone—or something that looked pretty much like a cell phone but that I imagined had a few extra magical features—out of his shirt pocket and pushed a couple of buttons. "Sam, meet us at the barn behind Katie's house," he said into the phone. "And be careful. You know about her mother." The way Owen had to hold the phone away from his ear told me that Sam definitely remembered my mother. She'd hit him in the face with her purse when she was in New York at Thanksgiving, thinking he was an overgrown bat.

I went to get my truck, and Owen followed me out to the house. I pulled up into the horse pasture behind the barn so the truck wouldn't be visible from inside the house, then once Owen had parked, I led the way into the barn. The dogs came running up to greet us, but then came to an abrupt halt a few yards away, almost like they'd sensed that this was something they didn't want to get involved with.

Owen shoved Dean down to sit on a wooden crate inside the barn, looming over him. "What were you trying to pull? Did you really think you could get away with it?" he yelled. I couldn't help but wince and take a step backward. Owen almost never raised his voice.

"Get away with what?" Dean asked, trying—and failing—to look innocent. I recognized the tactic from childhood. He wanted to make sure he knew what our parents thought he'd done so he wouldn't accidentally admit to something they didn't know about yet.

I was about to list his crimes when Daisy, our old mare, stuck her head into the barn to see what the commotion was. Dean patted his leg in what I knew was a signal for her to come to him. He'd always been her favorite, and I guessed he thought he'd found an escape route. But Daisy went straight to Owen, nuzzling his neck in a way that made me just a little jealous. Dean took advantage of the distraction and jumped off the crate, running for the door on the side of the barn closest to the house. Owen barely jerked his head and that door slammed shut. Before Dean could run for the other exit, Owen gave a hand signal and Daisy went to stand blocking the barn entrance. She pawed at the ground with a foreleg and her ears flattened against her head when Dean moved as though to run in her direction. Dean's eyes bugged out, and I could see it dawning on him exactly what he might be dealing with in Owen.

He went back to the crate and took a seat, as though that had been what he had planned to do all along. "So, what is it you think I've been doing?" he asked.

I took a deep breath, then shouted, "What have you been doing? For starters, you've been freaking Mom out. What was up with all that dancing on the square wearing Teddy's old Jedi robes?" I'd finally recognized the robes and realized where they must have gone. "And then panhandling? Really? That was so tacky. Oh yeah, and the window at the motel. What was up with that?"

"But those are all minor," Owen put in. "Pickpocketing and burglary, however, took things a step too far. Magic used to commit crime is automatically classified as dark magic, regardless of which forces you channel to carry it out. Influencing people to your benefit, as you were doing while panhandling, is more of a gray area, but crime is definitely over the line."

All the color drained from Dean's face. "How—how did you know?" he asked, his voice shaking.

"I watched you dancing around the courthouse," I said. "And to think you were going to let them lock Mom up in the loony bin for reporting what she saw, when you knew all along that what she saw was for real. That was really low."

"No one was supposed to see that. And Mom really was nuts about some of that stuff, like what she thought she saw Gene Ward doing. Everyone knows his dad has an account at the pharmacy."

I refused to get sidetracked from his crimes. "I also saw you at the theater. You were the one who sent the snake illusion after Nita and me, weren't you?"

"I was only having a little fun. It wouldn't have hurt you."

"Ask Nita if it was fun. I didn't even see the snake."

"You didn't?"

"That's why you shouldn't play with things you don't understand," Owen said, pacing as he talked. "For instance, did you know that there are people your magic doesn't affect, who can see what you're doing, no matter what spell you use to hide yourself? That might have been good for you to know before you made a public spectacle of yourself."

Dean looked at me. "You?"

"Yeah, and Mom, too, only she doesn't know it. And there's a strong possibility that there are others in our family, too." I turned to Owen. "Speaking of which, how is it that he's magical when Mom and I are immune?"

"It's not entirely unheard of. It all involves the same gene—the immunity is actually caused by a mutation of the magical gene, but then that itself becomes an inherited trait. It's possible for both traits to exist in the same family. I'm not sure exactly how it works. Magical genetics isn't my area of expertise."

Although he'd answered the question I asked, my real question remained: How come my brother got to be magical? It was no fair. I thought I was the special one in the family with my magical immunity, and Dean had trumped me by having actual magical powers. But I kept my pouting to myself so I wouldn't sound like a bratty baby sister.

"Who are you, anyway?" Dean asked. "I take it you're not really here as Katie's boyfriend. You're here to track me down, right?"

"I'm here for a number of reasons," Owen said neutrally, glancing at me. "One of which was to determine who was doing unauthorized magic in a place with no registered magic users. The timing of your magical activity in this location was highly suspicious, considering Katie's position."

Dean turned to look at me. "You're mixed up in all this magic stuff?"

"At a very high level," I said, trying not to sound like I was gloating about knowing more about magic than he did, even if he was the one with the powers. "It's a long story, and I won't get into all the details, but Owen and I both work for a company called Magic, Spells, and Illusions, Incorporated. Well, Owen does. I used to. You might think of it as the Microsoft of magic—they come up with and sell most of the spells used in the magical world. They needed me because of my magical immunity. There's a rogue wizard out there trying to get darker spells into the market as our competition, and we're—our company—trying to stop him. I had to come back here because he was targeting me in New York."

"He's the one running your magic school, and I came here to get to the bottom of it all," Owen added. "But that doesn't get you off the hook. You've been using magic to commit crimes, and I can't let that slide, no matter who you are."

"And who are you?"

"I'm . . ." Owen's voice trailed off, as though he wasn't sure of the answer to the question. "I'm a fully trained and qualified wizard," he said at last. "The kind of stuff you're doing, I learned how to do by the time I was five. Of course, I didn't apply it in quite the same way you have. Now I run the theoretical magic division in the research and development department at MSI. I study old spells and try to find ways to apply them to modern life, in addition to creating new spells for specific situations. And I'm more or less leading our efforts to counter this rogue wizard, since he used to work with me and I know how he thinks." I noticed that he left out the part where he was probably the most powerful wizard of his generation.

"What should we do with him?" I asked Owen. "We should probably turn him over to the police, but then that would require explaining how he committed the crimes."

"Hey!" Dean protested. "How do you know I'm the one who robbed the stores? Maybe there's another wizard around town."

"You had all the stolen stuff in your house," I reminded him.

"So, magic really doesn't work on you?" he asked me, turning the subject away from his guilt. Then he raised his arms and chanted some mumbo jumbo. I felt the magic surround me, but as usual, it didn't affect me a bit. I copped a casual pose, even yawned in mock boredom.

Owen let it go on awhile, then waved a hand. "Enough of that," he said. I felt the magic die down. "You don't want to accidentally set the barn on fire with us in it."

"You mean I could do that?"

"You have so little control over your power that you're more likely to do the exact opposite of what you want than to actually accomplish anything. Now, where were we? Ah yes, we were explaining to you how stupid you were."

"And trying to decide what to do with him," I added.

"What we're going to do is teach him a lesson or two, and then get some information out of him."

"You're not going to torture me, are you?" Dean asked, starting to look truly frightened.

"I don't have to torture you," Owen said wearily. "You'll tell me what I want to know without me laying a hand on you. That's a point you don't seem to be grasping."

Outside the barn, the dogs sent up a chorus of barks. A second later, Sam swooped into the barn and perched on a rafter. Dean screamed—a high-pitched, girly scream—and fell off his crate. "That—that thing! What is it? Get it away!"

Sam dropped to the ground in front of Dean, folding his wings back. "That 'thing' is a gargoyle," he said. "Or, if you want to be politically correct about it, I'm a carved-stone American. Ancient guardian of churches, now serving as head of security for Magic, Spells, and Illusions, Incorporated. Sam's the name, investigatin's my game." He glanced over at Owen and me. "I take it this is our perp."

"Sam, this is my brother, Dean. And yeah, he's our perp."

Sam came closer to Dean, studying him intently. "Seein' as how he's your brother, Katie-bug, I won't tear his limbs off, just as a favor to you."

"Oh, I don't think special treatment would be fair at all," I said, trying to keep a straight face. "You do what you think is right, Sam."

"Okay, dollface, but only if you say so."

Dean screamed again and scrambled to cower in the corner against a hay bale. He shook visibly.

"You had no idea there were magical creatures, did you?" Owen asked. There was a trace of pity in his voice. "That's yet another reason you shouldn't play with things you don't understand. Magic isn't a game. It has serious ramifications. Do you even know what it can do?"

Dean shook his head silently. When he spoke, his voice was high and childlike. "What can it do?"

"Anything you have the power, the skill, and the spell to accomplish." He held a hand out in front of him, and a glowing ball grew there. He then tossed it up, where it hung just beneath the barn's ceiling, shedding light on the shadowed surfaces. "What would you like to see?"

"Can you pull a rabbit out of a hat?"

"He did it once in FAO Schwarz," I said. "And that's stage magic, which he can also do. What you're not getting is that this is real. There are people who work at magical companies, live in magical enclaves, and use magic for every aspect of their day-to-day lives. Instead of cooking, they zap something into existence. They turn on their lights by waving a hand instead of flipping a switch. They summon subway trains when they need them—and that's when they're not riding flying carpets."

"Here, you look like you could use a drink," Owen said, and a split second later, a tall glass with beads of condensation on the outside appeared in his hand. Dean crawled back onto his crate and took it from him.

I continued with my lecture. "There are magical creatures like the gargoyles, along with fairies, elves, and gnomes, walking the streets of New York like anyone else, and no one knows because they can hide themselves behind disguise illusions that make them look human."

Dean looked awed, but he also seemed to relax. The tension in his shoulders eased into his more usual slouch. "What is it you want to know?"

"Where did you first learn about magic, and what did they teach you?" Owen asked.

"If I cooperate, will you take it easy on me?"

"I think a lot of that depends on you. I can't allow you to be a threat to yourself or anyone else. But you could go a long way toward convincing me you've learned a lesson by cooperating. How did you get involved in this?"

"I saw an ad in a magazine. It said if you could see that ad, then it meant you had power and you should learn how to use it. I could see it, so I thought what the heck, I might as well check it out."

Owen and I exchanged a look. "I hope you have the material that was sent to you," Owen said, sitting wearily on a hay bale.

"Of course. I still need the references, and I haven't finished the course."

"Do you remember which magazine you saw it in?" I asked.

"One of those magazines for guys—not the porn kind, but with sexy pictures of actresses and some articles. I don't remember which one, but I'm pretty sure it was the March issue."

"Oh, boy," I said, joining Owen on his hay bale. "Maybe you should zap up some drinks for the rest of us. The ad I saw earlier was only regional, but if they're running recruitment ads in national magazines like that, then this could get ugly. There might be amateur wizards wreaking havoc all over the country, and we only know about it because I happened to be here."

"If it's in that kind of magazine, I wonder how Rod missed it," Owen mused. "I think he gets all of them."

"He's been dating Marcia since New Year's Eve. Either he doesn't need them anymore, or she got mad enough about him having them that he decided to give them up."

"I need to see your course materials and that magazine, if you still have it," Owen said.

"You can take my truck, since it's really your truck, after all," I said. "You still seem to have a set of keys."

"And you trust me, after all that? How do you know I won't take off?"

"Because I'll be coming with you," Sam announced.

Dean went pale again. "I can't drive around with that, uh, gargoyle with me."

"Relax, pal, no one will see me. Hidin' from ordinary folk is my specialty. We can chat about how sweet your sister is to pass the time on the drive."

Dean didn't look too happy about his companion, but he went without further protest. When they were gone, Owen ran a frustrated hand through his hair. "How did we miss this? Idris is teaching magic by correspondence course to maybe thousands of unidentified wizards across the country—people who'll have no idea of the difference between light and dark magic, who'll have no restrictions on how they use the magic. If this is any indication, we could have our hands full very, very soon."

"I thought most people with magical powers were identified at birth. You said it runs in families."

"Yeah, well, look at you and your family, never having the slightest idea what any of you were until you went to a place where magic was strong and there was something for you to see. Who knows how many magical families we've lost over the years as everyone spread out to places where there is no real magical culture or where the power sources are weaker."

"At least it doesn't look like Idris is specifically targeting me if he's going national," I said, trying to inject a dose of hope. "It's just pure dumb luck that my brother happened to see his ad so that we could figure out what's going on. I guess the big question is, how do we deal with something like this?"

He heaved a deep sigh. "I have no idea."

"Maybe we could do our own ads, offer better training and guidance. If we don't steal his customers, at least we might attract a different class of people so we'd have our own army."

"That could work, I suppose." He shook his head. "I don't know, honestly. I already had enough to deal with. This is too much to think about."

"No one said you had to do it all yourself," I reminded him. "Not everything is your responsibility. There are other people who can handle this now that you've uncovered it."

We sat like that for a while, Daisy watching us steadily. I thought I should pat his back or put an arm around him, or something. A friend would have done that kind of thing, right? But I got the feeling that he wouldn't find the contact soothing. Being next to him was the best I could do, and I tried to enjoy the rare moment of quiet togetherness while I could, even if he was distracted. Now that our mystery was solved, I had a feeling Owen would be going back to New York soon, before we had a chance to figure out whether me staying here was worthwhile.

My breath caught in my throat when Owen put his hand on top of mine where it rested between us on the hay bale. Coming from him, it was an unexpected gesture. He wasn't a very touchy person. "Are you okay?" he asked.

"Okay? Why wouldn't I be okay?"

"Because your brother turned out to be our magical would-be master criminal."

Oh yeah, that. I'd been rather sidetracked by thinking about Owen leaving town without me and wondering if clinging to him when he tried to leave would make me look desperate. "I don't know," I said with a shrug. "It's a lot to take in. I'm still finding it hard to believe. He always was a bit of a con artist, but a criminal? And then magical on top of it? This was supposed to be my normal place, you know? Where I went to get *away* from magical mayhem." I shook my head, at a loss to put what I was really feeling into words. He gave my hand a squeeze and I tried not to sigh wistfully. I was in really bad shape if he could nearly make me swoon just by touching my hand.

Dean and Sam returned way too soon for me. Sam flew to a rafter and perched there as Dean dumped a pile of booklets, papers, and a magazine in Owen's lap. While Owen flipped through the booklets, Web printouts, and brochures, I picked up the magazine and turned past all the pictures of scantily clad young starlets and ads for body spray to the back where the less splashy ads were. Sure enough, there was an ad like the one I'd seen in the regional magazine.

"These materials are actually quite comprehensive," Owen said. "You should learn some of the basics if you follow them properly. The problem is that there's no context, no guidance for how to use the power, and certainly no mention that there's any kind of magical code of conduct. It would be like teaching someone the basic skills of how to do surgery without teaching about when and why surgery might be neces-sary. You'd have people who knew how to remove or cut apart organs with no idea of the proper reasons or situations for doing so. A bright person with a good moral compass might figure it out, but imagine a real sadist with that kind of training."

"Yeah, it would be awful if someone found out he had magical pow-ers and then used them to rip off other people," I said with a dark glare at my brother. "And it seems like not even years of Sunday school pre-vented that behavior."

"Okay, okay, I'll put the stuff back," Dean said. "That is, if I can get it away from Sherri. I finally had her happy with me because I was giv-ing her everything she wanted."

"No, you had her worried because she thinks you're involved in something illegal," I corrected. "And hey, what do you know, she was right."

Someone cleared his throat, and we all looked up to see Teddy standing in the doorway. "What's going on here?" he asked.

Thirteen

Dean immediately went on the defensive, and he was the master, so I let him handle it. "And what are you doing here?" he asked. "Did Mom send you out to spy on Katie?"

Teddy rubbed his ear and looked away, avoiding eye contact with the rest of us. "Well, yeah. She saw the car and the truck, but nobody was in the house. Which was why I cleared my throat first, to give you some warning." He glanced over at Owen and me, with books and magazines lying open in our laps, and then at Dean and added, "I must say, this isn't what I was expecting. You know, Sis, I'm almost disappointed in you. Didn't your older brothers set a better example for you about what you should be doing alone in a barn with your significant other?"

"They're not alone," Dean said.

"I noticed that. Were you playing big brother watchdog, too? I thought you didn't approve of Owen."

"Minor misunderstanding," Dean insisted. "We're best buds now."

"I wouldn't take it that far," Owen muttered under his breath, so softly that only I could hear it.

Teddy came closer, his eyes narrowed as he studied us. "What are you guys doing, anyway, reading comic books?"

"Nah, just some brochures," I said. "Dean was asking our advice on something. How long were you lurking out there and clearing your throat?" I wondered what he'd overheard. We'd been talking about Dean's criminal behavior, and that was almost worse than Teddy hearing something about magic.

"Not too long. I know you well enough to know I wouldn't be interrupting much."

"Gee, thanks." I was fairly certain he meant it as a compliment, but it was discouraging when my own brothers couldn't imagine me as someone who might inspire a man to tackle me in a haystack.

"So, what are you guys up to?" Teddy asked. "And why are you doing it in the barn?"

I decided to let Dean handle that one. He was the glib one in the family. Besides, it was fun watching him twist in the wind. After what he'd put us through, I figured he deserved at least a little torture from his baby brother. He didn't miss a beat before saying, "We wanted the chance to talk without Mom bugging us. You know, the same reason we always used to hide out here even when we weren't doing anything wrong."

"I guess you never outgrow some things," Teddy agreed.

"Care to join us?" I asked, hoping he'd decline but sure things would look less suspicious if I invited him.

"No thanks. Unlike some people around here, I have work to do." He turned to go, then paused halfway to the door and turned back to us, as if to say something. But then he glanced upward and jumped back, stumbling and nearly falling. "What is that thing?" he blurted.

I tried for my most innocent look and hoped he wasn't talking about Sam. "What thing?"

"There, in the rafters. It's either the biggest bat I've ever seen or—or I don't know what. Wait, it's one of those gargoyles, like on a cathedral or something, but what is it doing in our barn?"

Oh, boy. It looked like I'd discovered yet another magical immune in the family if he could see Sam. I'd thought I was so special with my magical immunity, and at the rate I was going, I'd turn out to be the least special member of my family. But before I could go into a snit, I had to deal with Teddy. I tried to think of a rational explanation for a gargoyle in the barn. Scavenger hunt? Fraternity prank? Bad decision on eBay?

"What are you talking about?" Dean asked. "I don't see anything." I wondered if that was because Sam had veiled himself even to magical people or if Dean was trying to play innocent.

Unfortunately for Dean, Teddy had long ago learned that the more innocent Dean looked, the more guilty he was. "Okay, y'all are definitely up to something. What is it?"

"You're absolutely certain you see something that looks like a gargoyle perched on the rafter in our barn?" I asked. "And you still see it?"

"Yes! And it just looked down and winked at you." There was the slightest bit of hysterical edge in his voice.

Owen and I exchanged a look. We held eye contact for a while, having a silent conversation about what we should do next. Then with a deep sigh he said, "Sam, come on down and say hello to one of Katie's other brothers." To me he said, "He may be helpful in this."

Sam raised his wings and let himself glide down to the barn floor in front of Teddy. "Hi, I'm Sam. Glad to meet you. Your sister's a great gal."

Teddy took a step back, squeezed his eyes shut, rubbed them, then opened them again and blinked a few times. I waited for him to scream, yell, run away, or otherwise freak out, but he just breathed, "Whoa!" I should have known that a guy who'd spent his teens playing Dungeons and Dragons and reading fantasy novels would be more fascinated than upset by the revelation that magic might actually exist. After he'd verified and absorbed the fact that Sam was real, he asked, "Okay, so what is really going on here?"

Owen put down the magic booklets and stood up. "You saw Sam here sitting in the rafters, right?"

"Yeah. And I see him now. He talked to me."

Owen nodded. "Okay." He picked up a handkerchief, draped it across his left palm, then waved his right hand over it. "Now what do you see?"

"You've got a handkerchief draped across your hand."

"Dean, what do you see?" Owen asked.

"You turned the handkerchief into a dove. That's so cool! Can you teach me to do that? Maybe I could do magic shows, and then I could use it to make money instead of doing other stuff that you say I shouldn't."

Owen glared him into shutting up. Teddy laughed. "Boy, Dean, you've got some imagination. It's just a handkerchief. He didn't even fold it into a bird, like Katie tried to do with the napkins that one year for Thanksgiving when she read something in a magazine. Though, actually, this probably looks as much like a bird as Katie's napkins did."

"Shut up, Teddy," I warned. "I've got stories on you, too."

What Owen did next shut Teddy up far more effectively. He waved a hand over the handkerchief again, and this time it did turn into a bird. He held the bird for a long moment, giving everyone a chance to see that it really was a bird, and then with a gentle motion he sent it flying out of the barn.

Teddy gaped for a while, then he asked, "How'd you do that? I mean, I know it has something to do with having something up your sleeve, but you aren't walking around with birds up your sleeve all the time, are you?"

"Teddy, you idiot, it's magic," Dean said. "And I guess it doesn't work on you." He turned to Owen for verification, "Does it? Was that what that first trick was about, you made it look like you'd changed it into a bird, but it was only an illusion and it didn't work on him?"

"That does appear to be the case," Owen said mildly.

I could no longer fight back the snit that had been building up in me since I found out that Dean was a wizard. "I do not believe this!" I shouted, throwing my hands in the air. "Is everyone in my family going to get caught up in this? I was supposed to be getting away from all that stuff when I came back here, and it was here surrounding me all this time. I've got one brother taking magical correspondence courses and another brother who's immune to magic—not to mention Mom being able to see everything when she doesn't have a clue what's really going on, and goodness knows what's up with Granny—and I am sick of trying to explain it all and make it make sense."

Teddy, ever the peacemaker in the family, stepped toward me warily, like he might approach a mad dog. "Katie, honey, what's wrong?" he asked. "What's going on? And what's this about magic?"

I turned to Owen with a plea in my eyes I hoped he could read. "You explain it this time. I've run out of variations on the 'magic is real' speech." Before he could answer, I grabbed my purse and ran out of the barn to my truck. Owen was probably the best person to explain things to Teddy, anyway. They spoke the same language, and I was sure Teddy would ask for hours' worth of scientific-style proofs. By the time I got back, they'd probably be deep in discussions about theory. Owen and Teddy would be in hog heaven, and Dean would be bored out of his skull.

I wasn't sure why this had me so upset. I liked magic and magical people, and I'd spent most of my life feeling like I was too normal. I just wasn't quite ready to go all the way over the edge to where I no longer had any grip at all on the nonmagical world. My family was supposed to ground me, not be even weirder than my former working world had been. And, really, couldn't I manage to be special in just one little way without being overshadowed by my big brothers?

I drove straight to the motel. Nita was one of the few people I felt I could talk to who still had absolutely nothing to do with the magical world. Of course, at the rate things in my life were going, I'd soon find out that she was from another planet or was Wonder Woman's mild-mannered disguise. "Ohmigod, what happened?" she gasped when I entered the motel lobby. Without waiting for me to answer, she said, "I'll make tea."

"Nothing happened. Why? Do I look that bad?" I asked as she raised the counter so I could join her behind the desk.

She put on the electric teakettle. "He broke up with you, didn't he?" Her voice cracked with sympathetic tears. "Oh, Katie."

I sidestepped her hug. "Broke up? We aren't really together. We were barely together before I left New York, and I broke things off with him when I left." I knew it was a different story from what I'd told my family, but I didn't imagine her swapping stories with any of them, and in this case, something resembling the truth was my safest bet.

"Then, what is the problem? You came tearing in here like your tail was on fire, and you look ready to explode at any moment." She poured water over teabags, then turned back to me, waving a spoon. "Sit, and tell me everything."

I did as she ordered, for fear she'd hit me with the spoon. It was funny how calming her hyper presence could be. There was a certain peace in her bubbly mania. Soon, she handed me a mug full of spiced tea sweetened with honey. "Now, you'd probably better start at the beginning," she said as she took her own seat. "And don't leave anything out. I'm already mad at you for not even mentioning the hot guy until he showed up in town."

While I was still thinking of a way to explain what, exactly, it was that had me so upset, a car pulled into the motel driveway, making too fast a turn off the main road so that it fishtailed a little on the shoulder's loose gravel. It then came to a screeching stop under the motel office's canopy. When the driver got out of the car, I saw that he was tall and lanky, with clothes that fit so that he looked like he'd recently gone through an adolescent growth spurt. I knew exactly who he was. Phelan Idris, the rogue wizard who was giving us so much trouble, had come to town.

"Wow, a customer!" Nita said while I spilled my tea. "Nobody checks in on Mondays."

I didn't want him seeing me. Him not knowing that we knew he was here might give us the slightest advantage. "Oh, my tea!" I said, grabbing a handful of paper napkins from Nita's desk and dropping to the ground behind the counter just before the door chime rang. I halfheartedly mopped up my spilled tea while I listened.

"Hi, and welcome to the Cobb Motel!" Nita said cheerfully. "How may I help you?"

"You got any rooms?" he asked.

"How many nights?"

"I don't know. Maybe a few days."

"Okay, open-ended stay. We can do that. Smoking or non?"

"Smoking." Funny, I hadn't ever seen him smoke, but I imagined he might want a smoking room so he could mix up potions without raising suspicions.

"King bed or two double beds?"

"I want a room, okay? Not a game of twenty questions."

"I'm only trying to make sure you get what you want," Nita said, her voice still full of forced friendliness, but now with a little frost around the edges. "I'll give you a king room. Now, how will you be paying for that?"

"I've got a credit card."

"Great! Then I'll need a photo ID, as well, and you can fill this out. Don't worry about the car license number part. I'm not even sure why that's on the form." She gave me a funny look as she went to make a copy of his ID, and I hurried to look like I was still carefully mopping up the spilled tea. She returned from the back office, handed him his ID, his credit card, and a key. "Okay, Mr. Idris, you'll be in room twenty-five. You should be able to park right in front of your room. Enjoy your stay!"

Only when I'd heard the door chime and his car start did I stand up from behind the counter with my wad of damp paper napkins. "I can't believe I made such a mess," I said.

She raised an eyebrow. "I was wondering what you were doing down there. I almost thought you'd recognized him and were trying to hide, or something."

I started to say that I had no idea who he might be, then realized that maybe this was a good opportunity to give her a valid excuse for keeping an eye on him. "He did look familiar," I said.

She gasped and put a hand to her mouth. "You didn't see him on *America's Most Wanted,* did you? Maybe I should call the police. Do you think it would help or hurt business if word got around that a famous serial killer stayed here? I mean, as long as he didn't kill anyone while he stayed here. That would probably freak out potential customers. But if he got arrested here, that might get some attention, right? We'd at least have a few reporters staying here, and the motel name would get in the paper."

That was a little more excitement than I'd been aiming for. I'd forgotten how active Nita's imagination could be. "No, nothing like that," I corrected her before she could get carried away and call the police. "He just looks familiar. Maybe it's someone I know from New York."

She put a hand on one hip. "Why would someone from New York be here?"

Thinking fast, I came up with something I was sure would get her attention. "You know, he may be someone from this band I once saw in a club." Not that I frequently went to see bands in clubs, but that was certainly her image of my *Sex and the City* life in New York, so I went with it. "He could be on his way to Austin from Dallas for a concert or music festival, or something, and he might be taking the back roads to really get into the roots of the country."

Her eyes grew huge. "Oh, wow! A rock star in my motel! Just think, if he ever does hit the big time, that could make this place famous! We could make room twenty-five the—" she had to check the registration form "—the Phelan Idris room, and we could decorate it with concert pictures. We could make this the Rock and Roll Motel!" She flipped up the counter and ran to the lobby, where she could look out the side windows toward Idris's room, and I knew I had her hook, line, and sinker. She'd track every move he made. After watching for a few minutes, she turned to me. "Do you think you could watch the desk for a few minutes? I ought to get my camera. I'll need proof he stayed here if he gets famous. We have plenty of rooms, so if someone needs a reservation, get their info and give it to them. There's no way we'll have another person checking in this afternoon. I'll be back in a sec." She was gone before I had a chance to object.

When she was gone, I went back into the office and grabbed one of the extra keys for Idris's room off the key rack and pocketed it, glad that Nita's dad hadn't yet upgraded to card keys. Then I picked up the phone. I realized I hadn't asked for Owen's cell phone number, and he certainly hadn't volunteered it, but I knew Teddy's number, and they were probably still together, so I dialed that one.

"Hey, Sis," Teddy said when he answered. "Have you settled down any?"

"I'm fine. Is Owen there with you? I need to talk to him."

A second later, Owen came on the line. "Katie?"

"Idris just checked into the motel," I said without bothering with a greeting.

"He what? Are you sure?"

"I was right here when it happened, though he didn't see me, and it's his name on the register. There can't be more than one of him."

"But why is he here?" He sounded almost frantic, which was strange for him.

"Funny, that question didn't come up when he was asking for a smoking room with an open-ended stay."

"I'll get Sam on surveillance."

"He's in room twenty-five, and I think he'll already be under surveillance." The front door chimed, and I said, "I've got to go. We can discuss it later."

Nita was back, breathless and with flushed cheeks from her dash to the family home behind the motel. "Any calls or new guests?"

"Not a one."

"I already took a picture of his car, but it's a rental, so it doesn't really say anything important or meaningful about him. I guess we'll have to wait for him to come out." She dragged a couple of the lobby chairs over to the window, and I joined her. "Oh, I should have gotten snacks for our stakeout," she added as she settled into a chair, her camera at the ready. "So, were you ever going to tell me what you were so upset about when you got here?"

"Oh, just something with my brothers," I said dismissively, not really wanting to get into any issues with Owen at the moment. Then I had a brainstorm. My brothers. Of course. I knew exactly why Idris had come here. "And speaking of my brothers, I've left Owen alone with them for too long. I'd better get back home. You'll let me know if anything interesting happens?"

She didn't take her eyes away from the window when she responded, "Of course. This is the most exciting thing to happen to this place in ages."

"The band wasn't all that good," I said, already worried that I'd set her up for disappointment.

"It doesn't take much to be the most exciting thing to happen here," she replied dryly.

I was glad I'd parked on the side of the office away from Idris's room, so even if he was so bored or paranoid as to be staring out the window, he still wouldn't see me. When I got home, the barn was empty, so I headed into the house. The door to Dean and Teddy's old room was shut, and I had a feeling that's where the guys were. I knocked lightly on it and got out the "It's" part of "It's me" before the door swung open.

"That must be really handy," Teddy said. His eyes had a wide look of surprise and awe, like he was still taking everything in. He and Owen sat on one of the beds, most of the magic course pamphlets spread between them, while Dean sat on the other bed, watching the other two suspiciously. It almost looked like a slumber party for overgrown boys.

"So, I guess y'all are all squared away," I said, stepping into the room and shutting the door behind me, in case Mom came back or Granny showed up.

"Yeah, Owen gave me the whole story," Teddy said. "It's absolutely incredible, isn't it? I mean, all those years I spent playing Dungeons and Dragons, and it turns out to be real, and we never even knew. Just think of the trouble Dean could have gotten into if he knew he had magical powers all along. Though I guess he managed to get into enough trouble with them now."

"And think of how amazing my tattletale abilities would have been if I'd been able to catch him," I said. Then I turned to my other brother. "Dean, you wouldn't happen to have called anyone at your magical correspondence school about what's been going on, have you?"

"Well, there is a customer service number you're supposed to call when you're ready for the next lesson or if you have any problems."

"When was the last time you called it?"

"Um, uh, well, last night, when I couldn't get into the bank. You're supposed to let them know if something doesn't work, and being bounced off the door wasn't in the troubleshooting list, so I called right away, and then they transferred me to someone higher up, so I guess it was a bigger issue than I realized."

"That's why Idris is here, I bet," I said to Owen.

"What did you tell them?" Owen asked. He'd gone pale, and I could see the tension in the muscles around his jaw.

"I described what I was trying to do and what it felt like. Then they asked me if anything had changed around town—if there was anyone new. I said my sister's boyfriend was visiting." His voice trailed off, and he then added a sheepish, "Oops. But I didn't know it meant anything at the time. I was just excited because they'd let me talk to one of the main guys at the company. It would have been like running across a bug in Word, calling Microsoft tech support, and being transferred directly to Bill Gates in the middle of the night. So, uh, why does this matter?"

"Because the guy running Spellworks just showed up in town," I said. "He has to know you're my brother, and that means he has to know Owen's here and was behind the wards on the bank." It rankled me more than a little that Phelan Idris had known my brother had magical powers before I did.

"He got here fast enough," Owen said.

I shrugged. "Well, this might be an even bigger crisis for him than it is for us. Us finding out in this way could put a stop to his little magic school before he hits critical mass. You know, it was really stupid of him to actually sign up one of my brothers."

"That's typical," Owen said. "He couldn't resist getting a reaction out of you and showing off. As usual, he got sidetracked by looking for a reaction instead of following through."

I sat on the end of Teddy's bed. "Did I really screw things up for you, Katie?" Dean asked. He actually sounded contrite.

"No, in the long run you've helped. If you hadn't been mixed up in all this, we might not have found out about this scheme until it was too late. It would have been nice if we could have avoided having Idris come here, but here may be the best place to deal with him. It's harder to do magic here without the proper lines of power, and when it comes to raw magical resources, there aren't too many people who can top Owen."

"Ooh, time for the magical showdown at the O-K Corral?" Teddy asked, brightening.

"I hope not," Owen said, "but I'll still probably need your help."

Then a voice from downstairs called out, "Is anyone home?" It was Granny.

I got up and went to the top of the stairs. "What is it, Granny?" I asked.

"I tried to go to the bank to deposit my pension check, and they wouldn't let me in the door."

I turned around to find the guys standing behind me. "I guess the wards are still up," I whispered to Owen.

"Well, Dad always said she was a witch," Teddy said under his breath.

Fourteen

I glared at Teddy, then forced a smile and headed down the stairs, wincing as I crossed the squeaky patch. "But Granny, the bank is closed for the day," I said when I reached her, hoping that maybe there'd been a misunderstanding. "Remember, the lobby closes at three."

She rapped her cane on the floor. "I know that. And I was there in plenty of time, but I couldn't get through the doorway. People were walking past me left and right, but I couldn't go through. The bank's been charmed, it has. Someone wants to keep the magical folk out." She looked up at where the guys still stood at the top of the stairs and pointed her cane straight at Owen. "It was you who did it. I felt your magic."

I was all ready to spin an explanation, but Owen started down the stairs, the other guys following him. Once he'd passed the squeaky spot, he said, "I'm sorry about that. I should have lifted the wards already, but I wanted to be sure the bank was protected, with everything that's been going on. I'll take care of it tonight to make sure you can go there. You should be able to deposit your check tomorrow morning." His voice was calm and even, as if he were having a perfectly ordinary conversation.

That took Granny aback. She was used to being ignored, contradicted, and humored, but never taken seriously. "So, you were sent here to protect us from the scoundrel who's been using magic against us," she said, gazing steadily at him.

"Yes, I was."

"You've got strong magic in you, stronger than anything I've ever felt." She lapsed into that fake Irish accent that made it difficult for Teddy, Dean, and me not to laugh, but Owen kept a perfectly straight face. "I know a trick or two my Gran taught me, but nothing like what you do. You stopped our culprit, did you?"

"Yes, I believe I did. He won't be causing any more problems."

Her gaze darted immediately to Dean, who didn't react quickly enough to put on a fake innocent expression. Guilt was written all over his face. Her eyes narrowed. "You! I should have known. You always were a troublemaker." She rapped him across the knees with her cane, making him jump and yelp in pain.

"Abusing the gift like that is dangerous," she went on, ignoring Dean as he rubbed his knees. "Meddling with power can get you burned, and using it for personal gain takes you closer to falling into the darkness. I'd have tried to teach you how to use it, but your mother thought I was crazy. She's got a different kind of sight, but she doesn't understand the gift the way I do."

"Wait a second," I said, "You knew all along about Dean?"

"Of course I did. I felt the magic in him from the time I first held him. You're like your mother, though. And Teddy, too. My Gran always said the family liked to keep a balance so we could keep each other in check, one side with the power and the other side with the vision."

"What about Frank Junior?" I asked, almost dreading the answer. With one brother a wizard and the other immune to magic, there was no telling what the third one might be.

"Oh, he's as normal as your father is. And thank goodness there's someone normal around here."

"I had to go to New York to learn about magic, and you knew all this time?"

She shook her head and tut-tutted. "I told you I don't know how many times, but did you listen? I even tried to warn you about what you'd find in the city." That partially explained why I didn't remember her warnings. The family had been so busy telling me about all the criminals and deviants I was sure to run into that one more wacky warning would have been beside the point.

"But Granny," Teddy said, "We thought those were just stories."

"Just stories! Honestly. These children have no respect for their elders." She turned back to Owen. "I assume you listen to your grandparents."

"I don't have any grandparents," he said, "but my foster mother is about your age."

"That explains it. You had to listen to your elders. Is there any coffee?" Without waiting for an answer, she spun and headed toward the kitchen fast enough that I wondered if she used magic to speed her pace.

"I'll make some," I said, hurrying to follow her. It was a good thing I'd had my meltdown earlier and got it out of my system. Otherwise, I'm not sure how I'd have reacted to finding out that my grandmother was magical and had known about all this stuff all along.

I got to the coffeemaker before Granny did and made a pot of half decaf, since I knew she wasn't supposed to have too much caffeine and she'd have already had at least four cups of coffee that day. We certainly didn't need her over caffeinated; she was bad enough as it was. For once, she didn't fight me over who should make the coffee. Instead, she seemed content to sit at the kitchen table and let us serve her.

That was probably because she wasn't through with Dean yet. She rapped him again across the knees, and he wisely took a step back so he'd be out of cane range. "Now that you've had your little fun and you've shown what you can do, you are going to give all those things back, aren't you?" she said. She phrased it as a question, but her tone of voice made it more of a command. "I'd hate to have to tell your mother what a disappointment you are."

"Yes, ma'am," Dean stammered. "I mean, I'd like to, but I'm not sure I can, not without getting caught. They've got better patrols now, and it was almost a fluke that I was able to do it in the first place."

"Well, if you did it, then maybe it's right for you to get caught. Better to be caught bringing things back, even if you have to go in during business hours with a box full of stolen goods, than to be caught with the loot in your house or on your wife's wrist. You'll not be able to prosper until this wrong is set right."

Dean groaned. "Oh no; Sherri. I'll never get those things away from her. And for once I was able to make her happy." Apparently, he hadn't heard a thing I'd said earlier. I suspected he was the one who was reluctant to return the goods, and Sherri was a convenient excuse.

A shriek from the back door proved me right. "Dean Chandler, are you in here?" Sherri then stomped into the kitchen, her hair wild and her eyes blazing. "Just what, exactly, do you think you've been up to?"

He took a step away from her, only to realize he'd returned himself to Granny's cane range, so he took another step sideways. "Up to what, honey?" he asked, so cool and innocent that butter wouldn't melt in his mouth.

"'Up to what?'" she mocked, her voice going up nearly an octave. "What have you got yourself mixed up in, huh? And don't play innocent with me. I know you're up to something."

Dean's innocent expression faltered for a split second, but then he was back to his usual cocky grin. "Mind letting me in on what you know, darlin'?"

She raised her arm, showing a bare wrist. "I went to the jewelry store to get my new bracelet appraised, and guess what? They said it was stolen property. I told them someone had given it to me as a gift and turned it over to them."

"Wow, it really was stolen?" he asked, still maintaining the illusion of innocence. Granny leaned forward so she could reach him with her cane and gave him a good whack with it. "Ow!" he protested. "Okay, I got the stuff from a guy I know. I didn't know it was stolen, but I'll give it all back, I promise."

Normally, that was the point when Sherri melted, apologized for ever doubting him, and started calling him disgusting pet names like "snoogie woogums" while the rest of us tried not to throw up. This time, though, she tossed her hair back and said, "You'd better. I'm going to stay at Mom's for a few days, and when I come back, all that stuff better be out of my house, or I'll be packing up my things and leaving for good." With that, she turned and marched out of the kitchen, letting the back door slam behind her and leaving an uncomfortable silence in her wake.

"I don't think Sherri will mind if you give the stuff back," I said, breaking the silence before it got creepy.

"I guess not," Dean agreed, looking sheepish.

The coffeemaker stopped, and Owen, who was wisely staying out of the family discussion, found a mug and poured a cup for Granny. "I might be able to help return the goods," he said. "The magic is easy enough for me, and with Sam's help, we can hide the activity from the patrols for long enough to get in and out."

"I'll help, too," Teddy said. "I'm not sure what I can do other than stand lookout, but I think I ought to be there."

"You just want to watch and see how it works," I said.

"Well, yeah."

I looked to Owen, who shrugged. "We may need all the lookouts we can get."

Granny fixed Dean with a steely glare. "So you will make proper restitution?"

He looked like a ten-year-old who'd been caught stealing candy. "Yes, ma'am."

"And you won't use your power for nefarious purposes in the future?"

"No, ma'am."

"Good. We'll deal with your criminal nature once you've taken care of this." She turned to Teddy. "You'll have to see to it that he behaves. He can't pull a fast one on you."

Teddy grinned. As the next-to-youngest in the family and the youngest boy, being asked to play watchdog on his older brother was the fulfillment of a lifelong dream. "I'll watch him like a hawk."

"What'll you be watching, Teddy?" Mom asked as she came through the back door with an armload of groceries.

His mouth hung open, and he looked so guilty I was amazed she didn't notice. "I, uh, was talking about the next time Molly and Frank ask Beth and me to watch Davy. He gets into everything if you don't watch him."

She shook her head wearily as she put the grocery bags on the counter. "I swear, that child. If Molly would learn to say no and set some limits, it would do him a world of good. Now, boys, there are some more groceries outside you could carry in."

Dean, Teddy, and Owen moved to head for the back door, but Mom stopped Owen. "You're company. We won't put you to work." She flashed him a flirtatious smile. "That will have to wait for your next visit. By then, you'll count as family."

"I'll look forward to that, then." He turned to me and said, "Katie, weren't you going to show me that thing today?"

I wasn't sure where he was going with this, but I knew an escape plan when I heard one. "Oh yeah, that thing I was going to show you. How long until dinner, Mom?"

"At least a couple of hours."

"That should be plenty of time if we head out now. We'll be back in time for dinner." We passed the boys on the back steps as they came up with arms loaded with grocery bags. When we were out of earshot, I asked, "The thing?"

"I thought we'd pay a visit to our friend."

"Ah yes, the town welcoming committee should be there to greet him."

"I've been in Texas a few days, so I think I'm getting the hang of this southern hospitality. I'd feel bad if someone didn't welcome him to town."

We took his rental car and drove to the motel. "His car's parked in front of his room," I said. "So he's probably still here."

"That's good. I think we need to have a chat with him."

"You think he'll let us in the door?"

"He will if he doesn't know it's us."

"You might need to hide us in general. Nita's probably still staking out his room with a digital camera from the lobby window."

"Why would she do that?"

"I might have given her the impression that he was the lead singer of an up-and-coming rock band." We got out of the car, and I noticed that the door to the housekeeping closet was slightly ajar. I stepped in, grabbed an armload of towels, and said, "We could be housekeeping."

"Good idea."

On the way to Idris's room, Owen whispered something under his breath. I felt the tingle of magic building around us and wondered what we looked like. At a nod from Owen, I rapped on the door and called out, "Housekeeping!"

I held my breath while we waited for a response. After nearly a minute, I knocked again and jiggled the door handle. Then, finally, Idris opened the door a crack. "What is it?" he snapped.

"Fresh towels," I said, barging forward, Owen in my wake. Idris stepped reluctantly out of our way. He had a laptop computer, a cell phone, and a bunch of papers spread out on the bed, along with a Texas map. When we were well inside the room, the door abruptly slammed shut, even though no one touched it, and I felt the magic surrounding us fade away.

"You!" Idris cried out, staring in shock at Owen. I dropped the pile of towels on the foot of the bed, and he turned to notice me. "You, too! What are you doing here?"

Owen and I looked at each other. This wasn't quite the reaction we'd been expecting. I'd thought he'd be lying in wait for us, ready to pounce if we didn't get to him first. "You mean, in this room or here, in this town?" I asked.

"Here!" he sputtered.

"Well, I live here—I mean, I'm from here and my family is here," I said, "and he's here to stop your latest evil scheme. You didn't know that?"

He reached over and closed his laptop, then pulled a pillow over his papers. "Why would I know that?"

"Because you're here. Why else would you be here? This isn't the kind of place people decide to visit on a whim because they want to get away from it all. I mean, what are the odds that you'd show up here, of all places?"

He gathered his wits about him a little more securely, drawing himself to his full height to tower over Owen and crossing his arms over his chest. "That's none of your business."

"Actually, considering you've been teaching my brother how to do magic, it is." He looked truly blank, as though he had no idea what I was talking about. "Dean Chandler? The guy who called you in the middle of the night about some wards he ran into? I assume that's why you're here."

The expression on his face was priceless. Dad would say he looked like he'd been pole-axed. He forgot about towering over Owen and sat down on the bed. "That's your brother?"

"One of them. You didn't notice that we have the same last name and we're both from Texas?"

"You're from Texas?"

I turned to Owen. "I thought that was tattooed on my forehead. Everyone in Manhattan knows I'm from Texas."

"It's not really a rare last name, either," Idris mumbled. "I take it those wards he ran into were your work," he said to Owen.

"Yes, those were mine, and they did their job of stopping him before he could make a really big mistake. I thought that's why you were here, because you knew I was here."

"No, I'm here because there's no record of a wizard here, and my lessons haven't gone up to wards yet. I was worried I might have competition or that someone was on to one of my students and might expose him."

"Wait a second," I said, "you came all the way here to this town that's barely on the map and that most people in Texas haven't even heard of, just because you thought there might be another wizard here who could step in and steal your students or expose them for doing magic?"

He got the kind of expression Dean used to get when he realized he needed to come up with a good explanation for something, fast. Unfortunately for him, he wasn't nearly as smooth as Dean. "Well, um, uh, from the sounds of things, my student was attracting attention, and um, if someone warded the bank, it meant someone with power knew something was going on." He pulled a pillow into his lap and fiddled with it, then realized he'd removed the covering from his papers and moved it back. "I haven't taught dueling yet, so I wasn't sure my student would be able to take care of himself. He might have needed backup, and if a student got exposed, then it would ruin my operation."

"Your attempt to build a magical army of your own, you mean," Owen said. He didn't look like he was enjoying Idris's discomfort nearly as much as I was. He just looked tired and fed up.

Idris didn't deny Owen's assertion. "Yeah, if you want to put it that way. And, um, well, I was kind of looking for an excuse to get away from New York."

"Evil scheming is very hard work," I said in mock sympathy. "You need fresh country air to recharge yourself."

"It is! It was fun at first, but man, these people I'm dealing with are intense. I thought it was great to get the funding, but wow, now they want reports and results, and stuff. It's like if I don't have every magical person in the world as customers, I'm doing something wrong, and now they want me to find even more magical people so we can grow the market and outnumber your customer base. Oh yeah, and they use phrases like 'grow the market' and 'customer base,' which is so not my scene. It was a total buzzkill."

"That's what happens when you go into business," Owen said. "What did you expect?"

Idris acted like he hadn't heard him. He was on a roll. "And then there's this crazy broad who keeps meddling in my life. I can't even look at a woman without her showing up to get in the way. It's like someone cursed me. Do you know how long it's been since I've had any action?"

This time, I managed to keep a straight face while Owen cracked up. We both knew exactly who that crazy broad was, and that was a very accurate description for my erstwhile fairy godmother, who'd nearly driven Owen and me apart in her attempts to make sure we got together. I'd managed to get her on Idris's case to make sure he worked things out with his girlfriend, who was currently in MSI custody. Apparently fairy godmothers didn't think that forced separation was an excuse for infidelity.

"What?" Idris asked Owen.

"Oh, nothing," Owen said, fighting to suppress a smirk.

Idris turned to me. "So, my local student here is your brother? I guess that means you caught him and stopped him from doing anything else."

"Yeah, we kind of read him the riot act. He's seen the error of his ways. He won't be taking any more lessons from you, and he'll be warning the others about what you're really up to."

"He's also going to get some real training so that he can keep watch over this area for us, and he'll be registered with the Council," Owen added. "You might as well head back to New York. There's nothing for you to do here."

A look of panic crossed Idris's face. "I'll refund his money, but he'd better not be blabbing to the other students on my message boards. He can't do that to me! I carried out my end of the deal. I can't help it if he chose to use his power to commit crimes."

"Your lessons contained step-by-step instructions on how to commit specific crimes using specific spells," Owen pointed out. "The entire course was on using magic to get rich."

"That was only an example. When you do those problems about trains running into each other in math class, do you really think that means you're supposed to go out and crash trains into each other?"

"No," I said, "but if you're taking home economics and there's a cake recipe in a textbook, I do think it means you're supposed to follow those directions to bake a cake. It's not just a hypothetical example of what happens when you combine flour, sugar, and eggs."

"That's different! And you can't register him! I'll look like a failure."

"News flash," I said. "You are a failure. Maybe you should quit now while you're still ahead."

"I can't quit. Do you know what they'll do to me? I have to stop you. If you go through with this, you give me no choice. I swear, Palmer, this time I will bring you down."

Owen turned to look at him, staring at him silently for long enough that Idris started to sweat. Finally, Owen gave him a crooked grin. "This time, huh? You mean unlike all the other times?"

"I got away those times. The last time I almost got your girlfriend."

Owen shrugged. "Okay, then, I guess I'll have to take you into custody now." He took a step toward Idris, his hands raised. The sense of magic in use in the room grew stronger, and I stepped backward so I'd be out of the way of the magical fight that was about to break out. Just when it was getting intense enough to give me a headache, Idris vanished into thin air. Owen lunged toward where he'd been, but it was too late. "How'd he do that?" he asked. "I can't do that here, so there's no way he could do that."

"Well, he did. He's not here, so it's not like he just went invisible."

"This is not good," he said, the tension in his voice contradicting the incredible understatement of his words. He raised his hands again, his eyes half closed, like he was listening for something. After a while, he shook his head. "He used a lot of power, but I'm not sure where he got it."

I reached over and took his arm. "Come on, we're not getting anything done standing around here." With a weary sigh, he went along with me. On our way out of the room, I locked the door behind us, in case Idris hadn't taken his room key when he vanished. He'd have to use that much power again to get back into the room. I dropped the towels off in the housekeeping closet, then we got back into Owen's rental car.

"What do you think he'll do?" I asked.

"He may make a go of convincing your brother not to drop his program or let the other students know what's going on. Or he could challenge me to a duel on Main Street at high noon. With him, you never know."

Dean and Teddy were still hanging around at the house when we got back. They met us on the back porch. "What time should we meet tonight?" Teddy asked.

"A quarter to midnight behind the bank. We should all park in different places so it's not too obvious that someone's congregating," Owen said.

"Okay, quarter to midnight," Dean said, nodding. "Is that because there's more power at the witching hour of midnight?"

"No, it's because by then everyone here will be asleep, making it easier for us to sneak out, and there won't likely be anyone wandering downtown. It also seems to fall between two different police patrols of that area."

"Oh," Teddy said, looking disappointed. It was a shame how boring and ordinary magic often turned out to be.

"You're still planning to return those goods?" Owen asked Dean.

"Yeah. It doesn't look like I have a choice if I want to keep my wife." I bit my tongue to keep from saying that it wouldn't be a big loss. Besides, Sherri was turning out to be okay.

"Then make sure you've wiped off any fingerprints and wear gloves. Box everything up in separate boxes for each store."

Dean's eyes went wide, and the color drained from his face. "Fingerprints?"

"Don't you think they'd check if stolen goods suddenly reappeared and they still had no suspect? Returning the goods is a mitigating factor, but it doesn't erase the fact that you committed a crime."

"How are you going to explain to Beth why you're taking off in the middle of the night?" I asked Teddy.

"I'm always taking off in the middle of the night when I get an idea and head to the test crops," he said with a shrug. "She's used to it by now."

"I'll see you two tonight, then," Owen said.

"Do we need to bring anything?" Teddy asked.

"I've got it taken care of. Wear something dark that won't stand out too much if light hits it. And you'll need gloves, since we'll be handling stolen goods."

My brothers were waiting for us behind the bank shortly before midnight, both of them looking like cat burglars in their all-black clothing. Teddy was the most eager of the two. I wasn't sure if it was because of his curiosity about magic or because of Dean's reluctance to give back all his loot.

"We'll deal with the wards first, since that's our priority," Owen told them. "Then if we have time, if I have the energy, and if the coast is clear, we can start returning the stolen property. You did bring it, didn't you?" he asked Dean.

"It's in my trunk. Sherri had everything already boxed up."

"I hope you thought to wipe off her fingerprints so she won't be suspected," I said, finding it hard to believe I was actually looking out for Sherri.

"Of course I did."

"Good," Owen said. "Okay, here's the plan. Sam will veil the area, so no one who happens to pass by will see what we're doing. You should still be quiet and not do anything to draw attention to yourself because no veil is perfect. The less there is to see, the easier it is to disguise it. Stay out of my way, and if I tell you to do something, you'll do it without hesitation or question. Have you got that?" He sounded so firm and commanding that I might not have been able to resist tackling him if my brothers hadn't been there.

They nodded, apparently also getting that sense of power from him, but obviously with a totally different response. "Got it," Teddy said, while Dean gave a cocky salute.

We crept around the corner to the front of the bank, where Sam waited for us on the sidewalk. "I got you covered, boss," he said. "All of you. You did tell these two to keep it quiet?"

"Yes. It's under control." Owen turned to me and said, "I'd like you to be standing by. I probably won't need you because breaking wards is easier than setting them, but I'd rather be ready, just in case."

"I'll be here," I said.

As he went to work, I was torn between wanting to watch him and wanting to see how my brothers reacted to what he did. So far, they'd seen little more than parlor tricks, but this would be real magic on a level they hadn't yet experienced.

He sprinkled some shimmery powder in a line under the doorway, then stepped back, held his hands out, and did that half chanting/half singing thing he'd done when he set the wards. The wards again flared into visible light, then that light collapsed into the powder, which burst into blue-white flames that shot into the air.

Of course, that was the exact moment a police car drove by on patrol. When did our local police force become so effective?

Fifteen

"Oh, sh—shoot," Dean hissed, glancing at me as he corrected himself.

"We're running around at midnight and doing magic," I whispered back to him. "Do you think I'm going to tell Mom you used a bad word in front of me?"

"Hush!" Owen snapped.

I somehow doubted that with a wall of blue-white flame shooting to roof height, our whispering would be what alerted the cop to our presence, but I hushed, anyway. For all I knew, Sam might be able to veil the flame while it took too much extra power to muffle the sound.

The police car slowed to a crawl as it passed the bank, and I held my breath. I knew Sam was good at hiding things magically, but all that flame—along with the light it cast—had to be a challenge. Suddenly the flame collapsed in on itself, leaving no trace. Even the powder it had grown from was gone.

The police car kept moving at its frustratingly slow pace, but it didn't stop. When the car at last passed out of sight, there was a collective "whoosh" as all five of us let out our breath. Then Teddy turned to look at Owen. "That was so cool!" he said. "What did you do?"

"The energy that created the ward had to go somewhere, so it was absorbed into the powder and burned up," Owen explained.

I stepped in before the two of them could start discussing the chemistry and physics of magic. "Are you sure it worked?" I asked.

Owen gestured at Dean. "Come over here." Dean looked apprehensive, but he stepped forward. "Try to cross the threshold." Dean visibly steeled himself, then stepped forward. He was able to get all the way to the bank's door. "It worked," Owen reported. "Now, we need to get all those stolen things returned. Based on the pattern from previous nights, I think the police car will most likely return in half an hour, so let's hurry. I don't want to test the limits of Sam's veiling ability."

Dean and Teddy ran back to Dean's car to get the goods and returned loaded down. "This is the first batch," Dean said.

"How much did you steal?" I asked.

"I may have gotten a little carried away," Dean admitted.

"Which stores are those from?" Owen asked.

"I thought we'd start with the jewelry store, since that was the most valuable stuff."

We made a funny procession as we headed across the square to the jewelry store. Sam flew ahead. I followed behind him. Teddy and Dean with their overflowing boxes were in the middle, and Owen brought up the rear. We looked like a gang of inept reverse burglars.

"They didn't have a camera here, but there is a security system," Sam reported when we reached the jewelry store.

"Yeah, I was able to bypass it," Dean said. He looked a little too proud of himself for my comfort.

"That's not too difficult," Owen said. "The spell that dissolves the window actually keeps the sensors intact. You were sloppy, though. You overdid it on the windows. They should have come back as soon as you were in and out. That wasted power and drew attention to your actions." He faced the window, waved a hand, whispered a few words, and the glass vanished. "Okay, now put the stuff back in there." Dean went to climb through the window, but Owen shook his head. "No, just leave the boxes there. You want them to notice it's been returned. You don't have your name or anything identifying you on those boxes, do you?"

"These are the boxes I got from the store."

"Then put them in there."

Dean followed instructions. As soon as he was clear of the window, the glass reappeared. "You'll have to teach me how to do that," Dean said.

"Somehow, I don't think that would be such a good idea."

"I wouldn't do it to steal stuff again."

"Then why would you need to be able to do it?"

"This is amazing," Teddy gushed. "Now, how does the ratio of matter and energy work on this? Are you actually making the matter go away, like into an alternate dimension, or are you just separating the atoms so it looks like the glass isn't there, but all the matter actually still is?"

"Teddy, we don't have time for the scientific explanation," I said.

"Sorry. But can we talk about it later?" If they did, it wasn't a conversation I wanted to be anywhere near. Thinking about how magic worked gave me a headache.

We worked our way around the square, returning goods to all of the stores Dean had burgled magically. "What were you trying to do, open your own store?" I asked.

"Something like that. I thought I'd unload a lot of this stuff on eBay when it cooled down a little."

"You do know that cops monitor eBay to look for stolen goods showing up, right?"

"In this town? I'm not sure the cops know eBay exists."

"Jason's wife sells collectible dolls and antiques on eBay," I pointed out. "He'd know it exists."

"You took some extremely stupid risks," Owen said. "You shouldn't be doing anything with magic that brings unnecessary attention to yourself. That should be the first thing you learn, even before you start learning spells." I could tell the night's activities were draining him, even as he made it look easy. With each shop, the glass took a bit longer to disappear, and he walked more slowly to the next shop.

When we were almost done and Dean had retrieved the last load from the car, the police car returned. "Sam, have you still got us?" Owen asked.

"Yeah, but hold off on the hocus-pocus until he's gone."

We all froze in place, holding our breath as the police car made its circuit. Just when we thought we were in the clear, the car pulled up in front of the jewelry shop, and the officer got out to walk the square, swinging a flashlight ahead of him. He aimed the flashlight into the windows, where he was sure to spot the boxes.

"Now!" Owen hissed, getting Dean's attention. The window we were in front of had gone. Dean dropped the box he held as quickly and quietly as he could, then the glass returned.

From across the square, we heard, "Hey!" The police officer leaned against the window, getting a closer look. He must have discovered the returned goods. He went back to his car and got on the radio.

"I suggest we scram, now," Sam said. "I can bamboozle one of them, but not more with this many of us and at cop levels of scrutiny. Stick together, though. That makes it easier."

We clustered together and tiptoed away from the square, moving as one with Sam flying overhead. When we reached the spot behind the bank where we'd met, Owen said, "Now, go, but take the long way around instead of going straight home or looking like you were coming from here." My brothers took off, and Owen turned to Sam. "Keep an eye on things and let me know what happens here tonight."

"Sure thing, boss. Now you get some rest."

When he was gone, we made our way back to Owen's rental car. He tossed me the keys when we reached the car. "Do you mind driving? I'm not sure I'm up to it."

I noticed then that he was shaking. "You could have drawn power from me, or from Teddy," I said.

"I'll be okay. It was quicker and easier this way."

He fell asleep almost as soon as he got into the car, and I hoped we didn't get stopped this time, since I didn't have any Jedi mind tricks in my arsenal. I'd have to resort to crying. I let the car creep away from downtown without the headlights on until we were well out of the zone of suspicion. Then I took back roads to arrive home from the opposite direction, as though we were coming from out of town.

When I'd parked and killed the engine, I nudged Owen awake. "Are you wearing anything under that black sweatshirt that might look less suspicious?" I asked him.

"What? Why?" he mumbled sleepily.

"Because I don't think you need to be climbing trees or in and out of windows right now. And I think you need sugar. We could go in the back door, have a snack in the kitchen, and then if we get caught on the squeaky steps, we can say we just went downstairs for a midnight snack. The thought of food should distract Mom. She'll be so terrified about her guest going hungry that she'll insist on going downstairs and cooking you a three-course meal, and she'll forget to wonder why she didn't hear us going downstairs."

"Very good idea," he said, making no move to get out of the car.

I got out and went around to Owen's side, where I opened the door and pulled him out. I nudged him into a position leaning against the side of the car and unzipped his sweatshirt to discover a plain white T-shirt underneath. I pulled his sweatshirt off him, removed my own sweatshirt, and locked them and the bag of magic tricks in the trunk. I then got an arm around his waist and led him up the back steps into the kitchen.

Under the kitchen light, he looked even worse than I realized, very pale and drawn, and with his eyes sunk into dark circles. I put a kettle on to make cocoa, then found two packets of mix. While the water heated, I cut a couple of slices of cake and put one in front of him. "Eat!" I ordered.

He nibbled at the cake while I mixed up the cocoa, then I put a mug in his hands and made sure he took a few sips. By the time he finished half the mug, he looked a lot more human. That was reassuring enough that I was able to sit and drink my own cocoa.

"If doing all that had this effect on you, how did Dean do it?" I asked.

He finished his cake, and I got up to cut him another slice while he replied. "I imagine it took him all night, and there would have been fewer patrols then. It was harder for me to do magic tonight than it was yesterday. I've probably been using more power than is wise in a place like this, for too many days in a row. I shouldn't have done as many demonstrations as I did earlier in the day, and I may have gone overboard in controlling Dean. I probably could have done that physically, but I thought using magic would have more impact."

"I'm worried about you being weakened while Idris is in town and doing some pretty big tricks."

He shrugged. "He won't be able to keep that up for long, and he doesn't have any immunes to draw power from. I have you and Teddy. And your mother, if things get desperate, though I'd prefer it not come to that."

"Well, with any luck, Idris'll just hide out from the fairy godmother from hell and his new bosses for a few days and leave us alone so you can rest." I hesitated, then asked, "How long do you think you'll be staying?"

He flushed a pale shade of pink, but I couldn't think of what was so embarrassing about my question. "It depends. I was supposed to leave today, but I want to make sure we know what Idris does, and I won't leave as long as I know he's here. Do you think your parents will mind me staying a few days longer?"

"If you tried to leave before being here less than a week, my mom might hide your car keys."

A loud squeak on the stairs startled both of us into silence. A few moments later, Mom came into the kitchen in a bathrobe. "I thought I heard voices," she said.

"We were having a midnight snack," I hurried to explain. "We didn't mean to disturb you."

"Oh, it's no trouble. I might even join you." She then got a good look at Owen, and I found the play of emotions across her face to be fairly amusing. At first the mom instincts won as she noticed how sickly he looked. Then other instincts took over. The funny thing about Owen was that as gorgeous as he was, he somehow looked even more gorgeous when he wasn't looking his best. He was a sight to behold in a tuxedo, but in a T-shirt, his hair rumpled, unshaven, with his glasses on, and with dark circles under his eyes, he could stop traffic. There was a hint of danger to him then, lurking beneath his boy-next-door exterior. Even better, he was entirely unaware of this effect and didn't seem to notice when he was affecting women that way.

Then the mom instinct fought its way back to the surface. "Are you okay?" she asked. "You don't look like you're feeling too well."

"I must not be sleeping well away from home. I never realized I was so used to hearing traffic and sirens all night long," he said.

"I can make something for you, if you like. Maybe an omelet?"

He shook his head. "No, thank you. Katie made me some cocoa, and I had some cake. Now I think I'll get back to bed and try to get some sleep."

As much as I wanted to get into my own bed, I lingered with Mom for a while. "Are you sure he's okay?" she asked when the squeak on the stairs told us he'd made it to his room. "He doesn't look too good."

"I'm sure he's just tired," I said. "Remember how it took me a few weeks to get used to the quiet after I got back here. And it's never too restful sleeping in a strange place, especially in someone's home."

"You don't think it's anything we've said or done, do you?"

"Mom, he's fine. He's having a good time. I just think he's a little overwhelmed. He doesn't come from a big family, and he lives alone, so he's not used to having all these people around. But I think he's adjusting. He and Teddy really seem to be hitting it off."

"If you're sure."

"I'm sure." I kissed her on the cheek, then headed toward the stairs. "Now, I'm getting back to bed. Good night!"

It wasn't until I'd reached my room that I realized she hadn't even noticed the fact that both Owen and I had been fully dressed instead of in pajamas and bathrobes. And she hadn't noticed that she hadn't heard the squeak on our way down the stairs. For someone who could notice every detail of someone's outfit and remember how often in the last few months she'd worn it, Mom sometimes wasn't too observant.

There was no sign of Owen at breakfast the next morning. I hoped that meant he was sleeping in. I wrote a quick note and slid it under his door before I headed to the store for work. Sherri was already there, which was an "alert the media" kind of event, and she was surprisingly cheerful. "Wow, you're here!" I said, then immediately realized that probably didn't sound so nice.

"Why wouldn't I be?" she asked as she straightened the display of small impulse items around the cash register. "I do work here, don't I?"

"Well, yeah, I mean, uh, well, with everything you've been through, I thought you could have used a break." I thought that was a pretty good recovery from putting my foot in my mouth.

She rolled her eyes. "If my husband is going to be a good-for-nothing, I'd better be sure one of us pulls in an honest paycheck."

"I'm glad you're here. We'd be in a tough spot without you. And, um, it would be safe for you to go home now. We saw to that."

"I said I'd be gone a few days, and I will be. I'll go home when I said I would."

"Okay, then," I said as I headed to my own office with the beginnings of a grudging respect for Sherri. I never would have thought she had it in her. She might even be able to keep Dean in line in the future.

Owen called me about an hour after I got to the store. "I didn't mean to sleep so late," he said with an audible yawn.

"You needed it. How are you feeling now?"

"Almost back to normal."

"I should be able to get away from here in a couple of hours, so you take it easy until then. I hope Mom's not fussing over you too much."

"She is, but I don't mind. She made an incredible breakfast. She said I looked like I could use a good meal. I guess she forgot all those huge meals she's made in the past few days."

"She definitely shows her love by feeding people, so get used to being stuffed while you're around here. I'll see you soon."

About an hour after I talked to him, Nita called. "You are not going to believe the morning I've had," she said. Given her fondness for drama, it was entirely possible that she meant the phone had rung once, so I avoided jumping to conclusions, no matter how worried I was about what one of her guests might do.

"What is it?" I asked.

"I've been busy. Three people have checked in so far this morning, and I've made a couple more reservations. If this pace continues the rest of the day, I may have to see if the 'no vacancy' sign still works. We haven't had this many people check in on the same day since that big family reunion a couple of years ago."

"I wonder what's going on," I said, instantly even more suspicious.

"I think it may be the rest of the band! And maybe some fans. They all look kind of like the same types. It's a sort of emo group, right?"

I wasn't sure I even knew what "emo" was. "They're hard to classify," I hedged. "Keep me posted, here or at the house. I'm curious. Are any of the guys cute?"

She snorted with laughter. "Not even! I wouldn't go this low, even as desperate as I am, and even if they are in a band. Of course, none of them are Indian. Maybe they're here to work on an album in the peace and quiet. That'll really make the motel famous if the album is big. Oh wait, would you believe, here comes another one. Gotta go. I think I should get a bonus."

I was sure there were dozens of highly rational reasons why unattractive young men would suddenly flock to this town, but with Phelan Idris, patron saint of unattractive social outcasts, in residence, I was inclined to think there was something going on.

"I'm leaving for the day," I announced to Sherri as I grabbed my purse and headed out of the office. "I've got all the orders and invoices taken care of. Call me at the house if you need anything."

"Is something wrong?" she asked.

I was so surprised that she'd picked up on a subtle social clue from someone she wasn't flirting with that it took me a few seconds to come up with an answer. "Owen wasn't feeling well last night, so I don't want to leave him alone with Mom too long."

"Oh, yes, you should definitely go home, then." She sounded really and truly sympathetic, which a few days ago I would have considered nothing short of a miracle.

Owen was sitting on the front porch swing, two dogs at his feet, when I got home. "You look a lot better," I told him as I joined him on the swing.

"I'm feeling better. What are you doing home so early? If you keep this up, they may realize they can function without you."

"I'm trying to wean them off me so it won't be too hard to get away again." I waited for him to say something about me going back to New York with him when this was over, but he didn't, so I got to the reason

I'd come home so quickly. "I don't know for sure if this is relevant, but Nita said several people have checked in at the motel already this morning and she has a few more reservations. They're all young men, and she wasn't impressed by the ones she's seen so far."

"I take it this is unusual?"

"She usually checks in maybe a dozen people a week, at the most. I thought it was kind of suspicious that we're hit with a relative onslaught of the kind of people who are usually drawn to Idris the day after he gets here."

"You're right. There probably is something going on." He took the cell phone from his pocket and made a call. "Sam? Anything to report from last night?" He listened to the response and said, "Can you get back over to the motel and keep an eye on it? We've got a few new guests we aren't sure of. Thanks."

He closed the phone and returned it to his pocket, then said, "The police investigated pretty thoroughly last night, but they didn't seem to know what to do about a set of mysterious break-ins in which the stolen goods were returned. They were baffled, but they didn't have any suspects in mind."

"So it looks like Dean will get away with it. As usual."

"He may have escaped the police, but I don't think your grandmother is through with him." He grinned then, and he suddenly looked years younger with the worry and tension around his eyes easing a little. "Do I detect a hint of sibling rivalry there?"

"He always had a talent for getting away with murder. He might have started it all, but the rest of us got in trouble while he got off scot-free. Frank said he could roll in the manure pile and come out smelling like roses. Dean could smile at Mom, and she'd forget that he was even in trouble."

"But I thought it was the youngest—and especially the only girl—who could get away with things."

"Not in my family. I think I was held to a higher standard. Boys will be boys, you know, but girls are expected to be better than that. But I guess I did mostly stay out of trouble. I just always felt bad for Frank and Teddy getting in trouble so much when Dean got away with it."

The door opened and Mom stuck her head outside. "Phone for you, Katie. I think it's Nita."

"Coming," I said, trying to get off the swing gently so it didn't send Owen rocking too much. He looked better, but he still looked like he'd be better off sleeping for a week.

"Hey, what is it?" I asked when I got to the phone.

"Three more people checked in, and I have two more reservations. This is crazy."

"More band members?"

"Not unless they're reviving the big band in a postmodern way. There are too many of them. Do you usually get guy groupies? Or maybe they're like a new version of the Grateful Dead, with people who follow them everywhere. That would be cool, but Mom and Dad won't be okay if they're doing drugs in the motel or planning a concert in the parking lot."

"Are they giving you any trouble?"

"They're fine. I just don't have the staff for this. Say, you wouldn't want to pick up a housekeeping shift, would you? I don't need it today because all the rooms were already clean, but tomorrow's going to be a nightmare."

"I'll have to get back to you on that. Thanks for keeping me posted. Maybe we'll stop by later today to check out the commotion."

I returned to the porch and told Owen what Nita had reported. "You know, playing housekeeper might not be such a bad idea," I said. "It would give me an excuse to spy on these guys and see what's going on."

"But she said she didn't need help until tomorrow, and I hope we have a sense of what's going on before then."

"If Idris is rallying his troops, it's too bad we told him about Dean. We could have had a double agent."

"We could still have a double agent." I'd seen that look in his eyes before, and it made me nervous. Normally, he was totally sane and rational, but he had a well-hidden crazy streak, especially where Idris was concerned. It was probably a testosterone thing, so I didn't understand it.

"What do you mean?" I asked warily.

"Well, you were just telling me about some of your sibling issues growing up. It's not outside the realm of imagination that it could work both ways. What if he didn't care what his baby sister said about doing bad magic and only told you he'd given it up to appease you, and then he went right ahead with his plans?"

"Oh, you are sneaky. I'll give him a call."

I moved to head back into the house, but he handed me his cell phone. I called Dean's cell and said, "Have you actually posted any nasty stuff about Idris on that course message board?" I asked.

He groaned. "Sorry, Sis, I haven't gotten around to it yet."

"No, that's good. See if there's something going on about him rallying his troops in town. It seems like they're congregating. You need to go meet with him and tell him your sister and her crazy boyfriend are full of it, and you wouldn't listen to us anyway."

"And then report back to you everything they say? Got it. I'll give you all the details when I have them."

I closed the phone and handed it back to Owen. "Looks like we have us a double agent. I just hope we can trust him."

"You think he'll turn on us?"

I sighed and worried my lower lip with my teeth. I felt like a turncoat. This was my brother I was talking about, and as much as he sometimes irritated me, I did love him. But there were bigger things at stake here than family ties. "He's susceptible to flattery, so if Idris manages to get under his skin, it might affect his loyalty. You know, it's too bad we can't send Teddy as the spy. He'd fit right in with that crowd."

Owen fought back a yawn. "With the right preparation, I bet I could fake him as a magic user."

"But that wouldn't be a good use of your resources. You need to get some rest. I have a feeling it's going to be yet another crazy night."

Sure enough, I'd barely fallen asleep when the usual tapping on my window woke me. I hadn't planned to be going out, so I was in my pajamas instead of dressed for action. I opened the window, and Owen whispered, "I just heard from Dean and from Sam. Idris and his people are gathering on the courthouse square. It's definitely some kind of magical rally."

"And I take it we'd better be there, huh? Give me a second to put on some clothes." I closed the curtains, then pulled on my black jeans and a black long-sleeved T-shirt. If we kept this up, I was going to run out of dark clothes. My wardrobe wasn't designed for sneaking around in the middle of the night.

"It's too bad there's no Starbucks in this town," I said with a yawn as we neared the square.

"It wouldn't be open at this hour, anyway. I think even most of the ones in New York would be closed by now." Owen pulled into a parking space in the grocery store's rear loading area, then we went around the side of the buildings and approached the square, where Sam was waiting for us.

There were at least two dozen young men, including Dean, gathered around Idris, who stood in the gazebo. With some red-white-and-blue bunting behind him, he'd look like he was making a campaign speech. I supposed that was sort of what he was doing. Dean stood out in the group. He looked too handsome and self-assured. The rest of those guys, and they were all guys, seemed like they were probably making up for some sense of inadequacy. Dean was, too, I reasoned, but his inadequacies were better hidden.

Idris was in mid-speech, and his voice carried well to the bushes where we hid. "It's time for your final exam. If you pass this test, you will earn the title of wizard. I've brought in a top wizard from New York to test you. You'll have to find him and then defeat him in close magical combat. Now, I should warn you—he's very powerful, and it may take all of you working together, but that's part of the test."

He waved a hand, and a flickering image formed in the air next to him. It took a while to solidify, and Idris talked as the image took shape. "Here is the wizard you should be looking for. Defeat him, and you will be a true wizard." Finally, the image was recognizable. It was a picture of Owen.

Sixteen

Standing as close as I was to Owen, I could feel his muscles tensing, preparing to spring into action. I grabbed his arm and gave it a firm squeeze, hoping that would remind him that this really wasn't a good time to take all of them on at once. He looked at me and nodded, then after a few deep breaths, he relaxed and I let him go. With a tilt of his head, he indicated that we should leave, and we crept away, leaving the pep rally still in progress.

"This, you'll have to call in," Sam said once we were safely back at the car. "You'll need backup."

"I can handle it."

Sam shook his head. "Even if those guys aren't as powerful or trained as you are, you can't handle all of them by yourself if they're teaming up and gunning for you."

"I've got you and Katie's grandmother. And Dean on the inside. And I may be able to get some local allies. We're not that outnumbered."

"If you don't call and let the boss know what's going on, I will. Don't you think it would go better if he heard it straight from you?"

I felt like I was missing a crucial part of this conversation, but if my reading between the lines was accurate, then . . . "You're AWOL!" I blurted to Owen. "They don't know you're here, do they?"

"Oh, come on," Sam said. "You know the boss. Of course they know he's here. They just don't officially know."

"I thought I could wrap it all up over the weekend," Owen admitted, sounding like he was explaining why his homework wasn't done. "I called in sick on Friday, and I thought I could easily be back in the office by Tuesday, with everything taken care of."

"Yeah, and there wasn't anything suspicious about you calling in sick the morning after you spent the day begging the boss to let you come down here and make sure Katie was okay," Sam said.

If Sam hadn't already been made of stone, the look Owen gave him would have turned him that way. "We weren't having any luck finding or dealing with Idris in New York, so I thought I'd do better finding him here by going through his student. And I was right."

"But now you're outnumbered, with the bad guys gunning for you, and Idris seems to have some tricks up his sleeve, like that disappearing act he pulled," I argued. "So unless you're willing to run, you're going to need help."

"We can't afford to let him get away this time," Sam added.

Owen stood still for a while, then finally said, "Okay. I'll call. In the morning. It's pretty late now."

Sam snorted. "Like the boss isn't expecting this."

Owen held up his hands in surrender. "Okay, okay, I'll call. I knew I'd have to come clean at some point, but I would have preferred to do it with Idris or his junior wizard in custody."

"You do have the junior wizard," I reminded him. "That may help."

"Maybe I should get a little farther away from all the student wizards who are gunning for me before I take time out to make a phone call," he said.

"Don't worry, kiddo, I got you covered. Go right ahead and make that call," Sam said, a little too gleefully, earning himself another glare.

Owen went a few yards away, just out of earshot, and at least mimed talking on his cell phone. I watched him for a moment, then turned to Sam. "You were in on this?"

"Not really 'in.' I just agreed not to tell anyone he was here. He said it would only be for the weekend at first, but then he started tacking days onto it. Even if we hadn't seen what those goons were up to tonight, he'd have had to come clean pretty soon, or else I'd have had to rat him out."

"But why?"

Sam laughed. "Oh, dollface, and I thought you were so smart. It's 'cause of you! He nearly flipped when he heard about the bad guy going after you. I guess that was really your brother playing a prank on you, huh? The boss wanted to wait and see what happened after you figured out that Idris was involved. I was gonna keep an eye on you while they tried to find Idris in New York. But Palmer there was convinced Idris would be down here. And then he was the one I reached to tell about the stuff at the theater. I'm guessin' he didn't tell the boss about that."

"So he risked getting into huge trouble because he was worried about me?"

"I think he also wanted to make up for what happened the last time, you know, not letting his feelings get in the way of him being able to catch the bad guy again. Of course, the fact that he rushed down here to protect you doesn't help his case much, does it?"

"No, probably not," I said with a sigh. No wonder he hadn't said anything about me going back to New York. After this, they certainly weren't going to let me be close enough to him to be a distraction, unless they decided to lock me up safely somewhere they could keep an eye on me. Part of me was thrilled to have proof that he still cared for me, but I couldn't help but be a little bit scared. He might have had a crazy streak at times, but running off against orders wasn't like Owen. In fact, him being such a classic good boy was the main reason that he wasn't too scary, in spite of all the things he could do, like mess with people's minds and stop time.

Owen returned to us. "They're sending backup," he said. I couldn't tell from his tone of voice how he felt.

"So, how much trouble are you in?" Sam asked, and I was glad he did, so I didn't have to.

"I don't know. I'm supposed to stay out of sight and not engage either Idris or his minions."

I tugged on his sleeve. "Well, if you're going to do that, we'd better get home."

We managed to avoid the wizard gang and get back home to make our usual climb up the tree onto the porch roof. I seemed to be entering the house more often through my bedroom window than through the door these days. I'd just put one leg through the window when I noticed movement in my room. Someone was in there. I opened my mouth to scream in shock, but someone caught me from behind with a hand over my mouth. That could have been even more frightening, but I realized right away that it was Owen.

"What are you doing here, Mrs. Callahan?" he whispered.

I pried his hand off my mouth and blurted as softly as I could, "Granny?" Sure enough, my grandmother was sitting on my bed. "I thought you didn't like to drive at night," I added.

"Not liking to isn't the same as can't. But I'm not the one who should be answering questions, missy. Just what would you be doing climbing in through the window at this hour? Where have you been, and what have you been up to?"

Before we continued the conversation, I climbed the rest of the way inside, and Owen joined me. Granny patted the bed beside her, and we both sat down. "There's something going on in town," Owen said.

She nodded. "I thought so. Those were some strange-looking young men. They're using too much magic. They'll run us all dry. Now, what does this have to do with you?"

"My enemy is their leader."

"Oh, so it's a magical war that's brewing."

"I hope not."

"You'll need help."

"Owen can take care of it, Granny," I put in. I doubted he'd want the kind of help she could offer, unless she was going to scare off the junior wizards by shaking her cane at them and glaring.

"What kind of help do you think I can find?" Owen asked her. I was so used to people just humoring her that I couldn't get used to him having a serious conversation with her about the kind of stuff we usually ignored.

"We have the wee folk. I'll bet they're not happy to have their power sources drained by that lot."

"You mean the nature spirits? The naiads and dryads?"

"If that's what you call them. Yes, they live around the creek, more outside of town these days. But it takes special skill and a number of precautions to summon them safely."

"I'm familiar with the rituals."

She patted him on the leg. "I had a feeling you would be. You're a good boy. I've got some things that may be helpful to you. I'll bring them to you tomorrow." She braced her cane on the ground and stood up. "Now, I'd better get home before my daughter realizes I'm here. And you'd best get out of Katie's bedroom, young man. It's improper for you to be unchaperoned like this."

"Wait a second," I said, "you mean you came here in the middle of the night and waited for us to tell us there were strange wizards in town?"

"No, I came here because I noticed earlier today that the bark on that tree by the porch was scraped. Someone's been climbing up and down that way, and as you're the only one living at home these days, I had a feeling you were up to something. The best way to find out what you were up to was to catch you out and wait for you."

I looked out the window, toward the tree, then back at Granny. "You didn't . . ."

"Don't be silly. I came up the stairs, like a normal person."

"But how did you not wake up Mom and Dad? Those stairs squeak something awful."

She shook her head and tut-tutted. "It's not too difficult a spell to silence those steps. Don't tell me the great wizard here didn't think of that."

I looked over at Owen, and if I'd had night-vision goggles, I was pretty sure I could have seen the glow coming off his face. "But—but that would have been dishonest, deceiving my hosts," he stammered.

"And climbing in and out of windows in the middle of the night is honest?"

"But it's not magically dishonest."

She nodded. "Ah, you've been well taught. You know the rules. I'll see you two in the morning. Now, get to bed—in separate rooms, please."

When she'd gone and shut my bedroom door behind her, Owen said, "I honestly never thought of silencing the stairs. I know I can't make that squeaky spot in our house go quiet, but that's probably a spell Gloria put on it. I guess I assumed it would be the same way here."

"Climbing out the window is more fun."

"Speaking of which, I'd better go." His gaze lingered on me for a second. "I'm a little afraid of what your grandmother would do to me if she knew I was in here unchaperoned for too long. She's scarier than all those wizards who are gunning for me." I moved toward him to say good night, but before I got there, he'd already climbed back out the window.

Owen looked less exhausted and more like himself the following morning, aside from the slightest sense that he might be facing his own execution soon. Granny showed up while we were still eating breakfast, so I went off to work without worrying about how Owen would occupy himself in my absence. He had her eating out of his hand, and when it came to spending hours listening to her stories, it was better him than me. I hoped he had enough background knowledge to allow him to tell the truth from the stuff she made up. She couldn't describe a family event without getting details mixed up, so I wasn't sure how he'd get anything useful out of her ramblings about the wee folk.

Work went more or less without incident. On my way home, I drove by the square to see what the wizards were up to. They seemed to be roaming in groups of four or five, looking like they were searching for someone. The wandering groups made the townspeople nervous. People crossed the street to avoid passing them on the sidewalk. As I drove past the pharmacy, Lester was in the process of throwing a group out. I hoped Rainbow's candles had given them headaches or coughing spells, then I got an idea.

I pulled into a parking space in front of the pharmacy and ran inside. "Hey, Rainbow, do those aromatherapy candles come in votive sizes?"

"The full jar is a better value."

"That's okay, I need them for a pretty small space." I bought a bag of ten of the candles that were designed to balance your energy for a more even mood. I figured that encouraging romance with this bunch would be asking for trouble.

When I got home, Owen was out in the horse pasture, having what looked like a deep conversation with Daisy. "I swear, you're like something out of a Disney movie with all your animal friends," I said as I approached them. "When the little birds come sit on your shoulder and bring you news, I'm out of here."

"She was looking at me over the fence like she was sad and lonely."

I laughed and patted Daisy on the neck. "Meet the only horse I know of who can make puppy-dog eyes. She's basically an overgrown dog. I'm not sure she realizes she's a horse. How'd you learn to be so good with animals? Is that a magic thing?"

"I've never been that great with people. Animals are usually easier. As far as I know, it has nothing to do with magic. Well, except for the dragons. That was magic, and I didn't plan for that spell to have that effect."

"You also have that crazy Granny–taming ability. Speaking of Granny, did you get what you needed?"

"Oh yeah, a whole notebook full. I'll spend the afternoon cross-referencing what she told me with some of my materials, and then tonight we can go out on a little diplomatic mission. Is there any news on our magical visitors?"

I told him what I'd seen. "So far, it seems like they're sticking to downtown, so you should be safe out here. Maybe I could find you a hat and dark glasses as a disguise."

"I'm sure that won't be necessary."

"Just making the offer. While you're doing your research this afternoon, I think I'll help Nita at the motel."

"Why would you do that?"

"Well, there's the spying potential, and then there's this." I raised the bag of candles. "Take a whiff and see if they affect you even when they aren't burning." I opened the bag and he leaned over it, then recoiled instantly with a shudder. "Now, is that because of the magic, or because they smell nasty?"

He sneezed. "Both."

"Good," I said with a grin. "I thought they'd be a nice touch for our guests' rooms. Anything to throw them off balance. Now, have you had lunch yet?"

We were in the middle of making sandwiches when Mom got back. "Something really odd is going on downtown, and don't tell me I'm imagining things," she said as she came into the kitchen.

Oops. Owen and I shared a guilty look. I'd been so distracted by finding out that Dean and Granny were magical and Teddy was immune, that Idris had his geek brigade gathering, and that Owen was here without permission that I'd managed to forget that Mom was still immune and not in on the secret. She'd have seen all the nonsense on the square. "Nita said some really odd people had checked into the motel," I said. "She thinks it's a rock band hiding out here to write songs for an album."

"I'm not sure we want that sort of people in this town. I bet they brought their drugs with them." She was still grumbling as she went up the stairs.

"We'll have to be careful if we want to keep her out of things," Owen said.

I sighed. "I know. I'd assign one of the guys to look out for her, but I'm running out of brothers. And to think, I always thought I had too many of them."

The problem soon resolved itself when Granny showed up with an armload of books and family photo albums. "These may be of help to you," she said to Owen. She put the books on the kitchen table, then handed Owen a bottle full of murky liquid. "I also made you a potion. It's a recipe I got from my Gran. Best thing for restoring you after a lot of magic. You need to be careful about that in these parts. You can wear yourself out real fast." She settled in at the table, making herself at home, and I knew that Mom wouldn't stand a chance of getting away for the rest of the afternoon. Granny was better than a prison warden.

I felt like a chicken leaving Owen to deal with Granny alone, but they seemed to be getting along fine, so I didn't feel too bad about heading over to the motel. My main worry was that Granny might accidentally poison him with her magical home remedies while I was gone.

"You said you needed housekeeping help?" I said to Nita when I got there. Then I noticed the new decor in the lobby. The faded prints of local sights from an old chamber of commerce calendar were gone, replaced by framed album covers. Bright fringed throws covered the vinyl lobby chairs.

"Oh, bless you!" Nita said. "The housekeeper I did have quit this morning. She said she wasn't coming back until these guys left."

"Why? What did they do?"

She waved a hand in a dismissive gesture. "I'm not entirely sure, but I got the impression there was some kind of harassment going on. You know rock and rollers. I hate to make you face all that, but it seems like most of them are out for the afternoon."

"I'm sure I can cope." I gestured around the lobby. "I see you're already carrying out your new theme."

"Yeah, great, huh? Oh, and come look at this." She gestured me back behind the desk and pulled up some files on her computer. "I took these pictures Monday afternoon. He must have gone out for a long walk because he came straggling back later that day. Look at that thing he's wearing around his neck. It's not big enough to be proper bling, but it's too big to be a good man necklace."

I bent over and squinted at the photo of a tired, sweaty Idris as she enlarged the picture on the screen. His shirt was unbuttoned almost to his waist, which was not a pretty sight, and he had a medallion of some sort hanging on a leather cord around his neck. "There's no telling what it is," I said, wishing we could zoom in more and see if there was writing on it, but I knew it would only get fuzzy if we tried to enlarge the picture any more.

"I really don't know what to make of these guys. The leader's been holed up in his room most of the day, but I think he's out now. And I guess I'd better let you get to work."

"Just give me the key and tell me what to do."

"Make the beds, change out towels, wipe things down, empty the trash, put out new soap. We don't change linens daily unless someone asks for it. If anyone left a tip, keep it, but with this bunch, I wouldn't count on it." She made an exaggerated "what are you gonna do?" expression, then sighed. "Rock and rollers. At least nobody's really trashed a room yet."

She gave me a master key, and on my way to the housekeeping closet, I stopped by my truck to get the bag of candles. I put them on top of the housekeeping cart, which I made sure was stocked with soap and towels. Consulting the list, I went to the first room, knocked on the door, shouted, "Housekeeping," then when there was no reply, I opened the door.

It looked like someone had held a wild party in there. Before I did anything, I put out one of the candles and lit it. I hoped that having burned it at all would get more of the slightly off-target magic into the room for a maximum reaction. Then I snooped around. There wasn't much of interest to find. It could have been any twenty-something man's motel room, with dirty underwear left lying on the floor next to crumpled wet towels in the bathroom and clothes strewn around the bedroom. I couldn't find any evidence of magic or anything that looked like magical paraphernalia.

My spying done, I emptied the trash, made the bed, switched out the towels, and straightened the bathroom. Somehow I doubted that these guys were likely to notice the finer points of motel housekeeping, and this wasn't a mint-on-the-pillow establishment to begin with. I blew the candle out right before I moved on to the next room and left it sitting there on the dresser.

I went through the same routine with each of the other rooms. Most of the guests were doubling up, which meant twice the mess. It reminded me of my brothers' bedroom when we were growing up. I left two candles in Idris's room, one in the bedroom and the other in the bathroom, because I really wanted him to suffer. I was fairly certain I felt the tingle of magic as I entered his room. He was smart enough to ward his room with Owen around, though it was kind of a futile gesture when

I was around, too, but I didn't find anything particularly incriminating or useful in there.

Two hours later, I put the cart away and dragged myself back to the office to return the master key. "That's a harder job than you expect it to be," I said. "I left the dirty towels in the cart. Did you need me to wash them?"

"No, Mom takes care of the laundry. Thanks so much for your help."

I was on my way back to my truck when a rental car pulled up in front of the office. I paused, waiting to see if there were more members of Idris's gang arriving. But then a very familiar figure emerged from the car. It was Rod, Owen's best friend. I took that as a sign that Owen wasn't in too much trouble. Sending Rod was more like giving him a partner in crime than a babysitter. I was just about to run to greet him when another person got out of the car. It was Merlin, the CEO of MSI. That was kind of mind-blowing, when you thought about it, to consider that Merlin, *the* Merlin of Camelot fame, was standing outside the motel in Cobb, Texas. It also probably meant that either they thought this thing with Idris was a really big deal, or Owen was in really big trouble.

I darted around the corner of the office bungalow before they could see me and got into my truck. Then I hesitated, torn between conflicting loyalties. If I warned Owen, that would in a way be a betrayal of Merlin and the company. It wasn't a good idea for him to charge off and take matters into his own hands. On the other hand, I didn't work for MSI anymore, and Owen was my friend who had cared enough to risk his job to make sure I was okay. That sealed the deal. I started the truck and pulled out of the parking lot.

Owen met me in the driveway, with that uncanny knack of his for knowing where I'd be and when. He didn't look worried enough to have already known what was going on. "Your backup is here," I told him as I got out of the car.

"They haven't called me yet."

"I'm guessing it's a surprise. Owen, Merlin himself came. With Rod."

Normally, he turned various shades of pink and red with strong emotion, but this time he went a sickly gray color. "Oh. Where are they?"

"I saw them pulling up at the motel as I was leaving."

"Do they know you know they're here?"

"I don't think they saw me, and I didn't say anything to them."

He pulled his cell phone out of his pocket and checked it. "No missed calls and no messages." He pushed a couple of buttons, then said, "Sam?" There was a pause, and he swallowed hard before saying, "Yeah, I just heard. Go ahead and tell them everything, but try to give me a heads-up before . . . well, you know. Thanks." He flipped the phone closed, then said, "Sam's on his way to meet with them. But they haven't called me. I guess that puts me out of the loop, huh?"

"Or it means they don't want you going out and about with a gang of would-be wizards looking for you, and they know it's not a good idea to hold a magical convention around my family. Speaking of which, how did things go with Granny today? Did you get any useful stuff out of her?"

"Your grandmother really is a fountain of information."

"Mom would say she's a fountain of a lot of stuff."

"Well, true, not all of it is accurate. Her stories are heavily embellished, but there is a core of truth there, and I think there might be some things here that can help us."

"So you're going through with your plan?"

He shrugged. "I might as well, unless the boss tells me specifically otherwise. The more I can show I've accomplished, the better it's likely to turn out for me."

"I guess this means yet another midnight excursion."

"Yeah. I haven't been out so many nights since I was in school, with late-night magical training. Those midnight secret society meetings were murder."

That night, I followed the instructions Owen had given me. He'd said to wear something white, which was good because I'd run out of black clothes. I wore a flowing white peasant blouse with an old pair of jeans, because he'd also said things could get dirty and muddy. I left my hair down and put on some light floral perfume. If I didn't know how serious this situation was, I'd have suspected him of setting up a romantic rendezvous. Unfortunately, Owen's mind usually didn't work that way, so it was most likely that his instructions had more to do with attracting whatever local magical folk there were than with creating a romantic atmosphere.

When he knocked on my window—apparently he'd decided against magically dampening the sound of the squeaky stairs—he wore a white shirt untucked over faded jeans. He got some things out of his case, then asked, "Do you have any kind of portable musical instrument? Like a whistle, flute, pipes, or anything like that? I thought I had something in here, but I don't. This was one thing I didn't anticipate."

"I have my flute from high school band. At least, I think it's still around here." I found it on the top shelf of my closet and brought it down. "I have no idea what condition it's in."

"Can you still play it?"

"I'm sure I can get a few notes out, and I probably still have the school fight song memorized. I don't know what it will sound like, though. It's all in the lip, you know, and my lip is really out of shape."

He glanced at my mouth and smiled. "It doesn't have to be perfect. We just need the music."

In the very few times during my teen years that I'd climbed out my window to sneak away, I'd never imagined doing so with my band instrument. Come to think of it, I'd also never imagined it with a really hot guy. The magical world really was opposite land, where the things that had made me a dork in school were what now made me useful.

This time, instead of driving downtown, we drove through the town and then up the road a few miles before Owen pulled over onto the shoulder. He did something to the barbed-wire fence that made it possible for us to walk through it, then we crossed the field to get to the stand of trees that indicated there was water. It was the creek that went on to flow through the town.

The area around the creek was like an oasis in the desert. All around was flat prairie land, but the creek banks were rimmed with lush vegetation and trees. It was a miniforest stuck in the middle of a sea of grass. Owen held my hand to keep me steady as we made our way down the steep creek bank to stand at the water's edge.

The moon was bright, not quite full, but still enough to keep things from being pitch-black. Owen conjured a little hand fire to hover over his head and light what he was doing as he took things out of his pack. While he worked, I peered into the bushes and the creek water, looking for any signs of magical creatures. They wouldn't be able to hide from me using magic, but I couldn't see anything. I'd never seen anything remotely magical around here until a week or so ago, so I wasn't optimistic about this working. I was still afraid that Granny, magical or not, was mostly nuts and all the wee folk she'd seen were only in her head.

"Come over here," Owen called from where he stood on a flat rock that jutted out into the creek. He held a hand out to steady me as I climbed onto the rock with him. Then he took a pouch of powder from his pack and made a circle around us. "A protective measure," he said, "in case they aren't too happy about being disturbed."

"How reassuring," I said.

"I don't think they'd harm us, but we're not dealing with tamed beings here. Now, get your instrument out. We need to be ready in case they show up."

"Ready for what?"

"To offer them a gift. Music is very commonly welcomed, so that should work."

"I wish you'd told me in time to practice something," I said as I opened the case and put the flute together. "I'm not sure the Cobb High School fight song is going to do the trick."

Owen took the flute from me and put it on top of his pack, then he turned to face me. "And now, um, we have to do something that will attract them. There's, uh, a certain energy that may draw them."

I nodded, not sure where he was going with that, but then I remembered what he'd said when we'd investigated the creek in the town a few days ago, and before I had a chance to respond, he'd taken me in his arms and was kissing me.

It was as good as I'd remembered, whether or not it had any heart behind it. And I was pretty sure it had some heart behind it. You didn't kiss someone like that and not mean it. I knew I meant it when I kissed him back. The whole thing was rather wildly romantic, kissing on the water's edge in the moonlight. There was something primal and, yes, magical about it that made it dangerously easy to get carried away.

And then a voice from around the level of our feet said very loudly, "Ahem!"

Seventeen

We sprang apart—well, we separated our lips, but we still held onto each other pretty tightly. I didn't know about Owen, but my legs had gone all watery, and I wasn't sure I could have stayed upright if I hadn't been hanging onto him. Then when I got a good look at what was around us, I held onto him even tighter.

I almost felt like the heavens had come down to surround us. Pinpricks of light filled the creek's gully, going all the way up the banks on either side. They were in the trees above us and floating in the water below us. When I got a better look, I realized the pinpricks were the eyes of hundreds of little creatures. For most of them, all I could see was their eyes. Judging by what I could see, I was rather glad that most of them remained hidden.

The one who'd spoken to us was in the water. She leaned against the rock where we stood, barely outside Owen's barrier. She looked a lot like the fairies I knew, except she didn't have wings. Her hair was long and stringy, almost looking like seaweed, and it draped over her slender body. Aside from the strategically placed hair, the part of her that was visible above the water was naked. There were several more creatures like her—naiads, I assumed—in the water.

The ones in the trees were like nothing I'd ever seen before. They were roughly the same size and shape as the water creatures, but their skins were mottled like tree bark, and their hair was short and shaggy. Their fingers and toes were long and thin, a lot like the "fingers" on tree frogs, and they clung easily to trunks and tree branches. They must have been the dryads Owen mentioned.

There were also little sparks of light zipping in and out among the bushes on the creek banks. At first I thought they were fireflies, but then I realized they, too, were the eyes of creatures. These were tiny, and it was hard to see exactly what they looked like because they never stayed still long enough for me to see more than a blur of movement.

"I take it you wanted us to pop up, given that circle you created before you put on your show," the naiad who'd gotten our attention said. "If you'd only come here to make out, you wouldn't have bothered with the prep work, and boy, wouldn't that have made things interesting." She fluttered her eyelashes suggestively, then added, "And I think you might have been trying to signal the next river with the amount of aura you were sending out. My, such passion."

Owen released me and knelt to speak to her. "I've come to call upon your people for assistance," he said formally. I felt awfully exposed standing there, surrounded by all those not-necessarily-friendly faces, so I knelt beside Owen. He put his arm around me as he continued speaking. "There's new power here that doesn't belong, and I'll need help to send it away."

"Your power doesn't belong here, either," she said with a burbling laugh that reminded me of the sound of a small waterfall.

"I plan to leave of my own accord when this is over." He glanced at me and added, "I may return as a visitor, but I wouldn't be using magic then."

A gruffer voice spoke from above us. "The power has been drained. Our energy may soon be depleted."

We looked up and saw one of the dryads hanging from a limb over our heads. "Yeah, I noticed. That's why I'm here," Owen said. "There is an outsider teaching people here to use power. He brought even more people like him here, and he's determined not to let me stop him. I can't face all of them alone, but with your help, I should be able to drive them away and bring the situation back to normal for you again."

"We could drive them away ourselves," the dryad said.

"That would be perfectly all right with me," Owen said with a crooked smile. "Be my guest. But this is a trained wizard. I know him, and I can make plans against him to direct our fight so that we use no more power than necessary and bring harm to no one."

"And it's you alone, facing all those naughty power wasters?" the water creature burbled.

"I have allies. Merlin is here with me—Myrddin Emrys." I hoped he wasn't assuming too much. Sure, Merlin would be on our side against the bad guys, but would he go along with Owen's plan?

But dropping that name got their attention. They all perked up, and the little perpetual motion machines slowed down long enough for me to see they looked like wild miniature elves. I decided they must be pixies. "He has returned?" the dryad asked.

"He has," Owen confirmed. "He has work to do and is needed in this time." His voice had been soft and conversational, but when he spoke next, it was firm, with a trace of iron in it that reminded me of Merlin himself. "Now, will you help me?"

"What have you to offer us as a gift?" the naiad asked. I didn't like the way she looked at Owen. It made me wonder what offering she had in mind. After all, it had been our passion that drew her to us.

"We have music," Owen said.

There was a murmur among the gathered creatures, and then the dryad said, "That is acceptable. We will listen."

Owen nodded to me, and I picked up the flute. I was fairly sure I could still play "The Star Spangled Banner" from memory, but the flute part to that was mostly high trills, so on its own it wouldn't be very effective. Teddy had made me learn to play "Princess Leia's Theme" from *Star Wars,* but that seemed wrong to me, somehow. As I'd told Owen, about the only thing I was sure I could still play was the school fight song. After four years of playing it for every pep rally, at the start of every half of every football game, after every score, at the end of the game, and at random times when the team needed a boost, it was forever drilled into my psyche.

I took a deep breath and played a test note to make sure I could still play at all, then adjusted the alignment of the instrument. I made the mistake of looking out at my audience before I started playing, and it made me even more nervous than chair tests had back when I was in school. As scary as my band director had been, he was nothing like hundreds of magical creatures, and the outcome hadn't been nearly as important as the fate of this corner of the magical world.

The sound wasn't as bad as I'd feared once I started playing. Because "The Washington and Lee Swing" wasn't the sort of thing you'd think of for placating magical creatures, I slowed it down to give it a haunting, plaintive sound. That was also the only way I kept my fingers from getting tangled as they remembered nearly forgotten fingerings.

When the last note had died away, there was silence, except for the sound of running water. I had to resist the instinct to shout "C! H! S!" at the end of the song, as we had always done at football games. Then a series of clicks and whistles rang out. "Very nice," the naiad said. "We accept your offering. How may we help you?"

"I need you to be ready to come into the town when I summon you," Owen said. "I will bring our enemies to you. I don't want them killed or seriously hurt. I just want the apprentice wizards to be taken out of the equation so I can deal with their master without their interference."

"We will protect you and your lady," she said with a bow. With a sidelong glance at me, she added, "Though your lady needs no protection from magic. And when we have done as you asked, we would like more music, unless you have another gift for us." She batted her eyelashes meaningfully at Owen.

"Yes, of course," I hurried to respond. I could even practice something, now that I knew I needed to.

"Then we have an agreement. You may leave now, and we give you safe passage."

Owen broke the circle with his foot as I put my flute away. I would have preferred that he wait until we were ready to go, but it appeared to be a show of trust. I felt as though tiny hands were touching my hair and clothes while I waited for him to gather his things, but when he took me by the hand to lead me away from there, all the pinpricks of light parted, leaving us a clear path. The pixies followed us all the way to the car, keeping a respectful distance, which generally meant running in circles around us as we walked.

"I meet the most interesting people when I'm with you," I said once we were safely in the car and on our way home. I hoped the quip covered up the fact that I was shivering. I knew it wasn't from the cold, but I wasn't sure if it was a reaction to having been surrounded by all those creatures or if I was still feeling the aftereffects of that kiss. He'd barely touched me since he'd been here, so being hit with a kiss like that out of the blue had really done a number on me.

"I just hope we can count on them," he said, keeping his eyes on the road as he drove. "Spirits like that are notoriously unreliable. For one thing, they're very old, so time means little to them, and matters that are important to us look trivial to them. They get comfortable where they are and become less inclined to stir themselves. But they might show up to hear more music."

"I guess that means I need to find more music."

"What you did tonight was perfect."

"What I did tonight was play my school fight song at a slower tempo. Can't we just bring a CD player and give them something really good?"

He shook his head. "No, it's the act of creating music that has the effect on them. A recording doesn't work."

"I hope you actually have a plan for dealing with Idris working in that crazy genius brain of yours."

"Nothing elaborate. I'll merely give them what they want."

"Which is you."

"Exactly. And then I'll lead them to the creek area, where I'll have reinforcements."

"So your brilliant plan is to use yourself as bait."

"Sometimes there is brilliance in simplicity."

"And is the boss likely to go for that?"

"I guess we'll find out soon enough."

He went with me to work the next morning, against my objections. While the would-be wizard army hadn't yet made it to the feed-and-seed store, I didn't like him being out and about. He wouldn't even take the baseball cap I offered him. I wore the necklace that alerted me to magic in use, and I could tell he wasn't using an illusion to hide his appearance. That would have been a waste of power, but it might have kept him safer. At one time, I'd wondered if he was maybe a little too perfect, but as I got to know him better, I was learning that he was as flawed as the rest of us, one of his major flaws being that he was stubborn. Since I was a real prizewinner in that category myself, I supposed it took one to know one.

I was able to convince him to stay back in the office, where he was somewhat hidden from anyone who wandered into the store. Dean showed up for work on time, for a record-setting two days in a row, and came back to the office to talk to us. "You're driving them crazy, staying out of sight like that," he said to Owen. "After a whole day of searching, they haven't seen you yet. Some of them are starting to wonder if you really exist. One group went home this morning. I'm not sure if they were discouraged or just not feeling well. They were all complaining of headaches."

"That evens the odds a little," I said, trying to be optimistic. It sounded like my magical candles were doing their job.

"I'll give them a show later today to help bait the hook," Owen said. "What I'd like is to engineer a showdown tonight, get them all in one place, and then teach them a good lesson."

"There's a meeting this evening around sunset," Dean said. "That might be a good time to show up. What kind of lesson do you have planned?"

"The magical version of shock and awe. When I'm through with these people, they'll never want to go near magic again." There was a dangerous glint to his eyes that made me glad there wasn't nearly as much power to draw upon here as there was back in Manhattan. That meant he might not be able to do too much damage.

Sherri called from the front of the store, "Katie! Someone's here to see you."

I excused myself and went to the front register, where Rod and Merlin stood. Sherri was practically draped across the counter and drooling at Rod, who eyed her in return. He quickly moved his gaze away from her when I approached. I guessed it took a leopard awhile to change its spots completely. "I assumed we might find you at your family business," Merlin said.

"Yes, I'm here." My voice involuntarily went up in pitch from nerves.

"And I take it we might find Mr. Palmer here, as well?"

I wished I had a way to warn Owen, but I had a feeling he'd be expecting something like this. "Yes, he is. Come on back." Sherri gave us all a really funny look, but I decided to leave it to Dean to explain it to her.

The office was little more than a glorified broom closet, so adding two more people made it uncomfortably crowded. Still, it was probably the safest place to meet. Owen jumped to his feet when Merlin entered the room. He'd gone pale again. "Sir," he said in a hoarse voice.

"Ah, Mr. Palmer," Merlin said, his voice calm and casual, and not at all like he was chewing out a wayward employee. "I trust you've recovered from your illness." I knew it had to be sarcasm, but it sounded totally sincere. Owen gulped and nodded. "Good, because we will need your help to resolve this situation, and after that, we have much to discuss."

Owen gulped and nodded again. "Yes, sir."

Dean cleared his throat, so I introduced my brother to Merlin and Rod. "Meet our local wizard," Owen added.

"And Dean, this is Rod, another friend from New York who also works with us, and my former boss, Merlin."

"You mean, like in the stories?"

"One and the same," Merlin said. "Although I'm currently functioning under the name Ambrose Mervyn. It's a more contemporary translation of my original name."

Dean gaped at him. "You mean, you're the real Merlin?"

"It's a long story," I put in. "We can discuss it later."

"In the meantime," Merlin said, "We need to develop a plan for dealing with Mr. Idris."

Owen cleared his throat. "Um, actually, I sort of have something set up already. Dean says that Idris and his students will be meeting tonight on the town square at sunset. I've already gained the support of the local nature spirits to help us. They'll be along the creek in the city park. I'll show myself to the students, who are likely to give chase, and I can lead them into a trap. The naiads, dryads, and pixies will take care of the students, leaving us free to deal with Idris. It feels like the available power in this area keeps getting weaker and weaker, and he's stronger than I've ever seen him, so it may take all of us."

Merlin regarded him for a long moment. I almost thought I could see the wheels turning in his head as he evaluated the situation. The longer he stared at Owen, the redder Owen turned. Finally Merlin said, "You seem to have taken care of the planning for us. It's a good thing you were here in advance to set everything up."

"Yes, I suppose it is, sir," Owen said with a totally straight face.

"What's all this conspiring?" a voice said from the doorway. We all turned to see Granny standing there, leaning on her cane and glaring at us. Before I could introduce her, she caught sight of Merlin and smiled. "Well, hello there," she said. "And who might you be?"

"Uh, Granny," I said, "this is my boss, Mr. Ambrose Mervyn."

"Ah, Merlin," she said with a nod. "It's good to know you're back. You're not here to do anything foolish like put Arthur back on the throne, are you? I doubt he'd fit in well in a constitutional monarchy."

"That is purely legend. Arthur is well and truly permanently dead," he said with a smile.

I was still goggling over my grandmother talking about constitutional monarchies, so it took me a moment to remember to introduce her. "Sir, this is my grandmother, Bridget Callahan. And Granny, over there is my friend Rod."

"My good lady," Merlin said as he took her hand and kissed it, and she blushed and tittered like a schoolgirl. For a man his age, he was quite distinguished-looking, maybe even handsome, and he was probably the only person I knew who was older than Granny, although he was more than a thousand years older, so I could see how that might make her a little flustered. "You have a lovely granddaughter."

She turned to me. "I suppose you're up to more magical mischief making, with this new lot here."

"She knows?" Rod asked.

"She is. Magical, I mean," I replied.

"This family would make a fascinating study for the genealogy group," Owen said. "They seem to have the magical gene and the mutation for immunity in nearly equal numbers. I've seen some clans in the British Isles that function that way, but—"

Rod cut him off. "Owen! Later."

"Oh, right, sorry."

"We do have something going on that we have to plan for, Granny," I said.

She entered the room and sat in my desk chair. "Maybe I can help."

"That's really not necessary," Rod said.

She shot him a glare that could have curdled milk. "You lot have my grandchildren mixed up in this. You'll not shut me out."

"You've already been very helpful," Owen said gently. "You gave me perfect directions to find the local magical folk, and they're going to help us tonight."

"This all has to do with those strange young men loitering downtown, doesn't it?"

"Yes," I said. "And we'll be getting rid of them soon enough."

"Good. They have terrible manners." She stood and said, "Then I suppose I'll see you all this evening. You're outnumbered, so you need me. I'll have Teddy pick me up. I don't like to drive after dark. Be sure to eat a good dinner." And then she was gone before any of us could object.

"Now we see where Katie gets it," Rod observed dryly.

I whirled on him. "What's that supposed to mean?"

"Well, would you let yourself be left out of this?"

"Not on your life."

"I rest my case. How much help might she be?"

"I have no idea. I didn't know she was magical until a couple of days ago. I just thought she was crazy."

"She's got a pretty vast knowledge of folklore and folk magic," Owen said. "She's also got a few good protective charms and healing abilities." I remembered all the nasty herb teas she'd made me drink when I was sick as a child, and now I knew why her miracle cures never worked on me. She must have figured my immunity out, for she gave up on the teas after a few tries.

"It would seem that our magical assets include myself, Mr. Palmer, Mr. Gwaltney, and now Mrs. Callahan, as well as Sam," Merlin said.

"We also have Dean on the inside," Owen added.

"And then Miss Chandler as an immune."

"Plus my brother Teddy, who's also immune."

Merlin raised an eyebrow and said to Owen, "Now I see what you mean about an interesting family tree. And then we have whatever local creatures deign to show up. That's against how many of them?"

"About two dozen to start with, but a few of them left this morning," Dean reported.

"Mr. Idris is the only fully qualified wizard of the lot?" Merlin asked.

"As far as I can tell," Dean replied. "Not that I'm an expert, but the whole group seems to be students."

"Ah, then it looks as though the odds are in our favor. Shall we convene at the park half an hour before sunset?"

I finally managed to herd the magical cabal out of my office so I could get some work done and so the work of the store could continue. I couldn't imagine explaining to my dad why I was holed up in my office with a group of strangers during peak operating hours. Owen let out a huge whoosh of breath when they were all gone. "I guess I'm not fired," he said.

"Yeah, but the question is, will you have to stay after school when this is over?"

"Oh, this is definitely not the last I'll hear of this. How much trouble I'm in will depend on how things go tonight."

When I'd finished my work early that afternoon, I said to Owen, "Ready to go bait the hook?"

He sighed heavily. "We might as well."

"Having second thoughts?"

"Of course, but I can't think of anything else that would be as effective. I'm sure I'll be fine. I can take care of myself."

"Yeah, but we don't want you wearing yourself out before tonight. I'm worried about you."

"You are?" he asked with a raised eyebrow.

"Of course I am. Why do you think I'm here in the first place?"

"Saving me from myself, I know." He sounded almost dejected.

I patted him on the arm. "I mean that in a good way. Do you think I'd have willingly left New York and come back here for just anyone?" That earned me the slightest hint of a smile and an incredibly cute blush.

I'd parked my truck behind the store in the loading area so it wouldn't be as visible to anyone driving by. As we pulled out onto the road, Owen said, "Let's go by the square. See if any of them are there." There weren't nearly as many of the visitors wandering the square this afternoon, just a couple of groups. "Drive slowly by them," he said. Then he turned his face to the truck's window so he was fully visible.

One of the men in the group did a double take as I drove past, then he got the attention of the others and pointed. "Speed up now," Owen directed. I gunned the truck to drive away as the group of wannabe wizards took off running after us. I was almost out of their reach when I reached a stoplight that had just turned red. The tires squealed as I slammed on the brakes. It was an intersection with a major highway, so I wasn't about to try running that light.

The band of wizards had almost reached the truck, and my necklace buzzed to the point that it was painful. "They're using magic," I said.

"I know. I'm deflecting it."

Then they veered off to the side, and I let myself relax. Maybe they'd given up. But then a car roared around the corner of the square, heading toward us.

"Oh great, now they've got a car," I said, tapping my fingers on the steering wheel in worry and impatience. "I can't run the light."

"You don't have to."

"Well, in about fifteen seconds they're going to rear-end us unless we find another way to get out of here."

Eighteen

Just then, the light turned green. A car on the other road screeched to a stop, and the car following rear-ended it. I winced, but this was no time to stop and play good Samaritan. I floored the truck and made the turn onto the main road as fast as I could without losing control, since the old truck didn't turn on a dime. Then I made the mistake of looking in the rearview mirror. They were still behind us, having squeaked through the light just as it abruptly turned red, skipping the entire yellow stage. Something told me the light wasn't exactly on its normal cycle.

My truck could barely get up to highway speed, while they were driving a new sports car. That meant I wasn't going to be able to outrun them in a typical high-speed car chase. I did, however, have other advantages. I'd grown up in this town and knew its streets like the back of my hand. I turned sharply onto a side street, then made another quick turn. They roared past down the first street, and I turned again, cutting across the neighborhood and back to one of the main cross streets.

"I think someone else is following us," Owen said in the freakishly calm voice he got in tense situations. I was impressed with the way he didn't try to apply nonexistent brakes on his side of the cab when I made those fast turns. You'd have thought he was in car chases every day.

"They must have called in backup," I said, turning sharply onto another side street. And then I had to slam on the brakes as an old lady with a walker made her way slowly across the road to her mailbox. The bad guys were right behind us and closing in fast.

As soon as the lady was more than halfway across the street, I swerved to the wrong side of the road to go around her and continue down the street. Owen turned in his seat, muttering something in a foreign language, and my necklace nearly jumped off my neck. "What are you doing?" I asked.

"A little diversion," he said in his calm crisis tone.

I chanced a glance in the rearview mirror and saw the lady still standing at her mailbox. The car following us screeched to a halt, though, and one of the guys jumped out and ran to kneel in front of the car. The lady looked at him for a moment, then shrugged and made her way slowly back across the street. "Let me guess, they think they hit her," I said.

"Maybe it'll teach them a lesson about safe driving."

I turned back onto the main highway, hoping we might be able to get home now without being followed. Unfortunately, one of the pursuing cars turned onto the highway from a different road and resumed the chase. Soon, the other car was right behind them, and then a third car joined in.

"Where's Burt Reynolds when you need him?" I asked as I tried to think of something else to do. My repertoire of driving tricks was rather limited, especially in the old truck that could barely hit fifty and cornered like the *Titanic*.

"Rocky and Rollo would really come in handy right now," he said, referring to the two crazy gargoyles who sometimes worked as drivers for MSI. They had a tag-team method of driving that could be alarming, especially in Manhattan traffic. "Brake!" he shouted. I laughed, remembering the crazy drive we'd once taken with them and the way they called signals out to each other. "No, I mean it, brake!" he said.

I slammed on the brakes without even looking at what he was talking about, then after we'd come to a stop I saw an enormous old Cadillac whip onto the road. It looked like a ghost vehicle with no one behind the wheel, until I noticed a pair of eyes peering through the steering wheel and a bubble of bluish-white hair sticking up from behind the wheel. "Oh great, we had to run into Mrs. Gray's weekly grocery trip. They usually send out bulletins to clear the road while she's on it. She doesn't acknowledge the possibility of any other cars being on the road." In spite of the speed at which she pulled out in front of us, she proceeded to drive at about twenty miles an hour, turn signal still blinking furiously. That meant our pursuers were right on us.

My necklace went nuts. If I hadn't had the steering wheel in a death grip, I'd have pulled it off. I wasn't sure what they were throwing at us, but I was glad it didn't work on me. "Are you okay?" I asked Owen, who looked awfully pale.

"I'm fine. It's easy enough to deflect. It seems like they're trying to make me get out of the truck and go to them."

"Too bad I can't control all the door locks from here so I can keep you in the truck."

"If I wanted to leave the truck, I'm not sure you'd be able to stop me. But don't worry, I'm not going anywhere."

I whipped a right turn down another side street, made a couple of blocks back the way we'd come, then turned back onto the highway in the opposite direction of the way we'd been going, behind the car that had been following us. I gave a friendly wave to Jason, the local police officer, who passed us going the other direction.

A second or two later, I heard a short burst of siren and looked back to see Jason pulling over the last car from the line of pursuers. "They made a U-turn right in front of a police officer," Owen said with a grin. "Not very bright."

While Jason had the one car pulled over, the other two cars made legal moves to get back behind us before I had a chance to turn off again. This town didn't have nearly enough side streets, and they were spread too far apart.

"Another bright idea might really come in handy about now," I said through gritted teeth as I tried to evade the rest of the apprentice wizards while sticking to the speed limit in a residential area where kids and dogs were likely to dart out into the street without warning. There was so little traffic on the side streets in our town that you could usually get through a whole game of stickball without interruption, as long as you weren't playing during what passed for rush hour.

Owen got out his cell phone. "Sam? We could use some assistance. Are you up for scaring some wannabe wizards? Okay, great, and hurry." He put the phone back into his pocket. "Sam will be here in a moment."

Something occurred to me. "Where does Sam carry a cell phone?"

"He doesn't. This isn't your typical cell phone. It's also a direct magical communication device."

"Nifty."

I was about to ask another question, but something dark swooped down out of the sky, zoomed over us, and then I heard brakes squealing behind us. I looked in the rearview mirror to see the car behind us turning around—in yet another illegal U-turn that, unfortunately, Jason wasn't there to catch—and driving away rapidly with Sam in pursuit. "Gee, you'd think they'd never seen a gargoyle before," I joked. "Now we just have one more, and we need to get rid of him before we can go home. We don't want them finding our secret hideout."

The final pursuer drove a little more cautiously. My necklace kept humming, telling me that they were still trying to use magic on us. "Do you think they can damage the truck?" I asked. "Was there enough in what you saw of the correspondence course for them to blow out a tire or something like that?"

"Don't worry, I'm shielding the truck." He sounded strained, and I glanced over to see that he was even paler and had beads of sweat on his forehead and upper lip. I didn't think that was because of my driving.

"Do you have the energy for that?"

"Do we have much choice?"

"You could draw on me again."

"Not while you're driving."

"Oh. Right. Give me a second. I may have an idea."

I turned back onto the main highway, in the opposite direction from home. We passed the car Jason had pulled over, where he had all the car's occupants spread-eagled against his police cruiser. As we went by the motel on our way out of the other side of town, I held my breath, hoping no more of the junior wizards noticed and joined in the chase, but nobody seemed to be hanging around the motel.

Now was the time to pray for a stroke of good fortune. If I was in a hurry, I never failed to run into a funeral procession or a slow-moving hay hauler on the two-lane road and either have to pull over for the procession or get stuck driving fifteen miles an hour with hay blowing into my face until I reached a safe passing zone. Now, for a change, I wanted to run into one of those things.

"Oh, glory hallelujah," I breathed as we passed the small church on the outskirts of town. A funeral procession had formed, and the motorcycle officer escorting them was about to pull onto the highway to stop traffic. He waved me through with a grin, probably recognizing the truck as belonging to Dean. Then he pulled out onto the road and stopped our pursuer while the hearse, a limousine, and a whole line of cars made their slow, stately way onto the highway and to the cemetery a few miles away. "That should hold them a good ten minutes," I said. It was enough time for me to circle back around the town on farm-to-market roads and get home safely.

Owen slumped in his seat, and my necklace went still. I glanced over at him, and he'd gone a grayish shade of pale. "Are you okay?" I asked.

"I will be. It's draining to sustain that kind of magic around here, even worse than I realized. It's almost like there's nothing there at all right now. I can recharge a bit before tonight, and I don't think we'll have to worry too much about all our would-be wizards having too much force. If they haven't learned good control, they'll be burned out with one or two spells. In fact, the ones who were using magic while following us will probably be useless tonight."

The next time I glanced over at him, he was sound asleep, his head resting on the window. I tried to be careful about hitting bumps or taking turns too fast the rest of the way home.

I had to wake him up when I parked behind our house. He already looked a little better, but he was still pale. Mom noticed that the second he set foot in the kitchen. "Are you okay?" she asked, taking him by the arm.

"I think his allergies must be acting up," I said. Fortunately, Mom didn't question me.

"I'll make you some soup," she said. "I may even have some homemade chicken soup from last winter in the freezer. It won't take too long to heat it up. You just sit right down. Katie, you get him some juice."

She went off to dig around in the deep freeze in the laundry room, and I poured Owen a tall glass of orange juice. I figured he needed the sugar as much as he needed the vitamins. I noticed Granny's bottle of potion hidden in the back of the refrigerator, and I added a splash or two of that to the juice. The earlier dose she must have given him hadn't killed him yet, and there was always the chance it might help. Soon, he was being stuffed with soup, cheese and crackers, fruit salad, and cake for dessert. By the time he insisted he couldn't eat another bite, he looked much better. He still appeared tired, but his color was healthier. Mom didn't argue with him at all when he said he wanted to lie down for a while.

I could have used a nap myself, but I hadn't drained myself of power and I was afraid to have no one on the lookout when we had gangs of rogue wizards out hunting for Owen. I shocked Mom by volunteering to do the dishes after lunch. It wasn't because I was feeling particularly helpful, but rather because the kitchen window gave me a good view of the driveway.

While I washed, Mom fluttered around putting away the banquet's worth of food she'd taken out in her efforts to feed Owen. "Are you sure he's okay?" she asked. "Maybe he should see a doctor."

"He's fine. I just don't think he's sleeping well in a strange place, and then with the allergies on top of that it's leaving him a little run-down. Not to mention he was overdue for a vacation, so he has a lot of rest to catch up on."

"Well, I hate for him to get here, and then spend the whole time sick."

"He hasn't. He's just been a little tired a couple of times. You can quit worrying about him."

"Goodness knows, I have enough to worry about. Everyone's acting so strange lately, even you. But I suppose love makes you act funny, doesn't it?" she asked with a wink. "Speaking of which, I really think you ought to put in more effort. He's a nice boy, and very good-looking. Maybe you should wear more lipstick and do your face up a bit. I have some samples." When she wasn't busy meddling in everyone else's business and running the town through committees, she sold makeup through home parties and personal visits and never stopped trying to do makeovers on me.

"Mom, I'm fine the way I am. He likes the natural look. He's said he doesn't like women wearing a lot of makeup." Well, I was sure he would, if someone asked him.

"Just a little maybe? The spring collection had some nice, natural-looking colors."

"Mom!" I knew my voice had taken on an annoying teenage whine, so I tried again, this time sounding more like an adult, I hoped. "It's not me. Really. I think it might scare him if I suddenly looked like a Miss America contestant."

"Well, suit yourself. But you know, you haven't had much success before, so it could be time to change your ways." I couldn't respond to that without getting angry, so I chose to ignore it. She was still muttering under her breath as she went back to clearing off the kitchen table. The ring of the telephone interrupted her muttering. She answered, then handed me the phone. "It's Dean. He wants to talk to you. There must be something going on at the store."

We didn't have anything as fancy as a cordless telephone in the house. We'd only upgraded to push-button phones instead of rotary dials a few years ago when so many services started requiring touch-tone. That meant it was almost impossible to get away from Mom to talk on the phone. I was stuck talking on the kitchen phone, right in front of her. "Hi, Dean, what's up?" I said when I took the phone.

"The odds are a little more in our favor for tonight," he said.

"Why, what happened?"

"Well, three of them left in a hurry, totally freaked out. It seems they got a look at Sam and are now less sure they want to be mixed up in this. Then three more got arrested. I guess there was a traffic violation. Jason pulled them over, and then he found some contraband in their car—drugs of some type. I have a feeling it was herbs for potions instead of actual dope, but by the time they verify that, our fight should be over."

"That's good to hear," I said, trying to keep my voice neutral for Mom's benefit. "I'm glad that's been taken care of."

He laughed. "Let me guess, Mom is hovering and listening."

"Exactly."

"I thought you two were just supposed to raise some interest, not make that big a splash. They're all in awe of how powerful this wizard must be to have eluded them like that. But be honest, wasn't a lot of that due to your driving?"

"Maybe. I guess I'm not totally useless."

"Who'd have guessed, my little sister comes out ahead in a car chase."

"Thanks for the report. I'll see you later."

The moment I hung up the phone, Mom pounced. "Wasn't it sweet of Dean to check on you like that?"

"Yeah, it was really swell of him." I could tell she was dying to know what Dean had told me, but the phone rang again before I had a chance to make something up. I was closest, so I answered.

It was Nita. *"Help!"* she said. "I still don't have housekeeping help, and these people are animals. I've had a bunch check out already, but there are still too many here. Can you come do a few rooms for me? Pretty please, and I'll love you forever. I'll even buy lunch next time."

I wasn't sure that going to the motel in the truck the would-be wizards had been chasing was such a good idea, but the chance to spy on them was nearly irresistible. "I'll be right over." I hung up the phone and told Mom, "Nita needs housekeeping help, so I'm going over there. Can I borrow your car? I had a little trouble starting the truck earlier today."

The truck was unreliable enough that Mom didn't question me and just handed over her keys, which had the added benefit of ensuring that she wouldn't be wandering the town while the wizards were on the loose. I went upstairs to change shirts and do something different with my hair so I wouldn't be so obviously recognized as the driver of the truck they'd been pursuing. A Cobb Comets baseball cap with my ponytail pulled through the back worked wonders.

While I drove to the motel in Mom's car, I tried to think of ways to get rid of even more of our visiting wizards. I recognized one of the cars in the motel parking lot from the chase. Most of the spots were still empty, so the gangs must have been roving the streets still. As I made the rounds, I lit the magical candles in each room to get more of that jarring skewed spell into the air. I wasn't sure how much good that would do, but I figured every little bit would help. It sounded like we'd already lost a few wizards to headaches caused by the candles.

The guys who'd been in the car chase were in their room, and I held my breath as I went in with a pile of towels. As I'd expected, they barely looked at me. "I was wondering when housekeeping would finally show up," one of them said. I made sure to make a note of which one he was so I could tell Owen to give him a special blast.

"We're full, so it takes longer," I said, keeping my head down so my hat brim covered my face. "Now, would you like me to change your sheets or just make the bed?" That was my subtle way of saying that I couldn't do much about the bed while they were lying on it.

"Nah, don't worry about it. Just clean the bathroom and leave the towels."

On my way to the bathroom, I paused by the dresser and moved the candle behind a stack of pizza boxes, then lit it. The bathroom was enough to make me wish I had access to magical cleaning spells. I had three brothers, so you'd think I'd be used to what guys could do to a bathroom, but this was something else. I was really going to make Owen give them the full treatment. It was a good thing I had gloves. By the time I'd finished clearing out their science experiments and returned to the main room, they were all holding their heads and moaning. I had to suppress a smug smirk.

"Who'd have thought that doing magic was such hard work?" One of them said. "I'm so drained, and my head is killing me."

"Ssshhh!" another one said with a gesture in my direction.

"Oh, she probably doesn't even speak English."

Idiots, I thought, *never mind that I talked to you in English.* If I hadn't been worried that the candle would burn down and possibly start a fire in the room, which would be bad for Nita's family, I'd have left it burning. Instead, I blew it out as I passed, and the jerks never even noticed. I hoped I could sic a few pixies on them.

I finally got around to Idris's room. I didn't see his rental car anywhere nearby, but then all rental cars looked alike to me. At any rate, the parking spaces in front of room twenty-five were empty, so it looked like this would be a good chance to search his room thoroughly in his absence. I tapped on the door and said, "Housekeeping," then prepared to use my master key, but the door opened just before I got the key in the lock, and I was face to face with Phelan Idris, on my own and unguarded by anyone magical, as far as I could tell.

Nineteen

I kept my head down and held my breath, waiting for Idris to recognize me. But my nonmagical invisibility spell from being the "help" worked, and he just turned away from me after opening the door. "About time," he said. "I need new towels."

I hesitated. While his back was turned, I had the perfect opportunity to make a run for it. He could live without clean towels, and being alone in a motel room with Phelan Idris was very high on my list of experiences I could live without, so me running away was a win-win scenario. On the other hand, he hadn't recognized me, and this was the best chance we'd have to see what he was up to. There was no telling what I could discover from being in his motel room with him when his guard was down. Plus, it wasn't like he could use magic on me, and I had a feeling I'd come out ahead in a physical fight, thanks to my brothers teaching me a few dirty tricks. I took a deep breath and crossed the threshold, even as a little voice in the back of my head warned me that this probably wasn't the brightest thing I'd ever done.

His room wasn't quite as messy as some of the other rooms had been. It merely had a high level of clutter and an odd smell that wasn't stale pizza or dirty socks. Someone had been brewing potions in the bathtub, I suspected.

I put on the heaviest hick accent I could manage and lowered my voice to whiskey-and-cigarette tones. "Y'all have got us busier than a one-legged man in a butt-kicking contest," I said as I took some cleaning supplies with me back to the bathroom. I saw the magical candle on the dresser as I passed, but I figured trying to light it in front of him was too risky. He was an idiot in a lot of areas, but he did know his magic and he was likely to recognize it.

His bathroom wasn't frat-house filthy, but he'd definitely been up to something other than personal grooming in there. The towels and washcloths were a funny color, and they had a pungent smell. I dumped all the towels and washcloths into a plastic garbage bag to take to Owen for analysis. The chemical properties of potions could affect me even if the magic didn't, so I kept my rubber gloves on while I cleaned the sink and bathtub.

I couldn't resist looking at the toiletries spread out on the bathroom counter. It appeared that Idris was a devoted Rogaine user. He also wore the brand of body spray that was featured in the really annoying commercials where women lost control around men who wore it. His personal scent was "Player," which nearly sent me into uncontrollable giggles.

If he'd been brewing potions, he had to be up to something, and I needed to figure out what it was while I was in his room. I tried watching him out of the corner of my eye as I brought the bag of used towels out of the bathroom and stashed it on the edge of the housekeeping cart. Then I grabbed a stack of clean towels and headed back into the room.

He had papers spread over the bed and table, along with a bunch of what looked like necklaces. The closer I got to the table where the necklaces were, the more my own magical necklace vibrated. I immediately tripped on the carpet and sent my armload of towels flying around the room, letting a couple land on the bed and one land on the table.

"Oopsie!" I said, remembering to keep my voice low and my accent heavy. "That ol' rug just reached up and grabbed me." As I gathered towels, I made sure that I got one of the necklaces in the fold of a hand towel. "Now I guess I'd better get you some really fresh towels that haven't been all over the floor." I carried those towels back outside, slipping the necklace—which turned out to be a cheap Texas souvenir, the kind you can buy at the cash register at gas station convenience stores—into my pocket as I did so.

Idris fidgeted furiously while clenching his jaw as I carried yet another stack of towels to the bathroom and took my time arranging them. I whistled cheerily to myself while I worked, wandering in and out of the room to get a feather duster, which I used liberally all over the room, and then the vacuum cleaner. The feather duster was good at knocking things down so I could get a better look at them as I set them right—always just before Idris could get to me to keep me from touching them. With the vacuum cleaner cord I managed to wipe out everything he had spread out on the bed. A few pages of parchment found their way into the pocket of my apron while Idris sputtered and I apologized heartily.

"You have got to be the worst hotel maid ever!" he blurted after I toppled a pile of books.

That was my cue to burst into sobs. "Oh, please don't tell my boss. I need this job. I got three kids at home, and their daddy took off months ago. He was a no-account hard drinker who barely kept a job more than a week, but we needed what pay he did bring in. If I get fired here, my kids'll starve." I sniffled and ran a sleeve across my nose. "I'll just get out of your way now. Have a nice day, sir. No need to tip me, since I caused you so much trouble."

I'd almost made it to the door when he called out, "Hey, wait a second!" and caught me by the arm. I kept my head down and hoped he'd do something uncharacteristic like apologize, but instead he pulled the baseball cap off my head. It got tangled in my ponytail, so it didn't quite work as a dramatic moment of revelation, but it was enough to show my face. "You!" he shouted. "What are you doing here, spying on me?"

I drew myself up to my full height, jerked my arm out of his grasp, and put a hand on my hip in an indignant posture. "You were the one who invited me in. Didn't you recognize me? It's not like I'm in disguise." I gestured at my work clothes and set my baseball cap back on top of my head. "I really do work here. My friend's family owns this motel, and I'm doing her a favor since you and your gang of merry men scared off the housekeeping staff. Now, if you'll excuse me, I have work to do."

I almost made it to the door before it slammed shut on its own and he stepped in front of me. He couldn't use magic directly on me, but it looked like he could use magic on other things that could affect me. I should have thought of that sooner, but now wasn't the time for reevaluating this plan. While he guarded the door, I turned and ran for the bathroom. That took him by surprise, so it was a few seconds before he realized I was running away from him instead of trying to get past him. His hesitation gave me just enough time to be armed when he got to the bathroom.

I hit him right in the eyes with a big burst of "Player" the moment he showed his face in the bathroom doorway, then while he was still rubbing his eyes and fumbling blindly, I dropped to my hands and knees and crawled past him back into the main part of the room. Then I got back to my feet and sprinted for the door, hoping he hadn't used a spell to seal it shut. Fortunately, it did open, but before I could get out, the smell of "Player" hit me, meaning Idris wasn't far behind. He grabbed my wrist, pulling me back into the room. I backed away from him as much as I could with my wrist still in his grasp, but instead of pulling me back, he moved with me until I hit the wall, then he kept moving forward. The smell of his body spray was strong enough in that proximity to make my eyes water.

"I don't think I'll have to worry too much about Owen anymore," he said in a pleasant, conversational tone that was more menacing than a growl, "considering I've got you now, and we both know what he's willing to do to keep you safe."

That made me more angry than scared. I'd given up the best relationship I'd ever had, left the best job I'd ever had, and exiled myself to the middle of nowhere in order to avoid exactly this situation, and here I'd walked right into it. I tried edging away from Idris sideways, not only because the thought of his body against mine was so repulsive to me, but mostly because if he got close enough, he'd find all of his stuff that I'd stashed in my pockets and in the pockets of my housekeeping apron. Priority one was getting away. Priority two was getting away with all the things I'd found in his room.

He kept coming after me, giving me just enough leeway to move but never releasing his grasp. Then he made the mistake of getting too close to me at just the right angle, and that gave me the opening I was looking for. A well-placed knee to a sensitive spot made him release my wrist as he grabbed at himself, then while he was still doubled over, I darted out of the room, grabbed the housekeeping cart, and nearly ran into Sam.

"You okay, doll? You took an awful long time in there."

"I'm fine. Idris may not father children, though."

"Sweetheart, you've done the world a favor." Idris then came limping out of the room after me. I pushed the cart ahead of me and ran, letting Sam deal with him. I hadn't realized how fierce gargoyles could be. He gave a hissing roar and spread his wings to their fullest. Idris flinched, but he didn't run.

The door of the next room opened, and the jerks I'd seen earlier staggered out, clutching their heads, coughing, and choking, only to find themselves facing a very pissed-off Sam. They all screamed at the top of their lungs and took off running across the parking lot. There went three more from their side, I noted.

The commotion drew Nita out of the office, hefting a baseball bat. "What's going on?" she asked.

"No wonder your housekeeping staff quit," I said, then pointed at Idris. "This—this—this person just made a pass at me, and not a welcome one either."

"She assaulted me!" he said, still not standing completely upright.

"In self-defense. I'm not sure what he'd have done to me. He had me by the wrist and wouldn't let me go." I held out my arm to Nita.

As soon as she saw the red mark circling my wrist, she raised her bat at Idris, who flinched even more than he had at Sam in attack mode. "I want you out of here, now! No one treats my workers—or my friends—that way. I don't care how big a rock star you are!" From my spot next to Nita, I stuck my tongue out at Idris, who looked confused at the rock star reference. Sam was practically rolling on the ground in mirth, safely invisible from Nita, I assumed. I had to admit, it was a pretty good show.

This was a big test for Idris. He probably could have gone after Nita—if Sam let him—but using magic on the nonmagical in a way they might notice was strictly forbidden. If he tried to zap her with magic, then he really would have broken with the legitimate magical world. Apparently, though, he hadn't yet gone so far as to be willing to do that. "Let me get my stuff," he said, but she waved her bat again. "Okay, I'll, uh, come back later when things are calmer." Then he ran for the rental car that I now noticed was parked at the other end of the motel.

"Sorry about that," Nita said. "These guys have been jerks since they got here. I'll tell Dad and Ramesh about it so they can take care of them tonight."

"No problem. Thanks for coming to my rescue."

"So much for the Rock and Roll Motel idea," she said with a shrug. "I don't think they'll be famous enough for it to pay off, anyway."

While she went back to the office, I put the housekeeping cart away, except for the sack of tainted towels, which I threw into the trunk of Mom's car. Then I headed back home to report what I'd found.

Sam must have called ahead to Owen, for when I pulled into the drive-way and parked behind the house, a worried-looking Owen was there waiting for me. He took me by the shoulders and asked, "Are you okay?" It would have been nice if he'd taken that maybe one step further and actually hugged—or even kissed—me, but the fact that Dean and Teddy were there with him probably restrained him some.

"I'm fine. I was mostly putting on a show to get Idris in trouble. He's the one who'll be needing an ice pack. But I did bring you some presents."

He frowned in confusion. "Presents?"

I pulled the necklace from the pocket of my jeans. "Well, there's this. He had a bunch of these in his room, and they don't strike me as his usual style. They felt like magic, so I swiped one. It also looked like he'd been making potions in the bathtub, and it seemed like he cleaned up after himself with the room's towels, which I have for you in the trunk if you want to analyze them. Then there were some papers—"

"How many of these did he have?" Owen cut me off. He held the necklace in his hand, staring at it in horror.

"I didn't count them, but there were a bunch."

"No wonder I got so tired this afternoon. He must have been tying up every magical circuit in the area to make these. It also explains how he was able to magically teleport earlier, if he already had one."

"What is it?"

"He's turned this into a power magnet. It draws in available power and directs it to the user. It would have the effect of making the user more powerful while limiting access to power for everyone else around. And you said he had a bunch?"

"Yeah, probably enough for every member in his group. He was going to cheat!"

"This is bad. I'm not sure we can fight this."

"But he doesn't have them right now. Nita kicked him out of the motel, and she wouldn't let him get his stuff. He'll be back tonight, I'm sure, but we may be able to get to them before then. Remember, I have a key to his room." I turned to Teddy and said, "Go to the motel and grab every one of these that you see. The key to his room is in the drawer of my nightstand. Oh, and Nita may still be watching his room."

"I'll just tell her you dropped something when he attacked you and I came back to get it." He ran off to the house.

"I suspect I know what's on those towels, but it wouldn't hurt to verify," Owen said, walking around to the trunk of the car. I unlocked the trunk, and he opened the plastic bag and took a whiff. "Yeah, this was the potion that gave the amulets the power. We've got to make sure they don't have them."

Teddy came running out of the house, waving the motel key, and got into his truck. We watched him go, then Owen handed the necklace I'd given him to Dean. "You should have this, since you'll be in the middle of them. This should make any protective spell you do more powerful than almost anything they could throw against you. He did teach you at least one protective spell, didn't he?"

Dean nodded. "Lesson three."

Owen shook his head in disgust. "I really need to take a look at his curriculum. It's not what I'd recommend." Then he looked up at Dean. "You'd better go. Be careful, and try to warn me if anything else odd comes up."

As we watched Dean leave, Owen said, "I think he'll be okay. Not just tonight, but in general. We scared him straight on the magic front, and I think having the magic might make him more motivated in other areas. It'll force him to be more disciplined. Do you think you can distract your mother?"

The abrupt change in subject made me blink. "What?"

"We need to leave well before sunset, and I need to get some supplies out to the car, but I can't hide anything from your mother magically."

"I'll see what I can do."

Mom was busy in the kitchen when we went back inside the house. "Mmm, something smells good," I said. "What's for dinner? I'm starving."

"I've got a pot roast cooking. It'll be another hour before we're ready to eat, but don't go snacking and spoiling your appetite."

"Let me get cleaned up from working at the motel and I'll give you a hand." Owen followed me into the living room, where I headed for the front door. "We never use this door," I whispered, "but it should be a good way of sneaking in and out rather than going through the kitchen." I tugged at it without much luck, but he waved a hand and it opened easily for him. Then we went up to my room. I took off my baseball cap and went to the bathroom to wash my hands while he got busy with the magical case under my bed. I left him upstairs working as I went down to the kitchen.

"You can peel those carrots and potatoes," Mom said, gesturing with a meat fork from the stove, where she tended the roast. I sat at the kitchen table and went to work. Mom immediately took advantage of the opportunity to have me as a captive audience. "I hope you two have plans for this evening. You should get out and have fun. I can't believe you've spent so much of his visit working or hanging out at home."

"We are going out tonight, right after dinner."

"I'm glad to hear it. And I hope that's not what you're planning to wear. That boy came all the way from New York to see you, and you go around dressed like a farmhand."

"I'll change clothes before we go out. I just wore this to clean at the motel."

"And put on some makeup, too. I've got a new lipstick shade that should look good on you." She wiped her hands on a towel and turned as though to go get it, just as I looked up to see Owen coming down the stairs with his backpack and an armload of other supplies.

"You don't have to get it now," I hurried to say. "I'm going to take a shower before dinner. I'll put on makeup then." I held my breath, hoping she wouldn't insist on getting the lipstick now while she had a free moment. Owen had just reached the bottom of the stairs. Apparently, he'd used Granny's stair-silencing trick because I hadn't heard the telltale squeak.

The back door opened, and Granny came barreling into the kitchen. "Anything good for dinner tonight?" she asked.

That distracted Mom well enough that she didn't notice the sound of the front door opening and closing. "We're having pot roast, and you're welcome, as always, Mama," she said.

Granny caught my eye and winked. "I brought some tea," she said. "I think Owen might like it. Where is he?"

"He's resting, I'm sure," Mom said. "He hasn't been feeling well."

"That's why I brought the tea, to make him feel better." She winked at me again and headed out of the kitchen. "I'd better go bring some to him."

She was in on the secret, but I didn't trust her not to go blabbing it to everyone, so I stood up and got in her way. "That's okay, Granny. I'm sure he'll be down in a little while. Now, why don't you help me peel these carrots? That way I'll have time to go clean up and look nice before dinner."

"Oh, that reminds me," Mom said, "I was going to get that lipstick for you. Mama, can you watch the roast and do those vegetables? Katie's going out with Owen tonight, and I'd like her to look nice, for a change."

"I think he likes her fine the way she is," Granny muttered.

I figured this was the safest window of opportunity while Owen was outside, so I hustled Mom out to the living room and then up the stairs to her bedroom, where she kept her makeup samples. Mom jumped when I shut the bedroom door behind us. "I want to surprise him," I said.

"Oh, good point!" she said with a laugh. "Now, sit here." She patted the end of the bed, and then I had to endure her smearing and brushing stuff on my face. "See, you need to highlight your eyes more, and then some blush makes you look fresher and more alive." She dug in her case for a tiny tube of lipstick. "I think Rose Blossom is the best shade for you. It's pretty natural. Now, don't you look nicer?" She waved toward my reflection in her dresser mirror with a flourish.

I cringed at the look but forced a smile. "It's great. Now I'd better go help Granny peel those potatoes."

When we got downstairs, Owen was sitting at the table with Granny, who was pouring him a cup of tea. His eyes went wide when he saw my painted face, and then they went wider when he tasted the first sip of tea. Then he frowned thoughtfully and forced himself to drink the whole cup. I took that to mean he thought it might be beneficial.

Granny took off immediately after dinner. Owen and I headed out next, after Mom approved of my attire, hair, and makeup. At least I'd look good, whatever happened in the battle. When we got into town, Owen parked in the public lot behind the square, then we walked over to the park where we would make our last stand. The same creek where we'd met the local magical creatures the night before ran along the back of the park, with a steep slope leading to the water. A walking path led from the park to follow alongside the creek all the way through town. A small gazebo stood in the middle of the park's open space, and trees rimmed the park's perimeter, sheltering it from public view. In short, it was the perfect place for a romantic picnic. Or a magical battle.

Owen opened his backpack and spread its contents out on top of one of the park's picnic tables, then went about warding the sides of the park to keep out innocent bystanders and keep in any wizards we happened to trap. After he was done with that, he said, "We'd probably better summon our friends to give them time to get here." He took my hand to help me down from the table, then we walked hand in hand toward the creek. I wasn't sure if he meant to summon our friends the same way he had the night before, but I trembled in anticipation. I was sure he could feel it from holding my hand, and even if he didn't feel me shaking, he had to notice how clammy my hand got.

If he noticed, though, he didn't let on. We walked silently to the path that led down to the water's edge, where I waited for him to do something incredibly disappointing like putting his fingers to his lips and giving a sharp whistle or chanting a summoning spell. Instead he turned pink and stepped toward me. "You, ah, um, remember how this worked last night?"

I faked a dramatic sigh. "If I have to suffer for the sake of our cause, well, I guess that's just my cross to bear."

He surprised me by grinning in reply. "I have to admit, it's one of the least unpleasant things I've had to do in the line of duty." I wanted to ask him why, if it was so not unpleasant, he hadn't done it when it wasn't in the line of duty since he'd been here, but he was already kissing me and I forgot about saying anything.

Our first kiss had been under an enchantment. Our second had been in the middle of the company Christmas party. We'd had a few more since then, but not recently, before last night. I wasn't sure if it was because of the long drought or because of the magic in the air, but this was one of the better ones. When we finally separated, I whispered, "You know, that's good for more than just summoning nature spirits."

I didn't get to hear his response, for a burbling voice near our feet said, "Geez, use a bullhorn, why don't you? We said we'd be here." I turned to see the naiad from the night before clinging to the creek bank.

"Thank you for coming," Owen said. "I'll lead our enemies to you, and then you and your people should give them a good scare. I don't want anyone harmed permanently, though. I just want them never to want to have anything to do with magic ever again."

"We're looking forward to it," the naiad said. "The crew is on their way and should be here by sundown."

"Is anyone there?" a voice called from above. It was Rod. Owen released my hand as we made our way up the path to the park. Merlin was with him.

"Will we have our allies?" Merlin asked.

"They're on their way," Owen said. "I've just spoken to the naiad who's been dealing with us."

"Excellent. It appears that we're ready."

Granny arrived then, carrying a bottle with a scarlet thread wrapped around its neck. Teddy followed not too far behind, breathing hard in his effort to keep up with her. He carried a pillowcase with something in it.

Granny went right up to Merlin. "I trapped a sprite a few years back," she said, holding up the bottle. "It'll be mad when I let it go, so I'm thinking I throw the bottle into the midst of all them naughty boys and see what happens."

I cringed as Rod visibly stifled a laugh, but Merlin bowed gallantly to her. "Thank you for your efforts, good lady. I am certain that will be helpful."

She brandished her cane. "And if that doesn't work, I can swat a few backsides."

I leaned over to whisper to Owen, "A sprite?" In my experience, "sprite" was the term modern male fairies preferred, since there was a stigma involving men and the word "fairy."

"A legendary wild creature," he whispered in response. "Not the kind you're used to. Some don't even think they exist. They're right out of folklore and get the blame for all kinds of things. I'm curious to see what she really has in there."

"If she's got anything in there."

"If she caught a sprite, it could help us." He raised his voice to a more normal speaking level and addressed Teddy. "Did you find the things you were looking for in his room?"

Teddy raised the pillowcase. "Right here. There were eighteen of them. I got out of the room not too long before he came back and packed all his stuff away. There was a lot of yelling and cursing about having been robbed, let me tell you. That brought out Ramesh and his shotgun, so Idris didn't bother lodging a formal complaint."

"What is it?" Rod asked.

Owen took the pillowcase from Teddy and drew out one of the necklaces. "This." He tossed it to Rod, who immediately raised both eyebrows.

"You've got to be kidding. It's a good thing we got our hands on these. We'd have been toast if they'd been armed like this."

Merlin leaned over Rod's hand to study the necklace. "Very interesting work, but rather unorthodox." He straightened and pinned Owen with a sharp look, then asked, "What did you plan to do with them?"

"I gave one to Dean so he'd be armed while he's in the middle of them. I hope we can count on him not to abuse it. Otherwise, my main concern was that they not have them. This magic is too dark-tinged for me to feel comfortable using it." Suddenly, he smiled. "But I do have an idea."

He took off toward the creek, carrying the pillowcase. The rest of us hurried to follow him. Merlin lagged behind, escorting Granny. The naiad greeted us, not sounding too thrilled to see us. "I said we were coming. Keep your shorts on."

"I have a gift for you," Owen said, upending the pillowcase on the water's edge. "These will draw power to you and your people. I ask you not to use them too much tonight because the rest of us will need resources, but in the future, they should allow your people to control the magical elements in this area. You shouldn't face more problems with outsiders draining the power lines."

She pulled herself halfway out of the water and picked up one of the necklaces. Her eyes went wide as she held it. "This is a generous gift," she said. "We are in your debt." She turned her head and made a high-pitched sound that reminded me of dolphins. Soon, we were surrounded by pinpricks of light as all the magical creatures converged. "We will fight at your side tonight." Then she batted her eyes at Owen and lifted her seaweedy hair off her neck, completely baring her torso. "Now, if you'd be so kind as to help me put one on . . ."

He obliged, blushing slightly and avoiding looking at me. He needn't have been embarrassed on my account. I didn't feel particularly threatened by a chick who lived in the water, unless she pulled some Little Mermaid stunt to be with him. The cheap metal Lone Star necklace looked out of place on her unearthly form, and I tried not to wish that it turned her skin green.

Sam swooped in then and said, "Looks like the party's about to begin over at the courthouse. And funny, the gang's a lot smaller than it was." If he'd had feathers, he would have preened, he looked so proud.

"I guess I'll go be the bait," Owen said. "I'll need Katie with me. The rest of you, stand by."

Merlin stepped up in front of Owen, staring him in the eye. Most of the time, Merlin seemed like a kindly, cheerful older gentleman, the sort you could imagine playing Santa at the children's hospital every Christmas. But every so often, without saying or doing anything in particular, there was something about him that made you well aware that he was a legendary sorcerer from more than a thousand years ago. This was one of those times, and I could tell from the way Owen stood that he sensed that, too. "I will be able to rely on you in this?" Merlin asked him.

"Yes, sir."

"You remember what your priority is, and that your personal concerns have to be secondary?"

Owen glanced ever so slightly at me, then said, "Yes, I do." I couldn't help but gulp. Merlin was basically reminding him that he was supposed to catch the bad guy instead of rescuing me, and while I was in favor of that in theory, it made it kind of suck to be me.

"Very well, then." Merlin then stepped aside, and Owen moved to catch up with me.

When we reached the courthouse square, he took my hand. "Do you see anything?"

"Yeah, the League of Extraordinary Dolts is gathered around the Confederate War Veterans statue, with the chief dolt doing his Hitler oratorical impression, complete with spittle. Why, you don't see it?"

He shook his head. "He must be filtering against me."

"I guess that goes with the territory of being public enemy number one."

We moved closer so I could hear what was going on. I relayed the gist of it to Owen, feeling like one of those simultaneous translators at the United Nations must in having to listen and talk at the same time.

"He sounds pretty frantic," I said. "He's yelling at them for failing him because they weren't able to catch you. They're not fit to call themselves wizards, but at least they're better than all those who were even weaker and ran away in fright."

Idris worked himself up into a good fever pitch, then yelled, "I'm finished with all of you if you don't catch that wizard tonight."

I passed that on to Owen, who said, "That sounds like my cue." I led him to where I was sure he'd be visible even if he couldn't see them. He cleared his throat, then said in a loud, clear voice, "If you want me so badly, Phelan, why don't you get me yourself instead of sending your lackeys after me?"

Twenty

It took a couple of seconds for them to react. First, their heads turned in our general direction. Their eyes widened, and they blinked, then frowned, as though they were comparing Owen in real life to the picture Idris had shown them. The ones who'd actually seen him in person earlier in the day during the car chase had already left town, so there wasn't anyone in the group who could verify Owen's identity. In all fairness, he was a little shorter in real life than you might imagine he would be, based on his picture.

"There he is! Get him!" Idris shouted, pointing at Owen. "None of you will ever be real wizards unless you can capture him and bring him to me."

Owen bent his head to whisper to me, "What's going on?"

"I guess he hasn't dropped the veil," I said. "They're all gawking at you, and Idris is saying they should go get you."

"Ah, thank you." Then he spoke to Idris. "Are you afraid I'll beat you again?" I nudged him to turn a few degrees so he'd actually be facing the person he was addressing. If Idris hadn't been such a jerk, he might have let Owen see what was going on.

"I think I came out ahead last time," Idris said.

I relayed the message to Owen, who replied, "You escaped. I'm not sure I'd call that 'coming out ahead.' Scurrying away like a sewer rat isn't my idea of a victory."

"I like my odds now, since you're more than a bit outnumbered here." I counted eighteen student wizards, not including Dean, plus Idris, which probably meant the odds were in our favor when you considered who the people on our side were. But I wasn't going to tell Idris that. That was part of the surprise.

Idris turned again to his people. "Well, what are you waiting for? The person you're supposed to be catching is right there in front of you. Do I have to draw you a map?"

Moving almost as one, they rose and headed in our direction. At first, it was a few tentative steps forward, but then they gathered momentum and surged toward us. I didn't feel I needed to relay Idris's instruction to Owen. Instead, I tugged on Owen's hand and yelled, "Run." I wasn't sure whether he was able to see the wizards coming at us, but I didn't want to take any chances.

The student wizards ran through the Magic 101 spell book, throwing one thing after another at Owen as we fled. There was enough magic in the air to give me goose bumps. They must have dropped their veil because Owen deflected their spells easily without pointers from me. It helped that they had to say the spells clearly and out loud, sounding like first-graders reading from a primer. That gave Owen plenty of time to have his own counterspell ready in an instant. He'd probably had to practice fending off this kind of attack in the magical equivalent of Cub Scouts.

The wizards behind us shouted in triumph as we ran from the square toward the park. They were sure they had their quarry on the run. I heard Dean's voice cry out, "Follow him!" They didn't need much urging. They were already convinced they were moments away from earning the designation of real wizard for their achievement in capturing their mentor's archenemy. I almost felt sorry for them. They knew no more about what they were messing with than Dean had before we set him straight.

We ran straight for the creek and down the path leading to the shore. When the first of the wizards reached the creek bank path all hell broke loose. The lead naiad rose from the middle of the creek and gave that creepy dolphin call. At her signal, several naiads popped out of the water near the creek bank to grab student wizards by their ankles and pull them into the water, where they sputtered for breath as the naiads dunked them repeatedly. The rest of the students were so freaked out by the naiads that they didn't notice the dryads in the trees above them. Dryads dropped from the trees onto the student wizards below with un-earthly howls. Others pelted the wizards with twigs.

The students behind the first group saw what was happening and tried to turn and run back up the path to the park, but they were blocked on the narrow path by the students who brought up the rear. A big traffic jam formed, which made them easy prey for the pixies, who popped out of the bushes to poke at their ankles and calves with sharp sticks as they giggled in delight.

"I guess we'd better go see how the rest of the fight is going," Owen said.

"Do we have to? This part is pretty fun."

"I want to catch Idris this time, and this is probably my best chance."

"If he even shows up. I didn't see him in the group chasing us."

"I don't think he'll be able to make himself stay away. He's not stu-pid enough to think that this bunch will really do much good. He'll let them tire me out, and then he'll face me himself."

Since the path was still jammed, Owen and I climbed the creek

bank, finding handholds on trees and roots as we made our way upward. We emerged into the park to see a magical battle in full force. The
students who'd been blocked from going down the path to the creek
had been caught by Rod, Merlin, and Sam, who'd all emerged from their
hiding places with Teddy and Granny and were blocking the park's one
unwarded exit so that no one who wanted to run from naiads, dryads,
and pixies could get away. The panicked would-be wizards who no
longer wanted any part of this added to the chaos, getting in the way of
those who were still gung-ho enough to want to catch Owen.

Judging by the guys running in circles, their eyes wild with terror,
and the grin on Rod's face as he stood waving his hands in languid ges-
tures, I got the impression that Rod was sending horrific illusions after
them. Those guys were probably facing things out of their worst night-
mares. Merlin stood calmly by the exit, with Granny at his side, waving
a hand every so often to deflect a spell or to block someone from getting
away. Merlin's attention seemed to be more on Owen than on the fight
itself. I got the feeling this was some huge test that would determine
Owen's future with the company after his crazy AWOL stunt.

At the moment, though, Idris wasn't there, and the pixies were
keeping the fight away from Owen, which I hoped would help him save
his strength for when it would really be needed. So far, the battle was
going our way, with us having the advantage on land and in the water.
We even had our own air force. Sam swooped down from the sky to
buzz the battling wizards. He had a laughing pixie riding his back. The
pixie blasted the students' backsides with magical sparks, making them
leap into the air as each blast of sparks hit them. Meanwhile, more pixies swarmed the ground, getting underfoot and tripping people left and
right. Anyone who fell down was in big trouble. He might find his
shoelaces tied together or his jeans unbuttoned so that when he tried to
stand, his pants would fall down and then he'd fall over so the pixies
could get him for more mischief.

Then one of the students saw Owen and yelled, "Hey, there he is!"

Soon, we had all the students who weren't currently entangled with a magical creature, running from an illusion, or in Sam's strafing path after us. Owen sent a fireball into the crowd, dispersing them like a bunch of bowling pins hit by a well-placed ball. "Did you novices really think you could take me on?" he shouted. He sounded awfully intimidating, unless you knew he was a total sweetheart who was almost meek about doing magic, like he didn't want to be noticed.

One of the student wizards sent his own fireball flying back at Owen. This ball was much smaller and dimmer than Owen's had been, and it flickered in and out. Owen reached up and snagged it like he was catching a pop fly, then he held it hovering above his hand. As he held it, it grew bigger and brighter. Then with a flick of his wrist, he tossed it back at the wizard who'd formed it. "Nice try," Owen said as the fireball hit its target and the student fell over. When he hit the ground, a trio of pixies gleefully pounced.

While Owen fought, I looked around for any sign of Idris. I could imagine him being coward enough to make other people fight his battles, but I couldn't imagine him not being there for the fight at all. Then again, this was Idris we were talking about. He had the attention span of a gnat and could very well have been sidetracked by something shiny on the way from the courthouse square to the park. If a pretty girl had walked by, we might not see him for hours, so long as she wasn't repelled by his body spray or by his personality. For all I knew, he was off at the Dairy Queen having a banana split and wouldn't remember that there was a fight going on until he finished.

I felt a surge of magic coming toward me and whirled to see what it was just as Owen neatly deflected it. He was tiring now, breathing hard, with sweat-dampened hair clinging to his forehead. "Are you okay?" I asked him.

He nodded as he raised his hand and muttered something that sent a student wizard staggering away. "I'm fine. I don't think I'm tiring as much as these guys are."

"Maybe you should have kept one of the necklaces."

"No!" I was surprised at the vehemence of his response. "Dabbling in that level of darkness isn't worth it."

"You gave one to Dean. You weren't going to risk letting him go over to the dark side, were you?"

"Dean isn't me." He pulled me out of the way of an oncoming attacker and then sent that attacker flying to land on his back, where the pixies immediately swarmed him. "The more power you have and the more power you're able to tap into, the more dangerous dark magic is. It's practically harmless for Dean. For me, it's a line I don't dare cross."

Owen was quite possibly one of the nicest guys in the known universe, and he wasn't particularly ambitious about power, so I had a hard time picturing him turning into the magical equivalent of Darth Vader. I had a feeling his foster parents had instilled a healthy fear into him as a preventative measure. Bad magic was dangerous enough that you didn't want to rely on someone's discernment, not when that someone was as powerful as Owen was.

Owen tugged at my sleeve. "I want you to walk through the middle of the fight. It's all magic, so they can't hurt you. I don't think they know about immunes, so they won't understand why they can't affect you. Play it up. See if you can get Ted to do the same thing. They'll think you're the most powerful wizards ever. I want them to feel so outclassed that they're afraid to come near magic again."

Although I knew intellectually that all those flying fireballs and influence spells would have no effect on me, that didn't mean walking out into them was my idea of fun. I took a deep breath, put on a serene expression, and headed into the middle of the action. It took a lot of self-control not to flinch at the things that came flying my way. Instead, I bestowed beatific smiles on the student wizards who waved their hands in my general direction. The expressions on their faces as spells passed harmlessly around me were priceless. I couldn't remember anyone ever looking at me with that kind of awe.

That gave me the confidence to really play it up. Every so often I held out my own hand, as though I was deliberately deflecting something instead of just being unaffected. Once I even stopped and laid my hand on top of the head of a student who seemed to be throwing everything but the kitchen sink at me, to no avail. "Give it up," I said sweetly to him. "Your pitiful magic can't harm the likes of me." He went pale and fell to his knees.

Finally I reached Teddy, who stood near Granny. "What's with the Our Lady of Perpetual Smugness routine?" he asked me.

"They don't seem to know about people who are immune to magic, so Owen thought it would freak them out if they couldn't affect me."

"It seems to have worked."

"Want to play?"

"I might as well. I don't seem to be doing much otherwise. I've warned Merlin and Rod about a couple of things, but they're way ahead of me. Hey, do you think anyone will write stories and songs one day about this epic fight of good against evil?"

"Not unless you feel like doing it. And it's more like good against annoying, which is less epic."

I hung out beside Granny while he stepped into the melee, and I soon saw how I must have looked. He didn't have quite the experience with magical immunity that I did, so it took him a while to stop flinching when it looked like something might hit him. Soon, though, he caught on to how protected he was, and then he started showing off with theatrical motions to supposedly deflect the magic. All those years as dungeon master had finally paid off for him. I would have bet he wished Dean hadn't swiped his old Jedi cloak.

Rod and Granny continued to guard the exit. The terrified reactions of student wizards running back to the battle gave me the impression that Rod had cooked up some impressive illusions. Granny mostly swung her cane and shouted, and I was rather glad I couldn't hear exactly what she was saying. I was sure they were curses of some kind, but whether they were the magical variety wasn't quite clear in the chaos.

As absolute proof that Idris had left out a few crucial facts about magic, some of the students swarmed around Merlin. Compared to Owen's spectacular showboating, Merlin didn't seem to be doing much of anything. If you didn't know he was *the* Merlin, you might have mistaken him for an ordinary old man and very likely our side's weakest link. It would have been one of the dumbest mistakes you ever made.

Four of the student wizards closed in on us. "Hey, Grandpa," one of them said. "Aren't you going to join the fight, or are you just gonna stay here with Grandma and watch?"

"You really don't want him to join in," I muttered, too low for them to hear.

"I'm quite enjoying it as a spectator," Merlin said cheerfully. "This is some of the best entertainment I've had in months, even better than the last movie I saw about that young Harry Potter."

"I guess magic is one of those things that you lose with age, huh, Pops?" another one of the guys said.

I shook my head sadly. *Stupid, stupid, stupid,* I thought. They were such jerks that they didn't deserve a proper warning. Merlin waved a careless hand and the whole group immediately turned into little white rabbits. Their noses twitched furiously in what had to be a panic. Granny didn't help matters by saying, "My gran had an excellent recipe for rabbit stew. I haven't had it in years." She hefted her cane as if to club a couple of rabbits. The rabbits hopped away from the scary woman with the big stick, only to run into Owen's wards, which sent them hopping back to cower and shiver in a circle. Merlin then turned them back into humans, but they stayed right where they were, nearly catatonic with fright. After that, the rest of the student wizards stayed well away from Merlin, which allowed him to resume watching Owen.

I made my way back across the battlefield to Owen's side. This time

I had to pay more attention to where I stepped than to what was flying through the air. A number of the student wizards were on the ground, either utterly exhausted and magically spent or so bombarded by pixies that they couldn't move. The attrition in their forces meant Owen wasn't quite so beleaguered. Now he only had to fight off three guys at a time.

That appeared to be enough, though. It wasn't my imagination; he really was moving more slowly now. It was completely dark, with only moon and starlight illuminating the park, along with the occasional burst of magical light, but I was sure he looked pale. Even his vast resources had to run out after a half hour or so of this kind of activity.

He sent the three attackers flying away from him with an impatient wave of his hand and paused to wipe his forehead with his sleeve as the pixies pounced. Moments later, a few more students joined the fight. These were the more determined ones who hadn't yet been scared off or defeated. I hated that Owen had to face them now, when he was tired. Then again, I supposed they were tired, too.

I took his hand as the students surrounded us. He gave me a nod of thanks, and then our palms grew warm where they met. The extra power allowed him to dispatch those guys easily. He was no longer trying to put on a show. He was merely getting them out of his way as quickly as possible. These guys slumped to the ground, sound asleep. They didn't even stir when the pixies picked through their pockets.

Owen released my hand. "Thanks. That helped."

"Are you sure you're okay?"

"I'm tired, but I don't feel like I'm in any danger."

There was a burst of light and sound from the other side of the park, where Merlin, Rod, and Granny were. It looked like the fighting had intensified over there, but I couldn't see any of the students. Almost all of them were out of the fight by now. Next to me, Owen tensed and took a step back toward the trees. "What is it?" I asked.

He shook his head. "I don't know, but I don't like it." He threw a fireball in the air, and it exploded like a firework, lighting the whole park. "What do you see?" he asked.

A figure was walking through the park. Merlin, Granny, and Rod didn't seem to see it at all. I could, though. It looked like Idris had finally finished his banana split and shown up. "It's Idris," I said.

He walked straight toward us, a smug grin on his face. "You either need to find better students, or they need better teachers," Owen said when I nudged him to let him know that Idris was near.

"Still leaning on the girlfriend, huh, Owen?" Idris said.

"Better than tricking flunkies into doing what I can't," Owen replied. I took his response to mean that Idris had unveiled himself to Owen. "Give it up, why don't you? Your army is out of it, and the power lines here aren't strong enough for you to do much against me."

"Under normal circumstances, maybe. But who said these are normal circumstances?" Idris tugged on a leather thong around his neck and pulled out the necklace Nita had noticed in her photograph. At our look of surprise, he said, "What? You thought I hadn't already made one for myself?"

Twenty-One

I should have anticipated he'd do something like that. Of course Idris would have made one for himself first and kept it on, but I wasn't sure what we could have done about it, short of having Teddy strip him of anything that looked suspicious while Ramesh covered him with his shotgun and Nita held her baseball bat over his head. I hadn't even known that there were magical magnifiers back when I first saw that photo of Idris, though that did explain how he'd been able to teleport. I supposed we could have had a contingency plan in place, but that was all twenty-twenty hindsight when a fresh Idris faced us, wearing that necklace, and Owen was so visibly exhausted.

I grabbed Owen's hand and nodded to him. It was just in time as Idris sent a wave of power at us that gave me goose bumps. Our joined hands went white-hot as Owen deflected it, and while Idris had to react to his own spell coming back to him, Owen took a step back, even closer to the trees around the creek bed. I had a feeling he was either getting closer to our allies, or he was getting closer to one of those necklaces.

A wall of magical fire rushed at us, and Owen doused it. Having him draw power from me had been pleasant—even kind of sexy—before, but this bordered on painful, the difference between a nice, hot bath and a tub of scalding water. I also felt the drain of energy. I wasn't sure how much more I could take.

"Are you still relying on your girlfriend to get you out of tight spots?" Idris asked with a sneer. Owen didn't waste his breath replying. Instead, he waved his hand and the earth under Idris's feet shook, forcing him to jump backward.

While they fought, I looked frantically around for our allies. You'd think that the size of the battle they were fighting would have drawn some attention. We should have had spectators by now, but in the fading light of Owen's fireball, I saw the others still clustered around the entrance, watching the student wizards, who were lined up like prisoners. They didn't seem to realize what was going on.

That figured. Idris must have veiled us from the others. That was the only way he'd have been willing to take Owen on. It also explained how he'd reached us in spite of walking right past Rod and Merlin. Teddy might have seen everything, but he didn't know Idris and wouldn't know that Owen might be in trouble.

I was about to yell for help when someone else called out, "Yoo hoo! There you are!" It was an all-too-familiar voice. I cringed reflexively when I turned to see a fairy godmother hovering nearby and shaking her wand at Idris. "You didn't think you could escape from me, did you?" she scolded. It was Ethelinda, who'd nearly driven me batty while she tried to be my fairy godmother. Now she was working on behalf of Idris's sometime girlfriend, but it didn't look like she'd changed much since I'd last seen her. She'd made an attempt at Western wear, with a Dale Evans outfit on top of layers of other mismatched clothes and a tattered cowboy hat on her head with her tarnished tiara clinging precariously to it.

Idris reacted more violently to seeing her than he had to any magic

Owen had thrown at him. "You! What are you doing here?" he shouted, backing away from her with a look of panic in his eyes.

She tittered at him. "Why, keeping an eye on you, of course. A business trip is no excuse for being unfaithful to your one true love."

"I wasn't being unfaithful! I was just talking." His voice went up in pitch, practically whining.

She shook her head sadly. "That's how it usually starts. Just talking." Then she noticed me. "Katie! And Owen, too. It's good to see you're still together. That was one of my better triumphs." She waved her wand in the general direction of our joined hands.

She'd actually done us some good by coming on the scene, for a change. Idris might have been veiling us from our reinforcements, but he wasn't able to hide her, and Merlin, Granny, and Teddy all joined us to see what was going on. Rod stayed by the park entrance, watching the prisoners. The conquered students who'd managed to pick themselves up from the ground but who hadn't yet been officially captured also came toward us, staggering and reeling from exhaustion even as they were drawn by curiosity. Dean was among them, looking a little fresher but acting as tired as the others.

The ground swarmed with pixies, who came to check Ethelinda out and stayed to torment Idris. They untied his shoes and stuffed pebbles in them, then tugged down his socks and stretched out the elastic so they sagged around his ankles. He danced frantically, trying to get rid of them. Acorns and twigs came flying from the trees behind us, hitting Idris with frightening accuracy. Owen released my hand and nudged me away, freeing both hands to get back into the fight while Idris was distracted.

Our human allies reached us then. Teddy couldn't do much, and Granny just waved her cane and her sprite jar, but Merlin knew what he was doing. Idris did a fairly impressive imitation of a whirling dervish as he spun and leapt, trying to counter spells coming at him from both Owen and Merlin at once, along with all the little threats from the pixies at his feet. His necklace may have amplified his power, but it didn't give him the ability to handle multiple threats at the same time.

I was engrossed in watching the fight when someone grabbed me. "Oh, come on," I started to protest before my captor put a hand over my mouth. I tried biting, but couldn't catch anything other than my own lip with my teeth. Then I tried stepping on his feet, but that wasn't very effective when I was wearing sneakers.

"Back down, or she gets it!" my captor called out. I couldn't see who it was, but guessed it had to be one of Idris's students, and probably one of the honor-roll members at that, since he seemed to have figured out that magic didn't work on me. Instead, he used brute force. The feeling of something cold and sharp against my neck told me he was using normal weapons, too. I quit struggling so I didn't accidentally slit my own throat.

The fight came to a screeching halt. The look of devastation on Owen's face when he saw my predicament brought tears to my eyes. I couldn't believe I'd put him in this position again.

Ethelinda was the first person to react audibly. "Oh my! I can't bear to look!" she cried out before vanishing. *Gee, thanks a lot,* I thought. Some good she was.

Idris laughed, sounding almost hysterical. "Wow, you're in a spot, aren't you?" he taunted Owen. "If you want to catch me, it means watching your girlfriend die a horrible death at the hands of . . . who are you, again?" he asked the student holding me.

"McCreary, sir," my captor said.

"McCreary. Good man. You pass." Idris returned his attention to Owen. "If you make any kind of move toward capturing me, the girl gets it—" he mimed a slice across the throat "—from McCreary here. But if you save your girlfriend, you have to let me go, and you'll know you've lost again."

I might have been able to think my way out of a more elaborate trap, but there was absolutely nothing I could do now. It didn't look like anyone else had any better ideas, either. Even the pixies were still, looking to Owen for guidance.

Merlin was the one who stepped forward and addressed Idris solemnly. "Your inability to care about others is more dangerous than any spell you've tried to develop. If that is the way you see the world, all the magic you do will be stained with darkness."

Idris laughed at him. "Nice one, Pops. Since this magic thing doesn't seem to be working out so well for you in this millennium, maybe you could go into writing greeting cards. Now, since no one seems to be willing to shed this little lady's blood, I'm going to walk out of here, and you're going to let me." As he walked past me, he paused and said, "Nothing personal. You just made a really bad choice in boyfriends. Too bad, because you'd be kind of cute if you wore more makeup."

If I hadn't had a knife to my throat, those would have been fighting words. I had to settle for glaring at him. I wasn't the only one glaring. Merlin fixed Owen with a stern stare that clearly told him he would be the one to have to deal with this. If we got through this okay, I had a feeling Owen would never, ever rebel against his boss again. The price was way too high. Then Owen met my eyes with a long gaze that took my breath away and almost made me forget someone was holding a knife to my throat. He looked like he was the one in mortal peril, the anguish was so great. This seemed to be good-bye. I felt like I should say something meaningful. What was that bit from the end of *A Tale of Two Cities*, something about this being a far better thing to do? Or maybe the classic "We'll always have Paris." That would be meaningful between us because we'd talked about *Casablanca* being his favorite movie.

Instead, though, the words that came out of my mouth were, "Say hi to the dragons for me." Those weren't what I'd have normally chosen to be my last words, but the glint that went into his eyes made me suspect they wouldn't be my final words, after all.

Owen said something softly and sternly, and I immediately felt the knife drop away from my throat. And then I felt a pair of arms go around me, not in a threatening hold, but rather in a big hug. "Aww, you're so soft and cuddly," McCreary said in a voice that sounded like he was soon going to be petting me, squeezing me, and calling me George. If the dragons Owen had magically tamed could talk, I imagined this would be what they'd sound like. The moment the knife left my throat, Owen went after Idris.

Something hit me then, a sense of magic that had no effect on me other than to make me shiver, but it made my captor relax his hold on me. I turned away from watching Owen to see Dean readying a fireball. "Get your hands off my sister, you creep," he said. He didn't have to ask twice. I stumbled as the guy released me, but Dean stepped forward to catch me. "Are you okay?" he asked. I nodded, and he said, "I'm glad Owen gave me that necklace. I've never been able to do anything like that before."

Owen and Idris were back locked in combat. Merlin stood nearby, but his attention wasn't on the fight. Instead, he held his hands out, chanting. One by one, the remaining student wizards, including the prisoners, stopped in their tracks, wherever they were, and then slumped to the ground. It looked like he was eliminating the risk of anyone else jumping into the fray with magic or any other assistance. I was totally in favor of that. I moved toward the fight, but Dean held me back, sheltering me in his arms. "Don't risk putting him in that kind of spot again," he said. I knew he was right, but I didn't have to like it. I vowed to find the meanest, sneakiest martial art around and become a master at it. Even if I couldn't do magic, I'd make the next person who tried to use me as a hostage regret it.

The fight wasn't going as well as I would have hoped. With the magical magnifier, Idris was a lot fresher than Owen, which made up for Owen's usual advantages of strength and skill. Owen looked flat-out exhausted, but determined not to give up. "He can't keep going like that," Dean muttered. He released his grasp on me and pulled his necklace off. "Owen, catch!" he yelled.

The necklace sailed through the air, and Owen caught it easily with one hand. He stared at it for a moment, and then I noticed Merlin staring at him. I remembered what Owen had said about the dangers of using magic like that. But didn't desperate circumstances call for desperate measures?

Apparently not. Owen shook his head and tossed the necklace aside. "No, not that way," he said softly, but so clearly that his voice carried across the park. Merlin looked pleased as he continued dealing with students. Owen had apparently passed the test, but he hadn't yet won the fight. A laughing Idris came after him with renewed vigor. Owen retreated, running back toward the creek where he had hope of more help from the nature spirits, but he was too exhausted to run very far or very fast, and when he tripped and fell, he hit the ground and didn't make it up again. Merlin finished dealing with the students and turned to aid Owen, but he was moving slowly and looked exhausted. Merlin was powerful, but he was also very, very old. He raised his hands to fight Idris, but the spell he threw at Idris wasn't enough to be more than an irritant.

I couldn't bear to watch, but I couldn't tear myself away. I looked around for anything that could help Owen and realized that Granny, with her bottle full of sprite, was the only other magical person still standing. "Granny, your sprite!" I called out, hoping this was one of the things she was right about instead of being crazy. She stepped toward Idris, threw her bottle in the air, and swatted it with her cane like she was hitting a baseball for fielding practice. The bottle shattered in midair, the shards falling around Idris. Owen stayed on the ground, scrambling out of the way. I pulled away from Dean and ran to Owen, hauling him to his feet. He wrapped his arm tightly around my waist, almost cutting off my breathing, but I was so glad that both of us were still alive that I didn't mind. With our arms around each other, I helped him back to where Dean stood.

Idris ignored his escaping quarry, he was so busy brushing himself off. At first I thought he might be brushing glass away, but then I realized that the bottle hadn't been empty. Something had been in there, and that something was now free. It was hard to tell what that something was, it was moving so fast, like the cartoon Tasmanian devil, a whirlwind of destruction uttering incoherent snarls of rage and madness. Blood flew, along with bits and pieces of what I assumed were Idris's clothes.

Granny came over to join Owen, Dean, and me. "They don't like being captured, and they take it out on anyone they can as soon as they're free," she said with grim satisfaction. "Besides, being cooped up in a bottle like that is enough to drive anyone crazy. I forgot how long ago it was I caught that thing."

Idris fell to his knees. "I give! Stop it! I surrender!" Merlin said something sharp in a foreign language and snapped his fingers, and the sprite's mayhem ceased as the sprite vanished. Idris was left bloodied, his clothing shredded. He whimpered a little in relief once he realized the sprite was gone. Then he did something I never would have expected: He broke into sobs. "Oh please, you've got to help me. I need your protection. I throw myself on your mercy."

Merlin stepped out of the way before Idris could grab onto his pants leg and cry on his shoes. Then he said sternly to Idris, "So, you surrender yourself to us? You place yourself under our power so that your power becomes our own and cannot be used against us?" There was something about his tone and the precise formality of his words that told me this was a ritual of some sort, possibly even a binding one.

Idris pulled off his necklace and handed it to Merlin, then he clasped his hands together and said, "I surrender myself to you. I place myself under your power so that my power becomes your own and cannot be used against you and yours."

Merlin nodded. "Very well. Now, what is it that you need our protection against?"

"These people I've been working for. I want out. It's going too far. I

280 · Shanna Swendson

was having fun before, doing my own thing, you know, but they're serious. I don't know, it's like they really want to take over the world, or something, and they were using me to get it started. And guess who'd have taken the blame if they got caught or if something went wrong. But I didn't know how to get out. These people would track me down and come after me if I tried to get away. They were like the Firm, you know, only with magic. No one leaves, and all that. I'm in huge trouble for failing. They might even kill me for not raising a proper army. You're the only one who might be able to protect me."

Owen and I came over to stand beside Merlin. "You'll tell us everything you know?" Owen asked.

Idris scooted around on his knees to face Owen. "I don't know much. I only met the moneybags lady in person. I think she's got a boss beyond that, and that's the person calling the shots, but I don't know who that is. I do know I'm scared of him."

"We will protect you in return for whatever assistance you can provide us." Merlin gestured Rod to come join us. "Mr. Gwaltney, will you see to him?"

Rod did something complicated with his fingers, and soon a thread of liquid light twined around Idris's wrists. Then he pulled Idris to his feet and walked him over to where the other prisoners were.

Merlin faced the gathered prisoners, revived them with a snap of his fingers, and said firmly, "It is over. This ends now." His voice had the weight of a millennium of authority, and it seemed to resonate with the prisoners even if they didn't know who he really was.

Owen released his hold on me and stepped forward. "I hope you realize now that what you were playing with is dangerous and not to be used lightly. There's so much you don't know, and that lack of knowledge could have gotten you killed."

One of the prisoners spoke up. "Could you teach us the stuff we really need to know?"

Owen turned to Merlin, a questioning eyebrow raised.

"Why not?" Rod asked. "I doubt we've interrupted their entire magical training scheme. We might as well do our own training and do it right so we'll have our own allies to call on if we need them."

"We may be able to train you," Owen said, turning his attention back to the prisoners. "But you should know that you won't have much power to do anything in this town. Finding sources of power will probably be a part of your revised curriculum."

"You are now free to go, so long as you vow never to use your magic to do harm or to influence others for your personal gain," Merlin said. "If you swear this, it is binding. If you will not swear this, you will join Mr. Idris in our custody."

They all raised their hands and swore. "Now, before you leave, I'll need to get your contact info if you want to continue training," Rod said. He stood near the exit with his Palm Pilot, entering data. Most of them stopped to give him the information, but several just ran. I had a feeling they were going to pretend they'd never discovered magic.

When all was done, we trooped back to the creek bank to thank our friends. "Do I need to bring my flute?" I asked Owen.

"I don't think so. Those necklaces were more than enough payment for their aid."

"Good, because I didn't want to play the school fight song again."

"But it would have been appropriate tonight," he joked, already sounding stronger.

The head naiad met us at the water's edge. "You won a great victory tonight—with our help, of course. My people actually had a lot of fun. Give us a shout next time you're in town." She winked at me and added, "I'm sure your lady would agree to helping you summon us. We will make good use of the tools you gave us. We are now even, with neither side owing any debt." With that, she disappeared beneath the surface of the water, and the few remaining pinpricks of light along the sides of the creek followed her.

Then we all turned and headed back toward our respective vehicles.

"We will return to New York tomorrow," Merlin told Owen as we walked. "I won't expect you back in the office until Monday. You need the rest, and I imagine you have some business here you need to conclude." He gave me a sidelong look as he said that, but I was afraid Owen was too beat to pick up on the hint.

While Rod shoved Idris into the backseat of their rental car, Merlin took my hands and said, "You have been most helpful, as always, and I have enjoyed meeting your family." He winked and added, "If I were a few centuries younger, I might be tempted to stay a couple of days longer myself, and become better acquainted with your grandmother."

"When you get to be a certain age, what's a few centuries?" I said with a laugh, even as I cringed at the idea of my grandmother dating my boss. Or former boss. Maybe.

He grew more somber again. "You are welcome to return whenever you see fit. After these events, I'm no longer convinced that you're any safer anywhere else, and you more than make up in assistance what you might cost in distraction or danger. But you must do what you—and what Mr. Palmer—believe is best. He is the one who seems to suffer the most."

"Thank you, sir. I'll keep that in mind." It sounded like the ball was in my court. Or maybe Owen's court. I knew where I stood, but I still didn't know what he felt. Did he feel relief at having me out of the way and presumably out of danger, or did he want me with him? It looked like we were going to have to talk about it, but clearly not tonight.

By the time I'd said good-bye to Rod and Merlin, Owen was already at his rental car and ready to go. "Do you want me to drive?" I asked. He looked to be close to passing out, and he just nodded and sat in the passenger seat.

When we got back to the house, he automatically headed for the tree on the edge of the porch, but I caught him. "Remember, we left legitimately. And it's not even all that late." It just felt like it, we'd been through so much.

"Oh, good," he sighed. "I wasn't sure I could make it up that tree. I'm not entirely sure I can make it up the stairs."

I took his arm. "I think it's time for more cake, maybe some ice cream. And then, just think, we get to sleep through an entire night."

"Wow, I'd forgotten what that was like."

"I can't believe it's all over now."

"We've saved the day again," he said with a laugh that sounded like he'd been drinking. He must have been giddy with exhaustion and relief. "And now, it's time to get back to normal."

That's what I'd been afraid of. I'd come to the conclusion that normal was way overrated.

Twenty-Two

I didn't want to go to work the next morning, but it would have been hard to explain that this was the first day I hadn't had to do what amounted to at least two jobs in days. Things worked out, however, when Mom got a look at Owen the next morning at breakfast. "Oh, you poor thing! Those allergies must be killing you. Katie, you can't leave a guest at home alone when he's sick. I'll tell your father you aren't going to work today. You stay and look after your friend."

I could only imagine what she'd have said if she'd seen him the night before. Today he looked pale and tired, not nearly as shattered as he'd been before he got a good six hours' worth of sleep.

"I'm fine," he insisted. "But I would appreciate having Katie stay home with me. I have to go back tomorrow, so this is my last day here."

That set off a whole new round of fussing. I'd heard Merlin tell him that he didn't have to be back at work until Monday, and this was only Friday, so I wasn't sure why he felt he had to leave so soon. I supposed he might want to catch up on his rest in the peace of his own home and have a whole free day before he went back to work. Being around my family wasn't restful for anyone. At least he'd said he wanted to spend the day with me. I took that as a positive sign.

When Mom had rushed off to her meetings and Owen and I were left alone with our second cups of coffee at the kitchen table, I said, "So, you're heading back tomorrow, huh?"

"Yeah, I think that's best. I'll have been gone more than a week."

"That makes sense," I said, nodding. "And I guess your cat and your dragons miss you."

He smiled. "I don't know about the dragons, but Loony may not let me back in the house. I don't think I've ever been away from her this long. Fortunately, it looks like I have a job to go back to. There's nothing like catching the bad guy for getting myself out of trouble. I'll have to send your grandmother flowers to thank her for her sprite."

I waited for him to say something about me coming back with him, but he didn't. I knew Merlin had said it was okay, but I needed to be sure of what Owen wanted. "Is there anything else you wanted to do while you're here, before you go?" I asked.

"Sleep?"

I laughed, trying to keep my tone light even though disappointment weighed me down. Would it have killed him to say he wanted to spend quality time with me without having to worry about dark magic, or possibly that he wanted to pick up where we'd left off before the naiad showed up? "Yeah, sleep does sound good."

"Did you get your front porch time?" he asked.

"What?" I asked, shaking my head.

"You said back in New York that you wanted some time to sit on the porch, or maybe in a hammock, and have nothing to do with magic for a while. Did you get that while you were here?"

"I guess so. I hadn't really thought about it. The first week or so I was here, I was treated like a guest, so I got spoiled and had time to relax—as much as I could amid all the craziness. I got to know my baby niece, which was nice. And then when they realized I was staying instead of just visiting, it was right back to being a member of the family instead of a guest, and I was back at work. There wasn't any magic for a while, but I'm not sure I'd call it restful." I sighed. "What about you? Did the craziness continue after I was gone, or did the disaster quota drop dramatically in my absence?"

"Well, I didn't have to drag anyone out of a burning building or a frozen pond. I haven't been trapped by dragons, stalked by a fairy godmother, or had hordes of mothers swarm after me, so I guess you could say things settled down after you left."

I let the ensuing silence hang in the air for a while, in case he wanted to add something about not being sure that the disasters were really directly related to me, after all, or maybe that he kind of enjoyed all the little crises because they were entertaining and better than being bored and alone. But he didn't say anything. I knew my only other option was to ask him flat-out if he wanted me to go back to New York, but I couldn't bring myself to do it. What if he said no?

After we cleaned up from breakfast, we took a short ride around the town to make sure things were more or less back to normal. All of Nita's guests had checked out during the night or first thing in the morning, and there were no strange cloaked figures dancing on the courthouse square. When we stopped at Dairy Queen for lunch, there was some talk of kids setting off fireworks in the park, but otherwise, it appeared that a major magical battle had gone entirely unnoticed.

Mom held one of her big family dinners that night to say farewell to Owen. I watched him across the living room, chatting with all three of my brothers while he held Lucy. I'd been surprised earlier at how well he fit in with my family, but now I knew that wasn't as surprising as I'd thought. As odd as my family was proving to be, he fit in perfectly, magic and all.

The rest of the family said their farewells at the dinner, so we were alone when Owen left the next morning. The odd distance I'd noticed when he first arrived was back in full force as he prepared to leave, getting his magical case from under my bed and carrying his bags out to his car. He closed the trunk and gave it a pat, then turned to me and said, "So, I guess I'd better be going. Thank your parents for being such great hosts."

"I will. They loved having you here. I'm sure they'll be telling me right away to invite you back any time."

"And maybe the next time we won't be fighting magical battles."

"Let's hope not."

"Teddy and your grandmother will have to keep an eye on Dean. I think he'll be okay, but it wouldn't hurt to watch him."

"That's a good idea."

An awkward silence fell, and I wasn't sure what to do. Should I kiss him good-bye, hug him, shake his hand, or just wave? Did I make the first move, or should I let him? "It was good to see you," I said at last. "I really missed you." I figured that counted as a verbal first move. Whatever happened next was up to him.

"Yeah," he said, looking down at the ground and turning red. "It hasn't been the same without you."

I could come back! I wanted to scream, but I wasn't going to beg, not even for him.

He came around the car and opened the driver's-side door, then paused as he stood inside the open door, leaning against the top of it. "Thanks for your help, as usual."

"Say hi to everyone for me."

"I will." There was another long, uncomfortable silence. I wasn't sure what was going through his head, but I was imagining throwing myself at him and giving him a kiss that would have drawn every naiad in a three-county area. His cheeks turned even redder, which made me really wonder what he was thinking. After a pause he said hoarsely, "I'm sorry you had to go because I screwed up."

"It wasn't because—"

He smiled ruefully and shook his head. "I know you didn't blame me, but let's face it, that's the reason, because I have this bad tendency to lose perspective when it comes to you. But, you know, I have those same perspective problems whether you're near or far, and it's a whole lot easier and a lot less distracting for me to drop everything when you need help if you're near than if you're far away. I can't seem to get you out of my head wherever you are."

I was stunned silent—something I hadn't been sure was possible. With Owen, you often had to read between the lines. Had he just said what I thought he'd said? "So, you weren't mad at me for leaving?" I asked at last.

"I was mad at me for getting us into a situation where you felt you had to leave. And I guess I thought you were disappointed in me, like everyone else was."

"I was worried about you. I didn't want you to have to go through anything like that again, to have to make that choice again. And that didn't go so well, did it?"

"All's well that ends well. Whenever you're ready, I'd like to have you back." Before I could respond, he got into the car and shut the door. I stood in the driveway until his car was out of sight. When I couldn't even imagine a trace of him anymore, I went to my truck and drove to the store.

"Did Owen get away on time?" Dad asked when I got there.

"Yeah, his flight isn't until this evening, so he should have plenty of time, even with any security holdups."

"Good, good. Now, when will you be going back to New York?"

"Huh? What do you mean?"

"That's where you want to be, isn't it?"

"Well, yeah, but . . ."

"And could you work out something with your job?"

"I'm sure I could, but . . ."

"Then you need to be there. That's a good man you've got, and you'll get nowhere with each other at a distance like this. You're not afraid of something, are you?"

I'd been afraid he didn't really want me there, but that had gone out the window with what he'd just said. "No, I guess not." I realized then that I was afraid of more than that. I'd never let myself believe Owen could want me. This distance had become an excuse. I could play noble and stay down in Texas, with no danger of the relationship moving in either direction—getting closer together or breaking apart—and not take any chances. Or I could face things head-on, win or lose. "You know, I think he might be worth taking a chance on. I guess I'll see when I can book a plane ticket to go back."

Dad reached into his pocket and brought out an envelope. "You've been working hard all spring, which is one of our busy times, and you've got us back on track with all your systems. I haven't paid you nearly enough, so here's what I owe you. Buy yourself a plane ticket and go back tomorrow, if you want to."

I gulped and blinked away tears, then threw my arms around him. "Thanks, Dad. Now I guess I'd better see if I can get a seat."

I logged on to the airline website using the frequent flier number I'd signed up for in optimism before my first trip to New York, back when I'd imagined myself becoming a real jet-setter. I was surprised to find that there was already a ticket reserved for me, going to LaGuardia the next afternoon. I wasn't sure if it was Merlin or Owen, since both of them had those uncanny precognitive abilities, but either way, it was a pretty strong message.

I grabbed my things from the office and ran out into the store. "I've got a flight for tomorrow. I'd better get home and pack," I called out as I left.

Back at home, I ran up the stairs to my room, then stopped short in the doorway. Sitting on my bed was a single red stiletto pump. I'd had a pair of those shoes, once upon a time. I'd lost one of them during a particularly disastrous New Year's Eve party. This had to be that shoe, and Owen had been the one who had it all this time. I still had the other one in my closet as a reminder of the little bit of glamour I'd enjoyed in my New York life. I went straight to the closet to get it, but it wasn't there. Then I took another look at the shoe on my bed. It was the right shoe, the one I'd had all along. Still, the fact that the shoe was out there had to be a sign.

After I had everything packed, including the shoe, I got into my truck to make one last round around town. I dropped in on Nita at the motel. "Please slap me the next time I say I want excitement," she said. "I'm still recovering from this crazy week." I noticed that the rock-and-roll decor was gone and the old chamber of commerce calendar prints were back.

"Yeah, that was pretty crazy. Uh, there's something I need to tell you."

She clapped her hands together. "You're going back to New York!"

"How'd you know?"

"It was all over your face. You look happier now than you have in ages."

"You should come visit. I'm not sure where we'd put another person, but we'd think of something."

"I will, you can count on that. You're going after that guy, aren't you?"

"I'm going after a lot of things."

"Good! You know, I think I might even be inspired to do something, myself."

"I can't wait to hear what you come up with," I said before giving her a good-bye hug.

Teddy drove me to the airport in Dallas the next day. I was glad it was him because we could talk openly along the way. "Dean's already planning a trip to New York so he can get a couple of real magic lessons," he said as he drove.

"You'll keep an eye on him, won't you? I think he learned his lesson this time, and he did help save the day, but you know Dean. He's likely to slip and get lazy along the way."

"He'll get nothing past me, I promise. There isn't any training we're supposed to have as magical immunes, is there?"

"Not that I know of. You just have to learn to keep your eyes peeled and your ears open, and be aware of anything that seems wrong. You'll learn to sense magic if you're around it enough. It feels like a tingle or a shiver up the spine. When Granny says she feels like someone's walking over her grave, that's what it feels like. And you'll try to keep Mom out of trouble—and out of the loony bin?"

"That's a tall order. I hope it won't be a problem anymore, now that all the wizards are gone."

"All you need is a good cover story in case you do notice something."

"I'm glad you're going back," he said after a few miles of listening to the radio. "Not that I don't love having you here, but now that I've seen what's going on and what you can do, I think you belong there."

"I don't do anything."

"Yes, you do. You're the glue, the backbone, the stuff that holds everything together. I could see it during that fight. I was really impressed. My baby sister is all grown up."

"Stop it, please, before I hurl. I don't know how to deal with my brothers taking me seriously." He reached over and ruffled my hair, I whined in protest, and all was right with the world.

Once the plane landed at LaGuardia, time really seemed to slow to a standstill as all the people ahead of me took their own sweet time getting their carry-on bags out of the overhead bins and then inching down the aisle. The corridor to the baggage claim stretched out miles ahead of me, and then I was finally there. I searched the baggage claim area for Gemma and Marcia, whom I'd let know I was coming, but they were nowhere in sight.

Then I saw a familiar face. Make that two familiar and very odd faces belonging to a pair of goofy gargoyles. A skinny, bug-eyed one stood on the shoulders of a heftier, squatter one. I knew the rest of the people in baggage claim saw an odd-looking chauffeur. The one on top held a sign reading "Katie Chandler."

I made my way over to them. "Hey, Rocky and Rollo," I said.

"Greetings!" Rocky said. He jumped off Rollo's shoulders and added, "Go find your bags and Rolls here will carry them for you." I wasn't sure I wanted to know what ordinary people would see when the two of them split like that. I pulled my bags off the carousel, then Rollo levitated them over to Rocky, who led the way outside.

As I stepped out into the busy, noisy area full of honking cabs, town cars, and shuttle vans, I caught a glimpse of something bright red.

I focused on it and noticed that it was a red shoe. A red high-heeled stiletto. And holding it was one of the most handsome men I'd ever seen, dark-haired and blue-eyed, with a shy smile that could melt your heart. He stood leaning against a silver town car.

"Maybe you could help me with something," he said. "I'm looking for the lady who fits this shoe."

"Funny, I have a shoe just like that." I was rather proud of how calm and cool I sounded, even though my heart was pounding and I was afraid I'd either faint or cry.

I'm not sure who moved first, but soon we were in each other's arms, kissing like we'd been separated for months instead of only a day. In a way, I suppose we had been apart for months, our recent adventures aside.

"I'm glad you came back," he said when we finally pulled apart.

"I am, too."

Rocky and Rollo finished loading the trunk with my bags. "Okay, ready to head out, boss?" Rocky asked Owen.

Owen opened the back door. "After you," he said.

I got in the backseat, buckled my seat belt, and held on for the wild ride I knew was ahead of me in the crazy life I'd chosen.

SHANNA SWENDSON is the author of *Enchanted, Inc., Once Upon Stilettos,* and *Damsel Under Stress.* She's also contributed essays to books on such pop-culture topics as *Pride and Prejudice, Firefly,* and *Battlestar Galactica.* When she's not writing or watching television and movies so she can write about them, she enjoys cooking, traveling, singing, and looking for new hobbies to make her author bio longer and more interesting. She lives in Texas, but loves to play Southern belle in New York as often as possible. For more information on Shanna and her books, visit her website at www.shanna swendson.com.